MW01611629

Well written and a wonderful twist on a well-heeled trope. Thank you Mr. McLean for a great deal of laughs and a thought provoking book: what is the ultimate use/abuse of power and who is responsible?

David Willis (Oakland, CA United States)

Truly Hilarious. It is so difficult to find truly funny novels, but this book definitely is one of the best. If you like the "frustrated anti-hero" archetype, then you will love Edwin Windsor. Basil Fawlty as a consultant to supervillians.

Darryl Lashambe (London, Ontario Canada)

Normally funny books make me chuckle and that's about it. This book is the first book since 'Good Omens' to make me laugh so hard that I lost my place and then prevented me from reading further by putting tears in my eyes.

If you love superheroes and comics like I do, or hate them like my wife does, you'll find this book awesome.

Adam Haner "Sceri" (Portland, Oregon)

Brimming with anarchic wit, this book is a refreshingly original antidote to the reams of identikit superhero stories that have marched across our pages and screens over the last few years.

Glenn Murphy (Raleigh, NC, United States)

By Patrick McLean

Consultation with A Vampire
How to Succeed in Evil
How to Succeed in Evil: Hostile Takeover

Unkillable
Stories I Told Myself

How to Succeed in Evil

Evil

Patrick E. McLean

For Kristy

ACKNOWLEDGMENTS

As strange as it may be to say of a first edition, this book has a lot of fans. And I want to thank each and every one of them. I had thought that writing a novel was a lonely, thankless task. But, since I released a great deal of work-in-progress in the form of podcast and free audiobook versions, I found myself supported from unexpected quarters. It seemed that every time I would stumble and my morale would flag, a total stranger would send me words of encouragement. I can't capture the magic of it in words. It is, quite simply, a debt I can never repay.

A lot of people had faith in me, even when I had doubts. It's an odd thing to say at the beginning of a book titled *How to Succeed in Evil*, but it's the kind of thing that renews a faith in humanity. Well, at least parts of it. Thank you, one and all.

CHAPTER ONE
Song

It's a beautiful afternoon over Southern California. Up and down the coast, the waves are breaking well and thousands of otherwise responsible professionals have been lured by the call of the sea. The old-timers with their longboards won't acknowledge it outside the tribe, but they whisper it around beach fires and fish taco stands. This is the best they've seen it. A pure gift from the salt mother of us all, the goddess Ocean.

Amid the dreams of endless summer and perfect waves it's easy to overlook the balance of nature. It's a nice concept, but there's a reason Mother Nature is called a bitch. All of her gifts must be paid for. Good surf in Southern California is purchased with bad weather on the other side of the Pacific. And if these breaks are the best — the best in a lifetime — what does that mean for the other side of the world?

But, in the unreality of Southern California, the rich and the rich-in-time do not care. They ride effortlessly, gracefully, impossibly on waves crafted from the misery of others. The girls on the beach are well oiled. The volleyballs ping back and forth, forth and back as if time did not exist and all eternity was a sunny day. Truly, it is paradise. Paradise with a little bit of traffic. So is it any wonder that, for leisure or commerce, Singapore Airlines Flight 209 is inbound?

209 has had a hell of a trip. It was badly battered shortly after takeoff. Halfway across the Pacific, the number three engine overheated. The pilot, Captain Song, eased it back to 20% power. While it's not the first time he's had to baby an engine, this is surely the worst flight of his career. Flight 209 is also losing cabin pressure. Somewhere near the middle of the flight, Song was forced to descend to keep the cabin supplied with sufficient oxygen. This means he has regressed to the beginning of air travel. Unable to fly above the storms, he must now play a deadly game with the weather.

This day the Pacific is filled with low pressure areas. They form, dissolve and re-form faster than Song's navigator can keep track of them. They are pawns in a malevolent chess game. Song seeks to slip between them, to climb over them, even backtrack and fly around. He does not always succeed. Sometimes the storms converge on the plane like the fingers of an angry black hand. Even as they try to knock him from the sky, Captain Song curses them. He speaks to them with an intimate hatred and names them for demons in the tales his grandmother once told him.

The demons of the East are largely unknown to meteorologists. So they name these areas of low pressure "onions". This is because the closely packed isobars on a weather map resemble the layers of the pungent vegetable. Meteorologists watch them closely, hunting typhoons in the Pacific and hurricanes in the east. Surfers also watch the onions. These areas of low pressure are the source of the precious waves. The more powerful the onions, the farther out to sea they are and the longer they sit there, the better it is for the waves. Waves are formed by a series of complicated relationships beyond the limits of human comprehension. Marijuana-steeped conversations concerning questions of wave formation often take on mystical dimensions. Oceanographers and meteorologists can get even farther out there. They smoke math.

Even as Captain Song prays for these onions to rot away into the sea — to leave his ship and its cargo aloft on the uncertain waves of air — millions of people pray for these onions to abide and grow in strength. If you believe that God answers prayers, Captain Song and the 239 souls aboard Flight 209 are simply outnumbered. But perhaps there is room for higher ideals than majority rule. Song's cause is just. His prayer is fervent.

The storms remain.

By the time Flight 209 reaches the magical area of high pressure that always seems to settle over Southern California, Song can no longer feel his left hand. He has seen his ship through 10 hours of dangerous flying. He is soaked to the skin and his sweat has turned to ammonia. He has taken the weight of the entire task upon himself and prevailed. It's not that he does not trust his co-pilot. It's not that he does not have faith in his crew. He is simply the captain. The responsibility is his. He has more experience. He has more training. Song believes in duty. He believes that duty, his sense of honor harnessed to a purpose in the world, will make him something more than a man. The storm has passed, and it seems he is proven right.

In the tones of an ordinary flight on an ordinary day, he asks the co-pilot to take over. The co-pilot notices that Captain Song must use his right hand to pry his left hand off the wheel. Out of respect, he says nothing. Song's will has triumphed over the limitations of his body.

The co-pilot wonders if his own will would be strong enough. Somewhere deep inside him, he knows it would not. Captain Song leaves the cockpit and relieves himself. Now that he has a moment to consider it, his bladder is close to bursting. The relief is orgasmic. Even so, Song would have urinated in his seat if it had come to it. He washes his hands and feels every drop of water on his skin. He splashes water on his face and looks in the mirror. He knows the satisfaction that comes

3

from being tested — pushed beyond one's limits — and finding oneself equal to the challenge.

The moment is interrupted by the explosion of the number three engine. Song feels the blast ripple through the airframe and is back in the cockpit without drying his hands. Warning horns sound. The fire suppression system is activated. He can hear the screaming of the passengers. Most of the port wing is now gone, and the plane is losing altitude. The starboard engines have been throttled back, right full rudder is applied. Even as Song the man loses hope, Song the Captain does not. His will cannot be broken by circumstance.

Aircraft aluminum has no will. It has a predictable failure point, beyond which it will give no more. The wing has been through too much and, in accordance with the laws of physics and its technical specifications, it gives up. The co-pilot calls in a mayday, but he's so scared that he's screaming it in Chinese. Song puts a hand on his shoulder. At his touch, the copilot regains control of himself.

Song takes up the mayday, in very clear and slightly accented English. Los Angeles tower responds that all runways will be made available. Captain Song explains his situation more clearly. He does not know why he does this. It does not matter. Surely they are all dead. The flight recorder beneath his seat will explain everything after he is gone.

Song turns off the warning horns. If he is to die, at least he will not die with a headache. Small comfort. But comfort is comfort. The jet shudders again. The delicate equilibrium between full left rudder, full right stick, no left wing, and reduced power on the remaining engines can't hold much longer. Next to him, the copilot is chanting "Namo a mi tuo fo". The copilot believes that this chant allows one to obtain rebirth in Amitabha's Pure Land of the West.

On the beach, the well-fed and the safe lounge and watch the surfers in the light of the setting sun. If one were to squint, this could be the Pure Land of the West. The co-pilot may never see it, but if some part of his corpse can be recovered, it will probably be buried here.

Flight 209 is hit by a breath of air and tumbles from the sky. The plane has lost its lift characteristics and, in the eyes of physics, is now a falling body, rushing towards its terminal velocity. There is an equation that describes how long Captain Song has to live. He knows this math. Even though it is hopeless, he fights on. He fights for control of an uncontrollable plane. Song will do his duty unto death. Beyond death if he can. But there is nothing that a man can do. The fate of Flight 209 is bound by the laws of physics.

CHAPTER TWO
A Lot of Words He Doesn't Know

To the east of Flight 209, the laws of physics are under serious assault. The surface of the ocean parts in a perfectly straight line. Superheated seawater explodes into the air. An impossibility is headed west.

This impossibility is a man flying many times faster than the speed of sound. This man never had a chance to study physics. He doesn't know that what he's doing is impossible. He just does it. He is called Excelsior. In Latin the name means "ever higher". This impossible man does not know this. To be fair, there are a lot of words he doesn't know.

But what good are words in moments of disaster? The endless stretching instant as the car begins to skid. That high speed memory survivors play over and over again, looking for the meaning of it all. What words are equal to these moments? What words are of use? No? Please? Stop? Don't?

When the wheels lose traction and you look over at the innocent eyes in the car seat next to you, there are no words.

And this is where he is asked to go, this Excelsior. This is where he lives. Do we expect eloquence from the avalanche? From a mighty rocket? From the forces that shift the continents? No. We expect action. Power, undeniable. And this is what his powers have made him. A force of nature with the will of a man.

To be sure, there are other heroes. Other people with exceptional powers who have been called to help their fellow and (it must be admitted) lesser men and women. Some are more colorful. Some are more eloquent. But Excelsior has always been the most powerful.

In a perfect world, Excelsior would race towards flight 209 with a full heart. With humility. With fear. With angry tears in his eyes at the injustice of it all. He would be fully aware that each life on that plane was woven into the fabric of mankind. They might be sons, brothers, mothers, daughters, friends, or enemies, but in his heart he would recognize that each was part of the mass. Each one another's hope of redemption, of love, of care. And that when even one soul is cut from the cloth of humanity the entire garment is weaker, unravelled in pain and loss.

In a perfect world, Excelsior would recognize that there are no explanations for tragedy, just excuses that masquerade as facts. But then, if it were a perfect world, planes would not crash.

Excelsior is ignorant of all of this. Perhaps he is desensitized. But he flies towards this disaster (as he flies towards all disasters) not because people are at risk. He goes because he has been told to go. For him, Heroism has ceased to be the right thing to do. Doing what he is told is the right thing to do.

And today he's going also because he needs a win. He's been taking it on the chin lately. Not feeling like a hero. But what else could he be? He's the most heroic hero there has ever been. He's the first. The best. The strongest. Like as not, there will never be another like him.

But for all his power he is, like anyone else, held captive to his own feelings. And right now, he's excited about a plane crash. Mostly because the last one was so good.

It seems like a dream now, but it was 1944. A different age altogether. A bomber's controls failed and the plane dropped over New York City. Excelsior caught the B-29 and laid it down right in the middle of Broadway. Everyone cheered. He drank with the bomber crew. He found a pretty girl, flew her around the island of Manhattan, made love to her in a cloud, and went home to sleep it off. It had been a pure win.

And a pure win was what he needed now. To feel like himself again. To feel that it all made sense. Now if he had sex with a girl in a cloud she would get pregnant and sue him for paternity. How had it all gone so wrong?

But not today. He knows he will save this day. He imagines the cheering crowds. Some of them will have video cameras. The footage of his rescue will play over and over again on television and computer screens. He will not just be a hero again, he will feel like a hero again. He will watch himself on TV.

When he intercepts the plane it is at 6,000 feet, spinning and yawing and pitching out of control. Excelsior's stomach churns just to think about being trapped inside the metal frame. He thinks to himself that he has been through worse. But has he? He has never faced certain death. The beach, he thinks. Set the plane down on the beach. That will look good.

As the plane continues to fall, he imagines girls in bikinis. The sun glinting off aircraft aluminum. Survivors wandering through a volleyball game, trying to figure out why the afterlife looks like Southern California.

Before he dives towards the plane, he fills his lungs and cries, "EXCELSIOR!" He doesn't want there to be any doubt about who's actually saving this plane. But everything goes wrong. He can't throw a jaunty salute to the pilot or the passengers. The windows are rolling so fast they are just a blur. And he can't get ahold of the damn thing. As he darts in towards the fuselage, the spinning plane slaps him away with its one good wing. He's glad no one sees it.

Excelsior gets mad and knocks the wing off. The plane falls like a stone. Behind Excelsior the remaining fuel in the wing explodes in a bright fireball. It's now or never. No more time for battle cries or salutes.

Excelsior dives hard and gets under the plane. His fingers dig into the aluminum. The plane slows, but not fast enough. He strains. The ocean rushes closer. At this rate, he'll never make it.

Rivets pop out of the plane as he presses harder. It is a physical impossibility to lift something without a place to stand. But he does. The plane slows. But then, with the shriek of rending metal, the fuselage rips in the middle. The tail and the nose slam sharply together, trapping Excelsior in an aluminum sandwich of disaster. He is exempt from the laws of physics, but the plane is not.

The fuselage disintegrates. Pieces of bodies and pieces of the aircraft are everywhere. Excelsior can think of nothing. Dread and failure overcome him. Somehow, he spies a man in a uniform falling beneath him. He seems whole. Perhaps he is alive. But the water is so close.

He dives again. Perhaps he can still save one. One would be something. It wouldn't be victory, but it wouldn't be failure. He snatches for the pilot mere feet above the ocean. The grab is good. His fingers close around the man's wrist, and Excelsior launches himself skyward.

It is a feeling he wishes he could forget. Through the skin he can feel the muscles stretch. He feels the vibrating strings of the tendons give way. He feels, more than hears, the pop as the shoulder comes free from the socket. The body hits the water at over a hundred miles an hour.

For a moment, Excelsior is silhouetted against the setting sun clutching the arm he has managed to save.

No one will say it is his fault. And the few who will know the truth of it will say that he did all he could. But Excelsior knows different. He is the child of an age that knew right and wrong.

10

And even though he is surrounded by relativists, he remembers that a loss is a loss.

He stares down at the slick of blood and oil. Watches hunks of aircraft aluminum sink beneath the waves. He won't go to the beach. Maybe he'll head west for a while. Find an unmapped atoll and hide himself away in shame. It's the only thing he can think to do.

But he knows, the next time there is a call, the next time there is another chance to be a hero again, he will go.

Like a junkie, he cannot refuse.

CHAPTER THREE
"Vorld" Domination

Edwin Windsor leans back in his chair. His long form is all angles and ease. Well over seven feet of him stretches from immaculately polished wingtip to slightly loosened tie. At the end of this day, he displays the rumpled elegance of a man who is perfectly at ease in a suit. Examining his face, one might mistake him for a serene mystic of the East. Except for a wrinkle that surfaces between his eyebrows.

This is frustration. Client-induced frustration. Deep inside him, Edwin believes that his life would be perfect if not for his clients. But, unfortunately for Mr. Windsor, his life is his clients. He is a most unusual kind of consultant. In all their myriad shapes and forms, consultants are a kind of parasite. At best symbiotic but, in all cases, useless without a host.

Even though he knows it is hopeless, he must try again. He interrupts the flow of babble that has engulfed him.

"So, Dr. Loeb," he says, "tell me about your business plan."

Blood rushes to Dr. Loeb's shaven head. He is wearing a Nehru jacket that is a little too small. The collar seems to prevent the blood from returning to his torso. It festers and turns purple. Edwin thinks that Dr. Loeb's head resembles an obscene Christmas tree bulb. Perhaps he will have an aneurysm. This thought does not alarm Edwin. But if it has to happen, Edwin would prefer for it to happen outside of his office. Just when the pressure seems to reach intolerable levels, Dr. Loeb releases it by screaming, "VORLD DOMINATION!"

Dr. Loeb's face returns to a more reasonable shade. Now Edwin has a ringing in his ears. In an effort to clear some of the insanity from the room he says, "That's really more of a goal than a plan."

"DOMINATION! DOMINATION! DOMINATION!"

Clearly, Dr. Loeb is insane. All of Edwin's clients are insane, but not all of them are so obnoxious about it. Edwin tries to appease the man in the hopes that this interview might end sooner. "I'll just put down mergers and acquisitions," he says as he pretends to scribble something on a pad.

"Ja, JA. Acquisitions! I will overtake ze vorld. And if you help me mit my endeavoring, I vill grant to you a small island as your revard. Say, Aftsralia. Muhahahahahaha HAHA AHHAHAHAHAHAH!"

As the laughter continues, the wrinkle of frustration digs deeper into Edwin's forehead. Australia? How insulting. Edwin's standard arrangement is 35% of the post-laundered gross. Edwin is not in the real estate business. And even if he were, Edwin knows that Australia is a mere 5% of the Earth's surface. Australia is not enough. To say nothing of the fact that Edwin does not keep score in yards. He keeps score in dollars. 35% of the world's wealth. Now that is a goal.

Most important, taking over the world is an impossibility. The foolish conceit of a deluded mind. But his clients never seem to understand this. The less equipped they are to control themselves, the more they want to control the world. Why not start with a small island? A city block? An apartment building? One's own temper?

Edwin knows that reasonable goals are not buildings levelled, damsels abducted or heroes taunted — these are not the ends. They are the means. The end is wealth. For lack of a better term, money. Edwin can help the clients who have power or abilities and are willing to live by their own moral code. But this creature? This Dr. Loeb? All he seems to have is a shaved head and a formidable command of the cliches of villainy. This is a colossal waste of Edwin's time.

Sensing that Edwin's attention has wandered, Dr. Loeb shouts "AUSFSTRALIA!" again. He gargles on the word. Edwin flicks his eyes to Dr. Loeb. What is this obsession with land? True, it is the only thing they're not making any more of. But time — time is the only thing you can't buy. Edwin wonders why he is wasting his time with this idiot. One more try, he thinks, and then I will be done.

"Why are you yelling?" Edwin asks.

"I'm excited."

"Please try to control yourself."

"Vell, I, ja, okay."

"Now, I am also excited. Because if you are this excited, you must have a wonderful plan — a brilliant idea with which to take over the world. Please, tell me what it is, so I can help you."

"I have plans for a giant laser."

Please, don't say "in space," Edwin thinks. Anything but another giant laser in space scheme.

"A giant laser!" cries Dr. Loeb. His eyes dart from one side of the room to another, looking for those who would steal his secret and sinister plan. Seeing that the coast is clear, he bellows "IN SPACE!" Once again, maniacal laughter.

Edwin rubs the bridge of his nose and waits.

"You're not laughing," says Dr. Loeb.

"That is correct. I am not laughing."

"But why? Do you not see the beauty of my sinister plan? Is it not unstoppable?"

"Unstoppable?" Edwin asks. "It's unstartable." Edwin gets up, buttons his suit jacket and walks from the room. He has decided that Dr. Loeb is the ultimate waste of time. A sunk cost. A waste so wasteful, so irredeemable, the only rational thing to do is to make future decisions as if Dr. Loeb had never existed.

"You're coming back, right? I mean, ja?"

CHAPTER FOUR
Ghosts of Clients Past

No doubt, you are familiar with the cramped wight-warrens of the modern business world. Perhaps you are one of the unfortunates who spends your every working hour longing to escape these narrow, frustrated places where the smell of cheap carpet hangs low amid poorly ventilated cubes. These places where the lesser demons of distraction run riot through phone systems and email. These places where the plants are plastic, the worker apes hairless, hunched, and pale. And hopeless. Oh, so hopeless.

When these worker apes dream of their reward after death, their Heaven looks a lot like Edwin's office. It occupies the top of a high tower that has the benefit of the cleanest air and clearest light in the city. And if you didn't know what Edwin does, you could easily mistake it for a temple dedicated to a clearer and more civilized religion than the world has ever known.

Edwin's office is the size of a football field. On two sides, three-story windows reveal the city spread out below. Edwin's desk is a simple slab carved from the heart of a redwood tree. The surface is clean. Most notably, there is no computer.

This office is a place designed for the contemplation of lofty matters. If it were any kind of temple, it would be a temple of clarity. This is a room constructed to capture God-like intellect. Here one can nod to Apollo as he drives his blazing chariot across the sky. And here, Apollo will nod back.

This is the room Edwin abandons. Edwin is frustrated that he must relinquish such a space to Dr. Loeb. None of this shows on Edwin's face. None of it shows in Edwin's thoughts. But all the same, the carefully controlled emotions are there. They are pouring into a giant cistern of feeling hidden deep within him.

As Edwin walks the long hallway to his lobby, visages of past clients stare out at him from the walls.

Here, a picture of Aluminar, whose semi-metallic skin flashes as Edwin passes. Aluminar once attempted to mine the center of the Earth and convert part of its molten core into counterfeit nickels. Edwin had advised against this scheme, suggesting that if one was going to use the power to tunnel effortlessly through the Earth for mining, perhaps gold or oil would a more profitable objective. Aluminar had not seen it that way. He had never returned from his storybook attempt to reach the center of the Earth. Perhaps he was still down there? Or perhaps he had encountered one of the several elements that rendered him powerless and inert. Whatever the case, the hole he had created in the poor soil of Eastern Oregon had collapsed in on itself. And now, only a nameless sinkhole marked Aluminar's grave.

Next on the wall is The Voodoin'. Edwin had been able to persuade him that the proper use of his powers was to provide zombies as cheap temporary labor to large manufacturing concerns. It had been an exceptionally profitable scheme. But The Voodoin' had no love for business. He retired to his native Haiti where he indulged his first love, the sport of baseball. He exhumed the bodies of many famous baseball players and reanimated them so he could watch them play on his own bizarre field of dreams hidden deep in the mountains.

Perhaps most absurd among the collection is The Carolignian, a man who had the power to transform himself into a warrior monk from the time of Charlemagne by rubbing a bit of dead flesh that he claimed was the foreskin of St. Paul. Edwin had not asked questions. He had merely harnessed the man's powers to make money. But soon after the money started rolling in, the Carolignian had disregarded Edwin's advice, demanding of him "If God is for me, who can be against me?" As it turned out, a great many people could be against him. Edwin had never known the victory of secular humanism to be so bittersweet.

And finally, Brainitar. Brainitar had cost Edwin dearly, both financially and personally. He admitted, only to himself, that he had made a terrible mistake when he had been sucked in by Doctor Grapewigget's mad obsession. Steven Grapewigget had invented a way to remove his brain from his perfectly healthy body and implant it in an ageless, multi-function robotic pod. He hoped to prolong his life indefinitely and prove that this was the next logical stage in human evolution.

Edwin cared for none of that. But with the vast parallel-processing resources of the human brain now in a machine interface, he devised a way for Brainitar to plug directly into the futures market. Using a combination of Brainitar's unique insight and a massive array of supercomputers, he had devised a seemingly infallible trading scheme.

But it had never been implemented. A factor unknown and perhaps unknowable had ruined everything — the phantom itch. It was a phenomenon experienced by amputees, in which the missing limb was still felt to be there to such an extent that the amputee would feel heat, cold or itching sensations. As an unforeseen side effect of Brainitar's transplant, the memory of his entire body became an itch he could not scratch. The brain inside the jar was driven insane by ceaseless and uncontrollable sensation.

19

Long nights Edwin had lain awake, wondering what he could have done differently. How he could have detected this madness. Insanity was hard enough to see in a normal person who was attempting to cover it up, but how do you read it into the folds of a brain suspended in liquid? There were no facial expressions. No chance of human warmth or contact. None of the thousand bits of information that we all rely on in our everyday exchanges with others.

None of Edwin's clients had ever really followed his advice. But it was Brainitar who was most to blame for the spot in which Edwin found himself now. A great portion of Edwin's own fortune had been tied up in Braintiar's scheme. And when Brainitar had decided, inexplicably, to hold a large dam hostage, Edwin's investment was lost.

Because of Brainitar, Edwin now has cash flow problems. Once again Edwin is forced to wade through the sludge at the bottom of the barrel of evil as he searches for an untapped resource. Someone with talent. Someone with potential. Someone completely unlike Dr. Loeb.

Right now, Edwin wants to know how Dr. Loeb made it through his screening process.

CHAPTER FIVE
A Child of Faded Empire

In the midst of the cavernous, modern lobby, Edwin's secretary sits behind an early Victorian partner's desk. The herringbone accents, brass fittings, and top inlaid with hand-tooled leather is at odds with the modernist decor. But, as Agnes is fond of saying, one mustn't surrender to the modern merely because it is here. It is important to put up some kind of a fight.

Agnes is dignified, gracefully aged and looks a trifle like Winston Churchill in drag. If you mentioned the resemblance to Agnes, she would be flattered. She is an unreconstructed Limey and, as they say on the island seat of that lost empire, frightfully proud of it. There is no dual citizenship for Agnes. Heavens, no. Her loyalty is to the crown and what it stands for. And her prolonged stay in this heathen country has only strengthened her upper lip and her determination to set a more civilized example for the wayward colony.

At one time, an unfortunate person had seen fit to refer to Agnes as an "executive assistant." Agnes would have none of it. She denounced the term as "barbarous jargon," and declared herself uncomfortable with the prominence of the syllable "ass." She is a secretary. She does not merely assist. She keeps order. And perhaps it is her smoldering, blue-haired

21

rage for order that prevents her from jumping as Edwin storms into the lobby. Or perhaps it is that, after her long years of service to Edwin, she has seen it all.

"What is that?" Edwin asks, gesturing towards his office.

Agnes shuffles a few papers and ignores him.

"Agnes? How did that waste of time find its way on to my schedule?"

"I'm sorry, are you speaking to me?"

"Yes."

Agnes carefully collates the papers on her desk into a stack. She folds her hands and looks to Edwin with her chin high in the air. "Now, how can I help you, Mister Windsor."

"That lout in my office."

"Dr. Loeb, yes, what of him?"

"Why am I wasting my time on him? He has no powers. He's obviously an idiot. There's no potential there for us to make any money. Why did you not prune him from my schedule?"

"I'm not sure I care for your tone."

"Agnes, please."

"It's true," Agnes grants, "he is a trifle substandard. But we are in something of a dire strait here. Clients have been dropping left and right. Dr. Spocktopolis has gone completely around the bend. He is refusing his latest invoice."

"That's a collections issue."

"Yes, a matter for the Unstoppable Auger. Unfortunately, he seems to have let his name go to his head and has been stopped, rather decisively, by the authorities."

"Ah," says Edwin. He does not like mundane details. He likes them even less these days, when all the details are less than flattering.

"Ah, indeed," says Agnes, not without sympathy. "These are trying times for us all."

"Yes, but there is simply no way that buffoon can help us. And why does he affect such a horrible Austrian accent?"

22

"The accent is horrible, and out of place. Many of your clients want to be something they aren't, but I have a good feeling about this Dr. Loeb."

And there it is. A feeling. Agnes is very old and very dear to Edwin, but a feeling? Edwin has no time for feelings. Feelings are fickle, fallible. Feelings fall apart, melt away or reverse without the slightest warning or provocation. To build a decision on feelings is to set a foundation in quicksand. Feelings! Even data can be falsified or misleading. But logic is something you can always rely on. Logic is the bedrock upon which Edwin constructs his world.

"He's not a Doctor," says Edwin, "This is lunacy. Show the man from my office. I'm going to the club."

"Edwin! Please! This is no time for golf," Agnes protests. The elevator doors close behind Edwin and she falls silent. She is old, but she is determined to keep from talking to herself for as long as she can manage.

She turns back to her desk, and finds Dr. Loeb staring at her. "Excusing me, but vhere is Mr.... I mean, Herr Windsor... Vindsor. Where did he go?"

"Mr. Windsor has been called away on urgent business. But fear not, he has left instructions for me to reschedule your appointment for a later date."

Dr. Loeb jumps up and down enthusiastically. Oh dear, Agnes thinks, I must discover how this will pay. She smiles at the odd man in the Nehru jacket, swallows her distaste and asks him if he would care for a cup of tea.

CHAPTER SIX
It's a Par Four Life

Right now, the most important thing for you to know is that the dwarf is insane.

At one point in his life, the dwarf was wound very, very tight. He was driven. Consumed by the ambition to be the best trial lawyer ever. When he graduated top of his class from law school, no one made the obvious jokes. They were all afraid that someday they might have to face him in a courtroom. And they didn't want the dwarf angry at them. But all of his classmates thought to themselves, "Y'know, one day that dwarf is going to snap." The drive, the insane pressure, the self-denial and the fact that the dwarf in question was named Topper, all pointed in that direction.

And snap he did. A shrink might call it a psychotic break. A fat Italian guy named Tony might tell you that Topper had become a real menefreghista — a guy who just doesn't give a damn. But both Tony and the psychiatrist would miss the whole truth. The truth is that one day, the dwarf looked back over the terrain of his life and realized that he hadn't had any fun. He hadn't had a life. What he'd had was an obsession. An obsession that he didn't want anymore. So he decided to get a new one. Topper decided it was time to have some fun. Actually, Topper decided it was time to have all the fun.

Sure, Topper has his problems. Topper has his demons. And, as has been established, he's insane. But the second most important thing for you to know is this: the dwarf has more fun than anyone else involved in this story. Including you.

And right now, he's playing golf.

Topper waddles up to center of the tee box and stabs a tee into the ground as if putting the finishing touches on a back-alley murder. He clutches his driver as if he is afraid it's going to wriggle free from his grasp and abscond with his wallet. He waggles forward. He waggles backwards. He heaves the club at the ball in a bizarre jerking motion that only the most generous observer would call a swing. The club misses the ball completely.

Standing at a safe distance, Edwin says, "One." Topper does not hear him. Topper is already swinging again. And missing again. And again. After surviving three of Topper's attempts, the ball takes on an air of invulnerability. Topper searches for a way to play the whole thing off.

"Are you giving me strokes on this hole?" Topper asks.

"If it will help, I won't count those last three," says Edwin.

"What? Those were practice swings! Practice swings!"

This illustrates the fundamental difference between Edwin and his lawyer. To Edwin's way of thinking, if you are going to cheat at golf, why bother playing at all? The way Topper sees it, if you're going to play a game, you should go the extra mile and cheat at it. Winning is way more fun than practice. And the best way to win without practicing is to cheat. Ergo…. This is the simple, irrefutable logic of Topper's overcooked little brain.

Topper lines his left eye up on his ball and closes his right. He thinks he's doing this to maintain alignment at the point of impact, but it reads as a bad Clint Eastwood impersonation. "Okay ball," Topper says, "time to go for the big ride." Somehow Topper connects with the ball. It squibs along the right side of the fairway and comes to rest within bounds. Barely.

Topper turns and holds up his club. "You know, I don't think it's me. Seriously, I think this club is warped." Of course Topper is deluding himself, but that's more fun than dealing with reality.

Edwin takes the tee. He always gives Topper the honor of going first on the first hole. For the rest of the round, the order is determined by who had the lowest score on the previous hole. And, for the rest of the round, that will be Edwin. As Edwin surveys the hole, the wrinkle in between his eyebrows disappears. Something inside him unclenches. Here, more than anywhere else, is where the tall man is at home. There are no low door frames, no undersized chairs. This is a game on his scale. It is not measured in feet and inches, but in yards. And every shot is accounted for. That is important to Edwin. Everything must be accounted for.

The tall man stays within himself as he swings. The hinges of his tall form all conspire to describe a perfect arc with the head of the golf club. As the club makes contact, Edwin can feel the ball compress against the face of the club. The ball climbs into the long light of the afternoon, seeming to defy physics.

Topper mutters, "Nice drive." As they make their way down the fairway, Topper asks, "So what happened with your meeting?"

"Complete waste of time. He was an idiot."

"Hey, hey," says Topper, "complete idiots are some of my best clients. Excepting you of course." There is no joke here. Edwin is so smart that sometimes Topper gets a headache just from standing next to him. Topper doesn't want to think any more than he has to. Not anymore. He's done with all that.

"He had no talent whatsoever."

"No superpowers!" protested Topper, "Was he in the wrong office? How can somebody expect to be a villain if they don't have superpowers? Was he an idiot?"

Topper is so Topper that sometimes Edwin gets a headache just from standing next to him. Mostly from Topper's voice. Topper speaks a high, shrieking, Long Island patois that increases in pitch with his excitement. Topper is crude and uncouth and loud. Very, very loud. Edwin is not sure why he enjoys Topper's company.

If you ask Edwin about this, he will tell you that he maintains his association with Topper because the little man is such a good lawyer. A man in Edwin's profession certainly needs a good lawyer. But this is all rationalization. The smarter we are the more we trick ourselves.

The truth is, Topper has learned to suck every last drop of joy from the marrow of life. Edwin doesn't even know he is supposed to crack open the bones. You and I might call this state of mind depression. Edwin thinks it protects the clarity of his analysis. But however it is described, Topper's happiness, though often misguided and destructive, is infectious.

Edwin is silent for several holes. But then he says, as if it is a great unburdening, "It's always the same."

Topper is taken aback by this uncharacteristic display of emotion. "The same?"

"Yes, the same thing always happens. They never listen. They never listen to me."

"I get that a lot as well. But, I figure, so long as they got the money to pay me, they must be doing something right."

Edwin shakes his head slightly, "I'm not sure that's how it works."

Topper heads off into the woods in search of his ball. When he returns, countless strokes later, Edwin asks, "Do you like your clients?"

"Aw, big fella, are you sweet on me?" asks Topper. Edwin winces a little, anticipating the headache that surely must be close at hand.

"Not me, I mean in general, do you like your clients?"

"I like it when my clients pay," says Topper. "What else is there?"

"I just…"

"Ah, you're just having a bad day. It will all blow over by Monday. You'll go back to work and everything will be fine."

"What if I don't want to go back to work on Monday?"

"Then don't," says Topper with a violent shrug, "it's not like they can take your birthday away."

"I'm not sure this is the life I wanted," says Edwin. Topper has never had such a glimpse into his tall friend's inner workings. He is stunned by this admission. He is at a loss for words for nearly .03 seconds. For Topper, this is an eternity.

"What is this bullshit? I'm sorry my friend, but it's bullshit. You got no time to be second-guessing yourself. You gotta be like a shark. You gotta be like me. You want something? You go take a bite out of it. You don't like it?" Topper's face goes eerily blank as he pantomimes a dead-eyed shark spitting out a bit of chum. "You go find something else to take a bite out of. And seriously, how bad can your life be? When you get upset, you get to go play golf."

"It's worse than you can possibly imagine. This morning, as I was going over the financials of Dr. Loeb's operation, I pointed out that not only has he lost money, year-over-year, but even if all his nefarious schemes and evildoings work, he will only make a 5% return on his capital investment."

"Oooh."

"It's awful."

"Horrible."

"He didn't get it, and when I told him he could be making an 8–10% return in the market, his expression never changed.

29

He just kept smiling. Do you have any idea how much money he wants to waste on a secret lair?"

"Hey, a man's got to have a nice pad. Place to call home, to bring the ladies back to."

Edwin ignores this. "That's not even my point. I just can't take it anymore. They're all so inefficient and dangerously irrational. Stupid, that's the word I'm looking for, stupid."

Topper asks the obvious question. "If they're so stupid, why don't you just become a villain and force them all out of business?"

"Me?" Edwin laughs, "I'm no supervillain."

"Edwin, you are the smartest, unhappiest person I know. If that's not a breeding ground for villainy, I don't know what is. Did you have an unhappy childhood?"

"My childhood was wonderful," Edwin answers in a way that does not invite questions.

"Bullshit, bullshit. You must have gotten picked on because of your height."

"No Topper, they don't really pick on the big kids."

"A cheap shot? From you? Edwin, I expected more. Look, seriously, I think you should try it. Part-time at first. It could be fun. I tell you what, I'll even be your sidekick."

"Villains don't have sidekicks," Edwin says, "they have henchmen."

"Hmm, henchman feels a little small, what about Executive Vice President of Henchmenry?"

"Topper, I don't want henchmen."

"Oh, it'll be great. I'll carry a big friggin' gun. Bigger than me even."

Now Edwin wishes he was playing golf by himself. "No guns. There's nothing smart or subtle about guns."

"But we can do it, right?"

"Topper, I don't want to be a villain."

"Well, you don't want to be a consultant anymore either. You're gonna have to come up with some options."

30

Edwin stops his pre-swing routine. "Topper, I'm not going to become a villain, I'm far too smart for that." He re-addresses the ball. Edwin cocks his head and lines up on the ball with his left eye. His lips compress. The pause seems to last an eternity. And then the club starts back.

When the club reaches the very top of Edwin's backswing, his phone rings.

Edwin tries to check his swing, but it is too late. Everything falls apart and the unthinkable happens. Edwin hits three inches behind the ball. His ball pops up in the air and comes to rest a mere 15 yards from the tee. This is the first time Topper has ever seen Edwin totally blow a swing. He's so shocked, he can't even think of anything to say.

Edwin frowns at his ball and then answers the phone. On the other end Agnes says, "Enjoying the serenity of the golf course?"

"I was. What is it?"

"I am vindicated."

"What?"

"Edwin, the good Doctor Loeb..."

"Is he still there? Has he soiled the carpet?"

"Nothing of the sort. We had a very enjoyable tea. A nice chat. Edwin, his real name is Eustace Eugene Reilly the 3rd. So I did a little checking, and the short of it is, he's loaded."

"Ah. Exactly how loaded?"

Agnes tells him. The strange little man has access to such wealth, it takes several minutes for her to adequately convey how much money is involved. When she is done, Edwin has no response.

"So shall I set another appointment for you?"

"Yes, you shall. Send what details you have, and a car. I need to think this through."

Topper bristles. "What? You're not going to finish the round? I'm just starting to make my move! C'mon, you at least gotta finish this hole. I'll give you a mulligan."

"No Topper. There's money to be made."

CHAPTER SEVEN
There's Money and There is MONEY

Now Topper carries his double scotch (neat) from the bar and climbs up into the waiting Town Car. Inside, Edwin scans a dossier on Dr. Loeb. Edwin is looking for handles. Anything he can use as leverage. It's a very, very old game. Edwin is very, very good at it.

Topper is bored. He searches the backseat. He finds no television, no mini-bar, no heavily medicated women of questionable virtue. These are just a few of the reasons he prefers to travel by limousine. Edwin is a point A to point B kind of guy; all Topper cares about is the ride. And now his drink is empty. Great, Topper thinks, what a barren form of amusement this is going to be.

And then something remarkable happens. Edwin laughs. This laugh is not the rich laughter of strong men drinking lemonade and playing horseshoes on a summer afternoon. Nor is it the sharp, clear laughter of children on a playground. This is a laugh that manages to be sinister, sane, and free from irony. It scares Topper.

"E, what is it?" Topper asks, not sure that he wants to know the answer.

"Do you know the problem with money?" Edwin asks.

"I know my problem with money. I don't have enough of it."

"The problem with money isn't making it. The real problem is keeping it."

"Yeah, well..."

"Let's say you amass a sum of money."

"Say it? Let's do it. Let's amass a large sum of money. A couple million dollars."

"No, no," Edwin says with an air of disappointment, "not a dentist's retirement fund. I mean Money. Several billion."

"Okay. Okay. I like the way you think."

"What would be the first thing you would do?"

"I'd get a proper limousine so I could freshen up this drink."

"You would buy a limousine?"

"And a driver. No, wait, I'd buy the limo and rent the driver. You know, slavery's against the law and all that."

"There's more than one way to own a person," Edwin observes coldly. "But after the limo, a house or two? A few parties?"

"And a yacht. A great big one."

"And so on, and so on. Now, people imagine it takes a great deal of time to fritter away a great fortune but, in fact, it usually happens within two generations of the fortune being made. Because the qualities and characteristics of people who make a great deal of money are rarely passed on to their children."

"I gotcha, rich kids ain't hungry. But I'm not a rich kid. I've got nothing but appetites."

"That's the point. The human condition, actually." Edwin says "human condition" as if it applies to someone else, "For all but a very disciplined few, no matter how much you have, there's always something else that would make you happier."

"A bigger yacht?"

"And after that an island. And after that a bigger island. And a bigger island."

34

"And then Australia, I get it."

At the mention of Australia, Edwin winces. He never wants to hear Australia mentioned in a scheme again. "The thing about wealth is it only stays wealth if you continue to make money. Resources have a way of migrating to the people who are most productive."

"Hunh?"

"The people who do something with them. In a free, or free-ish, country this happens because the children of the people who built the fortune spend all the money on yachts and islands."

"And parties. Don't forget the wild parties."

Again, Edwin's patience is tested. At least Topper wasn't talking about a wild party in Australia. "Yes, well, my point is made."

"Point? What point? What are we even talking about here?"

Edwin removes a picture of Dr. Loeb from the folder. One of the "doctor's" eyes is half-closed. His shaven head and prominent ears complete the general "lost and confused" theme. "This is Eustace Eugene Reilly the Third, aka, Dr. Loeb."

"Is that a Nehru jacket?" Topper asks.

"I believe so."

"Wow, I thought those were extinct."

"Yes, his horrible taste in suits notwithstanding — "

"What? It's the first thing I noticed," says Topper.

Edwin wonders if Topper's ability to derail a train of thought is somehow instinctual, or perhaps glandular. Edwin shakes it off and presses on. "These are the pictures you should be looking at." Edwin holds up two more portraits. "Eustace's father and grandfather. Seems the great-great grandfather founded LAP."

"Lap. So, big deal. If he had founded the lap dance, that would be something."

"Lower Alabama Power."

35

"They have power in Lower Alabama?"

Topper has done it again. He has managed to irritate Edwin. Edwin is not aware that Topper lives for this. That Topper believes he is loosening up his overworked friend. "Please Topper, this isn't a cross-country trip. If you keep interrupting me…"

"I gotcha, I gotcha, the family made a lot of money in power."

Edwin flips to the last page of the file. "Take the idea of a lot of money and then double it."

"I bet their car has a minibar," says Topper.

Still Edwin bravely soldiers on, "The father continued to build on the fortune…"

"Edwin, my liver is shrinking. You can't imagine how painful it is."

"… father deceased, mother and only son surviving…"

"A sad tale," says Topper, as he eyes his dry glass mournfully.

"And within two generations, this fortune will be gone. A large portion will be absorbed in taxes. The rest will have found its way into the hands of people who use money as a tool. A tool to make more money."

"Yeah, yeah. So why were you laughing?"

"I was laughing because I realized that we don't have to wait. We can liberate that useful money right now. No reason not to make an already efficient process more efficient."

"You've got a strange sense of humor, E. So how are we gonna do it? We gonna steal the money?" Topper is genuinely excited by the prospect of some action.

"You mean like a smash and grab job?"

"Yeah, yeah! Smash and grab. Squealing tires. Mini-bar in the getaway car."

"No Topper, no smash and grab job. No squealing tires. How do you get something you want from someone?"

"Take it!"

36

"That's usually difficult, expensive — "

"And FUN!" Topper jumps up on the seat, unable to contain his excitement.

"And there is always a chance, usually a good chance, that a robbery will fail. It's much easier to figure out what someone wants — really wants, deep down in those places people don't talk about — and then sell it to them."

"What if they want the money?"

"Rich children only want the money when it's gone."

"Well, how do you figure out what they want?"

"You ask them." Edwin laughs again. This laugh is scarier than the first. For all the chit-chat, Topper still doesn't understand what's going on. But he knows Edwin well enough to know that somebody is in trouble.

And with that the conversation is finished and the sound of the car rolling over the road fills the space between the two men. In the silence, Topper wonders what it is Edwin really wants, deep down in those places people don't talk about.

CHAPTER EIGHT
Excelsior on the Beach

"Ah, shit — where is he?" Gus asks one of the men who is guarding the dark, empty beach.

"Over there, sir."

Gus spits, just on general principle, and trudges into the soft sand. Gus hates beaches. A beach is a place Marines charge onto to die. Active-duty Marines. Gus is retired. He's got no business charging anywhere. And at this point in his life, he shouldn't have to put up with things he doesn't like. Especially beaches.

Gus is so old that most of his friends are dead. But the ones who aren't, they just sit around. They get to be grumpy all in one spot. They get to complain about whatever they like. In fact, they're so old, they get away with saying anything they want. Not Gus. He's still in the harness. Still in the service of his country. He's linked by history and affection to the world's most powerful man, Excelsior.

Excelsior. Big friggin' baby. And Gus is too old to be dealing with babies. He's too old to measure his words. He's just too old. But he's one of the few people Excelsior listens to. Maybe the only one he trusts. So it falls to Gus. Gus is saddled with handling the big dope. But who will take over when Gus is gone? What will happen when Gus dies? Gus doesn't like to think about dying. Especially not on a beach. So he spits again.

The light leaks onto the sand from the small beach town above. Gus makes out the silhouette of a man sitting, hunched over himself in the dunes. Gus can see that the man is shaking. Jesus Christ. Gus hopes he isn't crying again. Gus can't stand it when Excelsior cries.

People often marvel at how Excelsior hasn't gotten any older with the passing years. Gus wonders why the big freak never became a man. Guess he didn't have to. God only knows what the public would do if they ever found out how moody and insecure their mighty hero really is.

Gus stands next to Excelsior and looks out to sea. After a moment, Gus realizes that there is a severed arm lying on the sand next to Excelsior. Gus grunts and lights a cigarette. The flash from the lighter makes the wrinkles on his face seem deeper than Abraham Lincoln's. After a long drag, Gus says, "Anybody see it?"

"Those things will kill you," mumbles Excelsior.

"Yeah? Is that right? Is that what did him in?" Gus points at the severed arm with his cigarette.

"No, I did," mumbles Excelsior

"What did you do?"

Excelsior looks up at Gus. His eyes are brimming with fresh tears. Gus tries not to sneer. "I ripped his arm off. I couldn't save him, Gus. I couldn't save any of them."

Gus feels awful about his next question, but it's his job. "Anybody get pictures of it?"

"Is that all you care about?"

"No, I care about a lot of things." This is a lie. Gus doesn't really care about much anymore. As far as he is concerned the world can go to hell in a hand basket. Just so long as it's quiet about it. Sure, Gus wants to do the right thing. For most of his life he has been fervently patriotic. He's done more right and noble things than an ordinary person has even thought of. But, honestly, he just can't bear the goddamned aggravation anymore. He takes a long drag on the cigarette and lets the smoke out with the words, "So what's it gonna take?"

Excelsior blinks twice, not sure what's going on. "What?" Excelsior asks.

"What's it gonna take this time? What's it gonna take to get you up off your ass and back in the game?"

"Game? You think it was a game to those people on that plane?"

Actually, Gus does think it's a game. It's all a big game with rules that aren't fair. In fact, the game is so unfair, Gus can't even quit. But Gus knows it's the wrong thing to say. So he lies. "No. I don't think it was a game to them. I know their count. I've read their names. But I don't give a damn about them. And neither do you. You know why? They're dead. They're of absolutely no use to me or anybody else. In fact, now they are just a giant pain in the ass. We're gonna have to raise the plane from the bottom of the ocean, recover the flight recorders and comb the wreckage for remains. Do you have any idea what a pain in the ass it is to salvage a plane from those depths?"

"I'll do it."

"No you won't either. That's why there are dive teams. That's why there are aeronautical boards. You gonna find out what went wrong with the plane or the pilot? You gonna redesign a jet engine? Rewrite a service manual? Retrain pilots?"

"No," says Excelsior, as if he were a sullen teenager.

"That's right, because you're not any good at those things, are you?"

"No."

"You've never even been to college."

"You wouldn't let me go," Excelsior says.

"You're damn right. Because it's your job to be smart. It's not my job to be smart. That's what we got smart people

41

for!" Gus is yelling. His words sound like they have been played on a barbed-wire fiddle with a bastard-file bow. His yell degenerates into a barely controllable cough. Excelsior feels pity.

"Gus, I screwed up."

Gus might be old, but his will is steel. He shuts off the cough and says, "Yeah kid, it happens. Happens all the time. World's an imperfect place."

"It's been happening to me a lot."

"What can I tell you? You got streaks just like baseball players."

"But I don't like screwing up. I don't like looking bad."

"Well, nobody saw this one, so you're not going to look bad."

"Yeah but I know. I know what I did."

"Then be A MAN! Tough it out. We all make choices. We all got regrets." There is another coughing fit. Gus fights it down and continues, "But you live with it. You patch it up and move on."

"But what about the next plane?"

Gus softens his tone. "Son, it wasn't your fault. You didn't build the plane, you didn't fly the plane. And when it started to go down, you were the chance that came after their last chance. Now I can see you're feeling mighty low about this, and I am sorry, but if you never tried, they'd be just as dead."

"Maybe I should just stop trying." Alarm bells go off in Gus's head. This isn't working. Gus's whole job is to handle the big guy. Make sure he keeps trying. To this end, Gus is authorized to use whatever methods he see fit. Flattery, bribery, football metaphors, even appeals to reason — anything, just so long as it keeps the big guy in the game.

"You can't stop trying." Gus says, playing for time.

"Yeah, well what good does it do?"

"What good does it do? Son, you're a symbol. A shining beacon of hope for all those ordinary people out there. Look

42

up at that hill." Gus gestures at the thousands of houses that dot the landscape. "You're a symbol to all of those people. You make them feel safe at night. And around the world, you're a symbol of America's greatness. You can't quit, boy. You can't let all those people down, because you're... you're..." Gus waits for it.

"Excelsior?" says Excelsior.

"Who?" Gus shouts.

"Excelsior!"

"That's right. You're the big man. Bigger than this. Hell, you're the big man so those little people don't have to be. Because they can't be. So what are you gonna do?"

"I'm gonna walk it off?"

"You're gonna suck it up!"

"I'm gonna take one for the team."

"All of that. You're gonna get right back on that horse. That big white horse. And you're gonna ride off into the sunset. So that when the little people need you again, you'll be there for them."

"Yeah!"

"Hell yeah," says Gus. Excelsior stands up. The breeze catches his cape. It floats free, exposing the logo on his chest, that strange device of heraldry from a bygone age. Excelsior is a hero again.

Mission accomplished, thinks Gus. "Now get your sorry ass off this beach so I can go home. This cold is murder on my arthritis."

"Sorry Gus. I really am."

"Don't be sorry." Gus doesn't want to listen to this sensitive-guy bullshit. "Just, just get outta here. And," Gus flicks his cigarette butt at the severed arm, "throw that thing into the middle of the ocean, will ya?"

"But it's somebody's arm."

"Not anymore, it's an ex-somebody's arm."

Excelsior picks up the arm and flies out to sea with it. Gus watches him go. When he's far enough away, Gus shakes his head. That freak is held together with spit and bailing wire, he thinks.

As Gus walks off the beach, he prays that he doesn't live long enough to see Excelsior crack.

CHAPTER NINE
A Giant Laser in Space

Dr. Loeb is wrong about a lot of things. For example, Dr. Loeb believes that he sounds like an Austrian mastermind. He believes that, through hard work, he has eradicated all trace of the Lower Alabama Cracker he was born with. He believes the long hours he has spent watching Arnold Schwarzenegger movies has paid off. Dr. Loeb is wrong about a lot of things.

Right now, Dr. Loeb is meeting Topper. When he says "I ham pleased to meet you," his accent wanders back and forth in the linguistic no man's land that lies along the Alabamo-Austrian border.

As always, Topper says what's on his mind, "What gives? What's with the accent?"

Edwin is not comfortable with this exchange. People either love Topper or hate him. There is no middle of the road. This could go badly.

"Vaht do you mean?" Dr. Loeb asks, losing control of his accent in his misguided attempt to cross the deep chasms of the vowel sounds.

Topper juts his chin out aggressively. This is not a good sign. "Why are you talking like that? Aren't you just some kind of Lowland Alabama Redneck?" Edwin holds his breath.

"Aw sheet man, I ain't gonna skeer nobody talkin like dis. Least-wise not trying to take over the world. Like, man, when you're dropping a guy in a shark tank, you cain't say, 'Hey man, feed 'at bitch t'em sharks over ere.' You gotta say something cool like 'Difpose off him!'" Dr. Loeb looks to Edwin for confirmation. "Right man?"

"Yes-s-s-s," says Edwin. "Topper if you'll excuse us?"

Topper does not move. He stares at Dr. Loeb. Dr. Loeb is not sure why, but he is uncomfortable under the little man's gaze.

"Dispose of him?" Topper asks. "Dispose of him?"

"Yeah man. Y'know. 'Dispos hof hem! Ziss infstant!'"

Topper's face broadens into a smile. "Yeah," he says, "Yeah. You're gonna be all right." He slaps Dr. Loeb on the arm and heads for the door.

"Thank you Topper. We have plans to make," Edwin says, as he feels some of the tension leave his shoulders.

Dr. Loeb perks right up. "Awww man! A plottin' and schemin'!"

Now both Edwin and Topper stare at Dr. Loeb as if a plant is growing out of his head. As Topper leaves the room he mutters under his breath, "Holy crap, he's as crazy as a fruit bat in a badminton net."

"Would it be okay if'n I talked in the evil accent some more?" Dr. Loeb asks.

Edwin forces a smile. "Whatever makes you comfortable."

"So, you haf come to realize ze vizdom of my plank?"

"Yes, your pla...n. The giant laser in space. There are difficulties, but the idea is not completely without merit." Edwin struggles to get it out. He detests lying in all forms.

"Vat? You just put ze lazar into space!"

"Yes, yes, right there. You've touched on an interesting point. For the moment, we'll ignore the expense, and near impossibility, of constructing a laser in the megawatt range, and focus on the transport issues. How, exactly, would you put it into space?"

"Vee vould put it on ze rocket."

"It's very expensive to put something on a rocket. And something as heavy as your death laser — you were planning on calling it a death laser or something like that, weren't you?"

"Lazeradicator."

"Ah yes, much more colorful. Something as heavy and substantial as a Lazeradicator," Edwin says this last word as if it is something awful that he can neither spit out or nor swallow, "would assuredly require more than one rocket. That's multiple rockets, plus assembly once the parts are in space."

"So, se Space Shuttle," says Dr. Loeb, feeling like he is catching on.

"I think it is unlikely that NASA would be keen on helping you with your laser project."

"Lazeradicator."

"Yes, it's a fine name, but that's not the problem. No matter what you call it, you can't sneak it past NASA. And even if you could, it would cost you $10,000 per pound just to get your unbuildable laser into space. How much does it weigh?"

"I don't know."

Edwin is encouraged by this response. It suggests that Dr. Loeb has not lost contact, entirely, with reality. "That's because it can't be built. Now, I'm all for vision and daring — especially when these qualities are combined with patience and intelligence. But, really, it's like this. You can find a solution to one impossible problem. But two impossible problems? The complexities don't add. They multiply."

Dr. Loeb gives him a blank look. Edwin wonders if this is because Dr. Loeb has never heard of multiplication.

"I'm saying that it can't be done."

"But I have a lot of money," says Dr. Loeb.

"And you should keep it. Someday, you will have a good idea. That money will be used to finance it." Someday, thinks Edwin, is the day that never comes. "Let's try it another way. What would you do with your laser?"

"I vould destroy Vashington!"

"Why?"

"Vhat do you mean? It's Vashington!"

"Yes, and since the British burned it in 1814, it has remained inviolate. And increasingly picturesque."

"So?"

"How do you plan to make money from destroying the capital of the United States of America?"

"Vell, then I vould be feared."

"Then you would be broke. Having spent all your money on a laser, and getting it into space, you would then destroy a perfectly good city and get nothing in return."

"But, but, but... "

All the motorboat noises in the world aren't going to get Dr. Loeb out of this one. Edwin folds his hands and pronounces his stern judgement. "Your business model is deeply flawed. I cannot see the benefit, much less the possibility, of a giant laser in space."

For the first time during the whole session, Dr. Loeb does not have a ready and horribly ill-informed reply. He cocks his head. The accent falls away completely. "So what am I gonna do?"

"You're going to make me a small promise," says Edwin, "Can you do that?"

Dr. Loeb nods.

"You must promise me that, from now on, if we can't think of a good reason for you to do something, you won't do it."

"What do you mean?"

"Well, let's try it another way. Why do you want to take over the world?"

48

"That's what I'm supposed to do. I am a villain." Dr. Loeb says this like it is the most natural and obvious thing in the world. "I have a secret lair. I have ziss jacket. Ze right haircut. I am ze evil mastermind."

"Okay. Okay. Right there. Let's say you took over the world."

"Yes. Ja, I like ziss," says Dr. Loeb, clapping his fat hands together.

"You are lord and master of all creation," says Edwin.

"Domination!" he says, nodding so vigorously his jowls seem in danger of breaking free and rolling down his neck.

"What then?"

Dr. Loeb's mouth hangs open. He has no answer.

"What good would it do, to control the whole world?"

"But, that's what I'm zupposed to do!"

"Why?"

"Because, well, everybody knows ziss. Ze supervillain iz to take over the world."

"Of course. But why?"

"What do you mean?"

"It seems like a prudent question. You're about to devote a considerable amount of your time and effort to reach a goal. Is this goal worthwhile?"

"I did not become ze villain, ze super-villain I am, to be prudent."

"That's good. That's the kind of thing that helps me. Now," Edwin leans in to emphasize his question, "why did you become a villain?"

Dr. Loeb has no idea. Edwin lets him struggle with the question for a while. Of course, Edwin knows the answer. He knew long before Dr. Loeb sat down. The only question in Edwin's mind is — can he get Dr. Loeb to recognize the answer? It's a long shot, but if Dr. Loeb can have a moment of clarity, then a world of possibilities will be created for both of them.

49

You see, Dr. Loeb (by birth, Eustace Eugene Reilly the Third) is but a dilettante in the world of evil. A tourist, if you will. Or more precisely, a spoiled child who, by virtue of a sizable trust fund, has become a very spoiled adult. He has no sense of accomplishment. There are not many obstacles for the super-rich. There are precious few things for the young scion of a wealthy family to test his mettle upon. Eustace does not care for polo or sailing. He is bad at business. Charity work does not suit him. But he has managed to find something to call his own. That it is absurd and counter-productive does not deterrent for Eustace. In fact, that is what makes being an Evil Genius all the more attractive to him.

This is because Eustace's mother, Iphigenia Reilly, is controlling, shrewd and manipulative. The widow Reilly sees to it that her son has what the rich refer to as "a little money," but has denied him any substantial funds. Of course, Iphigenia will tell you that she loves her son unconditionally. This means that anything other than her love comes with conditions. If Iphigenia were given to introspection, she might realize that she would have been much happier with a child who was genetically modified to remain an infant. Since Eustace hit puberty, she has consoled herself with a series of small furry dogs.

Eustace has been driven to more and more bizarre forms of rebellion in his efforts to get his mother's attention. But until this moment he has not dared to utter his most secret hope. A hope which Edwin means to twist to his own purpose.

All of Eustace's defenses and fantasies are stripped away. He speaks softly. "I became a villain to get back at my mother."

Edwin smiles. Now he is getting somewhere. Edwin doesn't believe in revenge. There's rarely a profit in it. But Iphigenia Reilly possesses a mind-boggling amount of money. For the first time in the interview, Edwin uses Dr. Loeb's real name. "Now, Eustace, what will it be like when you have your revenge?"

"She, she, she'll have to do what I tell her." Eustace looks around nervously, expecting his mother to catch him in the middle of this confession.

"Control. You would have control."

"Yes," he says, "domination."

"Domination," says Edwin.

Tears of gratitude well up in Eustace's eyes. Then the fear comes over him again. "Can we really do it?"

Edwin is going to explain that if Eustace will listen to him, and hire the right kind of lawyer, they have a very good chance of success. But he is interrupted by an explosion at the back of the room.

"MOTHER!" cries Eustace in terror.

The dust settles. At the other end of the room is a figure clad in spandex. "It is I, Superlative Man!"

"He iz come to do battle with me!" Eustace cries with joy in his voice. "I am ze villain, ze sinister Dr. Loeb, and he must stop me. You take your life in your hands when you tangle mit ze fearsome intellect of ZE LOEB!"

Edwin tries. "Uh, Superlative Man, is it? It's not clear that my client is guilty of breaking any laws."

Superlative Man doesn't buy it. "What are you trying to say? He's evil. Just look at him. No self-respecting or law-abiding citizen would dare dress like that."

Insanely, Dr. Loeb agrees with him. "I am EVIL! He must stop me before I strike again! Manful COMBAT!"

Edwin tries again. "Eustace, that is, Dr. Loeb, you might want to rethink this. He's got a good 40 pounds on you and he just shouldered his way through a wall."

But it is no use. The high redoubts of Fort Reason are overwhelmed when the man clad in spandex yells, "Superlative Man, into the fray!"

Edwin pushes his chair back from the table. As the two men brawl, Edwin uses the intercom. "Agnes. Things are winding down in here. I'll need a full contract package — "

Superlative Man holds Dr. Loeb over his head and slams him into the conference room table.

"What was that? Yes, yes, absolutely — an accidental death and dismemberment waiver. And I believe Dr. Loeb will require prompt medical attention. Thank you."

For all his posturing, things aren't going well for Dr. Loeb. He is pinned under Superlative Man's knee. In pain, he gives up on all pretense and distress. An uninterrupted stream of Lower Alabama profanity pours forth from Eustace's slobbering gob-hole. Such filth, thinks Edwin. Such a remarkable knowledge of the anatomy of farm animals.

Superlative Man wrenches Dr. Loeb's arm hard against its socket. "Yield, villain, yield!" Dr. Loeb's shoulder lets go with a sickening crunch. The profanity drops off to a whimper.

Ah, that's nice, thinks Edwin. And then he produces a small nickel-plated pistol from his desk drawer and shoots Superlative Man in the leg. Superlative Man cries out in shock and surprise. The blood drains from his face and he collapses on the floor.

"You shot me!?!" he says, in firm command of the obvious.

Dr. Loeb looks at Edwin through a haze of pain, his arm sticking out at an absurd angle behind his back. Before he loses consciousness he says, "Thank you."

Edwin replaces the gun in the drawer. "No thanks required. It will be added to your bill."

"You have been busy," says Agnes as she stands in the doorway and surveys the carnage. "Is that the tang of cordite in the air? Destructive meeting, I take it?"

"No, no. An excellent meeting. However, it has left Dr. Loeb in need of medical attention."

"And what shall we do with this other poor unfortunate?" Agnes dials 911 as she speaks.

Edwin looks down at the man in the costume. Superlative Man. Of course, he is no superhero. There is nothing superlative about him whatsoever. He is an out-of-work actor trying to earn some extra cash. Edwin feels a stirring of some unidentifiable emotion for him. Not pity. Of course not pity. Whatever it is, he puts it from his mind.

"He should be handled with some discretion," says Edwin. No doubt when the actor returns to consciousness, he will be terribly upset about being shot. It is not Edwin's fault that the actor did not thoroughly read the death and dismemberment rider.

Edwin does not approve of violence. It is too unpredictable, too hard to control. But he needed a way to earn Dr. Loeb's trust beyond all question. He doesn't think that this farce is a bad solution, but he feels that he has somehow fallen short. He feels that, if he'd had a little more time, he would have been able to develop a more elegant solution.

"He has bled rather a lot," Edwin observes.

Agnes covers the phone with her hand and says, "Yes dear, that is my next phone call. Unfortunately, 911 does not dispatch carpet cleaning services." Agnes pauses thoughtfully. "But when you think of it.... Excuse me, do you — " An outraged squawking comes through the phone. "Well then, we'll just have the ambulance."

Agnes hangs up the phone. "You see, this is precisely what happens when you do not take the time to develop and discipline a quality serving class. That woman was unapologetically rude. I will never understand why such a bright, sensitive man such as yourself has chosen to make this savage country your home."

"It's where the work is," Edwin says, "and now it seems I must go to Alabama."

"Heavens, no! Edwin, I forbid you to go."

Edwin looks at her.

"Of course, what I mean to say is..."

"I know what you mean to say. It will be fine, Agnes."

"I predict disaster. I predict disaster."

53

"Yes. You always predict disaster. You have long been calling for the downfall of Western Civilization."

"No, no, Edwin. Not calling for. Bemoaning. Bewailing. I am Cassandra, crying out in the savage wilderness of America."

CHAPTER TEN
What do You Want Mr. Windsor?

Edwin ducks as he exits the jet. He feels a pain in his back. There's not an airplane door in the world that was built for someone of his stature. Outside, the atmosphere of the place hits him. The humidity, the heavy sweetness in the air, the sharp tang of aviation fuel — all of it combines to make it known, not just intellectually but physically, that Edwin has come to Lower Alabama. He watches Dr. Loeb's shaven head reflecting sunlight as the odd man rushes to the car.

Edwin rolls his neck, trying to loosen the muscles in the middle of his back. Halfway down the stairs, the heat and the humidity really kick in. Edwin mops his forehead with his handkerchief. There is a voice in his head that tells him this trip is a mistake. Edwin tries to ignore it. It is not easy.

The city slides by the car windows and soon they are in the country. Here, there are ill omens. A possum dead and strung out across the road. Vultures that hop out of the way rather than struggle to rise in the thick air. The trees, gnarled and ancient, disturb Edwin in a way he cannot articulate.

It's not that Edwin dislikes nature, he simply prefers the clean lines and precise angles of the city. Art, Architecture, Commerce, all the higher functions of mankind are displayed to maximum advantage in a city. Here, things burble and suck. They feed on one another and swell in the heat. How could anyone hold a crease in a suit in this climate? How could one even hold a thought? Edwin wonders if the humidity is swelling his brain.

As they pull off the road onto a tree-lined private drive, Dr. Loeb says, "Ah, vee ar hear!" In reaction to this bizarre homecoming, Eustace has intensified his accent. His words are now so thick and imprecise that Edwin cannot understand what the odd man says. This is a comfort to Edwin.

As a rule, Edwin does not think about clichés. He inhabits a world of possible cause and probable effect. So, the magnitude of cliché at the end of the tree-lined drive is lost on him. There is a two-story white plantation house that has been built, rebuilt and restored to the specifications of an antebellum wet dream. It has white columns, a white balcony and countless other frilly touches of extra whiteness that seem to be tacked on just in case you forget what color person is in charge around here.

As they exit the car, a well-kept woman in her 60s presents herself on the balcony. She waves to them with the corner of her white shawl. She speaks, in the rich, broad tones of a gracious, educated and sugary Southern accent: "Why Eustace, you have returned." It almost sounds like she is a loving mother who has missed her son. Almost.

At the sight of his mother and the sound of his real name, Dr. Loeb becomes embarrassed and defensive. "Rease porgive zizz voman," he says awkwardly. "Xhee iz de-rang-d. Sinks xhee izt moin marver."

"And I see you have brought a friend!" Eustace's mother exclaims with delight.

"Zizz ist Herr Vindsor!"

"I must confess. I haven't the slightest idea what the strange fruit of my loins just said."

"I am Edwin Windsor. It is a pleasure to meet you."

"Mr. Windsor, please forgive my son. He's de-ranged. But I expect you already knew that. Come in, come in. I shall be glad to receive you in the fo-yay."

A large black man, wearing a long-suffering expression as if it is his uniform, emerges from the house and takes the luggage. Edwin follows.

As he enters, Edwin is slapped with a wave of cold air created by unseen air conditioning units. He is further assaulted by the sight of Iphigenia Reilly floating down a curved staircase in a pretty fair approximation of "Gone with the Wind." This cliché is also lost on Edwin. But he can see that this woman is going to be formidable. Or, at the very least, formidably ridiculous.

In the awkward pause, Dr. Loeb attempts to excuse himself. "I must see to my verk."

"Is that any way to greet your mother?" Iphigenia asks. "You don't call. You don't write. And you know how I worry."

"High vas avsorbed mit verk. I Vust Vee to it kuh-now."

"You will not see to your work or anything else. Alabaster, take him to his room and see that he does not leave. I will deal with him later." The large black man tucks Eustace under his arm and walks away.

Dr. Loeb breaks character. "But Mom-MA!"

Iphigenia dismisses him with a wave of her hand and then turns her attention to Edwin. "I am sorry you had to see that. He was so sweet when he was just a boy. But as he grew... bless his heart." Edwin is very careful to maintain a neutral expression. The entire game could be lost right here.

Iphigenia leads Edwin into a painfully formal sitting room. "Do you have any children, Mr. Windsor?"

"No."

"Well you simply must have some. They are such a delight," she looks out the window, "when they are young." Now she turns back to Edwin, and with the full wattage of charm that only generations of gracious living can provide she says, "But

57

heavens, where are my manners? Would you care for some tea?"

"Yes, thank you."

She rings a small bell and soon Alabaster arrives with two glasses of iced tea on an ornate silver tray. Iphigenia takes a sip and sighs with theatrical delight. "Now Mr. Windsor, tell me, how is it that you have come to know my su-suss--uh..." Unable to finish the word "son," she trails off when she sees that Edwin is holding his glass of iced tea between his thumb and forefinger as if it is a dead thing he has found underneath his chair.

"This tea is cold," Edwin says.

"Iced. It's called iced tea."

"Would it be possible to have a proper cup of tea? A Darjeeling or an Earl Grey perhaps?"

"Alabaster, what other kinds of tea do we have?"

"Pekoe," the large man says clearly, but without expression.

"Will that suffice?" Iphigenia asks in a way that seems hospitable, yet somehow winds up indicating that she thinks Edwin is horribly rude.

Edwin is unable to hide his distaste. Orange pekoe tea, surely brewed from tea bags, which invariably contain the lowest grade of tea. It would be little more than the dust and twigs and foot sweat from the floor of an Indian tea-sorting room. "That will be fine," Edwin manages to say.

Alabaster leaves. "His family has been in my family for five generations," Iphigenia explains with pride. "But, how rude of me. You haven't come here to discuss history, have you? Tell me, how is it that a man like you has become," and here she pauses for effect, "friends with my son."

"Your son has sought me out for my advice."

"And you have advised him to continue with his costume and ridiculous accent?" Iphigenia asks.

"Of course not," Edwin says as he accepts a cup of tea. His delicate fingers direct the cup to his mouth. Edwin drinks with a refinement that Iphigenia finds irresistible. In this moment she sees him to be an intelligent, cultured man. She is not sure what the tall man's game is, but those three short, sensible words have begun an attraction. "I have tried to rid your son of any delusions or affectations," Edwin says as he replaces the teacup in its saucer. "Evil is not a game. It is serious and profitable business."

"You know, there are so few truly tall men in Lower Alabama." Iphigenia blushes. She thinks that she must seem silly, so she tries to play it off. "I'm afraid I find it simply too hot for regular tea. I've found that, in this climate, there's little else to do but drink iced tea, fan oneself, and commit indiscretions."

Edwin doesn't understand what's going on. The hideous woman's advances are a piece of data that fit no known set. Perhaps later this observation will be of some use. For now, he sips his tea and allows the silence work on her.

"So what exactly is it that you do, Mr. Windsor?"

"I am an Evil Efficiency Consultant. I help villains become more — "

"Villainous?" Iphigenia says, unable to contain herself.

"Profitable." Edwin says the word as if it is motive and justification all in one.

"Terrorism, extortion, kidnapping, revenge, that sort of thing?"

"On occasion, but most of those cash acquisition strategies are far, far too crude. Take, for example, a man who can run very, very fast. Say, twice the speed of sound."

"You mean like The Fla — "

"Names are unimportant, but yes, The Flamer is one such man. And his problem is not learning to run faster or farther. He has mastered his power. The question is, where should he run and why?"

"I'm not sure I follow you. If I recall, The Flamer is a hero."

"Ah, propaganda. The Flamer is confused. Not a bad man, but hardly what I would consider a hero. What do you know about hospitals?"

"Ah have endowed several," she says magnanimously.

"Then consider the problem of an emergency room. On any given night an emergency room has far fewer doctors than patients. All of the patients require medical care. But not all of them can be seen at the same time. So which patient goes first?"

"Well, the person who is the most hurt."

"Exactly. The term is Triage."

"Oh, that is French. You know, my ancestors were French."

"Yes, from the verb trier, to sort or sift. To discriminate. In my eyes, this word means to use a scarce resource for the greatest profit. The Flamer has no triage. He enjoys stopping street crime. So that's what he does. In his mind that is what being a hero is all about."

"What's wrong with it?"

"Nothing. As far as it goes. Which is not nearly far enough. But he makes an excellent object lesson. I encourage my clients not to waste their time on small, violent crimes. There's not enough money in them. That way, I remove irresponsible and self-serving nuisances like The Flamer from their path."

"But his outfits are so colorful."

"Yes, but he does not help others from a selfless motive. He helps others only because it suits him."

"But he does help people."

"In a limited and irrelevant fashion, yes."

"So you want my son to become a villain? Your kind of villain?" Iphigenia is on her guard again.

"Dear woman," Edwin says through a shark's smile, "All I want is for your son to be happy."

CHAPTER ELEVEN
Cindi with an i

Excelsior hates the sound of silverware scraping across plates. Silverware contacting teeth is even worse. It puts him on edge. He's trying to enjoy a nice dinner with a beautiful woman. But every slurp and suck, burp and gargle in the busy restaurant is right in his ear. His hearing seems to get better when he's dressed in ordinary clothes. And he's traveling incognito tonight, just trying to be an ordinary schmuck like the rest of us.

Beautiful women throw themselves at Excelsior all the time. He doesn't quite understand it but like rockstars, daredevils, fighters, and all men of power, it works in his favor. So he doesn't ask too many questions.

The problem is that these women aren't interested in him. They want the symbol. They want to make love to a force of nature. Not to him. Not to who he really is. Not whoever he might be without the powers or the costume. And the thing that scares Excelsior, deep down, is that he can't remember who he is without the cape. And he wants to know. He wants someone to love him. Whatever he is when he's not being a symbol.

So, he takes off the costume and poses as an ordinary man. A man who must face the age-old problem of finding a mate.

Her name is Cindi, with an "i". She makes a point of explaining that to people. As if it was some kind of bizarre Indian name. Two Elk. Clouds against the Moon. Cindi with an "i". She is attractive (if you're not picky), charming (if you're not listening) and young (by candlelight). As they look at the menu, she giggles at nothing at all.

Still giggling, she holds up an appetizer fork. "Tiny," she says. More giggles.

"Yeah, it's small," Excelsior says awkwardly. He looks at the menu. He can't read it. It's in French. But looking at the menu gives him something to do.

"Yeah!" More giggles.

The waiter knows, instinctively, that they don't belong there. He drapes his contempt in kindness. "Take all the time you need with the menu, Monsieur." This gets Excelsior. He's not used to people being snotty to him. He feels the heat build up behind his eyes. All he has to do is let it go to reduce this guy to cinders. He reels it back in. What is he thinking? He is a hero. The good guys don't do that kind of thing. Besides, he's taking a night off. Doesn't he deserve a night off? A long weekend now and again? Nobody can work all the time. How are you supposed to make friends, have a relationship? Or even just get your rocks off? Excelsior isn't exactly human, but he has needs.

Excelsior orders the cheapest bottle of champagne and some oysters. Cindi with an "i" doesn't like oysters, so Excelsior orders her some french fries. The waiter nods and says "Pommes frites," with a judicious balance of agreement and contempt. What a jerk. Excelsior doesn't want frites. He wants fries. But after a few drinks, a few oysters, the evening is almost agreeable. He seems to be making progress with Cindi with an "i".

Then the pager goes off.

When he's not in costume, Excelsior often gets teased about carrying a pager. "Call me old fashioned. It works," is what he says. But works isn't the half of it. The box clipped to his belt will receive a signal anywhere on the globe. Not only does it work under 300 feet of solid rock, it works when 300 feet of solid rock is trying to crush it. It will even receive a signal on the moon. Excelsior is pretty sure he can destroy it, but it has to be the toughest man-made object he's ever encountered. In a perverse way, he's proud of the device.

Excelsior has never consciously considered that the pager is the wrong end of the leash, but once he dreamed that he threw it into the furnace of the sun. Even in his dream, the pager went off. It called him away from its own destruction.

When the pager goes off, it means that he has to go. Whatever is on the other end of that vibration, it is important. If he doesn't go, right now, people will die. They may be brave men struggling for their lives, or innocents and children, but whoever they are, they are in danger. To be fair, they never use this thing frivolously. And isn't it a privilege to carry this pager? To be able to help? Then why is he so angry?

For all her faults, Cindi with an "i" is there. She is ready, willing and eager. As she leans forward, Excelsior wonders if her bare thighs are pressing against the leather of her seat. He wonders if she is wearing panties. He uses his X-ray vision to look through the table and answer his question.

Again the pager vibrates like the soulless, unforgiving thing that it is.

As the smug waiter passes, Excelsior grabs his arm. Not hard enough to break it, but hard enough to bruise. "I need a shot of bourbon and the check." The waiter winces in pain, but still the corners of his mouth drop in contempt. Excelsior gives the arm another little squeeze. He can feel the bones grinding together. "It's important," says Excelsior, "and it needs to be the very next thing you do."

The blood drains from the waiter's face and he nods. Excelsior releases his arm.

"What's the matter?" asks Cindi with an "i".

"I'm sorry baby. Daddy's got to go," Excelsior holds up the pager, "important business."

"You've always got important business. What about me? Aren't I important business?" She leans over the table and showcases her breasts. Surely they are some of the finest that money can buy.

"I'm sorry. This kind of business doesn't wait."

"Whatever. I think you're gay."

"I am not gay."

"We've been on what, three dates? And you always run off before you have to take care of the most important business!"

"Look, my work is complicated."

"Your work. Your small penis."

"But..."

"And you never have any fun. And you never buy me any cocaine."

"What?"

"You're no fun," pouts Cindi with an "i".

"This conversation is over."

"You bet your small penis it's over. Don't call me again."

She storms off. Excelsior will have to look for true love elsewhere. The waiter sets the check down and leaves quickly. Excelsior does not look up at him. If he had caught even the slightest hint of a smile he would have burned the waiter down in front of everybody. His eyes grow hot again. Sometimes it comes out as lasers, sometimes as tears. Either way, choking back the emotion is the smart thing to do.

Excelsior knocks back the drink and throws money at the check. He thinks it's ridiculous that he should have to pay the check. How many times has he saved this city? And what thanks? I mean really, a key to the city? A key that opens no doors.

As he wings his way out of town, the question rattles around in his head: Does he wear the costume, or does the costume wear him?

64

CHAPTER TWELVE
Edwin Dresses for Dinner

To Edwin's way of thinking the ultimate end of formal dress is to show the human form in its best light — to present one's self to advantage. And, to that end, any garment should lend authority, gravity and dignity. It should minimize weakness and vice, maximize strength and virtue. And to fully focus the force of personality through the lens of fabric, a man requires a tailor.

And not just any tailor. What is required is a remarkable man. An artist working faithfully in a rapidly disappearing art, deeply rooted in a tradition that stretches back through the centuries. A tradition that includes countless suits, crafted to fit countless numbers of men — gentlemen and rogues, saints and killers — the just and the unjust alike. When viewed at this level the tailor's art encompasses not merely needle and thread, scissors and fabric, but the whole cloth of mankind in all its shapes and sizes. And this is exactly the altitude from which Mr. Giles, Edwin's tailor, considers his craft.

Mr. Giles is descended from a long line of Saville Row tailors. So the material he has measured most carefully is the cloth of his own life. Each suit he has made has taken over 1,000 stitches. Each stitch has been made by hand. With measuring, fitting, and adjustments these thousand stitches absorb about 100 hours.

So 100 hours per suit, divided into perhaps 50 working years, makes 20 suits a year. A few allowances for quality, tuning up old suits, having a nice weekend, and working at a reasonable pace — this is, after all, a marathon, not a vulgar sprint — and Mr. Giles has calculated the span of his own life. He believes he will live to make 1000 perfect suits.

Fortunately, Mr. Giles has no modern ideas about retirement. Many, many people have worked hard to make him the craftsman he is. And he is happy to be absorbed in a long and honorable tradition. He will work until he can no longer maintain the standard. And his fervent wish is to die in the harness, on the job, with the feel of the fabric between his fingers. When he lets go his grip on this world, the last thing he wants to feel is a fine worsted wool slipping between his fingers as he goes.

The suit that Edwin lays out on the four-poster bed is suit number seven hundred and twenty-one.

When this particular suit was fitted, Mr. Giles explained to Edwin that cloth that he had selected, or spoken for (and hence the term "bespoke" tailoring) was the last of a very old fabric. A fine fabric, and one that he had used to cut a suit for Edwin's father. At this mention of his dead father, Edwin had stiffened slightly, causing the cuff of his pants to rise 1/32nd of an inch by Mr. Giles's measurements. For Mr. Giles, this 1/32nd of an inch was a vast gulf filled with meaning. The good tailor quickly changed the subject to silence. Edwin had not thought of his father since.

But now, alone in a strange land and confronted with the fabric again, Edwin's thoughts turn to his father. He remembers him only in fragments, but always with a wry smile and an air of feckless joy. Happy, that is it, he remembers his father as being happy.

Edwin looks at the fabric carefully. It is a light grey wool with subtle flecks of green throughout. The fabric is remarkable in itself, but nothing when compared with the garment complete. To fully appreciate the suit, one has to note how it slides effortlessly over the canvas of fabric that forms the structure of the jacket. It has not been bonded together with chemical glue as mass-produced, off-the-rack suits are. No, this suit moves and rolls, flows naturally like skin. It is not an exaggeration to describe this garment as being alive.

Mr. Giles has cut several other suits for the younger Mr. Windsor. Although Mr. Giles enjoyed Edwin's father's custom for many years and came to know the man, he never again spoke of him to Edwin. It had been such a tragedy for a young boy. And, if the truth be told, it had hung his frame with a certain melancholy so that the suits Mr. Giles cut for Edwin were impossibly elegant. Wrought with a sadness, cast in the light of a great house in decline. And for each suit, when he had taken the measurements, he had heard something sacred and sad in the proportions.

With a deft hand Edwin throws a full Windsor knot into the silk tie. Two tugs and the knot is perfected. He folds the collar, double folds his shirt cuffs and inserts cufflinks. The links are nothing ostentatious or outrageous, just delicate circles, complete in themselves. Socks, pants, shoes, belt. Then he slides into the jacket and tugs his shirt cuffs free. Edwin takes a moment to admire the cut of the suit in the mirror. How diminished the suit had been without the wearer. But now, it is complete. And Edwin is completed by it. The art of the tailor is in the intersection, in the dance of fabric and occupant.

There is something terribly appropriate in dressing for dinner, Edwin reflects. Composing one's self in order to be with others. For whatever faults Iphigenia Reilly might have (and misplaced lust is surely one of them) she did retain a sense of propriety. Of gracious living, if that were a phrase Edwin could use. And as long as a sense of this, a vestige of style and sensibility remained in the world, all hope could not be lost. Progress could be made.

Edwin leaves the room with a spring in his step.

CHAPTER THIRTEEN
Empress Josephine?

For years Edwin has guarded himself against the weakness of optimism. He has often seen false confidence punished in others by the relentless and unforgiving world. He has often heard cries of, "I'm invincible!" quickly followed by smaller, less forceful statements like "please, stop, don't, I have a family." But if you could ask him, as he descends Iphigenia's ostentatious antebellum staircase, he might admit a certain — well, not hope, you understand, but let's just say Edwin is prepared to believe that a glass exists. And further, that this glass holds liquid.

A servant directs Edwin towards the dining room. As Edwin walks he tugs a shirt cuff back into place. He has no real hopes for the cuisine, but he is hungry. At least his lower nature will be gratified.

The doors to the dining room swing open. And once again, Edwin realizes what an absurd emotion hope really is. As a younger man Edwin had often wondered why the progress of the human race was so slow, inconsistent and easily reversed. Why did the great minds not make the obvious leaps sooner? And why, when these leaps were made, did the great mass of men refuse to accept them? How, in any god's name, was the library at Alexandria allowed to burn?

Before him is the answer to these questions. In the center of the room, on a raised dais, being fed fruit and fanned by well-oiled young men in loincloths is Iphigenia Reilly. She is dressed, Edwin can only assume, as the Empress Josephine. A different man would be surprised, would break stride, gasp or perhaps even be struck blind from the sheer absurdity of it all. Edwin grinds his molars together and presses on.

"Why, Edwin dearest, how nice of you to come throw yourself at my feet. I've even saved you a cushion. Isn't that thoughtful of me?"

Edwin does not throw himself anywhere. Instead, he walks to the table and seats himself with great care. His size makes the low surface and delicate Louis XIII chair awkward and uncomfortable. But it is no matter. This is obviously a room in which dignity does not stand a chance.

"Where," Edwin asks, "is the boy?"

Iphigenia's laughter echoes in the high-ceilinged room. "I thought we could find some time to be alone together. To share our thoughts and speak of our feelings. Our feelings as adults."

"I appreciate that. But I am here in a business capacity."

"Oh, Mr. Windsor, never mind about the boy, I'm the REAL villain in the family."

Edwin says nothing. He even tries to think nothing. He merely looks at Iphigenia, and let's the silence work on her.

"Mr. Windsor, do you know what it is to be a woman in the South? In Lower Alabama? Raised and reared through the times I have known?"

Edwin doesn't even move.

"Of course you do not. But mine is the sex which is born to suffer. And the very blood that flows in my veins is born to misfortune. Is it so unreasonable that I would resist my fate? Would you not do the same in my shoes?"

In spite of his best efforts, Edwin blinks.

"Mr. Windsor, my husband was a dim, oafish creature. And I poisoned him myself. Does that surprise you? That evil should have such a beautiful and deceptive countenance?"

This does not surprise Edwin. In fact, it rather bores him. This is now a colossal time suck. Edwin is short on money. Which, of course, means that he is short on time. Better to cut his losses now.

Edwin removes the napkin from his lap, folds it and places it on the empty plate in front of him. "I take this monologue to mean that dinner is not forthcoming." He stands and buttons his jacket. "Madame, I will require your car to take me to the airport."

Iphigenia laughs so loudly she startles one of the well-oiled men who is fanning her. "Really Mr. Windsor, you surprise me in your naiveté. It is one thing to reject my sweet tea, it is entirely another to reject my hospitality."

"I have neither talents nor time to waste."

"Really now. And what else would you waste your time and talents on?"

"Something, anything that would show a profit."

"I do not lack money. Do you think I have any scruples?"

Edwin considers carefully. "No."

"Then scheme a scheme for me Mr. Windsor. That is what you do isn't it? Scheming schemes, never taking action." She looks lasciviously at one of the young men fanning her. "Seems terribly, what's the word I'm looking for, impotent?"

"Do you have any special gifts or talents I should be made aware of?"

"Other than my feminine wiles?" She bats her eyes at Edwin in a hideous fashion, "I have a tremendous amount of money and no scruples. Surely that is as thorough an ingredient list as you need for evil. And I am bored Mr. Windsor. Terribly bored." She holds up her hands. "These are far too idle. Be the devil for my playthings won't you?"

Edwin can't help himself. Distaste wells into his face like a bruise. Iphigenia does not react well to this.

"Alabaster! See that he has what he needs." The large black man moves to Edwin's side. "And relieve him of his cellphone. We wouldn't want him to have any distractions."

Edwin unbuttons his coat and produces his cellphone. "I have never cared for the devices," he says, as if all is right with the world.

As Iphigenia watches Edwin leave the room, there is no question in her mind that she has done the right thing. If her idiot son can be a villain, then she can be ten times the villain. This Edwin Windsor will merely be the tool, a technician in her employ. Besides, she does so enjoy making him uncomfortable.

CHAPTER FOURTEEN
Following the Protocol

Topper is missing his tall friend. Perhaps friend is not the exact word we are looking for here. Edwin doesn't seem to have friends in the usual sense of the word, but Topper likes him all the same. There is no denying that Edwin is a source of fascinating clients.

What Topper can't understand about Edwin is how a guy who is surrounded by such interesting people and opportunities can be so dull. Edwin never lets himself go. Never lets it all hang out. Surely Edwin must have urges? Topper has urges. And if there is one thing that Topper believes — one firm principle amid the shifting quicksand of the little lawyer's moral life — it's that you have to enjoy yourself. Topper believes that repression causes thin lips, sexless women and cancer.

Topper doesn't think it's wrong that Edwin pours so much of himself into his work. It's good to like your work. In fact, Topper is having a great day at work. As a negotiation tactic, he has just thrown a chair through the side of a 500 gallon reef tank. Clearly, Topper enjoys his work. But at the end of the day, when the work is done, a man needs something else. A man needs vices.

The way Topper sees it, that's how the whole system works. If you don't have vices, then you save money. And a man who saves money — who doesn't gamble or drink or do drugs or spend money on professional female companionship — well, in Topper's mind this is a man who will always be less creative and productive than a man who is profligate in his ways.

Why would a Puritan need to work hard? Early to bed, early to rise. Whatever. But get yourself on the wrong side of a loanshark or develop a serious jones for a real high-quality, first-class, expensive bender: these are the urges that inspire a man to greater efforts. You work hard to have the expensive extras. And you work even harder to pay them off before your legs are broken. This is the spirit that has made America great. This and the time-honored principle of sticking it to the other guy.

As Topper enters the lobby he says to Agnes, "Hey toots, how's tricks?"

Agnes does not look up from what she is reading. "Deceptive, I should think. And no substitute for a sound strategy."

"Work, work, work. That's all it ever is up here. C'mon, what say you and me take a break? Hit the strip club for lunch?"

"I am afraid I will have to politely decline your revolting invitation."

"So, is he back yet?"

"No," says Agnes. She still hasn't looked at Topper.

"When is he coming back?"

"I don't know."

"What do you mean you don't know?" Topper asks. "You know everything about him."

"He hasn't called," Agnes says with an air of great boredom.

"He hasn't called?"

"Ah, there is an echo in here," she says, looking into the high corners of the room.

"What do you mean he hasn't called?"

"Perhaps a rug would dampen it."

"He hasn't called? Is he in trouble?"

"Or some tapestries."

"He's in trouble. He's got to be in trouble."

"Ah, but I fear Edwin would not care for tapestries. Perhaps one of those newfangled white noise generators?"

"YOU CRAZY BROAD EDWIN'S IN TROUBLE! ANSWER MY QUESTION!"

Agnes pauses to let Topper complete a twitching and cursing fit. Once again she has reduced him to a state of apoplexy. Mission accomplished, she thinks to herself. But she cannot not resist one last dig. "Quite enough noise in here already."

Topper sucks air into his lungs in preparation for a full-on tantrum. Agnes feels it best to cut him off: "I have not attempted to call him because we have a protocol."

"Protocol? What's this protocol?" asks Topper.

"It's a set of rules that we have agreed to use when facing such situations."

"Arrrrrrrrrrrgh! I know that. You don't think I could pass the bar without knowing what a protocol is?"

"Pass the bar? Why, I always assumed you had merely walked underneath it."

"Ah, cheap shot you old bat. Tell me what's what or I'll let everybody know you're the reanimated mummy of Mary Poppins' grandma."

"If Edwin does not make contact in 36 hours, there are a series of steps that I take to resolve any untoward situation and recover him."

"Then what are you waiting for?"

"There are still five minutes remaining in the waiting period."

75

"Five minutes. FIVE MINUTES! You've got to be shitting me. We gotta go. We gotta go right now."

"Go whither and do which?"

Topper paced the wide marble floor furiously as he tried to piece a plan together. "We gotta go get him. We gotta get a shitload of guys. C'mon, this has to be in the plan, the protocol, whatever. Edwin's good at this. Guys, guns, some dynamite. A bulldozer to knock in some walls. Hell, an armored bulldozer. Yeah, yeah. And a Cadillac. A big friggin' Caddy to use as a getaway car. And make it a convertible 'cause Edwin's so tall."

"Truly, you think of everything," Agnes says as she calmly picks up the phone.

"Yeah, yeah. So that's in the plan. Right?"

Agnes shakes her head.

"Then who are you calling? Somebody with a crapload of Ninjas in black body armor or something? Oh, oh, it's gotta be somebody badass. Like a guy who farts laser beams out of his ears. A guy who can blow the side of a house in just by thinking about PEACHES!"

"No," says Agnes, "This is far more important."

"Who? Who is it?"

"I am calling Edwin's tailor."

CHAPTER FIFTEEN
Just a Consultant

Edwin is taken to a large room with good light. Once upon a time, an attempt had been made to make this room into a kind of conservatory for the musical edification for young Eustace. When Eustace had shown no interest or aptitude for music, the attempt had been abandoned. All that remains is a grand piano.

A guard is placed on his door but, to everyone's surprise, Edwin makes no attempt to escape. He hangs his jacket over a chair, rolls up his shirt sleeves and goes to work.

From Edwin's point of view, escape attempts are pointless. To begin with, he's not exactly sure where he is. And when you don't know where point A is, it's almost always impossible to get to point B. That makes any "heroic" effort a foolish risk to one's person and one's health.

Besides, Edwin has a problem to work on. Edwin is never so happy as when he is faced with an intricate and potentially lucrative problem to solve. He thinks it unlikely that this entire escapade will wind up being anything other than a waste. But, for the moment, this is out of his hands. So Edwin ignores everything that is beyond his control and does what he does best. He thinks.

For the first two days, Edwin's requests keep a team of assistants working around the clock. They gather information, collate data and print documents. Edwin is computer illiterate. Of course, that's not the way he says it. He will tell you that he is not easily fooled by computers, or seduced by any of the attendant fetishes of the cult of data. Data, in itself, is meaningless. For data to be of any use at all it requires a mind. A mind that, working from a coherent theoretical framework, can draw inferences, see patterns, use logic, overcome the narrow-minded thinking that infects a world of specialists.

Computer screens are too small for non-specialized thoughts. Edwin prefers to organize information in physical space. Tables, floors, walls. He has all the furniture removed from the room except for several large tables and a grand piano. While he thinks he constantly rearranges papers, books, pictures. He often changes where he stands or sits. Even the sweep of sunlight across the room indicates new connections. Edwin literally erects the structure of the challenge around him so that he can immerse himself in the problem.

At the end of the first day, two confused-looking young men in loincloths bring Edwin a cot. Edwin looks at the tiny bed. Then he looks down on the young men.

"We were just told to bring you a cot," one of them says.

"I will need another," says Edwin.

"They didn't tell us anything about that."

"Clearly, this is the best job you can hope to get."

"What's that supposed to mean?"

From the door of the room, Alabaster speaks. "Bring him another cot." The slave boys scurry off, leaving the two men to consider one another for a moment.

"This is not the best job you can hope to get. Why are you here?" asks Edwin.

"That old woman is shit crazy. But if she wants to pay me $140,000 a year so she can call me "Alabaster" and feel like she's living in Gone With the Wind, what do I care? I have two boys; they're both going to college and I'm going to retire in Aruba."

Edwin nods. Alabaster is the sanest man he has met in Alabama.

"So why don't you sleep in your room?" asks Alabaster.

Edwin turns back to the constellations of pages and images that cover the room behind him. "I don't want to leave the work."

Alabaster turns and leaves. He is certain that Edwin is as crazy as the rest of them. He doesn't have time to worry about the tall man. The house is running low on baby oil. Alabaster shakes his head and thinks of his sons. They will have a better life — a better life by far.

Exhausted from his labors, Edwin removes his pants and shirt, carefully folds them, and lays his long body down across the two cots. Under the weight of tremendous fatigue, the need for sleep takes over. But Edwin does not go without a fight. His mind still races. In his sleep he twitches, mutters and kicks out at odd angles. Edwin rarely sleeps for more than four hours at a time while working on a large project.

But as he sleeps, a book lies by the side of his bed. It is thick, heavy, and ponderously titled "Modern Power Distribution". On the back cover is a picture of the author, Thomas Putnam. Like the book, he is also thick and heavy. To compensate for his lack of chin, the learned Mr. Putnam wears a bristly mustache. While Edwin sleeps, Thomas Putnam and his compensatory mustache are being kidnapped. This is not Edwin's idea. He has suggested that it would be helpful to speak with Mr. Putnam. He might even have added that a phone call would suffice. But no matter. With the barest spark, the flames of Iphigenia's lunacy had been fanned.

Iphigenia's reasoning goes something like this: When you are a villain, you don't ask a technical expert if he has a spare moment to consult on your problem. You don't give him a phone call. There are conventions for all of this. You must

79

send in a strike team in a Nondescript White Van and grab the man while he is shopping, or perhaps playing with his children in the park. There is the black bag over the head, the futile yet inevitable struggle, the slamming of doors and the screeching of tires. Iphigenia thinks she is doing very well. She does not realize that these are the exact forms and tropes of villainy that Edwin rails against.

When Thomas Putnam is finally deposited in Edwin's room he is understandably upset. "What do you want with me!" Putnam demands through his mustache. Edwin looks at him. Then he walks over to the chair where his suit jacket is hanging.

"I demand to know what's going on here!"

Edwin dons his jacket, sighs deeply and answers as truthfully as he can. "If you must know, I am being held against my will by an oversexed antebellum nightmare of a woman because she believes that not only will I help her take over the world, I will also, upon due reflection, come to my senses and rule the world at her side as her consort."

This was not the answer Putnam was looking for. He tried again. "W-w-why have I been kidnapped?"

"Because these people are very stupid. I mentioned that it might be helpful if I could speak to you and…"

"What, you! You WHAT? Wait a minute. What in God's name is going on here?"

"I know," says Edwin, "it hurts to try make sense of it. I would have been happy with a phone call."

"This is an OUTRAGE, I, I, I…"

"I'm sorry for your inconvenience. Please try to calm down."

"INCONVENIENCE! I was at my son's BALL GAME! He saw his FATHER get KIDNAPPED!"

Edwin is already bored with the small talk, "Do you have a consulting fee?"

"WHAT?"

Edwin tries again, slower. "Do you have a consulting fee?"

"YES!"

"If we were to pay you, say, five times your normal consulting rate for this conversation, would that be sufficient incentive for you to stop yelling?"

"Uh, yeah," he says, stroking his mustache for reassurance. "But, please, what's going here? Who are these people?"

"You really don't want to know."

"Yes I do."

Edwin tries again. "As I explained, I am being held captive by an aged Francophilliac and her half-witted son. As far as I can tell, she longs to use her considerable wealth to see the antebellum South rise again in a ridiculous jihad of gracious living. And not only does she look to me for the plan through which her backward and inbred scheme can be realized, but she also demands my true love."

"You're right," says Putnam, "I really didn't want to know that."

"Yes, I'm usually right. Now," Edwin says, indicating a large map of North America that is marked with colored dots connected by an unruly matrix of fine lines, "do you recognize this?"

"It's the grid. Every power generation facility in North America."

"That is correct. Now, if my understanding is complete, this diagram means that every power generation facility is linked into the grid."

"Yes."

"Interconnected."

"Yes."

"Interdependent." For the first time since entering the room days ago, Edwin seats himself at the piano and begins to play.

"I wouldn't say that exactly, but close enough."

"So that a plant in New York might actually be generating power for a home in Florida."

"That's a stretch. You see, the energy used in transmission, dissipated in heat and radiated magnetic charge around the lines — "

"How do blackouts happen?"

"Well, it's complicated."

"Then tell me about the Lake Erie Loop. What happened with the Lake Erie Loop?"

"Well nobody really knows for sure. That blackout shut down the Northeast and the Midwest. It was blamed on a set of transmission lines that circle Lake Erie, but... well, I'm not sure what happened. There were investigations but..."

"Could it be that it was more politically expedient that a cause for the blackout never be found?"

"Yeah, that's probably it. Look, I charge people a lot of money to consult on power grid issues. But this system is so big — it crosses so many state and even national boundaries," he shrugged, "a lot of it is guesswork. It's worse in Europe."

"Please try to explain it to me."

"Look, in July 1996 a tree fell into a power line in Oregon. That took down 15 states."

"Remarkable," says Edwin. His fingers move faster across the keys. The music echoes beautifully through the empty room.

"Well, it was hot. People were using a lot of power for A/C. And the load on one power plant became too great, so it shut down. Which overloaded the next one. Boom, boom, boom, boom, like dominos."

"Or lemmings," Edwin says quietly.

"What?"

"Nothing." Edwin lifts his fingers from the keys and turns to face Putnam. "What is it called when power is, how shall I say, in harmony?"

"You mean, in 'phase.'"

"Yes, that's it."

"It's described by a sine function rotated through 180 degrees and when..."

"I've no need of a technical explanation. Now, power going down is one thing, but power going out of phase? What happens if power is out of phase?"

"How far out of phase?"

"180 degrees."

"A hundred and — are you nuts? It would cancel out; see if you have two waves, equal size, both headed in opposite directions. Wham."

"Calm water."

"Yeah, I guess. Nobody's stupid enough to do that."

Edwin drapes his long fingers over the keyboard and plays a chord. "Harmony, you see. But now, and just for an instant..." He shifts his fingers and the resulting chord is dissonant and wrong.

"But that could take down the whole grid. I mean you'd need a lot more than one power plant doing it. And all at the same time."

"And just for an instant?"

"Well, that's all you'd need, yeah."

"Thank you very much Mr. Putnam. Again, I am sorry for the inconvenience." Edwin rings a bell. In an instant, Alabaster appears in the doorway. "I am done with Mr. Putnam, Alabaster. Perhaps you could have him returned to his family in a slightly more civilized manner."

"I didn't want to kidnap him in the first place," says Alabaster. He shrugs in a way that suggests that these matters are largely out of his control.

"Do what you can," says Edwin.

As he is leaving, Putnam turns to Edwin and asks, "You're not really going to do it, are you?"

Edwin looks up from his papers. "Me? Heavens no. I don't do anything. I'm just a consultant. Like you."

With Putnam gone and the scheme complete in his mind, exhaustion overcomes Edwin. He goes to bed and sleeps for 14 hours. He is awakened by Alabaster shaking his shoulder.

"You've got to get up. She wants to see you."

Edwin sits up and considers appearing before a client in his current state, "I will require a shower and a shave first."

"No, sir. Ma'am powerful angry. She wants you right now."

"Ma'am?" Edwin asks.

Alabaster shrugs again. "She pays me $20 extra every time I call her Ma'am. I guess the habit stuck."

Edwin splashes water on his face, and cleans himself up as best he can. As he unrolls his sleeves he is moved to ask, "What is your real name?"

"Daniel."

"You won't mind if I don't call you Alabaster?"

"Nobody around here will know who you are talking about."

As Daniel helps him into his suit jacket, Edwin says, "That's fine. I'm afraid that no matter what I say, no one around here knows what I'm talking about."

CHAPTER SIXTEEN
Using the 'Asset'

Gus lights another cigarette. He takes a long drag and looks into the sky. In all the years Gus has known him, Excelsior has never just walked up. Would Gus walk if he could fly? Gus takes another drag and coughs some more. If Gus could fly, he'd probably just leave. But that's not the way it works. It feels like all the important decisions were made long ago and now Gus is just trying to live out his own epilogue with as little grief as possible.

There is a belch of diesel and a roaring noise as a generator comes to life. Arc lights cast harsh shadows across the decaying parking lot. Gus turns back to the nest of trailers and personnel that has sprung up in the last hour. Men in unofficial uniforms rush to and fro. Not a single one of them is without some kind of electronic doohingy. Typing and talking — struggling to get their thumbs on impossibly tiny little keys. And for what? Gus knows that they're all just talking to each other. And all while running around in the same damn parking lot. Why the hell are they running around? This isn't the runnin' around part. This is the waiting part.

He leans back against a car and watches minor bureaucrats swarm around him. He wouldn't give a damn for any of 'em. Not one tinker's damn. He coughs some more. Gus is too old for this shit. And yet they keep trotting him out to deal with the big man. That's one of the things they call Excelsior. The Big Man. Ha. When Gus found him he'd been a scared little boy in the middle of Kansas. Sure, he's gotten bigger since then. He's even figured out how to fly. He is way, way more powerful. But still, whenever Gus looks at Excelsior, all he sees is a scared little boy.

Shit, that was back in the days when they would send one guy to do a job. One guy and precious few regulations. Now they send a car full of guys and a trunk full of procedure manuals. And they still screw it up. Nobody has any initiative any more. Excelsior grows more powerful and all these drones grow weaker. Gus gives a bitter chuckle. The chuckle grows to a cough. And the coughing seizes him right down to his boots. As the air runs short, he wonders if this is finally it. But the coughing slows and the bright lights dance behind his eyes. Life, such as it is, goes on.

Radios crackle all around him. "The asset is inbound. Repeat, the asset is inbound." Men in jumpsuits scramble around frantically. As if what they do matters. As if what they do makes a difference at all. They're just ordinary men. Excelsior doesn't need their help.

Gus shakes his head. Is this what the world has really come to? The cars are fast and the men aren't worth a damn. Everybody has forgotten that life doesn't play by the rules. Every once in a while the bitch just tries to kill you. And sometimes you have to stand on it. Disable the safety and run it until it's red hot. No matter what the engineers say.

Maybe that's it. The world has gone to the engineers. Has to be it. When they first showed up they had slide rules. Now they have computers. Now nobody can take a crap without running it through a computer simulation. But for all their rules and their simulations and their levels upon levels of yes men, they still trot old Gus out to deal with Excelsior. That's 'cause the Big Man trusts Gus. That's 'cause Gus can look in his eyes and still see a scared little boy.

And right now, all these people — hell, they have a name for themselves, Bureau of Meta-Human Affairs or some such — all these college boy bastards scurry around not because they have something to do, but because they are afraid. If Excelsior wants, he can end all their lives. There's not a damn thing their simulations can do about it.

It's not something that's ever mentioned, but the fear is there all the same. Sure, it's all praises and service and propaganda when Excelsior shows up. But at the same time, everybody's bowels loosen a little bit. Gus laughs a little at this facade. The laugh becomes a cough.

"You shouldn't smoke," says one of the faceless drones or clones or whatever the hell they pass off as men these days. Gus looks right at it and he realizes that it's the head drone. A piggish little man everyone calls Director Smiles. In defiance, Gus hooks another cigarette in the corner of his ragged mouth.

"You got a light?"

"No, it's a filthy habit," Director Smiles says dismissively, "Now, let's talk about what we need from the asset."

"The asset?"

"Bishop Six."

"He has a name."

"Ah, Excelsior. We gave him that name. So we can give him another. And he is the most replaceable of us all."

Gus snorts. "Then why won't you bastards just let me go home?" Gus is getting riled. It's good. Makes him feel... not young, but less old.

"Duty," says the Director in a way that Gus finds especially maddening. "You must do your duty. And as for Bishop Six, of course he has certain powers, that is a fact. But without all of this," his gesture encompasses the field team rushing around them, "it would be to no avail. He cannot be in two places at once. The disasters he so loves to avert happen so fast that by

89

the time he learned of them the tragedies would be complete. He cannot reverse time."

"Sounds like a load of bullshit to me. There ain't nobody like him."

"Tensor, the Flamer, Cirrus — any of these could serve as our field operatives."

"They're weaker than he is."

"As Bishop Six is weaker than we are. How can one man contend with the compact mass of humanity? Thousands of operatives connected at the speed of light through broadband communications networks," he unclips some foul gadget from his belt and holds it up with pride. "Surely, Bishop Six can capture any one man. But which man? With this, I can take a picture and transmit it to the far side of the globe. Only then can our flying delivery boy capture the criminal and deliver him to our justice. Not his justice. Ours. The justice of ordinary, mediocre people."

Gus is tired of listening to this soft-handed man's talk. "Yeah, whatever."

Director Smiles flips open a binder. "Now, we'll just take a moment to go over the details one more time."

"He's not a details kind of guy."

"All the more reason for you to memorize the procedure — "

"Haw, haw, haw," Gus cuts him off. "Even if my memory was good enough to remember all that shit, I wouldn't do it. If you think it's so goddamned important, you talk to him about it."

"But you must. He listens to you."

"Probably because I don't waste his time with this bullshit," Gus says, blowing smoke in the fat little man's face.

"I am going to note your attitude in my report."

"You shouldn't threaten me like that. I'm an old man and I'm not sure that my heart can handle the strain. But you go ahead and tell him anything you like."

"Me? Oh, I could never. I mean, that's your job," Smiles says, flattening out his chins against his neck as he shakes his head in a vigorous No.

"Well, I'm not going to be around forever. Whattya scared or something?"

"Scared? Of Bishop Six? Don't be ridiculous."

Gus levers himself up off the car and advances on the small man. "Yeah, damn right you're scared. You're so used to snapping at people to get what you want, you forgot how to talk to them. Only you can't bully the strongest man in the world. Especially 'cause you're afraid of him."

"I am not. I am a rational man, and I understand that there are risks, of course, but I…"

"Bullshit. Back about a thousand years ago, I got to see a Hydrogen bomb. The boys called it 'Shrimp.' This bomb was being staged to the South Pacific and by coincidence Shrimp and I happened to be on the same base, at the same time. So the guy in charge of it asks me if I want to have a look. 'Sure,' I say, not wanting to look scared. They had it all alone in a hangar. And it didn't look all that threatening. All alone in a big, cold hanger. Just another piece of technology.

"Like your phone right there. But bigger, maybe like this trailer. There was no hum. There was no smell. There weren't even any lights. But I was scared anyway. 'Cause I thought that I knew what it could do."

"Yes, of course." says Director Smiles, impatient with the story already.

"But after they set it off, that's when I really got scared. You see all those guys in lab coats — all those guys with their binders and their big brains. They didn't know what it would do. Not for certain. Some said it might light the atmosphere on fire. And when they set it off, it was three times more powerful than they had calculated. I mean, when you say that a tree is going to grow a hundred apples and it grows 103, well, that's a mistake. You're just a little off. But when it grows 300? Well sir, that means you don't know shit about apple trees. And when the smartest guys don't know shit? That scares me.

"After that they stopped making bombs bigger. They were afraid they might crack the planet's crust. And even as I think back on it, it makes my palms sweat."

"But it didn't destroy the planet," says Director Smiles, thinking that he has a point.

"Scares me all the same. And Excelsior, The Big Guy, Bishop Six, the asset, whatever you want to call him. I know he can crack the planet. And so do you. So I know you're scared."

"But you're scared as well."

"Hell, son," says Gus, "I know I'm done. All I'm afraid of is the arthritis, constipation and not dying with my boots on."

"Your story is very colorful. But I assure you, as a rational man, doing his duty, I am not afraid."

A young man leans out of the telemetry trailer and yells, "Bishop Six 500 meters."

The director throws his binder at Gus and scurries off like a mouse. As he flees he yells, "Just see that he gets it done."

Gus tucks a fresh cigarette into his mouth and squints at the sky. High above him a bird moves through the air. No, not a bird. It's hard to get used to it. Even after all these years, Gus still can't make sense of it. Up in the sky, a man. Re-damn-diculous.

Excelsior settles to earth next to him.

"You look old, sir," says Excelsior.

"That's got nothing on how I feel," Gus replies.

There is the tiniest flash of light from Excelsior's eyes. Now Gus's cigarette is lit. Gus doesn't jump, at least he doesn't think he jumps. A man's not supposed to be able to light things with his eyes. He just isn't.

"What is it this time?" asks Excelsior.

Gus takes a long drag and exhales the word, "Hurricane."

"What?" asks Excelsior.

"Big son-of-a-bitch. Headed right for Miami."

"Why don't they evacuate?"

Gus flips through the binder. "I don't know. It's gotta be in here somewhere."

"Let me see that," says Excelsior. Instead of giving it to him, Gus throws it over his shoulder. He doesn't want Excelsior to see himself referred to as "the asset."

"Ah, it's all bullshit anyway," Gus says, bluffing his way through. "There's only two things it could be. One, they screwed up and didn't get the evacuation warning out in time. Or two, they're so used to counting on you, they didn't even bother to issue a warning. Either way, there's two and half million people who are depending on you."

"Two and a half million," Excelsior says, trying to get a handle on a number that large.

"Yeah, that's right."

"Gus, you know, I've never…"

"Ain't no time to be bashful, son. This is the time to get going. Those people need you."

"But what if? I mean, what if…" Excelsior says, thinking back to flight 209.

Gus gives Excelsior a look. "You're not going to let that happen." Excelsior drops his head to his chest. Jesus Christ, thinks Gus, not again. "You HEAR me? You're NOT going to let that happen."

Excelsior picks his head up. "No. I'm not."

Gus drops his cigarette on the ground and stubs it out. "Well, that's it then. Get to it."

Excelsior is gone in an instant.

CHAPTER SEVENTEEN
Edwin Makes his Pitch

Edwin breathes in. He breathes out and tries to release the tension from his shoulders. It doesn't work very well. The moment is upon him. Alabaster, who is Daniel, opens the large set of French doors that lead to the back of the property. The heat and humidity hit Edwin like a wet, sloppy fist.

In the distance Edwin sees that a pavilion of sorts had been erected. He hears the blare of a trumpet followed by cheering. Edwin looks to Alabaster/Daniel for some kind of context. Daniel just shakes his head. Edwin assumes that, once again, bad has gone to worse.

As they draw closer, Edwin sees that three teams of oiled boys are engaged in a pony race around a makeshift track. Iphigenia claps madly and squeals with delight as the young men jockey for position heading into the final corner. The number three team commands the lead on the inside. But at a crucial moment, one of the contestants loses his footing. The resulting crash takes out all of the contestants before they reach the finish line. An unjudgeable heap of bodies lies in the middle of the track. At least one broken limb protrudes from the mass.

Ah, thinks Edwin, Disaster. The theme of his trip.

This catastrophe in no way diminishes Iphigenia's enjoyment. She screams at the top of her leathery lungs and collapses onto her throne in a fit of hysterical laughter. She beckons a nearby slave-boy for something to drink. Edwin realizes that the figure seated next to her in a jester's outfit is her son Eustace. As Edwin approaches he can see that Eustace is chained to his mother's chair.

"Why Mister Windsor, how nice of you to join our little derby. Would you like me to run them for you again?"

Edwin looks at the boys picking themselves up off the ground. Several are bleeding. All of them have some kind of injury. They look exhausted. This dismal spectacle has surely gone on long enough.

"I don't care for sporting events. I don't enjoy leaving things to chance."

Iphigenia laughs. "You are such a serious, serious man, Mr. Windsor. You should inject some levity into your existence. Enjoy each breath instead of merely sucking them in and out between your teeth."

"I enjoy my work."

"And how goes your work? Have you schemed a scheme for us?" The use of the royal pronoun is not lost on Edwin.

"I have."

"Well, then by all means. The floor is yours to display our latest entertainment."

Edwin coughs and motions to Daniel. "Daniel, my papers."

"Daniel? Whoever are you talking to? Why, Alabaster! Have you been speaking nonsense in this man's presence?"

"No ma'am," Alabaster says.

"Are you lying to me, boy?" Daniel stiffens at the use of the word boy. He closes his eyes and sees a house high on a hill in Aruba and his anger subsides. "For that I shall have your paycheck flogged."

Edwin clears his throat and speaks, "Madame, when I asked you if you had any powers or abilities, you mentioned a lack of scruples — "

"Oh, how true," Iphagenia says, caressing a perfectly formed young boy who is holding her flagon of wine.

" — a considerable fortune, and boredom. But I have found that you have lied to me."

"Have I really? Why, I'm sure I didn't mean to."

"Fear not. I shall not flog your paycheck over it. But a lie of omission is a lie all the same." Edwin unfurls his map of power-generating facilities in North America. "It would appear that you have effective control over 24 electric power facilities throughout Alabama, is that not so?"

"Yes, well, that's just where the money comes from. The business is so dull."

"13 million gigawatts are at your command. Madame, you have considerably more at your disposal than mere financial assets."

"Well, perhaps I do. What do you propose? That I turn off the lights? Throughout Alabama?"

"No, Madame," Edwin scans the pointless decadence that surrounds him. "From what I have seen there is more than enough darkness in Alabama."

"What do you mean by that?!"

"I mean simply that there is no profit to be made in turning the lights off in Alabama."

"Well, any fool knows that. Why should I pay you to tell me that?" Iphigenia demands. In her mind she has become the very picture of royal wrath. She slobbers as she yells. Edwin is repulsed by the slobber, but unaffected by the wrath.

"Allow me to beg a bit more of your limited patience." And also limited intelligence and imagination, thinks Edwin. "As you are not inclined towards the family business, I will point out that these thin lines represent the transmission network, or power grid."

"I know that. I said it was boring, I did not say I was completely ignorant of it."

"Yes, and you know that if you turned off all of your power plants, electricity from the neighboring plants would flow through the grid and pick up the slack. There might be an area of increased dimness towards the middle of the state, but there are so few street lights and reading lamps in that region anyway," Edwin trails off with a wave of his hand.

"But," Edwin continues, with an air of growing excitement, "If you turned them off, rotated the phase of the power 180 degrees and then turned them back on again very quickly..."

Iphigenia does not understand. "What?"

"Yes, exactly. What?"

"What? I don't understand what would happen."

"Yes, that's the thing, I'm not sure anyone fully comprehends what would happen. But let me paint you a picture. On the beaches of Southern California, the blenders in smoothie stands would come to a halt. In New York, the lights would go out on Broadway. And everywhere in between, provided that it was night, darkness would fall across the land."

Iphigenia's eyes grow wide. Her lust for power, for evil, for wrongdoing is now a raging inferno. She staggers to her feet, which are now unaccustomed to walking because she has been carried around on a palanquin for so many days. She brings her swaying form under control and screams, "I can shut off the ENTIRE DAMN COUNTRY!"

Eustace is also caught up in the excitement. He leaps to his feet and shouts, "World DOMINATION! DOMINATION! DOMINATION!" Iphigenia be and his new conreaks a serving plate over his head. Eustace falls silent as hcussion collapse in a heap on the floor.

"So, Mr. Windsor, you are going to Washington to deliver my demands?"

The ground spins a little for Edwin. Why does this always happen to him? Why are they always so misguided? So foolish? He focuses his disappointment and contempt into a single word, "No."

"What do you mean, no? You've dreamt up this wonderful scheme, you fantastically evil man. Now we'll hold them to ransom. I could just kiss you."

"No," Edwin says, resisting the urge to gnash his teeth, "We will not hold anyone to ransom."

"Well, why not? You've given me the power to make my dreams come true. Finally a country of my own. The Kingdom of Lower Alabama! We shall take New Orleans and West Florida. And from there we shall have an empire. Resplendent in the former glory of the South."

Edwin pinches the bridge of his nose and summons his patience. "The reason we will not hold anyone to ransom is that, when you threaten someone with a destructive scheme, you must necessarily let them know your plan and, thereby, grant them a chance to stop you."

"Well then what am I to do with this newfound power to manipulate power?"

"I am glad you asked," says Edwin, clinging to the thinnest thread of hope. Because Iphigenia has asked, perhaps she will listen. "You are going to buy a widespread set of calls throughout the economy. Refining, manufacturing, retail, information technology — any operation where a sudden, unpredictable disruption of power will cause a dramatic spike in costs. Then, when you flip the switch and the market chaos ensues, trillions of dollars of wealth will flow to you through fronts and dummy corporations."

"Money? Money? What makes you think I want money? I've got more money than I know what to do with. I don't need money. What I need is the Empire of Lower Alabama before me on bended knee. Show me how I can take over Alabama, Louisiana and West Florida."

Edwin is very careful that his emotions do not register on his face. "Madame, I have labored for more days than I care to remember. I have presented you with a scheme that can easily make you the wealthiest woman in the world."

"I told you, I don't want money. I want control!"

"The easiest way to control something is to own it. And what's the point in fighting for something when you can simply buy it?"

"Silly boy, one cannot buy the hearts and minds of the people."

Edwin has no idea what Iphigenia is talking about. In his experience, the sad truth of human nature is not that people can be bought, but that they can bought for so little.

Iphigenia charges on. "One must conquer them! One must defend one's territory with cunning and force and might. Glorious battle that offers the chance of gallantry and heroics!"

Later, Edwin will realize that it was the word gallantry that tore it for him. Now he just says, "Madame, if you are too stupid to recognize your own advantage, I simply cannot help you."

Iphigenia presses her desiccated lips together and squints. "Mr. Windsor, I have shared my dream with you." She blinks back tears of the purest distilled crazy. "And you, sir, you have shat upon it. That is rude. Just very simply rude. And I am now upset." Iphigenia waves her hand and a great number of slave boys surround Edwin.

"I am thankful that you have come to the soon-to-be Empire of Lower Alabama. For that has given us the chance to teach you some manners. Alabaster, we order that he be confined with the pigs. Let us see how he enjoys being shat upon."

As they drag him away, Edwin asks Daniel, "You do realize that this is completely insane?"

"I see your lips moving," says Daniel, "but all I hear is Harvard and Yale. Harvard and Yale."

Edwin breathes out and lets himself be dragged.

CHAPTER EIGHTEEN
Search your Feelings

As a deeply theoretical man, Edwin has thought long and hard about hostage situations. Not only does he have clients to advise, but in his profession being taken hostage is bound to happen sooner or later. Key to Edwin's thinking is the idea that negotiation is overrated. Anyone who thinks that kidnapping is a good idea is irrational. And, with an irrational person, a rational process like negotiation is chancy at best.

The way Edwin sees it, taking a person, or anything else, to eventually get money is inefficient. If you want money, you should take money. But then, if you want money, why steal? There are any number of ways to borrow money. Money can also be earned. Money can be obtained through fraud. As a general rule one should not steal money when in need of money. One should only steal when it is overwhelmingly convenient.

In fact, theft in itself is crude. A remnant of the time when barbarous populations rode across windswept plains to sack entire civilizations. Why go to the trouble of taking something when, with a little imagination and planning, you can convince your victim to give it to you? And the theft of a person is worst of all. People are difficult to transport. Difficult to keep in good condition. And, worst of all, when people are taken, irrational value is attached to them.

"Consider," Edwin might say when explaining this to a client, "the most obnoxious child you have ever known. Perhaps you have been forced to endure the presence of such a creature at the lawn club luncheon or at a museum benefit. In the midst of your sorbet you have surely thought, 'I would pay handsomely to have that brat's vocal cords removed, table-side, before the desert course.'

"And let us further posit that this is not merely a bad day for this child but, in fact, he will undoubtedly grow to become the kind of unrestrained boor who laughs too hard at tasteless jokes and will one day beat his wife to death with a nine iron.

"All in all, this person is a benefit only to lawyers, and the apple of only his mother's well-medicated eye. But if you kidnap this monster at any point in his obnoxious life-cycle, the sympathy of untold millions will flow towards him. Even though society would be measurably better off without him. For this reason, kidnapping simply isn't worth the feelings of righteous indignation it evokes among the herd."

There are so few criminal schemes that will work. Edwin views all crimes as recipes. The right amount of this, the correct amount of that and, at the end, money. For all of his clients, Edwin tries to make sure that the amount of money at the end is far, far greater than the cost of the ingredients.

The costliest ingredient in kidnapping is secrecy. Not only do all of the conspirators have to keep quiet about the affair — a virtual impossibility with more than two people involved — but they also have to maintain the secrecy of the hostage's location. The entire scheme depends on it as a lever depends on its fulcrum.

So as he sits, shackled in the middle of a pig sty, Edwin has fewer worries than most people in his situation. He is being held at his last known location. And he knows that Agnes will call upon considerable resources to come to his aid. Not that she will have to. In this case, even a call to the local police might sort it out. Edwin smiles when he thinks of the logic of fighting incompetence with incompetence. So in this unusual circumstance, Edwin's greatest worry is for his suit.

As Edwin was dragged away, he hoped to have a chance to remove his jacket. But none came. He was thrown into the sty. And while his landing was soft, it was also incredibly filthy. Even as Edwin struggled to regain his feet, the slave boys swarmed him and crushed him once again to the liquid filth. Edwin pleaded with them, "Please. Please, spare the jacket." But the mob did not listen. Even though he did not resist, several sat on him while the others chained his feet.

After the initial violence, Edwin was left alone. The pigs, who wisely retreated from the human foolishness, now inspect the newest member of their sty. They snort and nudge Edwin. They quickly deem him harmless and inedible and return to wallowing in the mud. Filthy animals, some would say, but Edwin recognizes the native intelligence of these beasts. Pigs do not have sweat glands. Edwin is not exactly sure how he knows this, but this odd bit of trivium explains a great deal. The cesspool where he finds himself confined is the pig's air conditioning system. They cover themselves in mud to cool themselves, and to protect their skin from sunburn.

Edwin squints at the sun. Sunburn will be a problem. As well as dehydration. Another, more survival-minded man, would be covering his own delicate skin with mud right now. But Edwin does not descend to such behavior. He does not revert to the level of the savage. Better to die first, he thinks, than to give up what little dignity he has left. Edwin produces a spotless handkerchief from inside his jacket — a minor miracle, considering recent events — and cleans what filth he can from his face, hands and hair.

Edwin stands for as long as he is able, but eventually gravity pulls him down into the mud. The pigs wallow. Edwin broods.

The sun moves across the sky. Edwin dozes as best he can while sitting up.

"Oh my heavens. Mr. Windsor, bless your heart, you are a sight."

Edwin opens his eyes and sees Iphigenia holding an absurd parasol over her head. Around her, a retinue of slave boys fan their taffeta-wrapped queen. Edwin stands and straightens his ruined apparel as best he can, "Your hospitality, madame, leaves much to be desired."

"Oh, Mr. Windsor, it is you who have rejected my hospitality with your horrific manners."

"Whatever was I thinking?"

"Well, that's what I came here to talk to you about. You see, I believe that you are meant for far better things than this."

Edwin does not comment on the obvious.

"Do you regret your mistake of spurning me?" asks Iphigenia.

"I'm not sure I understand."

"Oh, Edwin, do not play coy with me. Search your feelings. Surely my nobility calls out to you, as yours cries out to mine. Come to your senses, my dear, and I can remove you from this squalor. Elevate you to your proper station. You shall become my consort, one of several, it is true, but we shall rule the world together."

Edwin had thought he was fully acquainted with all the ways that bad could go to worse, but at this moment he realizes he was mistaken. He clings to his professional demeanor. "While I do pride myself on thorough care of my clients, the arrangement you are suggesting is not a service I provide."

"But search your feelings. You must admit that you are attracted to me."

A wave of weariness ripples through Edwin's legs. He looks long and hard at Iphigenia. On her forehead he sees a droplet of sweat extrude itself through the layers of make up and sludge its way downward. Edwin realizes, with no small amount of horror, that he is more attracted to the pigs. There is no nobility here. Only unrepentant lunacy. All of Edwin's instincts recoil in horror. Still, he maintains control. He buttons the middle button on his suit jacket, draws himself to his full height and with great formality says, "No."

Iphigenia says nothing. The scene is still. Even the slave boys pause in their endless fanning. She presses her lips together and gets a far off look in her eye. For a moment it seems that she might cry. But then her hand darts out. A whip makes sharp contact with bare flesh. A slave boy cries out in pain and then the fanning resumes. "You are a fool, Edwin Windsor." With that she turns and walks away, her absurd retinue following in her wake. All but one.

There, with a fresh lump on his forehead, is Eustace, still in the jester's uniform. He hangs his head and arms over the fence and stares at Edwin. After a while he says, "Hey man, you're covered in pig shit."

"So your mother has let you go," says Edwin

"Yeah man, she's busy with her 'friends.'"

"I'm sure she is."

"You know, I believed you, man."

Like a shark smelling blood from miles away, Edwin senses weakness, leverage, an opening. "And you were right to. Your mother does not have half the control she imagines."

"Aw man, that ain't nothing but some bullshit. Momma got control. You said bad things about momma. Now momma got you too." Edwin just smiles. "Man, why you smiling?" asks Eustace, "you ass deep in shit."

"Your mother does not even have control of herself."

"What's that bullshit mean?"

"Eustace can't understand," says Edwin. Gently, he thinks. He must proceed gently.

"You calling me stupid?"

"That's not what I'm saying. I'm saying that Dr. Loeb knows what I'm talking about." Edwin hates himself a little for playing such an artless and obvious gambit. But there is no way to put a subtle move on a witless person. "Dr. Loeb understands what Eustace cannot. Ja, mein Herr?"

"Man, you crazy."

Edwin stands. "I may be chained in the middle of a pit of filth. I may be exhausted. My patience might be wearing thin. But I assure you, my sanity is intact. You are clean, rested, possessed of no self-discipline and more surely a prisoner of your mother than I could ever be."

Eustace looks away.

"So you have a choice to make. You may remain Eustace Eugene Reilly. Slave to your mother's desires. Never having a life or will of your own — "

"But I like it here."

"I'm sure that you do. It is comfortable. It is certain. Most of all, it is familiar. But you have a dream. A dream that you whispered to me in my office."

"Domination?" Eustace whispers, fearful of even speaking the word.

"Domination. You want control. And I can help you get it. But first you must control yourself. You must help yourself. You must help me."

"Ya'll want me to run and go get you a gun?"

"No, I don't need your help, Eustace. Eustace is weak. Eustace cannot even help himself. I need Dr. Loeb."

"What?"

"EUSTACE YOU ARE WEAK!"

Eustace jumps back as if he has been slapped. For a moment, Edwin thinks he has overplayed. But Eustace settles back down on the fence. "Yeah man. I sure am," Eustace admits. Edwin is still in the game.

"You are too weak to overcome your mother."

"Yeah."

"But the evil Doctor — " Edwin locks eyes with the awkward boy and says nothing. The moment stretches into a minute. The minute stretches into a time. Slowly, Eustace straightens.

"Ja." Eustace says quietly.

"He is strong."

"Kampfkraft," Eustace says a little louder.

"Yes, yes, cunning"

"Ja, JA. That voman is OUTFRAGEOUS!"

"Yes. Now unlock these chains and we can begin."

"You must promifse sometink first," says Dr. Loeb.

This is good, thinks Edwin. Dr. Loeb senses weakness and is using it to bargain. Vicious, yet rational. It is the kind of thing that Edwin can twist to his advantage. But Edwin is in a horrible position to negotiate. "What is that, Herr Doctor?"

"Ve vill built a lazer."

Edwin shakes his head, "We discussed this."

"There vill be no discuzzion!" Dr. Loeb punctuates each word with a slap of his hand. "YOU VILL HELP ME BUILD A GIANT LAZER IN SPACE!"

Edwin sighs. Under the weight of all this absurdity, he is amazed that he can remain standing.

CHAPTER NINETEEN
Nothing Right for Agnes

Agnes isn't having a good day. She's holding it together, but the fact that Edwin is in trouble is wearing on her more than her stiff upper lip will allow her to reveal.

To add to her strain, Topper has insisted upon coming along. "To the rescue!" he cried as he boarded the private jet. That was the first and last useful statement he had to offer. As soon as his little feet touched the lush carpet, an unending stream of bad ideas had rolled out of him.

"A stampede, that will do it."

"Wait, wait, a stampede of, not of cattle, but of guys dressed as Mexican wrestlers. That'll confuse the shit out of them."

"Ah, never mind, too complicated. Did you remember to pack a rocket launcher? No. Flamethrower? What? Why are you looking at me like that?"

Agnes knows that Edwin relies on Topper from time to time. And that, after his own fashion, Topper is loyal and trustworthy. But she does not approve of him. To Agnes, Topper is an undersized Barbarian with a law degree. She is certain that the little man's growth has been stunted by nothing other than his own debauchery. Yes, Topper is a good lawyer. But he is not the only good lawyer.

Restraint and perseverance are called for here. There are steps they can take — a great many steps — before it is time to call in the commandos. The important thing is not to increase the risk to Edwin. It is also important not to take action until they know, for certain, what the situation is.

From the plane, she attempts to call the Reilly residence several times. The phone rings and rings and rings. Agnes is beset by a maddening lack of information.

As the wheels touch down in Alabama, the protocol dictates that she make an appeal to the local authorities. Make the matter seem innocuous. An ordinary missing person case. She does not have a high estimation of local sheriffs, but it is a place to start. Agnes shares this idea with Topper. It is a logical, reasonable first step.

Topper says "Yer outta your old, wrinkly head. These rednecks aren't going to help you. They're probably all related. Haven't you seen any movies?"

"Well, what would you have us do?" asks Agnes, not really wanting to hear the answer.

"You go back home. I'll find some tanks, roll in there, blow the whole joint up and get him out."

"NO! You know very well how Edwin feels about senseless destruction."

"Yeah, but that's because he's an egghead. He's not a get-it-done kind of guy like me."

Topper cannot not persuade Agnes to see things his way. So, with the dwarf in tow, she marches into the Hims Chapel County Seat, through a door that reads Sheriff's Department, and in a loud voice asks "Is this the local constabulary?"

Earl, or more formally, Deputy Sheriff Earl Trotter, looks up at Agnes in a way that suggests he has no idea what a constable is, much less a constabulary, but is willing to adopt a shoot-first-ask-questions-later policy towards whatever it might be. His ears are set a little too high and his eyes are set a little too close together. When he asks, "Whut?" his features seem to jump off the top of his head.

"Law enforcement," says Agnes, "I am seeking the local authorities."

"That'd be sheriff Jessup."

"Is he about? I should like to file a complaint."

"Oh no, ma'am, he don't like complainers."

"Very well then, a missing persons report. I have reason to believe that my associate is being held to the North of here by — "

"Now just wait a minute Ma'am. Iff'n you know where he is, he ain't exactly missing now is he?" Earl looks at Topper realizing for the first time that there is a dwarf in the room. None of this makes sense to Earl.

"Deputy, a man is being held against his will!"

Earl's eyes flash back and forth between Topper and Agnes. "Well, ma'am, we in the profession would call that kidnapping."

"I care not what you call it."

"Well, it's important, cause we've got different forms for different things. See, if you had lost some livestock — "

"No, no, no, you dolt. A person, a man, has been kidnapped. And I need you to — "

Earl holds up his hand. Feeling that he is exercising his finely tuned powers of observation, Deputy Earl asks, "Ma'am, are you aware you are being tailed by a dwarf?"

"Painfully," says Agnes, wringing every bit of emotion out of the word.

"Screw this noise," says Topper, "This shitkicker's getting us nowhere." As Topper walks out, the last thing he hears is Earl saying, "Now ma'am, about how long do you reckon that rude little fella has been surveilling you?"

Agnes tries to explain, once again, about Edwin Windsor being held against his will. Earl wants none of it. "Ma'am, are

113

you sure you don't want to file a complaint against that rude little fella."

"No," says Agnes, "Remarkably, that annoying little man is the least of my troubles today. Now about this kidnapping."

"Oh Ma'am, I can't do nothing about that. You're just gonna have to talk to the sheriff."

"And where is he?"

"He's out, ma'am."

"When do you expect him to return?"

"Can't say. He comes and goes a lot. O-fficial business and all."

Agnes is not the kind of woman who can be dissuaded by a weak-chinned man. "Very well," she says, "I shall wait." And she plants herself in a chair as if she has every intention of growing roots.

The hours pass. The deputy is not comfortable with the strange English woman in his workspace. He had thought she would grow tired and bored and leave. But she does not. With each passing moment, Agnes is more at home in her environment. First, she flips through a magazine. Then she gathers all of the magazines in the sitting area, removes the subscription cards, and piles them alphabetically by subject. Next, she organizes the furniture. Wherever she steps, order follows.

The Deputy protests, "Hey, look, now just look, you can't — "

Agnes counters, "But it is such a frightful mess."

"But this is important po-lice business."

"All the more reason that it should not be shoddy."

Of course, Agnes knows exactly what she is doing. A little more time and she will have broken him completely. As she thinks this, she hears the rumble of heavy equipment. With her innate English instinct for tragedy, she knows Topper is about to ruin everything.

A blast of an air horn rattles the windows in the Hims Chapel Sheriff's office. Agnes hears the grinding of gears and an unmistakable, high-pitched cackle. The dwarf is afoot!

"Whut in the hell is that?" asks the deputy as he reaches for his gun belt.

Agnes does not answer. She drops a stack of files and bustles out the door as fast as her proper old feet will carry her.

Outside she sees a flatbed truck with a bulldozer on it accelerating hard towards the north end of town. As the truck roars past her, Topper throws her a little wave. He appears to be standing high above the wheel, on a naked woman's lap.

"Oh my God," says Agnes. She is certain that she has just seen the first Harbinger of the Apocalypse.

At the far end of main street, Topper flattens a few parking meters and a defenseless shrub. Squeezed onto the bench seat next to Topper are the Sheriff and a man named Clarence Johnson. The Sheriff is laughing so hard Topper can't even hear the engine. Hims Chapel is a very small, and very dull, place. This evening is already the third best time the Sheriff has ever had. And, just like the stripper that Topper is using to work the pedals for him, this night is frighteningly young.

After taking out the parking meters Topper overcorrects, hops a curb, mangles a stop sign and then manages to wrestle the rig back onto to the road.

"Whattya call this thing?" asks Topper.

"Suicide Knob," answers Clarence. He should know, it's his truck.

"I LIKE IT!" cries Topper.

From the reasonable end of town, Agnes watches the truck disappear. Coins from the parking meters rain down on the pavement, spinning and shimmering to a rest. As the sound of the truck fades into the distance Agnes asks the night, "How did this happen?"

115

The night does not answer. But in small towns, boredom is always to blame.

So it was that Topper, Clarence Johnson, and Sheriff Cooper wound up drinking together in a small sad strip club off Alabama State highway 109. They bought each other lap dances, talked the coarse language of men, and generally enjoyed themselves.

After he was pretty sure the Sheriff was drunk enough to tell the truth, Topper asked, "So whattya know about this Rielly woman?" Despite intoxication, Topper was still very much on the job.

"She owns most of the county. But I never did like her though. Rich. And not just rich, thinks she's better than everybody else. Looks down on people," slurred Sheriff Cooper.

"I hate people who look down on me," said Topper. They all laughed. "Except for her," Topper says, pointing at one of the women, "she can look down on me anytime."

"You a'right boy, you all right," said Sheriff Cooper. "I like a fella knows how to enjoy himself." Glasses of brown liquor clinked together and dived down throats.

"It's just a shame you're only half a man," said Clarence, needling Topper out of pure boredom.

"Half a man? Sheriff, you need to arrest this man. He's got bullshit pouring out of his mouth. Can't be sanitary." The men roared with laughter.

"No, no, I like you and everything little man, but it's not like you can do an honest days work," said Clarence.

"Honest day's work!" cried Topper. "I'm a friggin lawyer. If I did an honest days work, I'd be out of a job." Topper pointed to the sheriff, "And so would he!" More laughter.

Topper indicated a half-naked women walking by. "Finally, they bring out the good looking ones." The other men grunted their agreement. The women had not changed at all. The liquor had just worked its sacred and profane magic.

116

Clarence still wouldn't let it go. "Yeah, you'd have to be a lawyer. Me? I made my way by driving a truck. Then I bought a truck. Then I bought another truck and got somebody to drive the first one. I'm a self-made man."

"Not me," said the sheriff as he stared at pair of giant breasts, "My uncle got me this job."

Clarence pointed at Topper. His finger floated and bobbed in time with the slow waltz of alcohol sieving through his liver. "But you, little man, you couldn't drive a truck. No way." He held his hand out over the floor, "You must be at least this tall to ride this ride."

The Sheriff laughed a little too loud.

"Whattya mean I can't drive a truck?" Topper said, suddenly very serious.

"No way. No how."

"You mean like one of those trucks you've got out front? I can't drive one of those trucks? Is that what you mean?"

"That's what I mean."

"You gonna put some money behind that, or are you all talk?" Topper asked.

This got the Sheriff's attention. "Boys, boys, I'm afraid I can't let you gamble in this county, unless I'm in on it. I got 500 says the dwarf can't drive."

"I got five thousand says the dwarf can't drive. If anybody will cover it," said Clarence, thinking that he was calling Topper's bluff.

Topper smiled and pulled a gigantic roll of bills out of his pocket. "I'll cover all the action."

"There ain't no way in hell," said Clarence.

"Ah, bullshit. I'll drive your Tonka truck, all I need is a good pair of legs," Topper said, slapping the nearest stripper on the thigh. He peeled off a couple hundred and said, "C'mon Darlin', now I'm going to sit on your lap for a while."

117

CHAPTER TWENTY
Excelsior Fights the Hurricane

This time it's a hurricane. Whatever, thinks Excelsior. He is still pissed at that snotty waiter from that French restaurant. He's ready to uncork on just about anybody or anything. It's odd though, in 70 years they've never asked him to fight a hurricane.

Excelsior isn't sure he can pull it off. But so what? If he fails, maybe they'll stop calling him all the time. And then a black thought — what if he messes up on purpose? Just drops the ball? Would it be over? Could he take a night off? Love a woman? Have a family? Would they take the pager back? Maybe throwing the game is the smart thing to do. Because if he stops this hurricane, will they call him for every hurricane? But deep inside, he knows he can't throw the game.

Nobody understands. Nobody appreciates his situation. All those crazy bastards with gadgets and powers coming out of the woodwork. And he has to stop them. He doesn't know how his powers work, not really. And he certainly doesn't how some freaky alien ray gun works. And what about chemical warfare? His skin might be impenetrable but what about his lungs? The whole thing is risky. Excelsior meant higher, not indestructible. Not necessarily. And when he gets hit, or shot or bombed, it hurts. Excelsior is a good deal more nervous than most people know.

Last year, he had been hit with a beam weapon and was unable to feel his leg for two months. And then, after the "incident" with Sinestro, he forgot all the words he knew that began with the letter 'r'. He's still not sure he has them all back yet. At least he no longer locks up when somebody asks him if he needs a receipt.

Coming across the panhandle, Excelsior slows a little. Daytona rushes past him on the left. Orlando on his right. He skims the ground at 150 feet. Less chance of getting messed up in air traffic down here. The worst he might do is rattle some windows. He decides he doesn't care. A flick of a thought and he has broken the sound barrier. He can feel the air compress in a wedge in front of him. What is a mere mathematical consideration for students of aerodynamics is something he can actually feel with his fingertips. It's good. He's going to need to move a lot of air tonight.

Thinking it might be useful, he rips the top off a water tower in Hollywood, FL. But who knows? It's not like there's a playbook for this kind of thing. He grips the wedge of metal so tightly that steel seeps between his fingers. Then he sets his heroic jaw and accelerates.

The sound of the wind whipping past the edges of the metal is an angry, ceaseless ripping. He loves the sound. He is mighty. A god set to do battle with the elements. He gives it more speed. Below and behind him the windows of a strip mall shatter as he passes

As Miami Beach disappears beneath him, he tries to remember which way hurricanes spin. Clockwise? Counter? Does it matter? He decides to head directly into the wind and batter the storm into submission. Should he start from the bottom or the top? He decides it is best to cut it off at the knees like a quarterback you want to cripple. Get angry. Get tough. Time to end this thing's career.

Even as he amps himself up, he feels the air get colder and thicker. It takes a greater effort to maintain his speed. The sky and the sea become the same shade of grey. Visibility drops to zero. And then he hears the howl. As if the world is dying. The storm sounds hungry, eager to teach him a lesson about power.

It is 500 miles wide, 400,000 times bigger than a man. It is nothing more than a heartless, unpredictable, inevitable and remorseless set of natural coincidences. But to Excelsior it seems the storm has an evil will of its own. Excelsior is dwarfed, humbled by the wall of wind and water before him. And inside the costume, inside his bowels, he knows fear.

He puts it from his mind. Isn't he a hero? Heroes don't feel fear. Or don't have time to feel fear, flying that fast. There is nothing to do but fly the pattern. Get it done. He banks to the right and gives it all he is worth. In spite of the rain and the wind, the metal grows hot in his hands. He grips it tighter and loves the pain.

The sky explodes with moisture, as if the sea has been ripped from the ocean floor. He chokes on the air. Yet still he flies faster and faster in tighter and tighter spirals. He yells at the top of his lungs. His hands grip through the metal in several places. Of course he is more than human. But even he has limits. And reaching beyond the limits is a test of will, rather than power.

Around and around and around and around. Until finally the wind drops. He slows and catches a glimpse of the stars. He has broken the storm.

But this time, the laws of physics cannot be denied. Even as Excelsior stops circling, the fluid in the center of his skull keeps spinning at a frightening rate. Dizziness overcomes him. The horizon spins. The now flat ocean exchanges places with the sky again and again as he fights to make progress towards land.

He hits the beach like an artillery shell. Sand explodes outward. In the bottom of a crater, he vomits seawater.

Exhausted, he collapses into his own vomit. Is this victory? He doesn't care. All he wants to do is lie here for a moment.

Curious faces peer over the lip of the crater. There are a thousand questions they could ask, "Are you okay? Do you need anything? Can we help?" But when a small boy speaks from the crowd, he asks the question on everyone's mind.

"Did you save us?"

Excelsior nods as he wipes a strand of spittle from his chin. "Yeah kid. Today, I did."

Excelsior stands up. He doesn't want them to see him like this. But as soon as he's up, his legs give out. Only his ability to fly prevents him from collapsing onto the sand again. He throws the boy what he hopes is a jaunty salute, and heads up into the sky.

He flies East with all the speed he can manage. What he needs now is the sun. The light of the sun, which will somehow regenerate his powers. He had once joked with Gus that they should test his blood for chlorophyl. A good joke because there is no needle that will pierce his skin.

As he crosses the coast of Africa, he really begins to feel it. This time, he might not make it back to the light. Might have to lay himself out along the plain and wait for sunrise. But just as he gives up hope, he sees the first glimmer of dawn. At the speed he's going it takes only seconds for him to be engulfed in the light. He feels the power roar back into him. He doesn't know how. He doesn't know why. But in the light of a new day, he is somehow made whole again. What does he care of how and why? He stopped the hurricane. It's a pure win.

CHAPTER TWENTY-ONE
Marauding Through the Night

"Faster you dolt! Faster!" screams Agnes as if the British Empire were losing India all over again. The deputy doesn't need much encouragement to pour the gas to his rattly old patrol car. The flashing lights, the blaring sirens and the roar of the wheels against the road are really the only perks his job offers. Sometimes he drives far out into the county at night and pretends to be chasing someone. Just to relieve the boredom of it all.

But this? This is different. This is a real chase. And it is exciting. At first he had resisted the strange woman's urgings to chase down the truck. She had used all kinds of words he didn't understand. Words like "Miscreant" and "Commonweal." But when she said "Hot Pursuit" — well hell, wasn't that his job?

"Tallyho!" Agnes cries. She slaps the Deputy on the shoulder and points through a stand of scrub pines. There, on the far side of a long flat curve, is the Semi with a bulldozer on the back. The patrol car strains to create acceleration.

Inside the truck, Clarence has passed out cradling a bottle of bourbon. The sheriff has devoted all his attention to the stripper. Topper doesn't care. He has The Reilly Estate pulled up on the GPS and is making for it with as much speed as he can muster. Of course, this is complicated by the fact that he can't put his foot on the floor and is relying on the stripper's legs. Every few minutes he has to stomp on her knee to get her to return her foot to the pedal. This has been awkward, to say the least, but now the lunacy in the truck cab has settled into an orderly pattern. He kicks the stripper, the stripper moans, the sheriff thinks he's doing well and the truck goes faster.

But it is an inherently unstable system. If you take away any one of its components this diabolical apparatus will collapse under the weight of its own absurdity. This does not concern Topper. He doesn't like to think in terms of theory. All theory ever does for Topper is tell him what he can't do. And Topper doesn't like being told what to do.

Theory says that the bumblebee can't fly. But the little bumblsbee says, "Screw it!" and flies anyway. And if the bumblebee can get away with it, then Topper figures he can too. If this is the way it has to be, then this is the way it has to be. Topper doesn't care if he has to outdrink every redneck and shitkicker from here to the Mason Dixon Line. Edwin is in trouble, and Topper is going to come through for him.

Topper sees flashing blue lights in the truck's side mirror. He yells in the Sheriff's face, "It's the cops. You told me you were the law!"

The shouting brings Clarence back around. He doesn't immediately open his eyes, but instead reviews recent events. He remembers losing a bet. He remembers not liking it. He remembers drinking heavily. His sides hurt. Has he been in a fight? There had been laughter. Lots of laughter. Probably before losing the bet. He doesn't like to lose. Why would he laugh after losing? Something isn't right here, but everything is so sloshy in his head, Clarence can't begin to put these facts together. Until he hears the air horn.

And with the horn blast, a key fact drops into place. He's in a truck. He hears a child yell, "Holy Shit and thar she blows!

It's Liberace's outhouse!" But what kind of child would yell that?

Clarence opens his eyes. In front of them is a hill. At the bottom is a white plantation house covered with blurry — he rubs his eyes — frilly white bits. Focus doesn't make the place look any better to Clarence.

"Yessir," says the sheriff, "That's the Widow Reilly's place. Most ridiculous goddamned thing in the county."

Underneath the Sheriff's smoky, crackling laugh, Clarence hears a woman giggle. What is going on here? He almost has it, but clearly he is missing some key piece of information. He leans forward slowly. Nothing catastrophic happens, so he decides to turn his head. And then he sees a dwarf in a suit. The dwarf's tiny hands rest on the steering wheel and most of his body is cradled between a naked woman's fake breasts.

Topper pulls on the air horn again and it all falls into place for Clarence. As he opens his mouth to speak, he is slammed backwards into the seat. The truck roars forward as Topper shrieks, "Muwahhhhhhhh!" The horizon dips and bucks as the truck tears through the fields. Clearly something must be done. Can't anyone see that?

"Double Clutch. Double Clutchhhhhh!" cries Topper over the sound of grinding metal.

As the house grows larger and larger in the truck's front windshield, Clarence's common sense finally breaks through. It has been surrounded and outnumbered for most of the evening, but it has not given up. Now clear of the haze of alcohol and hormones and stupidity, it has just enough energy left over to send Clarence one clear message: "It's your truck."

Clarence dives across the sheriff and grabs the wheel. The wheel spins and it slings Topper into the window. Topper swears and spits and fights for control, but it is too late. This party has gone on too long. And now it is time for physics to step in.

In any high school physics class, they will tell you that inertia is the tendency of an object to remain at rest. This sounds very polite. Very Newtonian. But the fact is that inertia is an object's resistance to change. And resistance is never polite. When the object in question is 80,000 pounds of tractor, trailer and bulldozer, the resistance isn't just rude, it's vigorous.

In that same high school physics class they will prove this to you by bludgeoning you with all manner of word problems. And one of these word problems might go something like this: A 5,000 pound Tractor attached to a 75,000 pound trailer is traveling across an immaculately maintained lawn (coefficient of friction .024) at 50 feet per second towards an elaborately decorated manor house. If the tractor trailer is 125 feet away from the house, how many feet will the truck slide before (and after) hitting the house and completely destroying it? You may assume the house's mass is negligible, because the poor structure doesn't stand a chance.

Don't bother to sharpen a pencil or pull out scrap paper, because if you're ever faced with this problem in real life the only answer that will help you is "WE'RE ALL GONNA DIE!" Even a 6th grade dropout from the Alabama Public school system can tell you this.

"We all gonna die!" yells the stripper, finding the correct answer even though she is pretty sure higher math was what you did when you used numbers larger than 20.

Edwin Windsor and Dr. Loeb have left the pig sty. After a brief and pointless effort to clean himself, Edwin is now in search of transportation. He hears the sound of an air horn in the distance. Dr. Loeb asks, "What is zat?"

"I don't care," says Edwin. He strides towards a stand of scrub pine, thinking to conceal himself as he makes his way around to the garage. But when the air horn blows again, this

126

time louder and accompanied by the roar of a diesel engine, he cannot resist turning his head.

Descending the hill and rushing on to the front lawn is what appears to be a flatbed truck loaded with a bulldozer. The truck accelerates directly towards the house, but before it gets there the driver appears to have second thoughts. The cab flails one way, then another. But the cab is largely irrelevant, the mass of the trailer and bulldozer have been put into motion. The cab jackknifes and now the trailer drags it towards the house.

"Inertia," thinks Edwin.

The trailer hits the house sideways. The effect is impossible to adequately describe, but just imagine that someone has nuked the entire Victorian era. Frilly bits and doilies and bits of antique china fly everywhere. The entire first floor of the house is sheared from the foundation and shoved fifty feet backwards. The upper story comes crashing down on the truck.

In the patrol car, from a safe distance, Deputy Earl struggles to process the instantaneous conversion of a two-story Plantation House into a deconstructed, post-modern ranch. Try as he might, too many contradictory images and facts crowd his mind. So he sits there with his mouth open. After a moment he turns to Agnes for some kind of context or explanation.

As Agnes watches survivors emerge from the demolished house, she is consumed by thoughts of Edwin's safety. "You see," she asks the deputy, "Do you see what happens?"

The deputy just stares.

"Now," Agnes continues, "I am going to say I told you so. And then you are going to turn on your lights and we are going to race down there and restore order. Do you hear me, young man?"

The deputy has gone back to staring at the carnage. He manages to nod his head in agreement. "My sheriff's in there," is all he can say.

After a brief pause, Agnes says, "I told you so." The deputy turns on the lights and starts down the hill.

CHAPTER TWENTY-TWO
The Rescue

Topper falls out of the truck. It does not diminish his mood.
"WHHHHHHHHAHAHAHAHAHAHAHAHAHAHAHAH
AHA! That was awesome! Topper 1, Gone With the Wind
House 0!" After a brief victory dance, Topper searches for his
friend. "Edwin! Edwin! Where are you, big E? I'm here to
rescue you!"

Topper clambers over the frilly debris and walks towards a
man lying on the ground. It's not Edwin. It's a young man clad
only in a loincloth and a feathered headdress. He is bleeding
from his head. The injured boy looks up at Topper and asks,
"What happened?"

"I hit the house so hard I musta blown the clothes right off
of you!"

"I need a doctor."

"Yeah, you need a lot of things," Topper agrees. "But this
conversation bores me. Let's talk about what I need. I'm
looking for a tall guy. In a suit. Real serious. Looks like he's
never had any fun." The boy does not answer. He passes out.
"Oh, you're useless. Edwin! Edwin!"

Edwin emerges from the darkness. He is covered in filth, but
still manages to maintain his poise. Over his left arm he carries
what is left of his suit jacket. Any man who has just been

through Edwin's ordeal might be angry, perhaps even enraged, at the affront to dignity. But not Edwin. As he surveys the destruction, he finds it depressingly pointless. A fitting ending to the entire episode, yet deeply regrettable.

Topper is ecstatic. "Yes!" he cries, "I saved you! I'm a FRIGGIN' hero!"

Edwin sees a jacket hanger amid the rubble. He bends down and picks it up. As he puts his jacket on the hanger he says, "No rescue was required."

"What do you mean? Didn't you see the truck and the bulldozer and the BOOOM! Whattya want, a friggin' cavalry charge?"

"Yes, yes, extremely destructive. But what if I had been on the first floor?"

"Ah, first floor isn't tall enough for you," counters Topper. Edwin knows better than to explore the absurdity of Topper's logic.

"Why did you depart from protocol?"

"Agnes wouldn't tell me what it was!"

"No doubt out of fear that you would take matters into your own hands."

"Yeah, well, I did. And now you're rescued," says Topper.

Edwin frowns at Topper. Edwin frowns at the whole idea of the ends justifying the means. "Just because it worked out this time, doesn't mean it was a smart thing to do."

Topper stares up at Edwin with wide, surprisingly vulnerable eyes, "Oh, you bastard. Don't you take this away from me. You can't. I rescued you. Look! Just look at it!" Topper gestures wildly at the truck and bulldozer embedded in the wreckage of the collapsed plantation house. He admires the spectacle for a moment, then returns to pleading, "Edwin, please don't take this from me. I need this. I rescued you."

Edwin takes a deep breath. What does it matter? It's all a sunk cost now. "Very well Topper. You have rescued me.

Thank you ever so much. Now, where is Agnes? Not in the truck, I hope."

There is a shriek as the stripper falls out of the truck cab. As she staggers off, the Sheriff pleads with her from the door, "C'mon honey, come back. They's a sleeper cab in the back."

"She is most certainly not in the truck," says Edwin.

From across the ruined lawn Agnes cries, "Edwin!" As much as her dignity will permit, she rushes to Edwin's side. "Are you hurt? What have these Philistines done to you?"

"I am fine."

"Yeah," says Topper, his chest swelling with pride. "He's fine... 'cause I rescued him!"

"I am so sorry, Edwin, I could not stop him. I turned my back and..."

"It's all right, Agnes. It has all worked out for the best."

"Yeah! Thanks to Topper it's all one big fat happy ending," says Topper.

"Edwin, what has happened to your suit? And what is that awful smell?" asks Agnes.

"I am afraid that is the smell of pig."

"Oh my God."

Edwin holds up the jacket. It is utterly destroyed.

"I'm not sure we'll be able to find something off-the-rack at this late hour," says Agnes.

Edwin shudders at the thought of making do with something cut for the lowest common denominator.

Survivors of every kind emerge from the house. Some flee immediately. Others wander the grounds in mute amazement seeming to wonder, "Did the plane crash? How am I still alive? Wait... I wasn't in a plane. I was in a house. Houses don't fall out of the sky... do they?"

The sheriff recovers what little dignity remains of his office and asks the obvious question: "Where'd all these slippery faggots come from?"

Dr. Loeb emerges from the shadows to answer the Sheriff, "They haff been brought here and held against their vill. As haff I. I am afraid mine mater has quite lost her mind." He points to a figure wandering about on what is left of the front lawn.

The Sheriff turns and sees Iphigenia Reilly staggering around like a cross between a Can-Can girl and a Mardi Gras float that came in third in a demolition derby. All he wants is to go home and sleep it off. So he calls in the State Police. He calculates that his cousin — a good, dull, churchgoing man — has been sleeping for at least eight hours. Let him worry about it for a while.

"What are we going to do now?" asks Agnes.

Edwin puts an arm around Dr. Loeb's shoulders. "We are going to build a giant laser. In space." Edwin does not smile.

Alabaster, who is really Daniel, has not bothered to run. He knows it is over. He knew it was too good to be true. He sits on what is left of the front steps and waits for the hammer to fall. Every time he closes his eyes he sees visions of his sons working at Dairy Queen. Every time he opens them he realizes he is going to jail. Edwin walks over to him. Alabaster does not plead. He does not try to bargain. He just sits there and waits for the tall man to exact his revenge.

Edwin considers him for a moment. Then he says, "Daniel, you are an intelligent man and entirely without scruple. A totally self-interested agent who seems to care only about money." With a flick, Edwin presents his card. "If you find yourself in need of work, contact me. I can use a man like you."

Daniel takes the card, not entirely sure of what has just happened. Apparently he is not going to jail. So why does he feel like things just got worse?

Clarence decides that he's done with the entire state of Alabama. When the truck hit the house, he was tossed into the sleeper cab. Now that he's crawled out, he's decided he doesn't care about any of this. And why should he? He and his crew are due in Virginia day after next to tear apart a WWII-era generator factory for the Department of Defense. The DoD should have more than enough juice to get him out of whatever ridiculous jam this is. This bullshit is clearly somebody else's problem. So he fires up the truck and drives away. That night he scatters bits of plantation across three states.

CHAPTER TWENTY-THREE
23 Seconds

When Iphigenia is admitted to the emergency room she is diagnosed with dehydration and extreme sexual exhaustion. But by the time she is discharged, she is no longer in control of her fate. Topper works quickly. As it turns out, the judge with jurisdiction over Hims Chapel, Alabama is yet another of the Sheriff's cousins. And he thought that Topper was even funnier than the sheriff did.

Normally the argument required to deprive someone of their power of attorney and commit them involuntarily to a mental institution takes months. And in cases where staggeringly large amounts of money are involved, years can pass with no resolution. It is necessary to prove, beyond the shadow of a doubt, that the person in question is a danger to themselves or others.

This usually takes days of expert testimony, a careful presentation of meticulously prepared evidence and, quite often, the deliberation of a jury. But as Topper sips a glass of the Judge's fine bourbon, he makes his case with a handful of photographs and one sentence.

"She's friggin' crazy."

The judge laughs and signs the paper that transfers control of the entire Reilly estate to Eustace Eugene Reilly. The generous bribe also helps.

Then comes the obligatory stack of legal forms for Dr. Loeb to sign. Topper rattles through them quickly. "Yeah, yeah, yeah. Happy Mother's Day. Sign here. Initial here. Sign here, here and here." Somewhere in the middle of the thick stack of forms that Dr. Loeb signs to commit his mother is a very special contract. It looks like all the others. Across the top it says Power of Attorney. There are a lot of "Powers of" going on in this case. But this one is different. This form grants Edwin Windsor a complete power of attorney for all affairs of Eustace Reilly (d/b/a Dr. Loeb).

Of course, these legal machinations will not hold up to a concerted assault. But Iphigenia has gone around the bend, so she can initiate no legal action. They will be spared any trouble from Dr. Loeb by Edwin's special genius: restraint. Edwin isn't going to seize the money all at once. This isn't a smash-and-grab job. He will bleed it off slowly. Imperceptibly. Imperceptibly to Dr. Loeb at least. And along the way he will make certain that Dr. Loeb gets good value for his money. Edwin is going see that Dr. Loeb fully realizes the fantasy of being a powerful and successful supervillain. In Edwin's eyes it is a fair bargain. And he is certain that, if he could spare the several years it would take to explain the matter to Dr. Loeb, he would see it that way as well.

So it is that Dr. Loeb betrays his own mother, gains control over her and, for 23 seconds, is heir to one of the largest fortunes in the United States. But before he can squander a penny of it, Edwin snatches it from his grasp.

CHAPTER TWENTY-FOUR
A New Suit

Bone-weary, Edwin enters the private aviation terminal in Mobile, Alabama. As the automatic doors slide open, a wall of cool, processed air envelopes his body. Tendrils of vapor coalesce and spin through the thickened atmosphere outside. As the doors close, Edwin is almost able to forget the world outside the airport.

That is the point of the modern airport, isn't it? Featureless monotonic travel space providing uniformly grim comfort to the weary traveler. England, New England, New Delhi and Detroit, all the same. Where you might be going and where you might be delayed are indistinguishable until you exit the airport. And no matter how awful your locale, the mediocre plastic womb of the airport is always there for you.

For this and many other reasons, Edwin loathes airports. In fact, in this state of distress and undress, Edwin loathes everything. In a dirty undershirt, tattered and ruined pants, shoes still full of filth, he is a stark contrast to the uniformed plastic of the airport terminal. Edwin recognizes that fatigue and distress color his emotions and distort his thinking, but at this point, there is little he can do about it. The only thing for it is a hot shower and a proper change of clothes. Such necessities seem, at best, hours away; and what would be the point of cleaning up now? He can think of nothing more depressing than putting a clean body back into filthy attire.

On the far side of the terminal, Agnes is making arrangements with the flight crew. Edwin can hear that there has been some mixup with refueling. In her very polite way, Agnes is raking an airport official back and forth over the coals of her proper and righteous indignation. Edwin is confident that she will have it sorted out soon enough. Or, at the very least, she will have a roasted civil servant for her trophy case.

Nearby, Topper has passed out in an uncomfortable seat. There is a misleading innocence that gathers around him as he sleeps. Perhaps it is just his childlike size. But this veil of innocence is perforated by boozy snores that presage the titanic hangover condensing within him.

In his exhaustion, Edwin paces around the terminal. There is little point in sitting in one of the plastic terminal chairs. They are too small. Everything built for the public is simply the wrong scale for him. And Edwin, exhausted though he may be, will not offend dignity by sitting on the floor. Even the prospect of a rest seems as if it will be small consolation.

It is optimism (as much an analytical sin as pessimism) that has cost Edwin one of the few truly great bespoke tailored suits in the world. As great generals look back on massacres, Edwin considers the events that have led to the destruction of his suit. How could he have been so blind? How could he have thought that he was dealing with civilized people?

When Agnes asks such questions he brushes them off. But as Edwin paces the terminal, these questions hang on him like medals of defeat. Was he wrong to assume that people could be even remotely rational? Why does he see the world in a way foreign to those around him? Are the tasks he sets himself inherently hopeless?

Despair drapes the great man like a shroud. Of course, Edwin has made money. He always manages to make money. But what he can never seem to do is make sense of the world.

138

Even as he thinks these things, he knows it is the fatigue thinking them. But he cannot stop himself. He cannot even stop his pacing. Just like he cannot stop trying to talk sense to the insensible.

He crosses his hands behind his back and bows his head. Chin touching his chest he considers the tattered remnants of his suit pants. The light grey and clean, rational lines have been horribly blotted and marred by all manner of filth. The left pant is torn halfway up the calf. This is the garb of some sweaty, maladjusted and weak-minded adventurer. Can his current state really be the reward for his long efforts?

He hears the automatic door behind him open and close. As the crisp, measured clicks of dress shoe heels draw closer to him, he turns. The afternoon light reduces the approaching figure to a silhouette. The outline of a man in a bowler hat, carrying something draped across his arm.

Edwin smiles. Truly, Agnes thinks of everything.

"Mr. Giles," says Edwin, "I am so glad you can join us."

Mr. Giles returns a withering gaze that speak volumes. "Mr. Windsor, you look a fright. What have you done to my suit?"

"It is not my fault, I assure you. But I have, you should be glad to know, escaped unharmed."

Mr. Giles does not reply. Instead he removes his hat and drapes the garment bag across a row of seats. "I have heard of your plight. And, at the request of your secretary, I have traveled a great distance in a short time."

Edwin appraises himself in the mirror and likes what he sees. He has scrubbed his skin and now it glows a rosy pink. His time in the sun has given him a little color, and it lends him, if only temporarily, the air of a healthier, more physically adventuresome man. Perhaps one who enjoys the tedious pastime of yachting.

Mr. Giles has a different assessment. The jacket lies improperly across Edwin's shoulders. No one else may ever notice this flaw in the work, but for Mr. Giles, it cries out for adjustment. He is keenly aware that he has a finite number of suits left in him. And he wants each to be better than the last. "Shall have to tune the jacket a little," he says in a tone that attempts to downplay the seriousness of the matter.

"What's wrong with it?" Edwin asks as he turns and smooths the jacket across his midsection. The dark blue fabric moves like a second skin. The suit is magnificent.

"Hmm," says Giles. "You can wear it back to the city, but then you must give me some time with it."

"Very well." Edwin tugs gently on his shirt cuffs. He takes a moment to enjoy the somber, dark blue. Edwin has slogged through the filth and the absurdity to find himself in command of vast financial resources once again. Now, he can fund any scheme he deems reasonable. No more small time. No more attempting to explain the quality of the opportunities he can create to investors blinded by troublesome and antiquated morals.

"I should like another suit," Edwin says.

"Very good Mr. Windsor."

"Black, I should think."

"And the cut? And the collar?"

"I leave it in your capable hands, Mr. Giles."

Agnes enters the room. "The plane is ready." Edwin nods. Of course the plane is ready. Everything is ready. Now it is time to begin.

PART TWO

CHAPTER TWENTY-FIVE
Cotton Candy

If the rain falls on the just and the unjust alike, then does it not follow that the warmth of the sun should lift even the crudest spirit?

It's the kind of a question that a thinking person ponders as he or she goes for a stroll through the city after a light spring rain, filling lungs with a rare breath of fresh air, and seeking the common thread of humanity in the endless faces that stream by on a freshly washed sidewalk. It is not, however, what Barry is thinking. As he lumbers down the sidewalk, Barry is thinking about cotton candy.

Barry has been thinking about cotton candy for three weeks. Not off and on, but straight. At night he goes to sleep with visions of spun sugar dancing in his head. And when he wakes in the morning, the pink confection is still at the front of his mind. No matter where he goes or what he does, the thought of cotton candy is with him.

This thought had been introduced by an attempt at hypnotherapy. You see, Barry is a very violent man. And, as a condition of his parole, he has been ordered to see a psychiatrist. At his last visit, the psychiatrist asked Barry to think of a pleasant memory from his childhood. Barry had responded "Cotton candy."

"What is it about cotton candy?" asked the psychiatrist, feeling that he was finally getting somewhere with a difficult and uncommunicative patient.

"Stacy bought."

Now the psychiatrist is excited. Barry never really speaks in sentences longer than two words. To get two, two-word sentences in one session — let alone in a row — well, the shrink feels like he's really getting somewhere. So he decides to dig a little deeper in search of the mother lode. "Can you tell me another pleasant memory about Stacy?"

Unfortunately for the psychiatrist, and more unfortunately for his office, Barry doesn't have any other pleasant memories of Stacy. And as he searches for them through his small, very unorganized brain, he becomes uncomfortable. Barry starts breathing erratically. He snorts and shakes his head from side to side. "This is good," says the psychiatrist, "Work through it. Let it come."

Barry has no idea what this means. To be fair, even the shrink doesn't know what it means. It's just one of those things he says. But when Barry leaves his office by walking directly through a brick wall, all his clever mental health clichés desert him.

Barry has been recommended to Edwin Windsor by a former client who is currently being held in EnSuMac. EnSuMac is the unofficial term for the Enhanced Super Maximum prison where Barry was incarcerated. Edwin has developed an outstanding relationship with a few of the guards and inmates who have the eye and aptitude to spot talents that a man like Edwin can exploit. Barry shows remarkable potential. No one really knows how strong or destructive Barry really is, but in prison the guards went to great pains to make sure Barry didn't get angry.

The rumor is that Barry was granted early release, not because he reformed or changed in any way, but because the warden was not at all sure his prison could contain Barry. And

144

the warden is smart enough to know it's better not to have Barry's eventual escape on his record. Ship the problem to someone else. Even if someone else turns out to be a defenseless and unsuspecting public.

All of this information only serves to heighten Edwin's interest. He has watched Barry from afar, but has yet to interfere. Edwin believes that every man must make his own choices. All he can do is present the options more clearly. Ultimately, responsibility lies with the individual. Edwin is very careful not to get his hands dirty. After all, that is not his role. He is not a villain. He is merely a consultant.

Barry can almost remember that he has an appointment with Edwin. But it's not clear. His thoughts never are. But he has this generalized feeling that he has somewhere to be. He's pretty sure his destination is in the direction he is walking, but he can't get a grip on it. As he lumbers along the sidewalk, a beautiful little girl crosses his path. She is holding a beautiful little kitten. Barry has limited experience with beauty, so he doesn't really know what do to. He stops before he tramples her and just stands there, breathing through his mouth. The little girl is terrified. She holds the kitten up to Barry. "Do you want to pet my kitty? Her name is Candy."

As if it is the most natural thing in the world, Barry eats the kitten and keeps walking.

For a long time, Barry thinks about how scratchy cotton candy is. Then he remembers that the address of the place he needs to be is written down on a piece of paper in the wallet that hangs around his neck. For the next twenty minutes, he terrorizes passersby by walking up to them and shoving the wallet in their faces. "Where?" he demands. Eventually someone points him in the right direction.

The security guards at Windsor Tower have pretty much seen it all. Even before Barry shows them his paper, they are pointing towards the express elevator to the penthouse. The sooner they get this guy out of the lobby, the less likely whatever it is he's going to do will be their fault.

CHAPTER TWENTY-SIX
Barry BASH!

The elevator bell echoes through Edwin's cavernous lobby. Agnes does not look up. She has schooled herself to resist a great number of urges which she perceives as appeals to her animal nature. She does not drool when bells ring. Nor does she automatically look up from her work.

She makes her final notation in a file, closes it and looks up. "Do you have an app... Oh GOOD LORD! Ah-hem." Agnes struggles to regain control of herself. She is not the kind of person who is easily rattled. But when faced with a visage that clearly belongs to the Pleistocene era, she needs a moment. It is one thing to suspect that many of those you share the earth with are some species of subhuman, but to actually have a caveman walk through the door is something else entirely.

Barry's wide-spaced eyes and low, sloping forehead give no indications of intelligence. The general sheen of dullard in his eyes is enhanced by three letters, C R O, that are worked in scar tissue across his forehead.

Agnes decides it is best to proceed carefully. In a loud, slow voice, she asks, "Are. You. Lost?"

Barry shrugs.

"Do. You. Have. An. A. Point. Ment?"

Barry holds up the small wallet of papers that hangs around his neck. On the front, in large block letters, is his name.

"Of course," she mutters under her breath. She forces a smile and reaches for the appointment book.

In his office, Edwin sits quietly behind his desk, paging through a volume by a Polish man named Dzerzhinsky. When the intercom buzzes, he closes the book carefully and places it on the desk with some degree of reverence.

"Yes, Agnes?"

"It appears that a representative of the Union of Cavemen, Local Number Rock, is here about our yearly contribution of fire."

"Is his name Barry?" Edwin asks.

"The creature is so labeled."

Agnes shows Barry into Edwin's high, sunlit office. At this point, most people take a moment to comment on the decor, or marvel at the view. Barry just throws his carcass into a chair. The chair, a very tasteful and expensive piece that is hand-crafted from maple and artisan leather, collapses under Barry's weight. Barry doesn't seem to notice. Perhaps it is because this kind of thing happens to Barry all the time. Whatever the case, Barry looks at Edwin and sucks on his fist.

"I have heard that you are possessed of unusual talents," Edwin begins carefully.

Barry takes his fist out of his mouth and holds it above his head. A thin line of drool stretches from his mouth to the knuckle of his middle finger. Barry looks at the strand for a moment. When it snaps, he drops his arm downward and smashes a hole in the floor beside what is left of the chair. Edwin stretches over his desk and considers the damage. "Impressive," says Edwin.

Barry raises his hand to strike again. Edwin acts quickly "No, no, no. Another demonstration will not be necessary." Barry stops. He does not look happy, or at all familiar, with the exercise of self-control.

"I have been informed that you are at a loss for what to do with your talents."

"Barry BASH!" he roars.

"Yes, of course but what do you bash? Or more to the point, what should you bash?"

Barry shrugs.

"Well," says Edwin, rising from behind his desk, "I can help you with that." Edwin moves gracefully in front of a projector screen that is dropping from the ceiling. The title screen on the presentation reads, "Barry Banister, Bashing for Profit."

"Barry, you have a set of unique physical talents."

"Barry BASH!"

"Yes. That is exactly what I'm talking about. You are an incredibly destructive individual. And, if I may venture a personal insight, an incredibly misunderstood one as well. If I'm right, all your life people have told you not to break things."

Barry nodded.

"Yet all your life — "

"Barry BASH!" This time the floor escapes unharmed, but a Travertine topped end table is pulverized by a flick of Barry's finger. Edwin decides he'd better finish his pitch quickly, while he still has an office.

"That's right. And how much money have you made by bashing things?" Barry looks confused. In truth, "Barry BASH!" is his all-purpose response. But it doesn't seem appropriate here. Barry is a one-note kind of guy. But like a Neil Young guitar solo, he makes the most of a limited tonal range.

Edwin advances the presentation to the first slide. It is a picture of a gigantic sporting arena. "Now, as a general rule, I am not a fan of destruction. My purpose is to build wealth. Building wealth means creating value. Maximizing the scarce resources of time and talent."

Barry looks around the room for something else to break.

"But this is the exception to the rule. Municipal authorities paid nine million dollars to demolish this building." As he says this, the still picture transitions to video and Barry sees a series of precise detonations that result in the building's collapse.

Barry giggles and claps his hands together concussively. "BOOM!"

"Yes," Edwin says, "Boom. So what I propose is that we move you from the destruction business, to the de-construction business."

Barry gives Edwin another one of his world-class blank looks. Edwin loathes to be so blunt about it, but he recognizes that it is time to take a simpler tack. "Do you want to get paid to wreck buildings?"

Barry becomes excited again. He nods vigorously. "Barry BASH!"

Edwin directs Barry to a small table on the side of his office. On the table is a contract. On top of the contract is an ink pad. Edwin offers Barry a ball-peen hammer.

"Merely smash the ink on this contract and we have a deal."

Barry ignores the hammer and, laughing, smashes his fist clear through the table. Ink soaks into the contract. The deal is closed.

Edwin walks Barry to the elevator, talking mostly nonsense and using soothing, gentle tones. As the elevator doors close Edwin says, "We'll be in touch when we have a project." With Barry was safely out of the office and hurtling towards the ground floor, Edwin breathes a sigh of relief.

"What in God's name was that?" asks Agnes.

"That may be our most significant opportunity to date."

"What, you mean that brute with forehead villainous low?"

"Yes. He is powerful. And, I hope, not smart enough to ruin my plans for him with some terrible scheme of his own."

"He is rather hard on the office furniture."

"Yes, well. I trust you will lose no time in expensing the damage."

150

"Edwin, are you sure this is wise? He does not seem like a reasonable man. Or reasoning. Or even a man at all really."

"I understand your concern, but I assure you, I have the matter well in hand."

Agnes makes an unpleasant face.

"No, really. All of my earlier setbacks have the same root cause. I was expecting unintelligent people to do intelligent things. It was a lack of wisdom on my part. But that is the genius. Not only are we asking Barry do what he loves doing and is already very good at, but we simply cannot overestimate his intelligence. He has none."

"Edwin, he is a brute animal," says Agnes, not convinced.

"And animals can be trained."

"But how will you communicate with this creature? You are not a trainer. You do not think like a brute or savage."

Edwin smiles. "I have just the man for the job."

CHAPTER TWENTY-SEVEN
Enlisting the Little Savage

Topper struggles to keep up with his large friend. He takes three steps to every one. Every ten steps or so, Topper must jog to catch up. He seems even more frantic than usual.

"Topper, I have a special job for you," says Edwin.

"If it's a special job, why don't you hire a specialist?"

"I am. I mean, I have. And that specialist is you."

"Yeah, well, I'm a lawyer. And I don't particularly feel like being a lawyer right now."

"That's perfect, I don't want you to be a lawyer right now," says Edwin

"E, ya got me to thinkin' that day on the golf course. See, my life isn't like I thought it would be. I thought that being a lawyer would let you get away with stuff. That I would learn the rules and learn how to work them, y'know? I didn't think you'd have to obey them. I thought I'd just get to stick it to the other guy. I didn't want to play by somebody else's rules. That just sucks."

Edwin nods thoughtfully. He is gaining a new insight into his little friend. "So your caseload is manageable at the moment?"

"Manageable? I'm not the kind of guy who manages things. I make sure somebody else is there to catch the ball and then I feign total incompetence."

"I respect the efficiency of that."

"Yeah, so that frees me up to spend time on the really important things. Broads and booze and all the little extras that make life worth living. That's why I'm so relaxed and well-adjusted."

Edwin says nothing. Not only is there no point arguing with the little savage, he has found that having the discipline to say nothing at all is a powerful conversational tool. It makes most people so uncomfortable that they all but give in. Besides, there is far too much useless chatter in the world.

"So," Topper says, still struggling to keep up, "What's the play? And how do I help?" Edwin explains Barry's unique talents and his plan for them.

"So, we gotta find somebody who needs a building knocked over," Topper sums up.

Edwin waves a hand dismissively. "Merely an executional concern; I need someone to handle Barry."

"Yeah, but it's those executional concerns that bite you in the ass. Do you have a guy to pay you to knock a building down?"

"No, I generally don't associate with the laboring trades. But there is someone out there."

"En-henh. Well, I know a guy."

"You see, the easy problems solve themselves. That's why they are called the easy problems."

"So aside from hooking you up with a demolition deal, how am I supposed to help?"

"As you may have noticed, I am far more cerebral than you are."

"Dull is the word you're looking for. Unless you just want to come right out and call me stupid. And then I'm going to reach up and punch you in your freakishly tall shins, you lanky bastard." Topper pants as he catches up with Edwin again.

"What I'm trying to say, with great patience, is that I live mostly in my head. Whereas you feel life mostly in your — "

"Balls!"

"Stomach. The word I was looking for was stomach," Edwin says. "My point is that Barry is an appetitive creature. And as eloquent as I may be, I simply don't speak his language. I think you will have better luck communicating with him. On an operational basis, I mean."

"Okay, okay, I get it. And you're right. But can we stop for a second?" Topper points to the bar that they have conveniently stopped in front of. They go inside and Topper orders a double scotch rocks. Edwin has a glass of soda water.

"You sure you don't want a glass of milk?" asks the bartender.

"No," says Edwin, not paying enough attention to him to register the attempted joke.

Topper slugs back half his drink at one go. "Look, and this is just me talking off the top of my head here, but this scheme doesn't seem like you. Seems too small."

"Small?"

"Yeah, there's no angle. Really, just straight ahead? Knock a building over? I mean, they pay you to come up with that?"

"What's wrong with it?"

"Well, nothing. I mean, it's not that there's anything wrong with it. It's just not..."

"Ambitious?"

"That's it. Ambitious. It's not ambitious enough. I'm worried that you are losing your edge. I mean, Alabama was weird. It affected you. You're not as hungry as you used to be."

Edwin sips his soda water. "It has very little to do with hunger. I am being somewhat more careful. But that is because I am not in a position where I need to take aggressive risks. This is a simple plan. And simplicity is genius. This plan should generate plentiful, regular cash for my firm and my client. What could possibly be wrong with that?"

"Ah, safe, regular. All that bullshit again. It's like working for a living. Like all those stiffs out there." Topper gestures contemptuously with his drink and sloshes some Scotch across the bar. "Ah crap. This one has sprung a leak. Bartender, bring me another."

"Topper, you must understand. I enjoy my work."

"You enjoy your work? ENJOY your work. I'm calling bullshit. You're excited about this new client. But I predict you'll be just as miserable as you were. And the only reason you're excited is conditioning. Conditioned thinking, you gotta see through it. Be your own man. See you're only saying that because you can't see your way through to the world being any different. But you gotta throw off your conditioning. You gottta — " As Topper says this, a beautiful woman walks through the door. He stops talking and watches her sway her way through the high-topped tables and barstools.

When she has passed, Edwin asks, "You were saying?"

"Okay, okay whatever. I'm just saying I think we can do a little better."

"You have an idea?"

"Ideas, I got millions of them. But it's not just the idea. It's the vision." He slams his wallet down on the bar. "And I have a vision of money."

"Money?" Edwin asks, deciding to give Topper his head for the simple enjoyment of seeing where he would run.

"Yeah, money. Makes the world go around, right?"

"I believe the Earth spins because of the conservation of angular momentum, but keep going."

"Okay, even if angular what-ever-it-is makes the world go round, I'm pretty sure that money greases the wheels. So, you got this guy who can knock buildings over, right?"

"That is correct."

"I mean he can knock any building over. And you want him to knock over old buildings with nothing in them."

"For a price."

"Yeah, for a price. And for finding you one of those deals, I want a cut of it. You understand?"

"Of course."

"But what I really want is a bigger cut of a bigger deal."

"What exactly are you getting at?"

"You see last night, I get home about three in the morning — "

"Topper, please."

" — and Goldfinger is playing on some channel. You know, the James Bond movie."

"I've never seen it."

"NEVER SEEN IT!"

"I don't really care for movies."

"Oh, Edwin, how can you advise villains if you don't understand the style and panache of one of the greatest villains of all time? Auric Goldfinger!"

"You are referring to a fictional character, are you not?"

"Yeah, but so what? I mean, Jesus was a fictional character and look at the effect he had. And c'mon: the laser? The solid gold car? The 'No, Mr. Bond I expect you to die'?" Topper notices that the bartender is smiling. "See, see, this guy knows what I'm talking about."

Edwin decides it would be best to try silence again. But it is to no avail.

"So in the movie, you think Goldfinger is gonna rob Fort Knox."

"Rob Fort Knox? Rob it of its gold?"

"Yeah, because his heart is cold and loves only gold and his name is friggin' Goldfinger, right? But see, he's already got his own gold. So the theft is just a ruse. What he's really going to do is take over Fort Knox and detonate a dirty bomb inside. Irradiating the ENTIRE United States gold reserve."

"Hmmm," says Edwin.

"Hmmm? How about hell yeah? Isn't it a great idea?"

"Hmmm," says Edwin again.

"So there's one problem with his scheme. He gets caught."

"And what was the flaw in his plan?"

"Well, you could say it was Pussy Galore. She fell in love with Bond and switched sides. Which is how I would have done it in Bond's place. Used my legendary powers of seduction to save the free world. You know, if I was one of the good guys. Which I am not. I'm too much of a free agent."

Edwin rubs his temples.

"But the problem wasn't the hot broad. The problem was too many people. If it wasn't her it was going to be somebody else. See the more people you involve, the more likely it is that somebody screws it up."

Edwin freezes. Wisdom? From Topper? Could it be?

"So what would you do?" asks Edwin.

"So, you take this guy, Barry or whatever, strap a dirty bomb to him — some Polonius, Plutarchium, whatever. You wind him up. Tell him to go for the gold. He smashes through the wall, wham bam, and then when he gets to the gold — BEEP BEEP, 'Hey what's that funny noise?' And KaBLOOEY! That's it for Barry."

"Leaving no link to me."

"Exactly. And if you really want to make it good, all you have to do is put him in a turban. Everybody will think he's part of some jihad against the denser elements or something equally incomprehensible. Who knows what those Korons are thinking anyway?"

"Korons?"

"Morons with Korans. Korons. Towel-heads, camel jockeys. Taxi drivers. Assholes! You know who I'm talking about."

Explosions, senseless killing, widespread destruction, vile prejudice, it certainly is Topper's kind of plan. But Edwin is impressed to find a hint of subtlety in the operation. Subtlety is not something Edwin thought Topper was capable of. He makes a note to consider Topper more carefully in the future.

"So, before you do any of this, you buy a shitload of gold. Then, when the dollar tanks and the entire financial system collapses, the value of your gold skyrockets. Then you sell and buy up half the country for like $20 bucks. It's genius. It just needed me to inject a little realism. Y'know, verisimilitude."

"Hmmm."

"C'mon, you've got to admit, I've taken a good idea and made it better. And it's ambitious. It's audacious. Make a fortune by destroying the United States Dollar."

"I will grant you that it's not entirely a bad idea." Topper beams with pride. Finally Edwin has approved of one of his schemes. Topper feels like he's getting somewhere with the big egghead. At this rate, he might even be able to get Edwin to loosen up and have a good time. "But Topper," Edwin says, "it's already been done."

"WHAT? Nah. No way. I would have read about it."

"So, how much do you think this scheme of yours would devalue the dollar?"

"Oh, at least by half."

"Half?" Edwin snorts. "Half? That would scarcely get you on the board. Since its creation, the U.S. Dollar has lost 98% of its value. It's worth 2% of what it was. Sorry Topper, someone beat you to it."

"But how? Why didn't it make the news? When was the explosion?"

"There was no explosion, just a slow leak."

"So irradiating Fort Knox wouldn't throw the United States into turmoil?"

"Other than the fact that people might be disturbed by glowing racehorses, business would continue as usual."

"But the gold standard!"

"Oh Topper," Edwin laughs, "The dollar isn't backed by gold."

"What? Then these things are just pieces of paper," he cries, brandishing a fistful of notes.

"Yes."

"They're worthless?"

"Not exactly. You can exchange them for things like food and drink. So they are worth something."

"But what keeps people from realizing they're worthless? That you can't get anything for them unless the next guy takes it from you?"

"Nothing."

"Oooooh, that's evil."

"Yes, it is. One has to admire the ruthless professionalism of it. Only if you control a government can you get away with this magnitude of a crime. For the rest of us, we will simply have to content ourselves with lesser ambitions."

"This is all very complicated. I better stock up on a few things in case money doesn't work tomorrow. Wait. Wait. Gold. Gold will still be worth something. We should STILL knock over Fort Knox!"

"Ah, yes. But if you are going to steal gold, why go all the way to Kentucky? There's over 10,000 tons of the stuff in an underground depository twelve blocks away."

"I didn't know that."

"And even if it wasn't very, very secure, there is always the problem of how you move it."

"I'd carry it in my greedy little paws."

"I'm sure you would try Topper. But each bar of gold weighs 27 pounds. Which makes moving gold a slow proposition. Especially when you consider that the vault is constructed in such a way that it is very time consuming to get gold in or out. It requires, at this point, rather a lot of people. And as you pointed out, the more people, the more problem."

"But if you had a guy with superpowers. A really strong guy."

Edwin looks directly into Topper's avaricous soul, "That thought never leaves my mind. For a client of mine to gain control of 40% of the world's gold — "

"A CLIENT! Edwin, when are you going to start thinking about yourself? Lookin' after #1 like any good, red-blooded American should."

"Topper, I am not a criminal."

"You're a friggin' mastermind, that's what you are. All those facts crammed in that pointy head of yours."

Edwin sighs. This conversation is pointless. "Just accept that I do not break the law. I do not break the social contract. I do not break contracts of any kind. It's bad for business. But I advise those who choose to do so."

"You are a very, very strange man."

"Perhaps. But please, help me with this small thing. Help me with Barry. And we'll work up to currency manipulation eventually."

"Can we steal gold? Can we?"

"When the right set of powers come along, I will advise someone to steal the gold."

"Okay then. I'll help you," Topper downs the rest of his drink. "Now I got to go see a man about blowing up a building." Topper waddles out the door, sticking Edwin with the check.

CHAPTER TWENTY-EIGHT
Reasoning with Barry

Topper sets up a meeting for Edwin with R. Earl Lemahi. He is a half-Texan, half-Pakistani real estate magnate who has developed a number of sites around the city. But none bigger or more impressive than the Spackster project.

The Spackster building is one of the city's original skyscrapers. Only 20 stories tall, in its day it had been a marvel of engineering, but now its glory has faded. It's just another pile of dirty bricks with a cleverly disguised water tower on the roof.

Lemahi has surrounded the Spackster building on three sides with featureless boxes of expensive per-square-foot office space. These buildings are state of the art, and remarkable only in their soullessness. Edwin meets with Lemahi at the top of one of his prized buildings.

"Windsor," Lemahi says as he gestures towards the Spackster building, "I need this old pile of bricks taken down carefully and well. But I ain't never heard of you. Which makes me a mite nervous."

"And the fact that I'm offering to demolish the building for half the cost of anyone else? What does that do to your nerves?" Edwin says, cool as can be. It's not like this is his first negotiation.

163

"Makes them a damn sight steadier. I just wanted to come down here and look in your eye, boy. Make sure you were a serious man."

Edwin meets his gaze without flinching. These silly "men-of-business" games mean nothing to him. "And now that you have looked in my eyes?"

"Oh you're serious a'right. But I don't see no bond. And if you ain't bonded, you ain't doing this job." R. Earl leans back in his chair, pleased to think that he has put this smug bastard back on his heels.

Edwin's expression does not change. Edwin opens his briefcase and removes some documents. "You are right, I do not have a bond. My affairs are such that I am loathe to explain them to insurance inspectors. But I have placed $55 million in escrow. Far more than the decrepit Spackster building is worth. I hope you will agree that it is more than enough for you to indemnify yourself for any demolition related accidents."

R. Earl's eyes widen. He's obviously impressed with a man who can conjure up $55 million. "Yeah," says the gruff old man, biting off the word as if it was something he didn't want to swallow. "Now just don't screw it up. I've got a lot riding on this." The old man turns his back on Edwin, indicating that the meeting is over and that Edwin is dismissed. This annoys Edwin, but he leaves quietly.

Barry is in the high, bright room once again. Outside he can hear the wind blow. Inside he can feel the building move. He doesn't like tall places. He's clumsy and he falls down a lot. Right now he really is trying to pay attention to the words the Tall One is using, but it's hard. All those sounds. And what do they mean?

"So you see," Edwin says, speaking very slowly, "my associate will guide you on this new, and potentially very lucrative, path."

All Barry hears is "Bl you bla, my, blahblahb blah blahb you bl blah new, and blahblahbla, blah blahblahb blah." Barry squirms and blinks non-comprehension as if it is morse code.

The small one walks up to him. He smells funny. Like Dad. Barry doesn't know that Topper has steadied his nerves with quite a lot of scotch before this meeting. Not that Topper is worried, but any excuse to steady the nerves, you understand. "You didn't understand a word of that did you?" asks Topper. Barry doesn't get anything out of that sentence either, but he nods and smiles. The little one is smiling at him. Barry thinks it's funny.

"Yeah," Topper says to Edwin, "you got yourself a regular old rocket scientist here." Barry coughs again. Topper brings him a glass of water.

"Oh, I think I've gotten through to him," says Edwin. He hands Barry a picture of the Spackster building. Then he holds up a duplicate picture. He waits until Barry is looking at the picture he's holding. Then he tears it in half very slowly. He says "Demolish."

Barry drinks his glass of water and then crushes the glass.

Topper laughs. "Oh yeah, you got a real rapport going there." Topper laughs some more. His shrill notes put Edwin on edge. "Oh ho ho, big boy, you've got no clue do you?" Barry smiles and laughs along with Topper.

"I don't know about that," says Edwin.

Still chuckling, Topper winks at Edwin as he hands Barry a phone book. Topper takes a piece of the photo Edwin has torn in half and tears it again. Barry tears the phone book in half. Topper squeals with delight. "Oh, you are a strong boy!" As Barry nods Topper shoves a piece of candy in his open mouth. "Good boy."

Barry blinks twice and closes his mouth. He almost becomes angry, but when the sweet taste fills his mouth, he is happy.

"That doesn't mean he understood you," says Edwin

165

"What, you want me to get him to cut you a deck of cards?" says Topper.

Edwin shakes his head.

"So we can try it my way?"

Topper opens a cabinet and produces two identical cardboard models of the Spackster Building. "Bar-REE," Topper says with a sharply rising tone. At the high-pitched word, Barry perks up like a dog. Topper sets one of the models on the table in front of Barry. He places the other model on the floor in front of him.

Topper takes two steps backwards. He claps his hands together dramatically then he jumps into the air and screams "GENTRIFICATION!" When he lands, he slams both feet down on the cardboard model.

Barry giggles hysterically and brings his hand down on the other model, palm open. Not only is the model flattened, but the table beneath it splinters violently and cracks in half. Topper runs over to Barry's large, misshapen head and kisses it. "I love this boy!" Barry giggles some more.

Topper turns to Edwin, "I say we're ready." Topper scratches Barry behind the ear. "Good boy. Good boy."

Watching them, Edwin experiences a moment of doubt. But he dismisses it. After all, Barry is supposed to destroy a building. What is the worst that could happen? The building would remain standing? It wasn't like he could screw it up so badly that he would accidentally create another building.

CHAPTER TWENTY-NINE
Wrecking a Building

The day has come. Permits have been obtained. Streets have been cordoned. A crowd has gathered to watch the demolition of an historic building. In its day the Spackster building had been home to a full-service department store. Eight floors of glorious commerce named after its founder Hubert Spackster. When Hubert was in charge he liked to boast that there were only two things you couldn't get at Spackster's. Mothers and coffins. For everything else Hubert Spackster offered a layaway plan.

But those days are gone. It has been years since anything has been sold in the Spackster building other than sex and illicit drugs. Things have come full circle. Now mothers and dead bodies are available.

This has not exactly been a convenience for the neighbors, but it was what it was. Spackster's is the only place within three blocks that has yet to be swallowed by redevelopment. The stately, if crumbling, old building has been surrounded by taller and sleeker structures. And now, the time has come for the old place to make its final stand.

Edwin looks at this relic of the past. He is confident that the building doesn't stand a chance. A police Sergeant waddles over and says, "We're all clear Mr. Windsor, you can blow your building whenever you're ready."

"Thank you," says Edwin, "But explosions are dangerous. And explosives cost money."

"But I thought... yer sposta blow up this building aren't you? Says so right on the permit."

"Demolish. The permit does not specify how."

"Then howda heck are ya gonna?"

Edwin shakes his head. "Not how. Who."

Behind Edwin, the door to a mobile trailer is thrown open so hard that it leaves a dent in the siding. One of the hinges lets go with a horrible popping screech. The Sergeant flinches and grabs for his weapon. Edwin stands straight. He has become accustomed to the destructive path that Barry cuts through the world. The senselessness of it is no longer terrifying, it is merely tiresome.

Now that Barry has made an opening, he exits the trailer. But the force with which he has opened the door has also damaged the trailer's steps. No sooner does his foot touch the first step than the entire structure gives way. Barry lands on his face. In spite of himself, the Sergeant laughs.

But his laugh is cut short as Barry roars in frustration. In true, utterly senseless form, Barry rears back and punches the ground with all his might. The earth itself seems to recoil in terror. The pavement ripples, and cracks race along the ground. As the first of the car alarms goes off, a wall of glass in a nearby building explodes.

The Sergeant looks around frantically to see which building is going to fall on him. Edwin calmly flicks a piece of pavement from his well-tailored pant leg. "You see?" Edwin asks the Sergeant. The Sergeant nods in mute agreement, all the while wondering if they have a gun big enough to stop this guy. After pondering this for a minute, the Sergeant says, "Jesus."

Topper leaps down from the door of the trailer. He is high on life, destruction and several other substances. "Ah, HELL

YEAH!" he shrieks, "That's it. Get mad. Get mad at it. It's showtime."

Barry picks himself off the ground. Topper stands right in front of him and holds his open palm as high in the air as he can manage. "C'mon. You're a monster. You're an animal. WHOOOOOOO... ugh." Topper's high-spirited rant is cut short when Barry high-fives the little man and sends him rolling across the pavement. Topper comes to rest at Edwin's feet. He looks up and says, "We gotta get this kid in a boxing ring."

"Only if you can get him to throw the fight," says Edwin, "Otherwise we'll get no odds."

The Sergeant looks at Barry. Then he looks at Topper. Then back at Barry. Then at Edwin. It makes him seem less a person and more like some kind of spastic, over-caffeinated pigeon. When he realizes that both Edwin and Topper are staring him he says, "Are, are, are you sure you can control that thing?"

"Him? He's a pussy cat," says Topper, rubbing a spot on his head where it slammed against the pavement. "Hey, dumbass, get over here." Barry smiles and lumbers towards Topper.

The Sergeant flinches again. He thinks about calling for a S.W.A.T. team, just in case. But then he realizes that if this goes wrong, there's probably nothing a S.W.A.T team could do. It would be out of his hands and nobody could blame him.

"Come on dumbass, let's go mess up this building. Then we'll go get a double helping of pie."

"PUH-EYE!" bellows Barry.

"Yeah, yeah, pie. I know you like pie!" And with that Topper goes into a fit of verbal and physical gymnastics. He simultaneously curses and praises Barry. He moves quickly and erratically and incessantly, like the end of a piece of string dangled in front of a cat. All of this serves to keep Barry's attention. In this frantic manner Topper moves Barry towards the doomed structure one gesticulation at a time.

Edwin can not imagine how this communication is possible. It is as if Topper has a gift. The kind of a gift attributed to horse whisperers and snake charmers and wild-eyed mystics who spend most of their time in the dry, empty places of the world. There is only one way to say it. On some animalistic level, Topper and Barry have a connection.

As Barry nears the building, he becomes distracted. He looks down and sees two tiny flowers that have managed, against all odds and logic, to claw their way through a crack in the sidewalk. Their existence is impossible but, as so often happens in nature, no one has bothered to tell the flowers. It is enough to move a person with even the slightest amount of imagination to tears. One could see the flowers as a metaphor for beauty's eternal struggle to prevail in the harshest of conditions. Or as an example of how the gentler emotions can take root in even the rockiest and most uninspired of places. One could, but not Barry.

"Pretty," he says as lumbers to a stop. And there Barry, vicious brute with forehead villainous low, stoops to adore two tiny yellow flowers.

"Hey. Hey! HEY!" Topper stomps over to the flowers. "What is this? Flowers? What are you, some kind of sissy boy? Stopping to pick flowers? C'mon, we got buildings to mess up."

When Barry doesn't even look up. Topper gets mad. He slaps Barry across the top of his head. "C'mon, dumbass, leave the flowers alone." Barry still doesn't look up. With uncharacteristic gentleness, he caresses the petals with one sausage-like finger.

"Pretty," says Barry.

"Well piss in a parasol! If you like the flowers so much we'll take them with us." Topper reaches down to rip the flowers out of the earth, but he doesn't quite make it. Barry drops one of his meathooks on Topper's head. Topper is compressed into the ground. As the air escapes from his lungs he says, "Awk."

Barry lifts Topper off the ground. Legs flailing wildly, Topper commands, "Put me down. Put me down DUMBASS!"

"Flowers pretty," says Barry. Then he tosses Topper over his shoulder. Once again Topper tumbles across the pavement and lands at Edwin's feet.

"E, I don't like this job anymore," says Topper.

"I'm not sure I can care about that Topper," says Edwin, not taking his eyes off Barry.

"He squeezed my little brain," says Topper.

What an apt turn of phrase, thinks Edwin. "I am sorry Topper, but we have a schedule to keep and a building to destroy."

"Oh yeah, well I'd like to see you do better, Beanpole!" Edwin ignores the strange insult. Clearly Plan A is not working. Edwin is never without a Plan B. But Plan B and C and all the other secondary plans are always messier, riskier and less profitable than Plan A. So Edwin does something remarkable. He lets go of all his plans.

He quiets his thoughts and simply observes. He sees the building. He sees Barry. From the corner of his eye, he can see the Sergeant. He can perceive the Sergeant's indecision. Edwin can feel the situation becoming untenable. The moment has developed its own urgency. Something must be done.

Edwin pushes past this noise. He allows himself a greater calm. He uses his will to clear his mind. And at the bottom of it all — beyond all the worries and the factors and schemes and the judgements — is a breath of air that ruffles tiny flower petals.

The idea arrives fully formed. As if it has a will of its own. It is not completely accurate to say that the idea had Edwin, but that's the way it feels. Endorphins rush through Edwin's brain, confirming the joy of this Eureka moment.

"Ed, are you okay?" asks Topper.

Edwin walks. He brushes by Barry, who is still hunched over his flowers. Edwin approaches the Spackster building as any penitent might approach any temple of commerce on any day. The entrance is boarded and covered in graffiti. The remnants of a revolving door litter the sidewalk. But Edwin is not interested in the inside of the building. He is interested, for once, in the facade of things. And there, among the dirty stones, he finds what he needs.

A brick tumbles and grinds across the sidewalk. Before it comes to a rest, it shears the tiny flowers off at their base. Barry jerks his head up in outrage. And there stands Edwin pointing at the building as if, somehow, the building has just spat the brick on Barry's precious flowers.

Barry doesn't think much. Barry doesn't think often. And it goes without saying that Barry doesn't think very well. So when he sees that the little flowers have been crushed by a dingy yellow brick, and that there is large pile of dingy yellow bricks right in front of him, it's not hard for him to put two and two together and come up with — well, not four exactly, but a really, really big two. Which isn't the right answer, but for Barry it's close enough. He comes up swinging.

"MAAAAAAAAAAAAAAAAAAAAAAARRRRRGAHHHH HH!"

Fist hits bricks. Bricks lose. In fact, the bricks of the Spackster building lose so badly that they can't even qualify as bricks anymore. They are demoted to hot and highly confused dust so fast that the effect is indistinguishable from an explosion. Pieces of building whiz by Topper's head at a frightening velocity. Everybody runs. Even Edwin puts on an uncharacteristic hurry.

WABOOOOM! The west wall of the Spackster building gives way. Barry is buried in bricks and debris up to his neck. From his vantage point on the top of a police car, Topper can see Barry's head moving through the rubble like a periscope. Barry wades in deeper and takes out another support pillar.

The earth shudders as another section of the building comes tumbling down. "YEAH! YEAH! YEAH! WRECK THE JOINT!" Topper yells.

Topper's high voice carries through the noise of destruction. It is just the right pitch to be heard over the scrape of thousands of bricks upon thousands of other bricks, the tinkle of broken glass, and the basso profundo bellowing of Barry himself. Topper's voice reaches the spectators, the ordinary folk of the city who are sneaking a few moments from their lives with the expectation of seeing an implosion. They were expecting a quick orgasm of violence. But this is something different. This is something much better. The kind of thing many members of the crowd might order on Pay-Per-View. This is an orgy of destruction.

Topper's cry infects the crowd. Now thousands of people join in, "WRECK THE JOINT! WRECK THE JOINT!" as if the demolition is some kind of perverse sporting event. Topper feels the wall of noise pressing him forward before he understands what the crowd is saying. He turns and plays cheerleader.

Edwin does not take his eyes off Barry. Edwin now has a fear. It is too late to do anything about it. Another section of the building crashes down, sending up a tremendous wall of dust. Edwin covers his face with an immaculate handkerchief. Unable to see, the crowd falls silent.

"Aw c'mon," Topper shouts, "It was just getting GOOD!"

"Topper," says Edwin.

"Yeah," replies Topper, looking down on his friend from the top of a police car.

"I have a question." Before Edwin can give voice to his fear, he is interrupted by a deafening sound. It's a sound that one might describe as an impossibly large chandelier falling from its anchor point on the moon. But Edwin is far too practical a man to make this mistake. He knows what the sound really is. He puts a hand to his brow and bows his head.

As the dust parts the crowd erupts in a roar. There is Barry, laying into one of the newer, sleeker, tremendously more valuable buildings.

"WRECK THE JOINT! WRECK THE JOINT!" Topper screams as he smashes the blue lights on top of the police car.

"Topper please," Edwin says, not looking up.

"C'mon E. You gotta see this. This is awesome!"

Edwin watches Barry tip Lemahi Center Tower #3 into Lemahi Center Tower #4. Both buildings come raining down in an avalanche of shattered glass and twisted metal.

"HORAGGGGGGGGGGGGGGGGG!" yells Barry as he destroys millions of dollars worth of real estate.

Topper says, "I know those are the wrong buildings, but you gotta admit, the kid's got talent."

CHAPTER THIRTY
A Blackjack Toting Angel

"You moron! You incompetent! You, you, you complete toothless GOOB! I am going to break you. I'm going to break you and then I am going to have you ground up into little pieces, brewed into tea, drink you down and piss you out onto your own grave."

Edwin turns his face and catches a fleck of spittle on his cheek. It is not often that Edwin gets yelled at. The novelty wears off quickly. As Mr. Lamahi continues to vent his spleen, Edwin wipes the spittle from his face with a handkerchief.

Intellectually, Edwin is aware of the idea of sympathy. He can understand that Mr. Lemahi has poured all of his hard work and dreams of real estate success into this project. A project that has just been destroyed by the drooling, ham-fisted man-child that is Barry. He can understand that Mr. Lemahi is upset. He just doesn't care. Besides, all of this yelling is giving him a headache.

Edwin tries to calm Mr. Lemahi. "It's not a total loss is it? You have insurance. Acts of God and such."

"Damn it! There's not an insurance company on Earth that will cover what happened. Acts of Superpersons are not Acts of God. That goddamned clause just killed me! No, NO. YOU just killed me!"

"Please Mr. Lemahi, for your own good, you need to calm yourself. Perhaps some tea?"

"Calm myself! Are you threatening me?! Are you THREATENING ME?!"

"No, I am offering you tea. I — "

"No, shut up. You don't get to talk Windsor. You screwed it up. There's no other way to say it. So SHUT UP. Only I get to talk."

Edwin activates the intercom. "Agnes, we are in need of tea and scones."

The angry man doesn't stop talking. "25 years of my life in that project and 55 million in escrow isn't going to cover it. C'mon, c'mon say something. I want to hear what you have to say for yourself."

"I — "

"SHUT UP! I'm not through yelling at you yet."

Edwin pushes his chair back from his desk, crosses his legs and cups his chin in the palm of his hand. Truly, Mr. Lemahi is turning out to be a barren form of amusement. In the background Agnes shuffles in with a carefully prepared tray. "Would you care for tea, Mr. Lemahi?"

"Tea? TEA! Aren't you people listening? The only tea I want is made from his ground up BONES!"

"I'm afraid all I have is Darjeeling," says Agnes.

"Well you can take your Darjeeling and shove it up your dusty old — !"

From behind the teapot, Agnes produces a stun gun. Before Lemahi can finish his foul sentence, she gets him right in the neck. Lemahi goes from outrage to shock to a kind of vibrating fish face. His eyeballs roll back into his head and he slides out of the chair like a sack of meat. Which, given the trauma his nervous system has just endured, is pretty much what he is.

"Thank you, Agnes," says Edwin.

Agnes holds up the stun gun as an object of contemplation. "Call me old-fashioned, but I prefer a blackjack."

176

"As much as I respect you and your unique mix of talents, Agnes, it is an unavoidable fact that your strength is waning as you grow older."

"Oh posh. Strength? It's all technique. One should not blame the brush for the shortcomings of the artist."

"Mnnnnngah," says Lemahi as he struggles to regain a handle on the moment. He drags himself to a knee.

"You see? You see?" cries Agnes. "It is a shoddy product that does not work as advertised!" She zaps him again with the Taser. Lemahi rag-dolls to the floor. Edwin finds neither comedy nor tragedy in this. He watches the entire spectacle without emotion.

Now, a normal person, say a man on his way to buy a hot dog for lunch, would have been rendered unconscious by two blasts in the neck from a stun gun. But Lemahi is fueled by truly righteous and exceptional anger. And he is not to be denied. One hand claws at the side of the chair as he struggles to get his badly jangled nervous system to fire in some kind of coherent order. As he rises, red-faced and sputtering, Agnes says, "Oh good Lord!" and bustles out of the room.

Edwin is left alone with a crippled and angry man. "Windsssssssssir!" Lemahi slurs, hacking at his words like a stroke victim. "Urrrrrn ann idiot. An an an an an an — "

THOCK!

It is, Edwin thinks, an odd sort of sound. He looks up from his desk to see how it has been produced. There is Agnes, standing over the now definitively unconscious Lemahi. In her hand is a piece of lead wrapped in leather.

"There," says Agnes as if she has just set a quaint sea-side cottage to rights, "I feel better, don't you?"

Edwin does not feel better. He stares off into a point where the wall meets the ceiling.

"Edwin dearie, what is it?" Agnes asks. The battle axe of moments before has melted away into an angel of compassion. A blackjack toting angel, but an angel all the same.

177

"He is right," says Edwin.

"He is no such thing. He is rude and ignorant."

"But Agnes, don't you see? I know — I should have known better. To expect an irrational creature to act rationally..." Edwin trails off and Agnes lets the silence be. She pours Edwin a cup of the Darjeeling and quietly sets it on the desk beside him.

Edwin doesn't even look at it. Agnes says, "You shouldn't be so hard on yourself."

Edwin does not respond. After a while, Agnes leaves the room to arrange for the removal of Mr. Lemahi. As the cup of tea cools, Edwin sinks deeper and deeper into depression. And this funk is a malaise of why. Why had Edwin chosen to put himself in this position? It would have required little enough imagination to figure out what might go wrong. This most recent setback notwithstanding, was his entire conception flawed?

Could he truly expect the unrestrained and foolish to act rationally? Could he correct the flaws of a villainous world? Or was it destined to be that reason and logic would have little place under the sun? Edwin knows his logic is sound, that his ideas are good. But is the weakness and fallibility of men such that he can never succeed?

Days come and go. Edwin comes to work. Edwin goes home. He takes no calls and he holds no meetings. He sits in his office, staring into space, as the sun moves across the sky. Seeking his answer in the movement of shadows.

After long years of service, Agnes is highly attuned to Edwin's moods. At times she has felt his great brain churning on some problem as one might feel the thundering of a diesel engine buried beneath the deck plates of a ship. But now she can sense nothing. When she tries to talk with him, he dismisses her with an all-too-familiar wave of his hand. He has gone where she cannot follow. But she does not give up. She does the only thing she can think to do. She calls Topper.

178

CHAPTER THIRTY-ONE
Topper Gives a Pep Talk

Topper is not the kind of person who broods. Sure, he'll cry at the drop of a hat. Sure he'll rage and throw a fit for no reason at all. He will whipsaw back and forth across a range of emotions so extreme it could give an ordinary person the bends. But Topper never broods. The finer shades of a long, protracted ennui are unknown to him. As is the word ennui.

So when Topper hangs up the phone after talking with Agnes, his reaction is swift. "Bullshit," says Topper, "it's just nothing but bullshit."

The way Topper sees it, there is no reason to get stuck in a mood. The seasons change, the temperature changes, everything in the world changes. And if you fight it too much, you just screw yourself up. A man has to follow his urges. They come in on a radio from God. And you might not always understand them, but maybe you aren't supposed to.

All Topper knows for sure is every time he tries to think about his emotions, it gets him into trouble. But if he gets laid when he feels like getting laid and throws a tantrum when he feels like throwing a tantrum, somehow everything works out. He calls it advanced Zen. Eat when you're hungry. Sleep when you're tired. And when you feel like doing something, just do it already. Why resist?

"Guy just needs to get laid," Topper sums up as he exits the elevator at the top of Windsor Tower. He barges into Edwin's office. Without breaking stride he says, "All right, Beanpole. Time to snap out of it. We've already got one Lincoln Memorial, we don't need another."

Edwin sits low in his chair, the tips of his index fingers touching in front of his nose. He does not turn to look at Topper.

"What, now you're gonna give me the silent treatment? That's gonna get you nowhere. Because, let me tell you something. I'm louder than any silence."

Edwin looks up and to the right. As if he is recalling a piece of valuable information.

"Yeah, yeah. You just keep thinking. THINKING! THINKING! THINKING! That's the problem. You're unhappy because you're all of the time thinking and none of the time living!"

Edwin's gaze wanders to the ceiling.

"And just because I found that in a fortune cookie doesn't mean it's not true. What is it? Is it that you made a mistake? C'mon! I make mistakes all the time, you don't see it getting me down, do you? You can't give up!"

Edwin looks at Topper. He realizes that looking at Topper is a mistake. It only serves to encourage him.

"Yeah, yeah, look at me. See how short I am? You know, when they told me I was gonna be a dwarf, I said no way. I said un-hunh. I said screw you. And then they held out the book and showed me where it said, 4'5" and under is the classification for dwarf. And I said, there is no way I'm going to be a dwarf. You just watch me. And you know what I did? Do you?"

Edwin closes his eyes.

"I started hanging out with tall people. I started doing the things they did. I went out for the basketball team. I even thought lofty thoughts. Yeah, me. And I did this for a whole year. So I get back to the doctor and they measure me again. Still 4'4" and a half. They called me a dwarf. I called them assholes. Then I went out and bought shoes with a half inch lift. And forgot all about it.

"Which is what you need to do. Forget about it. It's a mistake, sure. Ya screwed it up. Everybody screws up. Who cares? Just roll on to the next thing. You just roll on. Get me? Roll on." Topper turns dramatically and heads towards the door. Any other man would be enjoying a false hope that Topper is done with his sermon, but Edwin knows better.

Sure enough, as soon as he reaches the office door, Topper spins on his heel and says, "And you know what happened? Three years later, I grew that extra inch. Hunh? Hunh? What does that tell you?" Topper pauses. Edwin does not react. Topper leaves the room with a "harumph."

With serenity restored to his office, Edwin wonders if Topper really has grown that extra inch. He makes a mental note to have Topper measured if the opportunity presents itself.

In the lobby, Topper takes a few deep breaths.

"Were you able to cheer him up?" asks Agnes.

Topper shakes his head.

"Well, I suppose we shall just have to ride it out again."

Topper asks, "What do you mean again?"

"It happened once before. Oh, that was a dreadful year."

"Year? You gotta be kidding me. He was like that for a year?"

"Well, it doesn't happen often," says Agnes defensively.

"Somebody's got to toughen that kid up."

"Oh, I am certain that is the answer," Agnes says, her tongue curling around the sarcasm.

"C'mon Agnes, I feel guilty enough about this as it is."

"Guilty enough? I scarcely think that is possible."

"I gotta make it right somehow."

"Oh, no," says Agnes, "You've had your chance. And, I might add, you have failed to bring him out of his funk."

"I can do it. I swear I can."

"I am as close to being sorry about this as I can be about anything that concerns you, but I have no more faith to waste on you."

"Aw, Agnes, I know I'm a screw-up. The trouble is I don't fit, see? I'm the wrong size."

"Really?" Agnes raises an eyebrow as she says, "I would have suspected that your trouble is that you fit all kinds of places where a decent person should never go."

"Oh, there you go again, always beating on me."

"If it is too much for you, I can only suggest that you put yourself out of my misery."

In defeat, and finding no solace, Topper scuttles into the elevator. "Fine, fine, you mean old bat. But I'm gonna make this right. You'll see."

"Away with you, you vociferous munchkin. I would sooner put out mine own eyes with a tuning fork than admit that you have done something correctly!"

Topper sticks his head out of the elevator. "Velociraptor what? What does that even mean?"

Agnes returns to her work with a dismissive gesture. "Just don't make things any worse than they already are."

CHAPTER THIRTY-TWO
Calling Forth Nemesis

Mighty forces call forth their own resistance. The bigger they are, the more they weigh. The harder they fall. The more friction they generate when they move. The faster they are, the harder they have to be able to brake to make the corner. Nature counterbalances the power she bestows. Sometimes not elegantly. Sometimes not obviously. But there is always a balance.

As Barry revels in his newfound might, he does not imagine that there might be some kind of a catch. After all, he has never been to college. He has never studied Greek drama. He's never heard of Nemesis, the forces of retribution called forth by the prideful actions of the hero to bring about his downfall. And even though he's not a hero, the same principle applies. Hubris is the nail that sticks out. Sooner or later, it gets pounded flat.

Barry has always been strong, but he's never known how strong. But then, he's never had occasion to put his strength to the test. Now that he's knocking down buildings, everything just feels right. In fact, it feels like buildings just aren't big enough any more. He needs bigger buildings. He needs mountains.

Of course, the police go berserk. They lay into Barry with everything they have. Pistols, rifles, shotguns, tear gas grenades, tasers — one guy even tries a can of restraining foam. The bullets bounce off. The tasers tickle. But when the Sergeant sees Barry eating the restraining foam like it's peanut butter, that tears it. Time to call for backup. And not just more guys. This is more than cops can deal with. It's time for a whole different kind of guy.

"Dispatch this is Charlie 3-1, Code 30P, Code 30P"

"Roger that Charlie 3-1," says the otherworldly voice of the dispatcher. "Confirm code three-zero papa." The voice of the dispatcher is as calm as if she were seated in a lotus blossom upon the right hand of Buddha himself.

There is an explosion. The Sergeant ducks. It's probably a gas main. But with this guy, how do you know? He keys the mike as the echos from the explosion finish bouncing off the buildings behind him. "Yes, goddamn it 30P! Request immediate back up!"

Just to be sure, the dispatcher checks the manual. She has never before received a Code 30P. Code 30 is the standard call for backup. Officer Needs Assistance. The addition of a "P" designates it as a call for backup with superpowers. She reads it twice to be sure. And then she passes it up to her supervisor. He checks the manual and then he passes it up.

The request keeps getting passed up, up and up. Eventually, it gets so high up the chain of command that it makes a small black box vibrate and beep on a nightstand. And next to the nightstand, Excelsior sleeps face down on the bed. He ignores the pager. It goes off again and again.

From across the room, a high-pitched warble comes from the strange logo emblazoned on Excelsior's skin-tight outfit. Excelsior opens his eyes. He wasn't aware they had placed a communicator in there. They must really be desperate if they are tipping their hand now.

He rolls over in bed, and smells it. It is the foulest stench imaginable. And it is coming from the layer of black slime that covers his outfit. Slime? Yeah, now it comes back to him. He had spent the better part of two days fighting some incredibly dense and rubbery creature that had crawled out of the Laurentian abyssal. Who knows what the hell it was? Let the scientists wade around in what was left of that foul, slime-covered beast and figure it out. All Excelsior knows is that he killed it. Well, he had broken off a lot of pieces and it had stopped moving. But the horrible thing had taken a toll on Excelsior. And now, from beyond the grave, it has filled Excelsior's bedroom with a stench that is a cross between the dumpster behind a discount sushi joint and a sinking oil tanker with a backed-up toilet.

From inside the filth-covered suit a man's voice says, "Bishop Six? Bishop Six, can you hear me?"

Excelsior sits up and rubs his face. This is a mistake. The smell gets stronger the higher you go in the room. Jesus, where had that thing been?

"Bishop Six, are you there? We need you."

"Yeawp. You sure do," Excelsior says through a yawn. "Call me back in an hour."

"Bishop Six! Bishop Six this is control. Are you receiving?"

He rolls over in bed and tries to ignore the voice. How much more do they want from him? He needs sleep, after all. Why can't they handle their own problems for once? Excelsior turns on the television. As the suit harasses him and the beeper rattles on the nightstand, he flips through the news channels. He's hoping he can see himself in action against that awful thing. That might motivate him to get out of bed. But, unbelievably, it seems his battle hasn't even made the news.

"Bishop Six, this is control."

The people on the other end aren't getting the message. "I said call me back in an hour." Ordinary people! No sense of gratitude. They don't want to know how weird and dangerous the world really is. They like to sleep soundly at night. And who could blame them? That's all he wants to do, get a little sleep. Maybe he should have let that slimy thing destroy Canada. It's not like Excelsior knows anybody in Canada. He doesn't even like hockey.

But Canada borders the United States. Which means that there was a chance that thing might have edged over into Vermont, or Michigan. So Excelsior had swung into action. He wears the Red, White and Blue, and is sworn to defend the US of A. Even the cold, flat parts that everybody moves away from when they get out of high school.

Excelsior flings the covers from the bed. He walks over to the suit and taps the logo. "This is Bishop Six, go ahead.

"Bishop Six, we've got a situation." They've always got a situation. "There's a man knocking down buildings."

"Just buildings?" asks Excelsior as he looks around for something to breathe through. The smell next to his costume is almost completely unbearable.

"Affirmative, just buildings."

"Isn't that what insurance is for?" wonders Excelsior. He hears scuffling noises as someone new grabs the microphone.

"Son, what in the hell have I told you about thinkin'?!" Gus's phlegmy drawl roars through the speaker. "Insurance is for acts of God and Nature, not superpowered freaks like you. No insurance company on earth will cover the pain in the ass damage you do."

"Aren't you dead yet?" Excelsior asks, somewhat in jest.

"I'm too mean to die. And too pretty." Excelsior hears Gus turn away from the microphone and cough for a while. "Now we've got a little problem up around 108th street."

"Gus, I'm running on two hours of sleep."

"Yeah, well I'm 155 years old and you don't hear me complaining."

"You didn't spend the last two days bashing your brains out against a monster from the bottom of the ocean."

186

"Hell, I tried for that duty. But I pulled the short straw and had to settle for dealing with your sorry ass." Excelsior smiles in spite of himself and the smell.

"All right. Let me get a cup of coffee in me. I'll pound this guy flat as a manhole cover and then you buy me lunch."

"Now listen, this one is a little different."

"Different?" Excelsior says with a snort, "They're all different aren't they, Gus? But they're all the same in the end. They all get pounded flat."

"No, you just listen to —"

"Yeah, yeah, yeah. 108th and what?"

"Spackster Ave., but listen, we've had — "

Gus's voice is cut off abruptly as beams of pure light leap from Excelsior's eyes and vaporize the costume. No point in saving it. No dry cleaner on Earth would have been able to get that smell out. But the smell that is coming from the ashes is even worse. Now the room smells like burnt, oily, fish hair. Time for another place to live. Excelsior goes to the closet for another suit. He's already thinking about lunch. He's gonna make Gus buy him a steak. A big one.

Excelsior steps out the window and is at Spackster and 108th Street in a blink. The destruction covers a block and a half. He had no idea it was this bad. The cops have seen him and pull back. They drag their wounded with them as they go. What happened here? Excelsior circles over the rubble, searching through the clouds of dust. He sees a squat figure, standing all alone. He doesn't look all that threatening. He looks big, sure, but he looks tired and a little lost. Somehow dissipated and harmless. Excelsior thinks about asking him if he needs help, but as soon as the guy sees Excelsior, he throws a steel I-beam at him.

Yup, thinks Excelsior, that's the bad guy. He fades back to catch the I-beam. The last thing he needs is that landing on a pre-school or something. Oh, he'd never hear the end of that. He heaves the beam over his shoulder and gets a good grip on

187

it. He doesn't want to hit the guy too hard with this thing —
then he'll just have to go chase him down. But, yeah, he's
gonna hit this guy in the face with an I-beam. Big fella should
be able to take it. After all, he just knocked down a bunch of
buildings.

Excelsior dips low, skimming six feet off the ground. This is
the part where the bad guy usually starts running. Only this
guy isn't running. He's not moving at all. He's just standing
there, looking stupid. Oh well, thinks Excelsior, batter up. And
he swings.

But when the I-beam connects with the guy, something
funny happens. The I-beam hits him and stops dead. The
force rebounds through the steel and Excelsior knocks the
wind out of himself. He's so shocked he falls down. What the
hell? That's never happened before. He looks up. The guy is
walking over to him. His face is a little red from where the I-
beam hit him, but other than that, he appears to be unharmed.

"Okay, buddy," Excelsior says as he starts to get up. But he
doesn't get there. The guy grabs his foot. He looks so harmless,
and is so nonchalant about it, Excelsior doesn't even see it
coming. People aren't supposed to grab him. They're
supposed to be afraid of him. Excelsior tries to twist free. But
he can't. He can't? He's almost got enough time to say "Hey!"
before the guy lofts him over his head and slams him into the
ground.

WHAM! WHAM! WHAM! WHAM! Back and forth, back
and forth. Even after the first couple of impacts, it's still kind of
a joke to Excelsior. He's never been beaten. And there's no
way this guy, with his messed up forehead and his eyes too
close together, is going to be the first. Enough is enough, thinks
Excelsior. He tries to fly away. But it doesn't work. The guy is
too heavy! How is that possible?

The earth keeps slapping him around. This is getting bad.
Excelsior panics. He starts flailing in every direction, but it's no
use. The guy just keeps bashing him against the ground. He

bashes Excelsior so many times that the remnants of a nearby building just give up and collapse completely. Everything goes dark for Excelsior.

Hiding behind a pile of rubble, Topper sees the whole thing. Cocky as he is, at this moment he's glad he's small. He had no idea Barry was so powerful. He thinks of all the times he slapped Barry and feels a little queasy. Barry grows bored with hammering the ground with Excelsior. He tosses the limp body over his shoulder like a child who is no longer interested in a toy.

"What a beast!" Topper thinks as he watches Barry lumber off. "What could possibly overcome a beast like that?" As soon as he asks the question, the answer becomes obvious.

CHAPTER THIRTY-THREE
How to Make Advantage from Avalanche

Edwin is not depressed. He is absorbed in thought. Since no one has said anything helpful to his present line of thinking, he has not seen the need to respond. In the fundamental monotasking of deep thought, all else is noise in the signal.

Edwin is certain that the world has become dumber as a result modern technology. There are simply too many interruptions. Deep thought — original thought — requires a quietude that is in danger of going extinct.

To make matters worse, the modern world has also been seduced by data. And why not? It is easier to crunch numbers than to reason. Numbers offer such reassurance. Reassurance and more. When you combine these numbers with the theoretical framework of the physical sciences, they seem to deliver the insight of a god.

The volume and pressure of a gas are inversely related. The motion of a body with a known velocity and mass can be described by a parabola. With these two bits of knowledge, even the dullest sheep can plug the right numbers into the right tables and use artillery to blow apart the world. Napoleon proved this when he used the intellectual wonder of calculus to conquer Europe.

But the concepts of the physical sciences are ill-applied to a world filled with acting men and women. The psychologic, the economic, these are matters for which no equation can reliably provide guidance. Today's statistical relationship is sure to be turned on its head tomorrow by a change of preference or fancy. Electrons can be excited, but they do not panic. Observe as many favorable conditions for a riot as you like — better yet, set them — and still, a riot may not occur. Most frustrating of all, you may never know why your plan of domestic unrest was foiled.

Edwin's father had been with British Intelligence during the war. He had become a master of the dirty tricks of the business. And, unwittingly, he had passed some of these skills on to his son.

Of course Edwin's father had not done this consciously or overtly. What kind of man would sow such seeds in his own child? But Edwin was exposed to a certain way of thinking. As a precocious child, eager for his father's affections, he had learned quickly and well. Even now, as Edwin sits in his high office, towering over the lesser people, his father's words are with him.

"No matter how smart you may be. No matter how much money you have at your disposal. No matter strength of arms or argument, you simply cannot force people to do a thing. It costs too much. For all the bombs we dropped, for all the lives that were lost, in the end, this is why the Nazis could not prevail. There is not enough money in the world to truly command and control a populace. All you can reasonably hope to do is create a situation where it is easier for people to do what you want than it is for them to do what you don't.

"Then, none will oppose or seek to thwart your aim. It will appear to them that you are merely helping them do what they want. In the end, there is no defense against cooperation."

In this pearl of remembered wisdom, Edwin sees the error of his ways. He has tried to control Barry. And he has done so without a proper mechanism for control. That was the flaw. It's not as terrible an error as it could have been. He had not attempted to work against Barry's native instincts, but he had tried to limit him to the destruction of a single building. Predictably, this had proved costly, unwieldy and impractical. Barry is not a surgical instrument. He is an avalanche. But how to take advantage of the avalanche?

Edwin watches hour after hour of news coverage of Barry's rampage. For the time being, the destruction has stopped. Hard-working news organizations are using all of their skills to whip people to a fever pitch, even though nothing is happening. They show clips of buildings collapsing, walls of dust engulfing fleeing people and pointless interview after pointless interview with the men and women on the street. As if the ordinary people matter.

It is what Edwin calls the hysterical blindness of democracy. How can the ordinary person matter in a world where some can knock over buildings and others can fly? Why do the sheep not see it? Why are they not outraged? Why do the sheep not rise up to trample the wolves?

As soon as he asks this question, the answer appears on the screen. A young man, with a tattoo of ram's horn covering half his face and bits of metal protruding from the other half, speaks with all the sincerity he can muster. "Yeah, I don't want anyone to, like, get hurt or anything. But I feel for him, you know what I'm saying? Sometimes I just want to bust shit up. Take it to the man. Like, like, all these corporations. He's like a, a symbol. Like a spokesperson. You know. For all the little people."

Surely this one is the smallest of the small, thinks Edwin. And still he identifies with the mighty. And in that insight the secret is revealed. They do not tear down their violent and destructive idols because they like to believe that they too are mighty.

Edwin's desk is covered with information about Barry. Pictures, school transcripts, protective services records, anything that has ever been committed to paper. And in the middle of it all is a picture of Barry in the 3rd grade. His hair is mussed and his smile looks wide enough to split his face. Scrawled across his forehead in red magic marker are the letters C R O. The letters are in a child's handwriting, but far from innocent. They knew they were taking advantage of the dumbest kid in the class.

The subtitle on the TV changes to "Riots Break Out." Now the camera crew follows the boy with the tattoo on his face from car to car as he stomps windshields and kicks in headlights. And there it is. How can one make money from a spokesmodel for destruction? For anarchy? For worse than anarchy.

Once the question is properly phrased, the answer is obvious.

"Agnes?" Edwin's voice cracks from days of disuse. He tries again, this time a little louder, "Agnes?" She comes quickly, fueled by the hope that her beloved Edwin has returned to himself. At first Edwin says nothing. He stands and unrolls his sleeves. He straightens his tie. Once again he dons his jacket of severe grey. Then he buttons the middle button and turns to his secretary.

"I need two things. I need a fashion designer, one with talent, but who will use English in a way that I can understand. And I need Barry's current location."

Agnes makes a note. "Designer, check. As for Barry, Topper has him."

Edwin's eyebrows shoot up. "Topper? Really? One can never be sure what he will do next."

"Yes," says Agnes, "but one can certainly fear."

CHAPTER THIRTY-FOUR
Down But Not Out

Excelsior lies on the ground in the center of a pulverized concrete outline of his body. Because Excelsior is so proud it will be difficult for him to ever admit that he was knocked unconscious, so let's just say that, right this moment, he's not very interested in opening his eyes. That is, until someone starts kicking him in the ribs.

Ordinarily, this kick wouldn't hurt Excelsior, but he's just been through the beating of his life (so far) and his ribs are a little tender. He cries out in pain. Then he opens his eyes and sees the ugliest man he has ever known.

"Jesus Gus, lay off." Gus does no such thing. He continues his generous application of shoe leather.

"C'mon lard-ass. No laying down on the job. You ah, ack, ack, ack," the cough silences Gus.

"Easy, Gus, easy," says Excelsior. He sits up and instantly regrets it.

Gus hacks and spits. Even before the hunk of lung butter hits the sidewalk, the old man crams another cigarette in the corner of his mouth. "C'mon pissant, you're not going to spread the blinding light of American sunshine lying down there on your duff."

"I don't feel so good."

195

Gus lights the cigarette. On the side of the lighter, the faded memory of an Airborne logo is almost visible. The smoke that Gus exhales from the first drag is so strong it is more blue than white. "Yeah, yeah, yeah," he continues, "now you know what I feel like when I get out of bed. Candyass. In the entire history of walking tall, kicking ass and shitting bullets, so far you're the only hero hasn't had to carry on after he's had a beat down. Time to tough, tough, auHooooo hough hough hough." Gus coughs his lungs down to a wheeze once again.

Excelsior gets to his feet. Jesus this hurts. He hasn't ever hurt like this before. He feels a little nauseous. This sucks. He reaches out to comfort Gus, but Gus slaps his hand away.

"TOUGHEN YOU UP," Gus roars with surprising force. "What, you turning fag on me now boy? Is that what you're doing? Don't you go all sensitive on me just because you got your ass kicked. That's how it starts. Saw a whole platoon go fag during the Battle of the Bulge."

"Up close and personal?"

"You keep joking, flyboy, I know what it means to take a beating and keep on going."

"Yeah, you look it."

"Aw, you're just jealous 'cause I'm so goddamned pretty," Gus's skin draws tight across his skull as his faceleather twists into a smile.

"Okay, okay. You win. You're tough. The only guy who could kick your ass was John Wayne."

"Bullshit. He was an actor. I'm the real thing."

"So where is he?" Excelsior asks as three vertebrae in his back realign with distressingly loud pops.

"You mean the guy who cleaned your clock?"

"No, the... I mean... yeah," Excelsior says. It finally sinks in that he has, for the first time, been defeated.

"He's over there a ways."

"All right," Excelsior says as he rolls his neck, "I'll be right back."

"No you don't. We've got orders."

"Orders?"

"We're falling back. We're going to regroup."

"Fall BACK?!" Excelsior discovers that it hurts to yell with a broken rib. He was also learning that it hurts to breath, hurts to stand, hurts to twist — in fact, he was beginning to get the idea that everything hurts when you have a broken rib. Was this the way ordinary people felt all the time?

"Protocol. We've got to come up with a game plan."

"But he just got lucky."

"No he didn't."

"You didn't even see what happened," says Excelsior.

"Saw the whole thing on satellite. You got your tights-wearing ass handed to you."

"I was careless."

"Like that's a surprise. Now listen to me, son," Excelsior hates it when Gus calls him son. They are almost the same age. He figures that Gus is upset because he's grown older while Excelsior hasn't. But Gus is always pissed, so how could he tell? Excelsior wonders if the only thing holding the old man together is anger.

"Son," Gus repeats himself to make sure he has Excelsior's attention, "we ain't ever seen anything you couldn't beat without really trying. Now, I know you'll get him. I know you will. You'll beat his ass until it glows like a ring-tailed baboon."

"Yeah, I will."

"But right now, we've got orders to pull back. Re-group and come up with a game plan. We keep making this thing angry and it's just going to destroy more of the city. Hurt more people. You don't want that, do you?"

Excelsior sulks. He says "No," when what he means is, "I don't care. I just want to get back into the fight."

Gus is pleased to hear rage and frustration in Excelsior's voice. Of course, they'd known this day would come. But you can never know — really know — how a man will react to

197

losing. In Gus's mind it was like combat. The guy you thought was the toughest hombre for miles around would sometimes go to pieces after the first artillery shell. Meanwhile, the little guy you figured was only good for making coffee would come walking back from the battle with a leg full of shrapnel and a spear full of scalps. Sure, Excelsior had lost, but it hadn't taken the fight out of him. That was good.

They walk off together. Gus tries not to cough. Excelsior tries not to limp.

CHAPTER THIRTY-FIVE
The Cromoglodon is Born

Deep within the brothel, Barry is sleeping. His gigantic chest heaves up and down in a way that is out of proportion with the tiny snoring noises he is making. Next to him, a blond girl named Selene hugs herself in a sheet and weeps with relief.

She doesn't know exactly how it can be, but the child-man sleeping next to her is responsible for the destruction outside. If he is angered, he could easily destroy this building and everyone in it. It isn't the most comfortable of situations, but it isn't exactly unfamiliar to Selene. All manner of powerful men come to the Evanston Street brothel. Men who could, with a word or a wave of a hand, also obliterate the building and everyone in it if they aren't kept happy. You don't need superpowers to do damage. But Selene knows many, many ways to make a man happy.

Selene has been with a lot of men. It has not always been pleasant, gentle or even consensual. But now she is lucky enough to work in a good establishment. The clientele is exclusive and the rates are high. A girl like Selene can do much worse. Most girls like Selene do.

Still, she has seen more than her share of hard times. And when they were lined up for Barry to take his pick, she prayed that one of the other girls would strike his fancy. In spite of her efforts to hide, or perhaps because of them, Barry was drawn to her. Selene is of a definite type — light skin, hair so blond it is almost white and impossibly pale blue eyes. To some men she is irresistible. Barry is one of these men.

She saw no spark of intelligence or mercy in his face. In fact, from the way he looked, Selene couldn't figure out why he was not drooling. When he wrapped his awkward arms around her, she feared the worst. But he had been gentle. Gentle, inexperienced and — most amazingly of all — tender. She would not have been surprised to learn that she had taken the man-child's virginity.

As they moved beneath the sheets, in spite of the tenderness, she could feel his pain. There were oh so many ways to wrong the flesh. And Selene knew that each of these wrongs left a mark. The damaged always recognize one another. She would have known Barry's pain even at the bottom of a dark ocean. When they joined, the impossibly dense cords of muscle in his back writhed beneath her fingertips.

Hours later, the door to Selene's room opens and clean light floods in. Selene gasps. Silhouetted in the doorway is a tall figure. Her pupils contract and adjust to the flood of light. Edwin enters the room.

Barry does not wake. Topper peeks out from behind Edwin's knee and says, "You see? I told you! I knew it would work. It was beauty killed the beast!" Topper's eyes linger on Selene. He loves women with that fresh from the bed look.

Selene looks away. She can remember being with him, even if Topper has forgotten. Some girls like the little man. They think he's cute or funny. But when Selene touched him, she felt anger crawling around underneath his skin. For weeks afterward she had nightmares of the anger breaking free and swarming into her body.

But Topper's anger is nothing compared to the tall one. He isn't hot with anger. He is cold. So very cold. Without really knowing why, she leans over and covers Barry with her arms.

"Please don't hurt him," she says to Edwin. "He didn't mean to do it."

Edwin looks at her with surprise as if noticing, for the first time, that someone else is in the room. "Mean to do it? I'm not sure he means to do anything, in the conventional sense. As for hurting him, I wouldn't know how. Not physically at least. And I'm sure I wouldn't know why. His talents are far too valuable to me." Selene doesn't like the way Edwin speaks. In his words she hears reasons, reasons, reasons, but no emotion. She realizes that if he can come up with a reason, he can do anything. There is no mercy in him. No warmth. Just cold.

Edwin turns and gestures to the people standing outside the room. They enter reluctantly. "Dress him." Edwin commands.

"But, but, but..." says the designer.

"We have a contract," Edwin says, "a contract you do not wish to break."

It takes three people to lift Barry and slip a shirt of unique fabric over his head. The material is completely black and clings like Spandex. It looks like an ordinary athletic T-shirt, but it is much, much more. Next come the pants, the same material but loose, like warm-up pants. And finally, a tight skull cap with the letters CRO in heavy gothic letters across the front.

Selene feared the worst when she saw Edwin in the doorway, but clothes? What is going on? She doesn't understand at all.

"Now," says Edwin to a man holding a tablet computer, "turn it on." The man taps the screen and Selene becomes scared again. She doesn't like any of this. She wishes she could hide between the mattresses. Why doesn't Barry wake up? But maybe that would make things worse.

Selene jumps when the garments make a high-pitched whine. "Can I go?" she asks.

"No," says Edwin, not bothering to look at her. "We may need you."

"Oh yes," says Topper, "She is exceptionally talented."

Barry's shirt changes from black to white and back again. A flurry of images and logos tear across the fabric. A diagnostic runs on the pants and hat. The images sweep outward to glowing white and then condense into a white dot in the center of his chest. The white dot bounces around the limits of the fabric like a pixel ball in a game of pong.

"Is that all you came here for? T-t-to make him into a television?" Selene asks.

"Yes," says Edwin. He turns and leaves the room.

From the hallway, Selene hears Topper ask, "Hey, Edwin, what's the C R O stand for?"

"Cromoglodon," says Edwin, naming the awful thing he has just made.

CHAPTER THIRTY-SIX
Taking a Meeting

Over the next few months, The Cromoglodon remains relatively calm. He destroys a few vehicles and breaks a few windows. He also tears down a statue of a Civil War general, but since nobody remembers who the statue commemorates, only the pigeons are put out.

In an unusual spasm of sensibility, law enforcement agencies are given a standing order to leave The Cromoglodon alone. Under no circumstances are they to attempt to apprehend him. Yes, he is bad. But he is so bad that attempting to catch him will only mean more pain and destruction. So the Feds claim jurisdiction and do nothing.

But this does not mean that The Cromoglodon's life is peaceful. He has created new movements in the herd. Inexplicably, The Cromoglodon is hot. Hotter even than the heroes that have tried to stop him. Magazines pay top dollar to paparazzi daring enough to get a shot of The Cromoglodon in action. When a photographer captures an image of Barry tearing a tour bus in half over his head, t-shirts are printed with the caption, "Who says the big city isn't friendly?"

The media has a field day. And why wouldn't they? It's been a slow news summer and The Cromoglodon is a ratings dream. The fearsome creature just keeps on giving. First, he's disaster news, then he becomes human interest and finally he crosses over into fashion and style. He is a hit. It becomes impossible to have a first-rate party without The Cromoglodon in attendance. And if he wrecks the joint (as he does, twice) it only serves to give new meaning to the term "smashing success."

When two news anchors are horribly injured trying to interview The Cromoglodon, their ratings shoot through the roof. Talk shows resound with questions like:

"How do you pronounce Cromoglodon?"

"What does it mean?"

"Why doesn't he have a spokesperson?"

"Do you know who's he dating?"

In this strange summer it seems the world has lost a sense of itself. And story after story is spoon-fed to lazy reporters and venial news directors by a well-oiled public relations machine. A machine that is designed, assembled and financed (through a dizzyingly complex structure of front companies) by none other than Edwin Windsor.

An op-ed piece in a major newspaper describes The Cromoglodon as "a superhero for the post-modern age. The ultimate deconstructionist." Another thoughtful journalist writes, "Who cares that he doesn't have a concern about outdated conventions of morality? He is a symbol to all the oppressed and disenfranchised. Striking at the system itself — the only hero strong enough to combat the real villain, instead of acting as a repressive extension of an oppressive consumer culture."

And when the frenzy reaches its height, Edwin strikes. But strike is too severe a word for what Edwin does. Edwin taps, precisely and with great effect. It all starts with a left turn.

"This isn't the way to my hotel," says the passenger. In the front seat of the town car, an Armenian kid pulls his chauffeur cap lower on his forehead.

"Is will be fine. I professionalism." Vasak figures everything will be better if he plays dumb.

"Hey, goddamn it, that's my hotel over there," Mike Hainer isn't used to the people who work for him, even the temporary help, making mistakes. He's a busy man. An important man. One with no time to fix other people's mistakes.

"Yehghvelch," Vasak says.

"Yegwich? What the hell is a Yegwich? Look this is simple, I need to go to the Plaza. Sprechenzie habla Plaza Hotel?"

Vasak nods and flashes him a moony grin. The hell with it, Hainer thinks. He'll get to the wrong hotel, have this guy fired and take a cab to the Plaza. So he'll be late for his next thing. It's not like he's never been late to a thing before. He returns his attention to the stack of papers in his lap.

For Mike, there is always a stack of papers or a person demanding his attention. Mike Hainer is in charge of a frighteningly large sporting goods conglomerate. And over the last 20 years, he has wrangled his company from an obscure manufacturer of running shoes into the premiere athletic brand in the world. The logo on his hand-tooled leather briefcase is the same logo that marks more than 80% of the world's finest athletes. From soccer to snowboarding, golf to gymnastics, Pysche has burned its brand on the world of sport.

But that's something of a problem. Pysche has grown so fast and been extended so far, Mike isn't sure there are any worlds left to conquer. The proposals in front of him include sponsoring tee ball leagues and hiring archaeologists to forge his logo within the centuries-old ruins of Mayan ball courts. Mike doesn't like any of these ideas. He is of the mind that it's time to invent a new sport. One that is faster-paced, has frequent breaks for commercials and will allow every aspect of the game to be sponsored. If he could just figure out a way to make the outcome of the game hang on how much fans bought during the game...

The towncar's undercarriage scrapes along the ground as Vasak drives into a below-ground parking deck. Finally, thinks Mike, this waste of time can come to an end. On to the next waste of time. Growth is always an uphill battle.

Vasak stops the car in the center of an empty level of the parking deck. "Where is this?" asks Mike. Vasak does not answer him. In keeping with his instructions, Vasak unbuckles his seat belt and leans across to the passenger seat. He feels around for the seat controls. He moves the passenger seat all the way forward. "What are you doing?" Mike demands.

Vasak opens the car door. He turns to his passenger and says, "Mechshelevdevel." Then he gets out of the car, locks it with the key fob and walks away with a happy bounce in his step.

"What is going on?" says Mike. It occurs to him that he might be in trouble. He tries the door. When it doesn't open, he gets angry. "Oh you Slavic Son of a Bitch! I'll have your job for this. When I get through you won't even be allowed to drive an ox cart full of dung in your native CrushinglyFuckingPooristan!"

Vasak doesn't break stride. He knows the angry man is right. He is going to lose his job for this. But a strange little man had paid him a lot of money to drive this limo. And the little man had promised a lot more when the car was delivered. What did Vasak care that Mr Hainer was upset? It was not like Vasak could afford to buy Psyche's shoes anyway. Besides, he was through with driving angry, dull business men around.

Hainer looks around the empty parking lot. He still doesn't fully comprehend what is going on, but he has seen enough bad in-flight thrillers to know that it might not be good. Is it the Russian mafia? Is this some kind of shakedown? He begins to get scared.

He yells until he is red in the face. He pounds on the window with his fist and then his shoe. He is so worked up, he does not hear the car locks click open. A tall, elegantly dressed man bends down and slides into seat next to him. Now he understands why Vasak moved the seat forward. This man is very, very tall.

The man unbuttons his jacket and says "Mr. Hainer. I have a proposal for you."

"And who in the hell are you?"

CHAPTER THIRTY-SEVEN
The Pitch

"Mr. Hainer, please try to calm yourself," says Edwin.

"Calm? I've been kidnapped! Evidently by you. Why would I listen to anything you have to say?" says Mark Hainer. He's indignant and feeling his own self-importance.

"Actually, you were kidnapped by an easily bribed, underpaid Armenian driver. I am just a good Samaritan who happened by and took pity upon you."

Hainer's eyes narrow. "You want money?" Edwin says nothing. "You don't want money? How much money do you want?"

"All of it. But that's the wrong question. The correct question is, what can I offer you in return?"

"This is bullshit." Hainer tries to open his door again.

"Mr. Hainer, I have a business proposal for you. And I want you to understand that I am a serious man who has no time to waste. So please forgive my having skipped the runaround from your secretary."

Hainer narrows his eyes. "I'm listening."

Edwin reaches forward and removes a stack of papers from the front seat. On the top of the stack is the justifiably famous picture of The Cromoglodon tearing a bus in half with his bare hands. "You are no doubt familiar with The Cromoglodon?"

"That freak? Yeah, my kid's nuts about him. That's why he wears black all the time. That's why he threw a birdbath through my screened-in porch. Wife wanted to kill him."

Edwin slips the photo to the bottom of the pile. The next page is filled with bullet points, a charts and a graph. Edwin hands it to Hainer. "This is the executive summary to a much larger scientific report I had worked up. It concludes that it may be impossible to measure The Cromoglodon's physical capacity. If you must gorge yourself on the details I can get you the rest. The upshot is this, not only is he the strongest man on Earth, he is most certainly the strongest man ever."

"Stronger than Excelsior? C'mon, nobody's stronger than Excelsior. Everybody knows that."

"If I could arbitrage everything that is known to be true but is actually false..." Edwin hands him a highly pixelated enlargement of a cellphone picture. It shows The Cromoglodon standing over Excelsior's limp body. "Excelsior attempted to contain him and failed. The FBI is flailing about at the limits of their understanding. And right now, the entire law enforcement community is operating under a no-pursuit policy. Why do you think this monster is still at large?"

"You certainly seem to know a lot about The Cromoglodon," says Mark. He has no idea where this is going, but as a master salesman he enjoys a good pitch.

"I represent him."

"Represent him!" Mark is unable to control his laughter. "You mean you're, like, his agent? He's going to play football or something?"

"Not exactly. I am a consultant, an advisor."

"Okay, whatever. How does this benefit me?"

"The Cromoglodon is simply the most powerful athlete on Earth."

"What? To be an athlete, you've got to play a sport. What sport does he play? Destruction isn't a sport."

210

"Perhaps not, but it has the media coverage of a professional sport. Here is a listing of media exposure, estimates of cumulative viewership and readership and, of course, an estimate of what it might cost you to buy that kind of coverage."

Edwin shows picture after picture after picture. The Cromoglodon emerging from the wreckage of a building, throwing a car, roaring pointlessly at the sky; each one has the Psyche logo displayed on The Cromoglodon's unique apparel. "All candid, all action and all prime placement."

"What? You want me to sponsor this abomination?"

Edwin says nothing. Hainer is smart, Edwin knows he will put the pieces together for himself.

"What did you say you were? Some kind of advisor? That has to be the worst advice I've ever heard. Associating Psyche with that, that menace? How much negative publicity do you think I can take? You expect me to come out with a line of destruction boots? My customers, the serious athletes and those who aspire to be, would leave me in droves! I'd be out of business in a year. And people would flock to those bastards at Apedis in droves. I don't even know if droves flock — but they'd leave us — hell, they'd run away from us barefoot. In my 35 years in the business, this is the worst idea I've ever heard. You sir, are an idiot."

Mark lurches violently in his seat. He moves towards the door, but when Edwin raises his hand, Mark stops. Edwin has one last piece of paper. When he turns it over a smile spreads across Mark Hainer's face. An evil giggle crawls out from the bottom of his bowels. "Oh ho. Ho ho ho, that's good, that's very good. Bravo."

It is the picture of The Cromoglodon tearing apart the tour bus but this time, blazoned across the middle of The Cromoglodon's chest are the corporate stripes of Apedis.

"It's reverse sponsorship," says Edwin, "You pay me, and I put any logo you wish on The Cromoglodon."

"No, no, no. That's the logo I want. That's the one. How much, and how do I know that it won't get back to me?"

"All of it. And I can provide complete deniability."

"All of it? That's rich. You get me a realistic number and you've got a deal. Now seriously, I've got to get to this dinner thing." He snatches the picture of The Cromoglodon wearing his competitor's logo from Edwin's hand.

"Can I keep this?"

"If you wish, but that may compromise your deniability."

"You're right," Mark says with an air of disappointment. He kisses the picture and hands it back to Edwin.

Having secured one deal, Edwin makes his way across town. He has a similar meeting scheduled with the head of Apedis. There is nothing like a bidding war to add a little realism to a price.

CHAPTER THIRTY-EIGHT
Excelsior Speaks

"Ladies and Gentlemen, the 'Heroes of Business' World Economic Summit is proud to present a man, well... certainly a man who is more than a man. One who is a hero to us all. The one and only Excelsior!"

A follow-spot illuminates a podium that stands all alone on a bare stage. On the front of the podium is the official logo of the event, an ungainly conglomeration of initials that read HoBWEC. Dramatic music filled with strings, rolling tympani and augustly muted French horns pours from hidden speakers. On some undetected cue, the spotlight rises. Slowly, the circle of illumination climbs the heavy back curtain. Up, up, up, impossibly up, as if the operator has suffered a stroke and is slowly crumpling to the floor, still clutching the handles, unwilling to loose his grip on the wheel even in the face of certain death.

The light comes to rest on an open hatch in the center of the auditorium's ceiling. The music swells in crescendo. The crowd sees feet drop into the auditorium. They go wild. The rich and the powerful, men of consequence and accomplishment, are cheering their heads off like little boys. As Excelsior descends, the cheering becomes louder. As if the crowd has suddenly doubled.

Excelsior waves down the applause and cheers. Shaking his head as if to say "No, no, not for me. You shouldn't." He does not betray how much he hates this kind of thing. How close he was to skipping out on the entire circus. In the dressing room he argued with Gus. "It's stupid. Having me fly in through the ceiling. It's demeaning. It's like having me jump through a hoop."

"Ah, bullshit. I can't even walk down a flight of stairs without my hip going out and you're bitching about being able to fly? Candy ass. Just calm down," said Gus, "go out there, make your damn speech, and we'll get out of here. And whatever you do, let's not have another Munich."

Munich. Gus always has to bring up Munich. Just can't let it go. It was another one of these bullshit speaking engagements. Excelsior did the same fly-onto-the-podium trick, then said a few words that were translated into German. And when it was over they put him in a receiving line. He was forced to shake hands with an endless line of dignitaries. That's when Yarlor the Terrible attacked. Right as he was shaking hands with the fat deputy minister of somewhere or another. At the time, of course, Excelsior had no idea that it was Yarlor. He just saw a bright blue flash coming at him from a clump of bushes on his left and he leapt into flight to avoid being hit.

As the ball of blue energy crackled harmlessly past him, he heard a man screaming in agony. Then the shriek of a woman crying out in terror. "I'm okay. I'm okay," he called down to reassure the people. Then he realized he was still holding onto the fat deputy minister's arm. But the rest of the man was no longer attached. If it had happened away from the event it might not have been so bad. But as Excelsior scanned the area for the source of the blue lightning, the press was making lightning of its own. Cameras flashed and flashed as they captured thousands of images of Excelsior silhouetted against a bright blue sky holding a severed arm in his right hand. It was a public relations disaster.

But Excelsior wasn't thinking about public relations. He saw Yarlor, holding a 13th century arquebus covered in glowing runes that crackled with lightning, fleeing the scene. This made Excelsior mad. He dropped the severed arm and swooped down on Yarlor in the blink of an eye. He tackled the villain so hard that Yarlor's spine broke in two places. He continued the motion of his dive back upward again and hurled Yarlor into the stratosphere. As he did, Excelsior bellowed in rage. Higher and higher Yarlor went, until the tiny speck of him was no longer visible from the ground.

But even as he vented his fury on Yarlor, the arm that Excelsior had ripped out (and subsequently dropped) was returned to its rightful owner in accordance with the law of gravity. Blissfully, or tragically, depending on your view of the human condition, the fat man was knocked unconscious when his own arm hit him in the head.

The cameras caught every minute from every angle. As Excelsior hung there in the sky listening to the squeal of the high-speed film drives, his conscience began to work on him. He had thrown a man to what would certainly be his death. Right now, as surely as the arm had tumbled to Earth, Yarlor was tumbling down from the upper atmosphere. But Excelsior wasn't a killer.

Gus was the killer. Or the people he directed. Excelsior never asked questions about what happened to the people and creatures he defeated after he was done with them. The government stepped in and took care of the mess. Once, when Excelsior had asked Gus what had happened to a man who called himself the Mean Streak, Gus had refused to answer. He'd given Excelsior a look that had chilled him to the bone. Even though Excelsior could burn Gus down with beams of heat from his eyes, it was Excelsior who'd had to look away. Excelsior never asked again.

But as he thought about Yarlor falling to his death through the open air, Excelsior decided that he didn't want to kill anyone. Not intentionally anyway. He wasn't sure he cared about this two-bit thug and his arcane device. But if Yarlor landed on somebody's house in Spain, Excelsior would feel bad about it. And he would never hear the end of it.

So Excelsior flew off into the sky above Munich. As he left he broke the sound barrier. The cataclysmic boom put a fitting end to the incident. He managed to catch Yarlor before he hit the ground. But by then the public relations damage was done.

As horrible as the press had been, Excelsior hoped it meant they would no longer trot him out and parade him around for public relations events. But it was a false hope. And now, here he is, speaking to HoBWEC. He steps to the podium and pauses.

He squints against the lights and looks lost before the crowd. The audience doesn't see it. They haven't come all this way and spent all this money to bear witness to a fallible creature. They have come to see a god who walks amongst them. A man who they believe can impose his will upon the wrongs of the world and make them right. These powerful men have been seduced by a greater power. And this is possible because Excelsior is cloaked in virtue.

Excelsior leans in to the mic and says, "So, I just flew in from Cleveland. And boy are my arms tired."

The room erupts in laughter. The crowd loves it. See, he's just a regular guy. But it's all a carefully created illusion. A public speaking coach spent three days trying to explain the joke to Excelsior. Finally he gave up.

"Thank you. Thank you." Excelsior says as he waits for the laughter to die down. "It's wonderful to see all of you in good spirits today. As you know, I'm not a comedian. Which is good, because I'm not here to be funny."

"Yeah, but could you ever beat up a heckler!" Laughter ripples through the crowd. Now Excelsior is confused. They aren't supposed to laugh here. The teleprompter doesn't say to wait for laughter.

216

Excelsior pauses a little longer than he should. Off-stage Gus is motioning frantically for him to continue. Better just to get it over with, Excelsior thinks.

"There are some who call me a hero. I'm not completely comfortable with that. I'm just a guy who was blessed with some talent. And I feel that means I should help out where I can. In fact, I think we should all help out where we can, don't you?

"And I'll tell you something else, and it might be the most important thing I have to say. I can't do as much as you think I can. You. You guys have the power to be the real heroes. No, no, I'm serious.

"Sure I can knock an asteroid out of space. Sure I've combated all manner of threats to our American Way of Life. Combatted and overcome. But I can only be in one place at a time. And, when you get right down to it, they don't let me stay in one place for very long these days. The world is a dangerous place, so I have to stay hoppin'.

"But what I want to tell you is you guys, the little guys, you're in there, y'know, wherever it is that you're in, day in and day out. And there's millions of you. There's only one of me. Think about that. There's only one of me. So not only do you guys," he tries for a dramatic pause, but it suffocates in cheese, "outnumber me. You guys, are my heroes."

The applause is polite, but not heartfelt. He is the hero. Who was he to take their heroes away? As Excelsior leaves the stage, he hears the Master of Ceremonies say, "Ladies and Gentlemen, please a big round of applause for the one, the only, the UNDEFEATED EXCELSIOR!"

Arrgh. Undefeated. Excelsior hates the word. Gus slaps him on the shoulder. "Good speech. Good speech. Now let's go shake some hands."

Excelsior's hatred for handshakes and small talk distracts him from self-loathing. Which is good, because they're on him

217

in a flash — the VIPs of the VIPs. They are all men of importance and accomplishment. They are all rich and envied.

Excelsior doesn't envy them. He doesn't want to work in the business world, so they mean nothing to him. He shakes hands, gently and carefully, steeling himself against any possible flinch reflex. "Thanks, thanks for coming out. Thanks for all you do. No, I mean it, you guys are the real heroes."

It goes well, until Rick Apedis. Excelsior shakes his hand like all the others. He mutters a few empty phrases before he realizes that the man isn't making small talk. "Wait, what did you say?"

"I said my company's image is being wrecked by The Cromoglodon."

Gus says, "Well, you got your logo all over him like he was a goddamned stock car. What do you expect if people are upset with you, sponsoring a menace like that?"

"I've noticed that you haven't stopped him," says Apedis.

Excelsior's face freezes. The man is right. Excelsior looks to Gus. Gus says something about security and priority and proportional response.

"That's bullshit," Apedis says. He points to Excelsior, "I think he hasn't stopped The Cromoglodon because he can't." The powerful men fall silent as they wait for Excelsior's response. The question hangs in the air. Is it possible to defeat the world's most powerful superhero?

Gus breaks the spell with his aw-shucks, West Texas drawl turned up to 11. "Of course he can stop that beast. But jes' how much of this city do you want to lose in the process? I mean, me? Hell, I don't care. I'm a rancher's son. Let our boy and that Cromogogomagomadon get a fussin' and feudin' — hammer this ol' town flat as West Texas. Suits me just fine. I'll move on in and raise cattle."

Gus gets one, strained laugh.

"No sir, we're waiting until we can get this brute out onto open ground where nobody's gonna get hurt, exceptin' of course the Gommagomacommadon hisself, then Excelsior here will batter him something fierce. But until sech time, Excelsior's gonna do what he's always done. Act in a way that protects the lives and the property of the citizens of the greatest country in the world. The United States of America. Let's hear it for the big fella. Excelsior!" And Gus starts applauding. Such a cheap trick, but it works. Out of habit, everyone in the room joins in the applause.

Gus leans close to Rick Apedis and says, "Why don't you step into the back and we'll finish this conversation." Before Rick can answer, he is flanked by two large men in suits.

In the back Rick is still angry. "Look, your little speech session doesn't change anything. I still don't think you can stop him."

"I can too stop him," says Excelsior, "if they'd let me."

Rick looks at Excelsior. Then he turns to Gus. "It's obvious I should be talking to you."

"Hey," says Excelsior.

"What do you want from us, Mr. Apedis? I told you, he's not going after The Cromoglodon."

"I think I have some say in that," says Excelsior.

Gus whirls on Excelsior. "I told you, it's not your job to think. That's what we have smart people for. Now be quiet and let me handle this."

"The problem is not The Cromoglodon," says Apedis.

"What do you think the problem is?" says Gus.

"A man named Edwin Windsor."

"Who's he?" blurts Excelsior. "What's his superpower?"

"He's very, very smart. You see, he's using The Cromoglodon to — "

"Blackmail you?" asks Gus.

"So to speak. He approached the head of Psyche and I for sponsorship rights to The Cromoglodon."

"But you said you didn't sponsor The Cromoglodon," says Gus.

"I didn't. Psyche did. Psyche sponsored The Cromoglodon with my logo."

"Oh," says Gus. "That is smart. And evil. Really, really evil."

"It's worse, it's a monthly contract, to the highest bidder. So next month..."

"...the price is going to be bid even higher."

"We can't afford to have any more damage to our image, so we must outbid. Whatever it takes. And this will go back and forth until both companies are broke. And then he will move on to the next industry."

Excelsior still doesn't get it. "Gus, we have to stop The Cromoglodon! You have to give me another shot. You gotta."

Gus shakes his head, "No. This rich bastard's right. The Cromoglodon's not our problem. Our problem is the guy who's calling the shots."

Rick Apedis taps Excelsior in the middle of the odd logo emblazoned on his chest. "You should never blame the puppet," he points to Gus, "when you can blame the man who pulls the strings."

"Yeah, yeah, you made your point. We'll look into it."

"I'll expect you do significantly better than that. I have a standing tee time with Jim Buchanan. Senator Jim Buchanan."

Gus scowls. Excelsior looks confused.

"Such an innocent. In addition to a terrible slice, Jim has oversight of your little agency here. Including the old man's pension and salary. He pulls both your strings. So FIX THIS."

Apedis walks off, feeling full of himself.

Excelsior decides he's had just about enough. He looks at Gus and says, "You know, you guys can't stop me either. What could you do, if I just decided to beat that jerk within an inch of his life?"

"Never happen. You don't have the stomach for it. Besides, I'd get to him first," Gus growls, searching through his pockets for a bottle of aspirin.

"No Gus, seriously, you can't stop me from going after The Cromoglodon. Do you have a contingency plan for that? For stopping me?"

Gus hooks his thumbs in his belt. He looks Excelsior right in the eye. "Somewhere, somebody's got a plan. There's probably a bunch of real smart assholes with soft hands thinking on it day and night. I bet you it's real complicated and expensive. Me, I don't like to think so much. So you get outta line and I'm just gonna whup you silly."

Excelsior smiles at the cocksure man. But his laughter trickles off when he realized Gus isn't laughing with him. There is no way on Earth that Gus could beat him in a fight. Gus is old. Older than dirt. And he's only human, after all. Then why is Excelsior uncomfortable? Why does he look away first?

CHAPTER THIRTY-NINE
A Giant Illusion in SPACE

It's the intersection of Dry and Nowhere. A high desert populated by animals who are forced to do things like lick their own eyeballs to survive. Only madmen come here. Well, madmen and guys in white lab coats... Okay, so madmen, guys in white lab coats, and general contractors? What the hell is going on here anyway?

In the middle of the desert, workmen are putting finishing touches on a very lovely house. It is white, two stories tall, and gives the appearance of having plenty of room for Mom, Dad, Junior, Sis, Baby and Spot. More than enough room, in fact. Because each member of the family is a two-dimensional cut out. Even the dog.

For this very special occasion, Dr. Loeb has adopted a costume of a lab coat and thick, elbow-length rubber gloves. He rushes about frantically, sweating and shouting orders that everyone ignores. In his mind, Dr. Loeb is the lynchpin that holds this entire enterprise together. Like the two-dimensional dog on the spray-painted lawn, it is a poor fantasy. But then, a hint of power is all that Dr. Loeb needs to keep him going. His clock isn't very accurate, but it's easy to wind.

"What is ZISS!" he screams, pointing to a rock that has been spray painted green instead of being cleared from the Simulated Lawn Area (SLA). "Haf I not TOLD you! Wirklichkeitstreue! Realism! Realizm in everysing."

The workmen ignore the tantrum. Like the heat and the dust, Dr. Loeb is just another inconvenience on this job site. A man in white overalls gets sick of listening to Dr. Loeb. He walks over and removes the rock from the lawn. "Sorry, Doc," he says.

Dr. Loeb yells after him, "And well you should be! Be thankful I do not haved killing you!" It is so hard finding quality henchmen these days, thinks Dr. Loeb. Then he stomps off to the blockhouse.

As Loeb enters the relative cool of the observation post, he snaps at one of the technicians. "Zou! Are zou monitorifing those clouds on the horifzon? Vill they intervere vith our test viring?"

The actor at the console turns around and looks at Dr. Loeb as if he's insane. Which, of course, he is. But before the actor can say anything, Edwin emerges from the cool darkness. "High cirrus. Nothing more than ice crystals that have lost their way in the upper atmosphere, Dr. Loeb. They will not interfere with the test of your satellite."

"Lazeradicator!"

"Lazeradicator, my mistake."

Of course the clouds will not affect the "satellite" test. There is no satellite. Hidden in the target house is a compact array of pyrotechnics equipment. When the theatrically large red button on the command console is pressed, it will trigger a flash of light, followed by an explosive fireball. As light moves too fast for the naked eye to detect its progress, it will appear to all the world and, most importantly, to Dr. Loeb that the test house has been vaporized by an impossibly powerful laser beam from space.

224

In the corner, another actor stares at two sine waves interacting at random on an oscilloscope. It's beginning to hurt his eyes. The sign above his station reads "Telemetry." Dr. Loeb is drawn to the flickering green light on the screen. He stares at the interplay of the squiggly lines and pretends to know what they mean. Doctor Loeb slaps his hands together and cries "Excellent! You are doing excellent work."

"Dr. Loeb, we have prepared a viewing chamber for you upstairs," Edwin says, trying to corral the child into his playpen. Just then a rumble very much, but not exactly, like thunder reverberates through the blockhouse. Edwin thinks that the explosion has been triggered prematurely, but through the reinforced glass he can see that the house is still there.

"You zee!" Dr Loeb cries, "Details. DETAILS! You have overlooked ze storm! I vill have you executed!" He slaps the man at the oscilloscope in the back of the head and hurries out of the blockhouse. Edwin looks to a man who is watching weather radar on yet another computer screen.

"I don't know what he is talking about. Radar's clear."

Outside, Dr. Loeb spins in frantic circles as he scans the horizon "Vere is the weather? Vere is the weather?" Edwin raises his eyes to the sky and sees a man descending from the sky, cape fluttering lightly in the wind.

"Excelsior," Dr. Loeb cries with perverse glee. "He has come to thwart my evil plan!"

How very odd, Edwin thinks, that Excelsior should pay a visit to the one client of his that he can be certain has broken no laws. Edwin meets the hero's approach with a calm and level gaze.

"Edwin Windsor," Excelsior says. It is not a question.

"MANFUL COMBAT!" Dr. Loeb cries as he flings himself at Excelsior's waist. Excelsior ignores him.

"I'm here to stop you, Mr. Windsor," Excelsior says in his most official hero voice.

"Stop me from doing what, exactly?"

"YOU WILL NEVER DEFEAT ME!" shrieks Dr. Loeb, slapping Excelsior's legs repeatedly with his rubber gloves.

The somewhat obscene slapping noise disturbs Excelsior. "Uh, what is this guy?" he asks.

"I'm sorry. He's harmless. Just try to ignore him," says Edwin. Excelsior does his best to tear his attention away from the spectacle clawing at his knees.

"It's The Cromoglodon. He needs to be stopped," says Excelsior.

"I'm not sure what this has to do with me," says Edwin.

"LOOK YA LITTLE FREAK, KNOCK IT OFF!" Excelsior yells so loud that it rattles the triple-paned windows in the blockhouse.

But Dr. Loeb is a game little rooster. "I will DEFEAT YOU," he cries as he redoubles his assault. Such as it is. Excelsior backhands Dr. Loeb the length of a football field. Dr. Loeb lies in the dust and moans quietly to himself.

"Thank you," says Edwin. "You were saying about The Cromoglodon?"

"We know you control him, Mr. Windsor. We've spoken with Apedis. This needs to be stopped. You need to stop him. Or I will."

"You are mistaken, I control no one. And I am not certain that he can be controlled."

"This is a courtesy visit, Mr. Windsor."

"Oh, courtesy, of course. May I offer you some refreshment?"

"I'm not joking."

"Neither am I. We have lemonade and a light lunch in the blockhouse."

"Do you know who I am?" asks Excelsior. "Do you know what I can do?"

"I know who you are. I know all you can do is what you are told."

"What?"

"Was it your idea to come here? To talk to me like this?"

"Well, no, but after conferring with — " Excelsior stammers, trying to think of something to say. Of course Edwin speaks the truth of it. It is all true. The last thing that Excelsior wanted to do is come to the desert and talk. But Gus made him. He said it was time to fire a shot over Edwin's bow.

"So, after being told to come here," Edwin continues.

"It's not like that."

"Really?" says Edwin, unblinking in the bright desert sun. "You really wouldn't rather be pounding away at The Cromoglodon right now? Perhaps standing over him brandishing a piece of reinforced concrete with which to knock him unconscious, or batter the life out of him once and for all?"

"I'm not a killer."

"No, you are not. You are hardly a moral agent at all."

"I don't even know what that means."

"You are a puppet. A puppet who is not even aware of his own strings."

Excelsior gets hot behind the eyes. He is sick of this. Sick of being called a puppet. And deep down, sick of it being true. But this is the only way he knows to live life. Even the thought of change terrifies him.

Fear wells up in Edwin. He wonders if he has gone too far, but his iron reason keeps a grip on his fear. This is the gambit. It must be played. And if he fails, there is no point in running or cowering.

Dr. Loeb finds his second wind. "YOU CANNOT STOP ME!" he cries as he scrambles to his feet, his thick rubber gloves smearing through the desert earth like newt pads. He runs inside the blockhouse. The tension is broken.

Excelsior watches Dr. Loeb go. "He's insane, right?"

"Yes." Edwin decides to try another tack. "You must be tired of having your life run by other people. How can you

227

possibly care that The Cromoglodon chooses to wear a particular brand of clothes? How does he harm anyone by doing that? It should be nothing to you when compared to the destruction and lives lost. Yet you are concerned with the welfare of a company. Clearly you are not a hero. You are something else. What are you?"

"I am a hero. I am THE hero."

"And who has convinced you of that?"

"What are you talking about? It's true!"

"Truth," Edwin says with disdain, "is easily manufactured. Let me ask another way. Are there any choices you make that are your own?"

"Yeah, I — " and here Excelsior is interrupted by a strange feeling.

"I cannot sympathize with you, because you are not a person. You are a thing. An instrument. A tool driven around by ideas not your own."

"You don't know," Excelsior says in something very like the voice of a five year old child. But he can think of nothing else to say. How does Edwin know?

"Who sent you here? Who is your controller?" As soon as he says it, Edwin realizes this is the wrong question to ask. It cannot be a singular person. It has to be a committee. Only a committee, bought and paid for by powerful people, could be this stupid.

Before Excelsior can respond there is a flash of light and the house behind them explodes. As debris rains down around them, Edwin calmly steps into the lee of the blockhouse and waits for the ringing in his ears to subside. Excelsior follows him and kept talking. Edwin understands none of it.

When his hearing returns, the first thing Edwin hears is Dr. Loeb. "MY LAZERADICATOR is a SUCCESS! My lovely all-powerful satellite in the sky!" Dr. Loeb stands with his hands on his hips and gloats over the destruction he believes his satellite-mounted laser had wrought.

Excelsior says, "I see your game Windsor. A Giant Laser in Space, eh? We'll see about that." There is a rush of air and a tremendous boom. Excelsior is gone.

He's back in an instant. He's holds a cylindrical satellite that has TELSAR IX painted on the side. "Now I've stopped you Windsor. Just like I'm going to stop The Cromoglodon." Excelsior crushes the satellite with his palms until it is no larger than a softball.

"NOOOOOOOO!" howls Dr. Loeb. He collapses upon the earth and works dirt into his scalp.

Confident in his victory, Excelsior flies off at a leisurely pace.

Edwin taps the hunk of aluminum with his foot. Undoubtedly, some meth addict in Nebraska is now bemoaning the loss of his satellite television signal, but Edwin fails to see how that harms him in any way. Edwin can think of no better way to cement the illusion of a non-existent satellite in Dr. Loeb's mind than the absurd farce that has just played out. Edwin steps back as the little man rushes over and clutches the destroyed satellite to his chest and sobs.

"Don't worry, Herr Doctor. We will rebuild. We will make it better," Edwin says. And this time, Edwin thinks, I will charge you more.

CHAPTER FORTY
Somewhere Over Kansas

As Excelsior flies east he is enveloped in high cumulonimbus clouds making their way across the prairie. Below him there might be rain showers or hail or tornadoes, but at this altitude there is only beauty. He checks his speed so he can enjoy his progress between the towering columns of water and the magnificent pillars of light that seem to hold up the sky. If this were a movie, music would be playing.

The lack of a film score does not trouble Excelsior. The song of victory thunders in his heart and the wind applauds in his ears. He feels at home. He is on an equal footing with the elements, and need not disguise his power. He isn't going to accidentally tear a layer off the atmosphere. Even if he flies through a cloud, the hole will repair itself. Here in the sky, everything is right with Excelsior.

Then the whispers start. At first, they're so soft he can't understand them. The rolling tympani and soaring strings in his heart are not overpowered, but they are tainted. Tainted by words. Somewhere over Kansas, he begins to question his victory. The whispers of doubt grow louder and louder.

"Puppet."

"Moral agent."

"Hero."

"Control."

Excelsior stops. He realizes that the words haunting him are in Edwin's voice. He pieces them into the conversation he has just had. He doesn't like the things that Edwin said. Edwin made him feel stupid. Excelsior knows he's not the brightest guy. That's okay. But he doesn't like feeling stupid. And he doesn't like feeling that Edwin is right.

And Edwin is right.

Excelsior can't remember the last time he took matters into his own hands. The last time he'd made a decision that really mattered. And he certainly can't remember making a decision against Gus's wishes. He loves the old man. Exceslior doesn't want to think about the day Gus will going to die, but when he hears that cough rattling through the old man's chest like a pile of dead leaves blowing across concrete...

Excelsior looks at the clouds for a long time. He tries to come up with a name for what he's feeling. Eventually, he gives up and keeps flying. He decides he will ask Gus about it. Gus is sure to be in a good mood. Not only has Excelsior delivered the message to Edwin, but he has managed to take out a dangerous space-based laser weapon at the same time. Pretty good day's work, thinks Excelsior.

He arcs high over the city and searches for the staging area. There it is, a parking lot filled with vans and trailers. They are ready to handle anything he might bring back. But this time, all he's bringing back is success.

Gus struggles down the steps of a modular trailer. "Jesus H. Tapdancing Christ! How come every time there's a shitstorm, you're smack in the middle of it?"

"What?"

"I gave you one job. One job, shit-for-brains, and you screwed it up."

"What?! I told him. I told him just like you told me!" Excelsior says. He's not sure what's going on.

"I am too old for this shit, you understand? Too OLD. Why did you destroy that satellite?"

"You mean the giant laser in space?"

"Laser? What laser? There was no space laser. I've got ThromCast on my ass because you tore something called GeoSynchronous Relay #7 out of the sky. Do you have any idea how much that satellite cost?"

"No."

"Of course you don't. But it's a lot. Tell me you just set it down somewhere. Gave it to somebody as a lawn ornament?"

"Uh, I crushed it into a small ball."

"You did WHAT? Why?"

"They blew up a house with it. The little man with the shaved head and the — "

"Just shut up. You just shut up."

"But Gus — "

"Shut up. You don't do anything. You don't say anything. I'll take care of it. You understand?"

"Look, it was — "

"That's talking. I don't want you to do that."

"But..."

Gus looks at him hard. Excelsior thinks about telling him off once and for all. Flying away and never coming back. Gus's hard guy act is interrupted by a coughing fit. He hacks and hacks and hacks. The color drains out of his face. His lips turn blue. Gus staggers. Excelsior catches him before he reaches the ground. "Help!" cries the most powerful man in the world.

EMTs rush over with equipment. After a few minutes with the oxygen mask, color returns to Gus's face.

"Gus, I'm sorry," says Excelsior.

Through the mask Gus says, "Just don't do anything. Just don't do anything until I tell you. Or until they figure out if I'm dead or not." An EMT reaches for the pack of cigarettes in Gus' breast pocket. "GODDAMN IT! Get your hands off of those. Who the hell do you think you are?"

"You shouldn't smoke," says the EMT.

"Yeah, but I do. So deal with it."

Excelsior watches them wheel Gus away. None of it makes sense. Why is Gus angry? Why can't he explain it to him? He was there. He saw the laser. He had seen the house explode. He had gone straight up and there was the satellite. Could he have gotten the wrong one? Maybe he should go back and check? No, that would just upset Gus more. Why does Gus get to do what he wants even though it's killing him?

Excelsior feels like he can't do anything right. Worst of all, can't do anything without permission. He doesn't understand any of it. But right then and there, he decides that it is Edwin Windsor's fault. Excelsior isn't going to do anything to upset his sick friend. He's not going to break the rules. But, he decides, when he gets a chance, he's going to get Edwin Windsor. The tall man has to pay. Excelsior just knows Edwin is behind it all.

PART THREE

CHAPTER FORTY-ONE
Mr. The Magnificent

Edwin has been doing well for himself. It shows in his office. The room has retained its essential clarity, but Edwin has adorned it with trophies of civilization. On one wall is a large bas relief sculpture of a man fighting a centaur. It is one of a handful of pieces looted from the Acropolis by Thomas Bruce, the 7th Earl of Elgin. Unlike the others, this particular frieze didn't quite make it into the British Museum. If it was recognized for what it was, art historians and museum curators would be quick to pronounce it priceless. But Edwin and his exceptionally discreet art dealer know otherwise. Everything has its price. Like the lesser piece by Rodin that occupies a pedestal by the west window. Or the medieval tapestry that depicts the Mongol sack of Baghdad in 1258.

In many ways, the tapestry is Edwin's favorite piece. It is both cautionary and inspiring. The Mongols tore across the surface of the earth like a pitiless force of nature. Ruthless and efficient, they used a practical code of laws and the barest handful of people to control the largest empire the world has ever known. And they did this by sparing valuable people and rewarding talent rather than tribal affiliation.

As Agnes passes the wall hanging, she doesn't think about any of this. She's surprised that Edwin has seen fit to obtain and display such a musty old rag. She approaches his desk and waits for Edwin to finish writing.

Edwin does not look up. "Yes?"

"Your 3 o'clock appointment is here."

"My 3 o'clock? I was not aware that I had any appointments today. "

"Well, yes, you did not have any appointments and now you have one."

Edwin looks up sharply.

"That's the thing with appointments," says Agnes, "You start off with none, and then, despite one's best efforts, they pop up like mushrooms."

"Agnes — "

"Edwin, please, I need you to meet with this man. He is the grand nephew of one of the women I play whist with. And, whist players being in short supply in this benighted country, it seemed a good idea to curry favor by — "

"Agnes, there are hundreds, if not thousands of people trying to waste my time. It is your job to keep them from doing it."

"Yes, but I was hoping — "

"Hope," says Edwin, "is a dangerous emotion."

"I was hoping — "

"Send the man away. I have no time for this foolishness," says Edwin.

"He calls himself Lifto."

"Agnes, please, I've already had my fill of nonsense from Dr. Loeb and his outrageous demands for a secret lair."

"That is your own fault. Build the child a playpen and have done with him."

"I will not. It serves no purpose."

"It will serve to remove him from your misery. Now let me give you a quick precis of your 3 o'clock appointment."

"You are a disappointment to me, Agnes," says Edwin. He regrets it as soon as he says it.

"Very well," says Agnes, stiffening with emotion. "I will show him out."

As Edwin watches her go he changes his mind. "Agnes. All right, I will see him."

"No, no, you are too right, I should not impose upon your precious time." Now she's sticking the dagger in. This aggravates Edwin even further. She's getting what she wants, but now she wants more? Emotions are so difficult and confusing. Edwin rises from his desk.

"Agnes, you are dismissed for the rest of the day." Edwin puts on his suit jacket and walks to the door of his office. Agnes blocks the way.

"Edwin, I am — "

Edwin is cold and formal. "You are in my way." Agnes says nothing. She steps out of Edwin's path and looks down at the floor.

As Edwin walks to the lobby, he smooths the lapel of his suit jacket and buttons the middle button. In the lobby a man stands and says, "I am Lifto the Magnificent!"

Lifto the Magnificent is not, in any conventional sense of the word, Magnificent. He is squat, hairy and wearing a purple unitard. He is excited. He's meeting Edwin Windsor. This must mean his career is finally taking off. He knows he has talent, what he needs is someone to help him reach the next level. He believes that Edwin is that man. This is very, very exciting.

When Lifto becomes excited, his complexion turns a deep shade of red that can only be described as purple's mortal enemy.

Edwin lies, "I am pleased to meet you Mr. Lifto."

"The Magnificent!" says Lifto.

"My mistake. Mr. The Magnificent."

Out of a sense of professionalism, Edwin takes Lifto into his office and goes through the motions. He discovers that Lifto's sole power is the ability to lift about 10,000 pounds. Lifto is inordinately proud of his ability. He also likes lifting cars so that pretty woman can have a place to park. It is his disturbed idea of chivalry. Lifto does not tell Edwin that after such feats he swells with pride, turns purple and fails miserably in his attempt to woo the freshly parked women.

Edwin quickly discovers that Lifto is a man with something to prove. He craves attention. This is unfortunate, because Edwin believes Lifto's real value is his anonymity.

Edwin has a way that Lifto can become a wildly successful. But it requires that he never, ever be famous. For the moment that Lifto became famous he would be an easy target for even the most minor of superheroes. Lifto can make a killing, but it will have to be a quiet killing. How to convince Lifto of this? Because not only does Lifto want to be famous, he thinks he already is.

Lifto tries to impress Edwin with a scheme of his own devising. His plan is to go on a car-throwing spree during which he will heave cars through the front windows of banks in a three-state area. He follows this rudimentary description of his plan with, "And rob them of course."

"I'm not sure that — " Edwin starts

"I rip the door off safe, take all money and leave. Maybe throw police car, maybe not. You know, uhh, details. What you think?" Although Edwin doesn't understand how it is possible, Lifto's broken, heavily accented English makes his plan sound even dumber than it actually is.

"I don't think it's a very good idea."

"No rob bank? But that where money is!" Lifto protests. He laughs as if he has said one of the most original things in the long-winded history of saying things. Lifto is disappointed when, instead of joining in the hearty guffaw, Edwin searches for a non-existent speck of dirt under his perfectly manicured fingernails.

"I just lift up safe and SMASH it on ground!"

Edwin sighs. This is probably as good a time as any. He says, "The problem is not the safe. Or police cars. Or lifting of any kind."

"No lifting?" Lifto asks.

"No. And no bank robbing either."

"No banks? But..." Lifto draws a deep breath. He's getting ready to tell his joke again. To make sure it is funny, this time he is going to tell it very loud. Edwin cuts him off.

"Yes, yes, that's where they keep the money. But if you rob banks, you lose money."

"That is no sense making."

"I'll try to explain. You see, if there was money in robbing banks, everyone would rob banks."

"But is all profit!"

Edwin presses a panel on the wall and a hidden whiteboard is revealed. He uncaps a marker and asks, "So how much cash do you expect to take in your average bank robbery?"

"$1,000,000?"

"Ah, ambition. Large numbers. I like that line of thought, but unfortunately the average bank robbery grosses only $5,000."

"5,000?"

"Yes, only $5,000. Hardly worth it."

"But $5,000 is lot of money."

"$5,000 wouldn't even pay for my suit. But let us assume," (wildly, thinks Edwin), "that you are above average and you are able to gross $10,000 for each bank robbery."

Edwin writes $10,000 on the board.

"But I to rob many, many bank!"

"Of course, that is your plan. And it is my point. Just stay with the numbers, Lifto. So, $10,000 is your benefit from robbing an individual bank. Now, what does it cost for you to rob a bank?"

"Nothing."

"Nothing?"

"Nothing! Lifto strong like bull. Easy for me to throw cars."

"Of course it is easy for you to throw cars. But while you are throwing cars and robbing banks you can't do anything else. It costs you time at the very least. But that's not what I'm worried about. I'm concerned with what it would cost you if you were caught." Edwin waits for it. He does not have to wait long.

"NO ONE CAN CATCH LIFTO THE MAGNIFICENT!"

"No, of course not. How silly of me. But let's just say it was possible. Not in the real world. But in the numbers. These are just numbers, Lifto. Like make-believe. So stay with me. Stay with the numbers."

"Okay."

"Now, hypothetically, how many years do you think — "

"But NO ONE CAN CATCH LIFTO!"

"The sentence for armed robbery, first offense, is usually 7 years."

"But I am to rob many banks!"

"Of course you are. So the sentence would be longer. Let's call it 20 years."

"That's better."

"Now, let's assume that instead of going to prison for those 20 years, you hold down a job." Lifto shakes his mane of hair indignantly. Lifto does not work for other men. He is a ruler of men. A mighty, hairy, lion. Edwin can see that he is losing him again. "A normal job. Say construction."

"Lifto does not do manual labor. I am in show business."

Edwin considers asking for clarification on this point. Lifting things is clearly manual, but perhaps Lifto does it only for pleasure. Edwin quickly abandons this line of thought. That way lies madness.

"All right then, what kind of hypothetical job would you like to have?" No good, still too close to madness. Edwin is finding it difficult to keep his mind clear.

242

With an air of great ceremony Lifto rises from his chair and proclaims, "Lifto will be King of Missouri!"

"Missouri is not currently hiring for that position." Stop, Edwin thinks. Do not try to follow his logic. Down that road lies madness.

"Oh," says Lifto, obviously disappointed. "Then I don't care. Something with people. Lifto is a people person."

"Reservations agent with a car rental company?"

"Yes, I think I would like that."

"So 20 years helping people with their rental cars, 40 hours a week at $10 an hour would be $400,000."

"$400,000! Without stealing anything?"

"Without stealing anything. So, we'll say the cost of getting caught would be the $400,000 you would give up in income.

"Now, let's say that you got away with the money 95% of the time. But there is still a 5% chance that you will end up in jail for 20 years."

"But NO ONE CAN — "

"Catch the mighty Lifto. Yes of course. But humor me. Stay with the numbers for just a moment longer. So 95% times a $10,000 benefit is $9,500. This is the incremental benefit to you of robbing a bank. That is, if our hypothetical Lifto were to rob an infinite number of banks."

"An INFINITE amount of money."

"Yes. Very good," (and very loud, thinks Edwin). "That would be an infinite amount of money."

"So I go rob banks now. Thank you."

"Wait, wait, we haven't factored in the cost yet."

"Lifto don't like costs."

"Neither do I, Lifto."

"Costs suck."

"Yes, they do. But we know that already. The only question left to us is how much do they actually 'suck' as you say. So, there is a 5% chance that you will get caught — I'm sorry, sorry, that the hypothetical Lifto will get caught — times

243

negative $400,000 is negative $20,000. So, over time, each time you rob a bank it costs you $20,000 dollars.

"But there's an infinite number of banks," says Lifto with dreams of filthy lucre glittering in his eyes.

"Yes, yes, so we add the costs and the benefits to learn what the true value of robbing a bank is to you and we see that, over time, it costs you -$10,500 each time you rob a bank."

"What!"

"The numbers do not lie, Lifto. In lieu of some special advantage like invisibility or an ability to walk through vault walls or even a telepathic ability to talk to coins — anything that might change this cost matrix — I cannot advise your entry into the bank robbing business."

"But this is just Hypothetical Lifto!"

"Yes, well, Hypothetical Lifto and Actual Lifto have quite a bit in common, I'm afraid."

"So you want for Lifto to work as receptionist?"

"No, I'm not saying that. I'm saying that if a crime makes you less money than working a regular job, perhaps you should find a different law to break."

Lifto is silent for a long time. Edwin can sense the tiny wheels of Lifto's mind turning. And even though they are most certainly missing a few teeth, Edwin is glad to have gotten them spinning. That is worth something isn't it? Edwin knows how foolish hope is, but for just a moment he indulges in it. Finally, Lifto lets out a long sigh and says, "I wish you had told Lifto sooner."

CHAPTER FORTY-TWO
Agnes vs. Mistivio

Agnes is still sitting her post in the lobby. She has refused to follow Edwin's instructions. But their disagreement is wearing on her. Edwin is right, of course. It is her job to keep his time clear and focused, but this was a favor. A favor to an old and dear friend. It should not be too much to ask. But the world has changed in many ways over the course of Agnes' lifetime. No matter how hard she tries, it never seems to make sense.

Agnes Plantagenet is old enough to remember a time without superheroes. A time with bad men, surely, but before Villains with a capital V. When the only costumes were uniforms, and everyone did their bit and went home. Of course there were heroes. But they had a quiet satisfaction about them. And their sense of accomplishment did not disappear with age, infirmity or the changing winds of fashion.

She can't pinpoint the exact moment that the world changed. The process has been gradual and insidious. And, if she's perfectly honest, she tries not to pay attention to popular lunacy. She had not realized how bad it had become until the televisions were installed in the lobby.

Of course, she understands the need to keep track of television coverage of The Cromoglodon for billing purposes. The variable nature of the beast's clothing has allowed the reverse sponsorship to become increasingly sophisticated. They have even been approached by a few companies who want to be positively associated with The Cromoglodon. Agnes sees this as yet another sign of the end times.

Every day the screens are filled with people running about in costumes with odd logos on various parts of their spandex clad bodies. They shout horrible slogans at one another as they fight in the most destructive manner imaginable. Agnes can't see it as anything other than a very disturbing game of, "Look at me! Look at me!"

How has it come to this? Perhaps she feels this way because the old always struggle to understand a changing world. These thoughts are reassuring, because they suggest to Agnes that things are as they should be. Most of the time, she suspects that something has gone horribly wrong.

Of course, there have always been exceptional people. Agnes can remember Sally Heckinsforth, the woman who had managed to win the Village of Hugglescote's gardening competition for 22 years in a row. Sally had a way with plants that was simply otherworldly. It was even said that she trained the ivy outside her kitchen window to make tea. Of course it was an exaggeration. But even if it had been true, the good Mrs. Heckinsforth would not have donned a skin-tight green suit and trained all the hedges in the village to throttle passersby for their change purses.

No. Mrs. Heckinsforth had been content with her garden and afternoon tea and outliving her husband and a thousand other ordinary acts which made for a life well lived. But these days, that doesn't seem to be enough. Agnes despairs.

Her mood has not been helped by the success of The Cromoglodon. As a result of his runaway popularity, all manner of wannabes have sought out Edwin. The job of insulating Edwin from all of them is wearing on her. On some days it has been impossible for her to get any other work done at all.

So when the elevator doors open, she knows what is coming. She doesn't know exactly what he will look like or what absurd powers he will claim, but she knows, as surely as a rough beast is slouching towards Bethlehem to be born, that another idiot is coming.

The elevator doors open to blackness. Utter darkness. Not a darkness that is darker than any mortal has ever known. Agnes guesses that is the desired effect. Why else would anyone disable the elevator's lights? An arm emerges from the darkness wrapped in a cloak of midnight blue. The arm drops and a smoke bomb bursts on the floor.

How utterly predictable, thinks Agnes as she watches the otherwise pristine lobby fill with smoke. How absolutely and completely not terrifying. How much more work for the cleaning crew.

A figure emerges from the smoke and, with a flourish of his cape, announces, "I am Mistevio!" He peers intently at Agnes over the corner of his high collar. He fancies that his eyes are dark pools in which the souls of lesser beings are swallowed. But Agnes is not afraid. She has long ago stopped reacting to men who wear eyeliner.

"Yes, Mr. Mistevio. And what can I do for you?"

"I am here to have a battle of wits with the one they call Windsor!"

"I fear Mr. Windsor would find little sport in such a contest."

"Do you dare to trifle with Mistevio, Master of the Darkness, Holder of Men's Souls, Sorcerer of Simulacra, Prism of Reality…"

Agnes can see that this man is unlikely to come to a timely conclusion on his own. So she cuts to the chase, "Do you have an appointment?"

"MISTEVIO needs no APPOINTMENT!"

"I take that to mean that you do not, in fact, have an appointment." Mistevio opens his eyes as wide as he can, and rocks his head side to side in a small, ridiculous motion.

Agnes holds up the appointment book. "Mr. Mischief, or whoever you are, is there any reason for me to check this appointment book?"

"Tell Windsor that I am here for him," Mistevio says, ending with his most sardonic laugh.

"I do not want to open this book to find that you have misled me."

Mistevio squints between eyeliner and mascara, "If you open the book, you will read what I wish you to read. If I wish you to see an appointment, you will see an appointment. If I wish you to believe that you are reading In Search of Lost Time by Marcel Proust, that is what you will find on the pages."

"I think I would require a much thicker appointment book."

"The strength of my mind will bend your reality to mine."

"Oh heavens, mind control."

"Mind control. Muahahahahahahahah!"

"Very well," says Agnes, "try me." She leans in and locks eyes with Mistevio. Contempt flows freely over the top of her reading glasses.

Mistevio does not wither. He reaches deeply into himself and imagines sinister forces pouring through his pupils, across the aether and into the very depths of Agnes' soul. Down to the small child within all of us that is afraid of dark rooms with open closet doors. Agnes' eyes defocus. Mistevio gets excited. This has never happened before. It is working! It is finally working!

But Agnes is not falling under Mistevio's spell. Agnes is watching the three television screens behind him. They all show a variation on the same theme. A man wrapped in leopard skin emerges from a bank. He lifts a car and hurls it towards the police. And then another. And another. There is also some amateur footage of a car crashing though a bank window. As the camcorder skews awkwardly to the right she can read the villain's lips so clearly she can almost hear the words, "I am Lifto!"

The bad video is replaced by animation that reads "Circus Man Crisis." This is bad, thinks Agnes, very, very bad.

Mistevio is completely unaware of the televisions behind him. His eyes are locked on his prey. And, all in all, he thinks he's doing pretty good. Agnes is in his thrall. That's what those books on mesmerism had called it, "thrall." Now it is time to command her.

"Arise, woman!"

Agnes ignores him completely. She is watching S.W.A.T. vans surround the building. As a helicopter flies by on the screen, she hears it outside her window.

"Arise!" Mistevio says. Perhaps Agnes is partially deaf. Perhaps Mistevio is just desperate. Agnes set her jaw and stands up. She turns on her heel and makes for Edwin's office. This is all her fault. If she had never asked him to meet with that horrible man.... She just hoped Edwin wouldn't be too angry with her.

"Woman, I have not commanded you to go!" Mistevio shouts, arms spread wide.

Agnes blinks and turns around. "My goodness, are you still here? I had forgotten about you completely."

Mistevio deflates. He is a failure. Worse, he is a non-threatening failure. He slinks across the lobby and presses the call button for the elevator. But the waiting proves too uncomfortable. He bows his head and scuttles into the stairwell. It is a long way to walk, but Mistevio is familiar with downward mobility.

CHAPTER FORTY-THREE
The Death of Culture

Lifto is uncomfortable under Edwin's gaze. The silence is terrifying. Why doesn't the tall man say anything?

Lifto was going to explain that he robbed several banks on his way over to the appointment but somehow he cannot. The words have frozen in his throat. And still, Edwin just stares at him. Outwardly, the tall man is emotionless.

Lifto knows he has screwed up. He can't imagine why he should be afraid of Edwin, but all the same he feels threatened. They say that Edwin is not a man to be trifled with. But they never say why. When the door opens, Lifto jumps.

Agnes says, "Edwin dear, a moment?"

Edwin rises from his chair and walks to the door.

"I'm terribly sorry, but it would appear that Mr. Lifto — " Agnes began

"The Magnificent," Lifto says without much force.

" — has been an exceptionally naughty boy."

"Yes, I know. He was just about to explain it to me." A helicopter roars by, rattling the windows.

"The authorities have surrounded the building. I'm afraid you will have to cut your meeting short."

"Your meeting, Agnes, yours," says Edwin. He looks out the window. Far, far below he sees tiny figures in riot gear cordoning off the streets. The police do not concern Edwin. They are well-trained and well-leashed. The real question is why are they waiting? Edwin's lobby should be overrun by men with mustaches and Lexan shields.

Edwin has no interest in protecting Lifto. Or even aiding him at all. There will be no stand-off. No negotiation. No daring last-minute escape. He will tell Lifto to turn himself in. But how to get Lifto to take his advice? "Agnes, are you pleased with yourself?"

"Edwin now is not the time."

"Small mistakes, Agnes. It is the small mistakes that compound into disaster."

"Edwin, I am sorry," Agnes says, losing her patience, "but what are we going to do?"

"I think you have done enough." Edwin is feeling powerless. He realizes he's taking it out on Agnes, but can't seem to do anything else. He watches the ants erect barricades far below and tries to get a handle on himself. There is a knock on the window.

Edwin looks up. On the other side of the glass floats...

"EXCELSIOR!" roars Lifto as he lifts Edwin's magnificent redwood desk over his head. His leopard-skin cape falls to the ground. Now the world has no defense against the sight of his absurd, bulging redness. "I will defeat you! Now all will know the true strength of Lifto the Magnificent!" Lifto steps forward and to hurl the desk through the window.

"STOP!" yells Agnes. As if the universe were a sensible, orderly place, everyone freezes.

Agnes advances on Lifto. "PUT. IT. DOWN." Lifto looks around uncertainly. He returns the desk to the ground.

"This office is filled with nice things and I will not see them wrecked by the horseplay of a few overgrown children!"

"Ma'am, you'd best stand aside," Excelsior says, the midwestern earnestness in his voice flattened by two inches of safety glass.

252

"And you," she exclaims, whirling on the flying hero without missing a beat, "of all people you should have the decency to use a door."

"What?"

"You know very well what I mean. You are a mere instant from destroying a three-story wall of glass in order to get to this, this — "

"LIFTO THE MAGNIFICENT," roars Lifto.

"Be SILENT!" shrieks Agnes. Lifto shrinks into the floor and wishes he was somewhere else. Edwin opens the balcony door. There is nothing to do but play it through. From far below he hears the wail of sirens.

"Excelsior, if you please," says Edwin, every bit the gracious host.

All of this is confusing to Excelsior. Usually when he apprehends a dangerous supervillain, he is subject to instant attack upon arrival. Air-to-air missiles. Laser beams. Courtesy just doesn't compute. He is certain it is some kind of trick. But even if it is, it's nice for a change. He floats over to the balcony and touches down gently.

"And be sure to wipe your feet!" Agnes says.

Excelsior takes two steps backwards and wipes his spotlessly clean boots.

"Now then. Welcome to Windsor and Associates. Mr. Windsor will see you now," says Agnes.

"Thank you, Agnes." Edwin is eager to play the host in an attempt to avoid the property damage that inevitably follows a clash of costumed apes. "Can we offer you something to drink?"

Excelsior points at Lifto, "I'm here for him."

"Excellent choice. Agnes, a pot of Oolong. We're going to sit down and talk this through." Agnes glares at everyone in the room and then leaves.

"Lifto does not talk," Lifto says, unaware of irony and its manufacture.

"You know, Mr. Windsor, people judge a man by the company he keeps," Excelsior says, doing his best to drip with folksy wisdom.

"People have also been known to judge a man by his appearance," Edwin retorts as he casts a dubious eye towards Excelsior's spandex.

"NO ONE CAN CATCH LIFTO!"

Excelsior circles around to the long end of the room. Lifto crouches behind the desk. "Now Lifto, you and I both know that's not true. Are you going to come quietly?"

Edwin rolls his eyes at the cliche. Edwin is sick of feeling powerless. He knows what is going to happen. He knows why. He knows everything that either side will say or do, but for all his intelligence, there is nothing he can do to stop it.

"Lifto, I advise you not to resist," says Edwin

"You want me to go QUIETLY!?"

"I'm not sure you are capable of doing anything quietly," says Edwin.

"Mr. Windsor, you should really be getting to a safe distance, so I can take care of some business." Excelsior says, not taking his eyes off Lifto.

Edwin steps directly in front of Excelsior. "You don't have to do this. You don't have to destroy my office."

"Yes I do. I catch the bad guys Mr. Windsor. That's what I do."

"NO ONE CAN CATCH LIFTO!"

"Then, by all means, catch him. Skip the battle."

"But, I have to bravely defeat him in single combat."

"You do not. Look, I don't care if you want to hurt him. But why not just grab him and fly away? Batter him senseless in a vacant lot. Perhaps the top of a mountain? Where property will not be damaged and Lifto will not be able to capture the inevitable hostage."

Excelsior thinks about this for a second.

"Whose side are you on?" asks Lifto.

"It's all the same to you, you can't be caught," snaps Edwin.

"But, I am paying you!" Something wasn't right here. Lifto couldn't put his finger on it. But something certainly wasn't right.

"If you can't be caught, why are you concerned about being caught?" says Edwin.

Now Lifto is totally boggled. While it's not possible to know the mind of another, we will not go too far astray if we imagine that Lifto is programmed in BASIC and the program reads like this:

```
5 REM I am Lifto's smarts-o-matic thought-thinking program.
10 goto 5
```

Edwin turns back to Excelsior. "So what do you think about my open area suggestion?"

"But then he wouldn't be able to elude me in a maze of narrow buildings," Excelsior says slowly.

"So you see the benefits?"

"It doesn't seem very sporting. And isn't your whole thing to help the villains?"

"Oh no, I'm not prejudiced. My services are available to anyone who will pay me."

"And villains pay better?"

"Something like that. Now, how about leaving my office in peace?" Edwin takes Excelsior's elbow and attempts to direct him towards the door.

"But, I must defeat Lifto," says Excelsior looking over his shoulder.

At the mention of his name, Lifto is knocked free of his infinite stupidity loop. He realizes that no one is paying attention to him.

"Hey, Lifto is HERE!"

"Yes, but you don't actually have to fight him to do that. And even if you do, you don't have to do that here." This a level of reasonability with which Excelsior is not comfortable.

"You're right. I don't have to. In fact, they've given me specific instructions not to harm you. But Mr. Windsor, I want to. Do you understand? I want to. I've been thinking about what you told me in the desert. And it made me angry. Angry, because you were right." Excelsior turns and considers a priceless Chinese vase that is displayed on a plain pedestal. "This is a very nice office for a criminal mastermind."

"I'm not a — " Edwin winces as Excelsior knocks the vase off the pedestal and it shatters on the floor. "I'm a consultant," he says through clenched teeth.

"You don't like that? You know, that's the first time I've seen you show an emotion, Mr. Windsor. Why so upset? I chose to do that. That's what you wanted, isn't it? For me to make my own choices?"

"I'm not sure destroying a part of the artistic heritage of mankind is what I had in mind," says Edwin.

Excelsior turns and considers the slab of beautifully carved marble on the wall. "Hmm, looks heavy."

"Heavy? The work of these unknown craftsmen represents the pinnacle of human achievement during the golden age of Greece. A time when wisdom and excellence were rewarded and the potential of mankind was properly channeled."

"Still, it looks heavy to me." Excelsior lifts the sculpture from the wall. "Ah, it's not so bad."

"Please be careful."

Excelsior locks eyes with Lifto. "Let's do this thing."

Lifto! LIFTO! LIEEEEEEEEFTO!" roars the hairy man as he lifts Edwin's desk from the floor once again.

Edwin dives for cover.

Lifto steps forward, holding the desk above his head. His plan is to throw the 600-pound desk across the room as one would snap a soccer ball back onto the field. But he doesn't quite make it. Excelsior bounds forward and shatters the desk with one mighty swipe of the Elgin Marble. The desk is thrown through the three story wall of glass.

Lifto plunges his hands into the floor and grabs one of the beams that forms the skeleton of the building. As he rips up a hunk of steel, Excelsior loses his footing and releases the sculpture. Edwin watches, powerless, as the slab of stone hits the floor and shatters.

Feeling a pain deep within him, Edwin closes his eyes. The floor heaves and twists underneath him. The sound of shearing metal comes to him from miles away. He opens his eyes and sees the world in slow motion. Excelsior has pounded Lifto into the floor. Lifto raises his powerful arms to free them from the concrete and the floor splits wide open. Edwin watches the crack run the length of his office and then into the center of the building.

"No! NO!" Edwin cries. But the sounds of impact and twisted metal are so loud that no one hears him. Edwin is filled with rage. Rage at his powerlessness. At the raw stupidity of it all. He wants to hurt them. To harm them. To put them down by force and restore order to his world. He even takes a step towards them. But of course, there is nothing he can do.

Except flee.

He races the crack along the hallway. In the floor he can feel the building vibrate as tremendous blows are struck. When he reaches the lobby Edwin sees the crack run all the way to the elevator shaft. No good. He dives into the stairwell. As he descends his feet barely touch the stairs.

The abuse of the building echoes throughout the shaft. The stairs buck under Edwin's feet and he collapses on a landing. A pain in his knee makes him nauseous. He lies there and fights for breath, worried that his heart may explode. He pounds the wall in frustration. Why? Why must he be a mere man? Why must he be so unbalanced? So strong of mind and weak of body? For the first time in many years, undisciplined thoughts tear through his mind.

He hears a terrible noise. The worst noise that he has ever heard in his life. Later, he will realize that this is the sound of a portion of the tower splitting from the rest of the building. It is the sound of building scraping against building. It is as if Edwin is trapped inside a violin on which God is playing a eulogy for the end of the world. He wonders if he will die. Then realizes he does not have a care for himself, but what of Agnes? What has happened to Agnes?

Edwin leaps to his feet and begins to climb. He ignores the pain in his chest and legs. Fear coats his hands with a cold sweat. From his chaotic thoughts he resolves a purpose. As the noise in his mind drops away and the pain in his knee grants him clarity, he feels something fierce kick within him. He sucks the stale air of the stairwell into his lungs and climbs.

"Agnes!" Edwin cries as he throws open the door to the lobby. The spectacle stops him cold. Half of his entrance is gone, along with what looks to be a third of the building. Inexplicably, some of the fire sprinklers have activated. Along the edge, exposed wires crackle and snap ominously. The wind claws at Edwin. In mere moments, his office has been transformed into a savage place. What little hope remains in Edwin's heart now drowns in bile.

"Agnes!" he cries again. As he approaches the edge, a large section of it gives way and tumbles into the empty air. The wind pulls at him seductively, beckoning the tall man into the abyss. For a moment, he considers yielding to the impulse and letting himself fall away from the cares of the world. Then he hears a soft cry.

He finds Agnes lying on the floor in the kitchen, collapsed in the ruins of her tea service.

"Edwin. You are unharmed?" Agnes asks with difficulty. Her face is drained and pale. Clearly she is in shock.

"Agnes, I'm sorry."

"Shh, shh, dear boy," Agnes says, coughing up a little blood, "Promise me…"

"Anything," says Edwin.

"Be good."

Edwin is unable to speak. The moments drag into minutes. Agnes closes her eyes and dies. He cradles her in his lap and says nothing.

He can hear sirens far below. In the distance are helicopters. As the last rays of sunlight fade, spotlights descend from the flying machines. They circle and circle, their lights highlighting all the tragedies that they are powerless to stop.

Perhaps Lifto still struggles against Excelsior. Perhaps the struggle is over and the rescue crews are simply dealing with the collateral damage. It matters not. Edwin knows the broad strokes of it. Lives have been lost. Property has been damaged. Resources have been squandered. Few, if any, will notice. They are too busy watching the explosions to ask what it might cost. It is entertainment for the masses already swollen with entertainments. Why have bread and circuses when you can have the Superpowered?

But Edwin will count the cost. He will count everything. As he holds Agnes and weeps, he even counts his tears.

CHAPTER FORTY-FOUR
Edwin Dresses for the Funeral

Steam rolls over the white tiles as Edwin Windsor stands, absolutely motionless, in the vortex of a six-headed shower. Although his long frame does not move within the womb-like embrace of the warm water, his mind ranges farther, ever farther. As if this white cell was not a bathroom, but rather a chamber in some sophisticated steam engine designed to harness the heat generated by his thoughts as they spin around the circumference of his brain.

Somewhere deep within himself, Edwin comes to a conclusion. His eyes open and his body becomes animated again. With the shower still running, Edwin steps onto the impossibly clean white tile. As he stands in front of the mirror, he can see himself only as a vague abstraction in the steamed surface. And there, before he even has a chance to grab a towel, a thought traverses the depths of his mind. Like a glimpse of a large fish in murky waters, he barely sees enough to describe it.

He searches his reflection. What if this undefined form — this sloppy, imprecise, ungraspable view of the world — is reality? What if sharp outlines are merely illusions created by strong minds? What if there is no precision? What if there are no terms? No categories? What if all of it is merely the play of light across a steamed mirror? Is that why everything seems to fall apart? Is that why it was all apart to begin with?

He wipes the mirror with a towel and opens the door to let the moist air out. He whips shaving cream to a lather with a badger hair brush and applies it to his face. The warmth of the lather and the reassurance of the ritual is soothing. Only after his face is prepared does he open the drawer. Alone in the center of the long drawer is the razor and nothing else.

He touches the cold steel to his neck, and for a moment, all thought focuses on the question of suicide. Of course he asks it. No man has ever felt an edge across his jugular and not, with varying degrees of sophistication, considered his own mortality. Crude men think of death as a bodily function, as unpleasant as kicking over a full bedpan. Ordinary men try to cover it over with bad analogies — a snake sloughing off the skin or the timeworn relation between caterpillar and butterfly. Religious men think of heaven. Impious men of unfinished revenge. But Edwin Windsor is not like any of these.

In Edwin's mind, death is exact. He can imagine it for what it is, a quick slip sideways, the sudden warmth on his neck and chest, lightheadedness, ringing in the ears, but no pain. Then the cold of the tile as he lies down and the warm stuff of his life sullies the floor. Peaceful. Inevitable. Definitive.

At the edge of this grim reverie, he imagines a function stretching out over time. The accretion of money and utility that all the moments of his life have brought and will bring. The part that came before is lost forever. Childhood and yesterday were, after all, only sunk costs. And the future, unknowable, but not inestimable. And where he stands in a perfectly white bathroom with a razor at his neck is the impossibly sharp edge of the now. Valued by the expectation of all future worth discounted back to this moment — a series, a summation, the equation of the value of his life. And with this in his mind he slides the razor along his skin, instead of through it.

The hair is parted from his face with a crackling whisper. He wonders if there isn't something else. Something unmeasurable. If he takes the summation and subtracts the crude utility of his life from it, will there be something left over? A something which makes all other measures truly and perfectly ridiculous? The immeasurable. The incommensurate. The soul. The a priori behind and yet still somehow beyond all biological demands.

Edwin splashes water on his face, and searches for his soul as plainly and practically as one might look for a spot that he has missed shaving. Edwin finds nothing.

In the next room he dons a broadcloth shirt and closes it with platinum cufflinks. He selects a black silk tie and turns to the new suit laid out on the bed. Mr. Giles has brought it himself, carried in his hands all the way from England. This time not at Agnes' request, but for her funeral. When Edwin had asked him if it needed further work, Mr. Giles had shook his head no. With great emotion, he said, "It is perfect."

The fabric of the suit is black. So black, it seems to suck light from the room. The line of the shoulders is so soft and alive, it moves like water deep underground on a moonless night. As Edwin slides the jacket over his shoulders it is as if darkness has been poured over his frame. He bends to tie a pair of shoes that have been hand-made for him by a wrinkled Italian cobbler who speaks no English.

Finally, he tucks a handkerchief into his breast pocket. Not a gaudy pocket square, but a full handkerchief of Egyptian white cotton. There will be tears, but Edwin will cry no more. His grief is absorbed by purpose. He adjusts his tie, tugs his cuffs into place, and goes to Agnes' funeral.

CHAPTER FORTY-FIVE
A Eulogy for Agnes

"Who can find a virtuous woman? For her worth is far above rubies," Edwin says. It is from Proverbs, 31:10. As Edwin says it, he can feel the dust of dry pages rolling around in his mouth. "I like to think that Agnes would have enjoyed those words, but I can not know. All I know is that I have lost." Edwin pauses, trying to find the words. But there is no adequate vocabulary of loss.

"I have lost," he says, attempting the sentence again. The words on the paper in front of him seem meaningless now. He cannot bring himself to say them. Everything feels heavy. His elegant frame sags. The strongest will might never bend, but even the hardest heart will surely break in the end.

And then, even though he knows it's not possible, he hears her voice. It swells within him. Filling, for the moment, the empty place in Edwin's soul.

"It was never supposed to be like this," he hears Agnes say. And then he feels his lips move, and the words come from his mouth.

"It was never supposed to be like this," says Edwin.

Now he says her words as she does. "The brave men and strong women of generations past did not sacrifice for this."

Now he knows the rest. He leaves Agnes behind, as he must. As is right and proper for a funeral, and speaks on his own.

"She, in particular, deserved better. She saw the best in all of us, even when the best wasn't there. I am sad to say that in many ways, her life must have been a terrible disappointment. But she never gave up. She never flagged in her defense of what was sensible. She believed that to the best and brightest among us, falls the duty of keeping the Grand Synthesis.

"In the end, the world did not come to her rescue. She was taken from us. She was taken from me. And we are all the poorer for it.

"When I was twelve, I lost my parents in a tragic accident that was beyond anyone's power to prevent. An unfair twist of an unfair universe. And I, being young, intelligent and privileged, could not comprehend it. And not comprehending, I gave up.

"It was Agnes, then, who came to my rescue. She did not coddle or comfort in the expected way. She gave me a question, 'Young Master Windsor,' she asked me, 'What will you do with your life?' I told her that there was nothing worth doing. That there was no point to any of it. Against the overwhelming forces of cruel fate and relentless time, a man could do nothing. We were all powerless. All else was comfortable illusion.

"And she told me that there is always a way to oppose, if not the instance, then the principle of a thing. And that it is in principle that true strength is found. The strength of character that can transform ordinary people into something more.

"At the time, I thought I knew what she meant. I was mistaken. And, at the time, I am certain I did not fool her. But finally, I have learned her lesson. I know what it means to oppose a thing. I know what it means to rise to meet a principle, however cruel and demanding it may be. No matter what it might require. I know what it means to become something more than you are in the service of an idea.

266

"It is small consolation. She is gone. And once again we are left behind to make what sense we can of the world."

Edwin steps down, but does not return to his seat. He walks to the back of the church and stands in the shadows. He observes the ritual, but derives no comfort from it. There is no belief or fantasy that can prevent him from seeing things as they are. Edwin knows his complicity. He knows he is an accomplice in the murder of Agnes Plantagenet. One of many. He does not want his guilt removed. He does not want his sin expiated. One does not expiate the truth.

When the service is over, the priest approaches Edwin. "Those were very kind words for a very special woman. I have always found Proverbs to be my solace in times of trial. Are you familiar with chapter two, verse ten? 'The way of the LORD is strength to the upright: destruction shall be to the workers of iniquity. The righteous shall never be removed: the wicked shall not inhabit the earth.'"

Edwin looks at the priest. "Unfortunately, my work does not leave me time to read popular fiction." The priest straightens up as if he has been slapped. He does a double-take. There is nothing humorous about Edwin's manner, yet there is no tone of insult. The priest walks away with his confusion, saying nothing else.

"Those sure were nice words," says Topper, "I'm not sure I know what they meant, but those sure were nice words there, E."

"Thank you Topper."

"So, we gonna get him?"

"Yes," says Edwin. "We're going to get him."

"Really?" says Topper, unable to believe that Edwin is agreeing to revenge. "That's great. 'Cause I know you're hurting. And there is nothing like a big old dish of comforting revenge to make you right with the world."

"Perhaps," says Edwin, "But the real question is, which him?"

"Whattya mean?"

"Who are we going to revenge ourselves upon?"

"Excelsior! Who else?"

"They are both at fault. It is only because Lifto resisted that there was a fight. It is only because of the pointless struggle that Agnes was harmed. We could just as well blame Lifto, or The Cromoglodon, or any of a host of villains or heroes."

"Yeah, but I still say we get Excelsior. Lifto's one of the good guys. I mean, one of the bad guys. I mean, he's on our side. Besides, Lifto's in prison. Not much point."

Edwin smiles. Topper doesn't get it. There are no good guys. There are no bad guys. There's just Edwin and everybody else. And the way Edwin feels right now, they don't stand a chance. Edwin doesn't explain this to Topper. Instead he says, "That's okay, Topper, we can get Excelsior. But I say we get them all, just to be safe."

"Oh, Edwin, I like the sound of that. This new you is, is — I don't know, but I like it. Does this mean I get to have a gun? A big friggin' gun? Bigger than me even?"

"No, Topper."

"No?" asks Topper, obviously disappointed. "But we're supposed to be the bad guys!"

"No, Topper. You can have a gun. I'm saying that I don't think they make a gun big enough for what I need you to do."

CHAPTER FORTY-SIX
Negatively Buoyant

The Cromoglodon wakes early and hungry after a hard night's work. It was cold last night, so he knocked a small apartment building over on himself to keep warm. He shrugs off the rubble with a tremendous yawn. His clothing is displaying an advertisement for orange juice. Definitely time for breakfast. He sets out in search of a diner or a grocery store to eat.

As he stumbles out into the empty street he is almost aware that something isn't right. He is accustomed to waking up to sirens or, at the very least, people screaming and running away from him. Today, there is none of that. The Cromoglodon spends most of his time being confused, so he figures that everything is normal.

The first rocket catches him in the ear.

"Take that, you son-of-a-bitch," Topper yells. He balances the smoking rocket launcher on his shoulder and hustles around the corner as fast as his short legs will carry him.

The Cromoglodon isn't hurt. The Cromoglodon isn't really even annoyed. After all, it's only a rocket. But Topper's got his attention. So he follows. When he turns the corner, a second volley of rockets takes him off his feet.

"Ahahahahahahahahahahahah!   You   block-headed bastard!" Topper yells at him from the next corner.

Still mostly curious, The Cromoglodon picks himself up and lumbers on. He follows the shrieking midget into a park. That's where he steps on the land mines. For all his toughness, The Cromoglodon has very sensitive feet. The land mines get to him. He bellows in pain. Now he's pissed.

"Oh shit," says Topper. Around the corner is a red MG. Topper leaps into the car and speeds away. The car is fast, but not quite fast enough. As The Cromoglodon gives chase, he's able to get a hand on the bumper. He pulls half of the trunk free. Topper gives it all he's got. He drives like an inspired madman — heedless of red lights, medians, newspaper boxes.

With The Cromoglodon close behind him, Topper barrels down a pier. When he reaches the decrepit warehouse at the end, Topper's foot never leaves the accelerator. He crashes through the back wall of the warehouse and sails into the harbor beyond. The car quickly sinks.

The Cromoglodon skids to a stop in the middle of the warehouse. The Cromoglodon can not swim. It is not a matter of knowing how. His incredibly tough structure is simply too dense to permit any buoyancy.

Edwin triggers the detonator.

The warehouse and The Cromoglodon explode and sink to the bottom of the harbor. The Cromoglodon does not sink like a stone. Stones don't struggle. Stones don't have lungs that burn for air. As stupid as he is, even The Cromoglodon is smart enough to realize that he is going to die. Fear, the true gut-wrenching, bowel-loosening fear of death is something that the invulnerable Cromoglodon has never been forced to consider. As he claws in vain against the dark water, the certainty of death sinks its reptilian teeth into The Cromoglodon's brain stem.

From the deck of a powerful motor yacht far out in the harbor, Edwin allows himself a brief smile and turns his attention to the radio. As the first dive team comes alongside in a zodiac raft with a soaked and shivering Topper, Edwin keys the mic. "Bravo team report."

"Bravo Actual, here. I think we've got him. If not I'd hate to know what else is stirring up all this muck. We're moving in."

"Negative, B-team, wait until favorable visibility conditions. Stay calm, safe and smart."

"Sir, whatever else he is, he is drowning and soon to die."

"Bravo Actual, whatever else he is, he deserves to die several times over. The medical team tells me that they will be able to revive him. The cold water will preserve him for several hours at least."

"Roger that. Holding."

"Holy Jesus, that was fun," says Topper. Edwin does not understand Topper's thrill-seeking behavior, but he is glad to see him happy.

"I'm glad you enjoyed your role," says Edwin.

"If I had known being a villain was this much fun, I never would have gone to law school. So now what?"

"We're going to wait until he is good and dead and then give him to the surgeon. And then, and only then, will we warm the brute and see if we can bring him back to life."

"I think you should just let the bastard suck water and drown," says Topper.

"Yes, I will take your blood thirst under advisement. You did beautifully by the way."

"Do you really think so? My aim was a little off with some of the rockets. I'll get it better next time."

Edwin doesn't bother to explain that there will be no next time. A plan that relies on extraordinary acts with less than 100% chance of success is not a good plan. Edwin is a little disappointed in himself that he couldn't come up with a better scheme. He longs for all his machinations to be inexorable rather than spectacular. Edwin does not mean to seize glory, but rather to crush it out of circumstance as an Anaconda kills its prey.

Eighteen hours later, The Cromoglodon is thawing on a slab. His head is now circumnavigated by a crown of fresh stitches and attached to high tension power lines. From Edwin's viewpoint, the stitches make his head look like a grisly baseball. Of course there are neater ways to place implants into a person's brain, but Edwin hadn't captured the beast for his looks. He had little trouble convincing the surgeon that speed was more important than aesthetics.

On the panel in front of Edwin are two switches. One switch will activate an automatic defibrillator, which will tickle The Cromoglodon's heart and bring him back to life. The other switch, will shunt half the city's power directly into The Cromoglodon's brain — probably killing him.

This kill switch is to be used only if the electrodes implanted in The Cromoglodon's brain prove to be ineffective. But for a moment Edwin's hand wavers between them. Of course, it would be wasteful to destroy such a powerful creature, but all of Edwin's purposes are cruel. His hand wavers as his demons wrestles with his better angels. The demons win. Edwin closes the switch that restarts the beast's heart.

As The Cromoglodon's eyes flutter and his vital signs gain strength, Topper climbs up onto his chest and slaps him across the face. "Rise and Shine!" The Cromoglodon awakes and instantly lunges for Topper. Edwin triggers the implants.

The surgeon who installed the implants argued that they should be placed in the pain center of The Cromoglodon's brain, but Edwin disagreed. He feared that, brute that he was, The Cromoglodon would be inured to pain. But fear, fear is something unknown to him; something The Cromoglodon is unequipped to deal with. The electricity triggers impossible and unknowable terrors within The Cromoglodon. Tears pour down his face. He attempts to curl up under a table that is half his size.

Edwin leaves the electrodes on for longer than he needs to. As he watches The Cromoglodon writhe on the floor, Edwin has an epiphany. Of course these creatures that surround him have the capacity to choose, but all their choices are bad. Edwin had believed that he could teach them, advise them, lead them to a truer path. Tip the scales of the world back to balance with a merest touch. Edwin realizes now that he had been mistaken. He can see now that he has been blinded by a sympathetic conceit. Now his thinking is clear and free from illusion. He quickly reaches the only possible conclusion.

In a time gone mad the only sane thing to do is to take over the world.

With The Cromoglodon cowering in fear, Topper returns to the room. "So, we're going to use him to get Excelsior. Is that the plan?"

"Not exactly."

"Then how are we going to get Excelsior? As much as I love that rocket launcher, I don't think it's going to be enough. What are we going to use on Excelsior?"

"The law."

"What?"

Edwin does not take his eyes off The Cromoglodon. "We're going to sue him."

"You're going to sue Excelsior. THE Excelsior?"

"Yes. You don't like the idea?"

"Well, sure, I like the idea. It just doesn't seem like enough."

Edwin turns away. "It's not. But it's a start."

CHAPTER FORTY-SEVEN
Serving the Process

For a suit to be brought against a person, he or she has to know that they are being sued. Usually, this is nothing more than a formality. A representative of the court, usually the plaintiff's attorney, presents the defendant with a special set of papers known as a process. Despite what television drama might lead you to believe, this is usually a pretty mundane affair. Someone walks up and hands the defendant (or sue-ee, if you are not fond of legal jargon) a stack of papers. Usually they say something like, "You're being sued," and walk off. As a general rule, they do not say anything like, "This is for what you did to Billy!" Or, "I told you we'd get you, you bastard!" Or even, "Have a nice day!"

But the standard process does not apply when it comes to someone like Excelsior. First of all, how do you find such a man? He does not keep regular office hours. And even if you do manage to locate him at the scene of a disaster chances are he will fly off before you can get to him. Sure, there is the occasional public speaking event, but security is tight, and there is still the flying-off problem. Topper had considered all of these things.

Oh, Topper is devil-may-care about a lot of things, but he is a meticulous and exacting lawyer. Because he hates to lose.

Worse than anything you have ever hated in your life, he hates to lose. And if he is to stand any chance at all, he must first get Excelsior in the courtroom. So he schemes a scheme. Topper thinks it is marvelous and subtle and on par with Edwin's best work. It isn't. But it is good. It is very good.

Excelsior has moved to a hotel on the West Side while a new apartment is being found for him. He spends his time much as he always does, lazing about and waiting for something to happen. And nothing has happened for several days. Absolutely nothing. He finds it hard to believe, but there has been no world-ending emergency, no alien attack, no earthquake, no sinister plot to foil. Another person might be glad, or thankful, or at least remembered that he had just been complaining about not having any time off. But not Excelsior. He's bored.

He turns on the television, looking for something. Anything. Anyone to save. He doesn't have to watch long. A local television channel has preempted regular programming with breaking news. Excelsior has no idea how long this emergency has been going on, but they've already created a name and a logo. "Bridge to Disaster!" That has to take a news channel at least ten minutes, right? Undoubtedly there is someone in a corner of the station frantically composing a theme song.

The screen shows helicopter footage of the Turnbuckle bridge. There, in the very middle, an accident has forced a red minivan through the guardrail. The vehicle teeters precipitously on the edge. The only thing holding the car back from an eight-hundred-foot drop into the water is a badly damaged guy wire.

Excelsior doesn't think too much of it. C'mon, it's just one car. He can see several fire trucks and police cars in the background. That's fine, Excelsior thinks, let the little people handle the light work. But then, just as he is about to change the channel, he sees the driver stick her head out the window.

276

She is beautiful. As she screams hysterically, her blonde hair flies in all directions. The car lurches closer to the edge of the bridge. As the woman points frantically at the back seat of the car, Excelsior notices that she's not wearing a wedding ring. The shot changes to a helicopter camera. There, on extreme zoom, Excelsior can see a child in a car seat.

Hmm, thinks Excelsior. Hot mom, with child, in danger. He should probably go check that out. In the back of his head, he hears Gus saying, "Just don't do ANYTHING!" He decides he doesn't care. He wants to save them. He wants the easy win and the gratitude of a beautiful woman. The adoration of the public. So he's going to do it. What were they going to do, punish him for saving a mother and child? He didn't think so. It's not much of a rebellion, but it's a start.

Excelsior flies low and fast along the surface of the water. It's more fun that way. When he reaches the bridge, he arcs high into the air so that everybody gets a chance to see him. A cheer goes up. That's right, he thinks, Excelsior is here to save the day. As if there is all the time in the world, he floats down and grabs the front of the car.

"My child! Save my child," the beautiful blond screams. She's even better looking in person.

"Don't worry, ma'am, Excelsior is here." He lifts the car and puts it back on the bridge. The crowd roars its approval. Excelsior laps it up. The adoration is deafening. He is the hero. It feels good. It is a pure win.

The woman struggles to open the back door and remove her baby from the car seat. Excelsior steps forward. "Allow me, ma'am." There is a screech of twisting metal as he effortlessly rips the door from the frame. Without looking, he tosses it off the bridge.

"Hey there, little fella, your mother is worried sick about you," Excelsior says as he leans into the car. But as he's

277

leaning across the seat, the child leaps up and shoves a handful of papers into his face.

"Surprise, you're being sued!" says Topper.

"What? What is this? What's going on here?"

"It's all in the papers. Don't try and figure it out for yourself. Take it to a professional."

"What about the woman?" Excelsior asks.

"Oh, her?" Topper looks as his watch. "She's paid up for another hour and a half. Have a ball."

"What? I don't understand any of this."

"That's why you need a professional," Topper says. "Now, if you'll excuse me." Topper steps down from the car and sees the crowd. This is a moment Topper cannot waste. "Hey everybody, let's have a big hand for Excelsior. He SAVED ME!" The crowd erupts into cheering again. Excelsior is still trying to make sense of the strange little man. Before he can ask any questions, Topper scurries off into the crowd.

"I'm dismissing your case," says the Judge.

"Dismissing my case?" says Topper, "But it hasn't even started! Besides, the defendant didn't send counsel. It's over, we win."

"This trial isn't even getting started. You don't have proof of service."

"Proof of service! Your Honor, please," Topper holds up a picture of himself waving to the crowd on the bridge. In the background of the picture, Excelsior is holding a stack of papers. He has a confused look on his face. "Not only do I have proof of service, service was covered on NBC, CBS, ABC, CNN and CNBC. How much more proof does the court require?"

"Yes, but whom did you serve papers to? The court will agree that you presented documents to a man in a costume. But this court does not recognize that you have correctly identified the party you wish to sue."

"What are you talking about? He's Excelsior. Everybody knows Excelsior."

"And everyone knows Mickey Mouse as well. And if you want to sue a man who wears a Mickey Mouse costume, you don't file suit against Mickey Mouse. You find out the man's name and file the proper legal papers in the proper legal manner. Your case is dismissed."

"This is a travesty! A friggin' tra-ves-ty. I don't have to put up with this kind of runaround."

"Yes, in fact, you do," says the judge. He drops the gavel.

"Son of a bitch." Topper grumbles as he storms from the courtroom. "I need an angle."

Twenty minutes later Topper has related the whole story to Edwin. "We're sunk. We're sunk before we even get out of the harbor."

"I am shocked," says Edwin, not shocked in the least.

"I know, right? You'd at least think they would play by their own rules."

"No, I am shocked that you managed to leave the courtroom without being held in contempt."

"What? Let my passion interfere with my work? Sir, I am a professional. But I don't know what to do with this. I'm stymied. We could try getting the case heard in another court, but if this is going to be their defense…"

Edwin smiles at his little friend. "Topper, don't worry. This is a simple problem. Easy to solve."

"Easy to solve? We can't even appeal because we never even got to trial! This is a complete failure of the legal system! What can we do?"

"Clearly they have forced our hand. We have no choice but to reveal Excelsior's secret identity," Edwin says as he picks up the phone.

Topper recoils in shock and amazement. "You know Excelsior's secret identity? You mean you've known all along?"

279

"I haven't the faintest idea who he is."

"But then how?"

"Shh, Topper, shhh."

The next day a two-page advertisement appears in the paper claiming that Excelsior is really Ron Koch, a city garbage man and known pedophile. Shortly after publication a completely nondescript lawyer arrives at Edwin's office and serves him with the papers for a defamation of character lawsuit. Somehow, the case is moved to the top of the docket, and Topper and Edwin stand in court two days later.

"Your Honor, this man has falsely accused one of America's great heroes of being a child molester. Decency itself has been wounded, and cries for redress in the amount of 1.3 million," says the counsel for Excelsior.

When the judge looks to the defense table, he is surprised to see Edwin Windsor writing a check.

"Does the defense have anything to say?" the Judge asks Topper.

"As much as it pains me to say it, Your Honor, we have no argument," says Topper.

Edwin rises and carries the check to the prosecution. He says, "You win."

The attorney looks at it and says, "It's too much. You made it out for 1.4 million? Why would you do that?"

"Call it a tip," says Edwin.

"Well, I don't know what just happened, but this very strange case is closed," says the Judge as he bangs his gavel.

"Why would you do that?" the government attorney asks Topper.

"'Cause now, my walleyed friend, we have precedent. If Excelsior doesn't need to reveal his true identity to sue us, then we don't need to know his true identity to sue him."

The attorney blinks his perfectly normal eyes twice, then realizes that Topper is right. "Oh, my God. What have we done?"

"Bingo Walleye, ya screwed up!" Topper looks towards Edwin. "He's not a trial lawyer. But he's very, very smart."

"Call the judge back," the attorney yells, "We've got to reopen the case!"

"Here's a copy of the papers I already served your client. I'll see you in court. You'll see me in your nightmares."

CHAPTER FORTY-EIGHT
Backrooms

There are those who think that the business of the law is conducted in the open air of the courtroom. That every discussion and decision is held in the hallowed halls of justice amid august assembly with wise fathers in togas chiseling words in stone so that Justice might be preserved through the ages. But it is not so. That's the nickel tour. That's civics class. That's the "Babies-come-from-Storks" explanation. And just like the miracle of birth, the reality of the manufacture of justice is much, much messier.

The trial is just the tip of the iceberg.

R. Lee McEllroy, representing Excelsior, comes from a long line of silver-tongued devils. He is well respected as a defense attorney, and highly regarded as a fixer. Topper knows him well, and has, at various times, carried a marker on McEllroy for debts he has acquired from him in a regular card game run by the Clerk of Court. McEllroy is an ideal choice as local counsel for the government's defense of Excelsior.

At first, R. Lee is a little in awe of Excelsior. After all, this is the man who stopped the Sprawl invasion almost single-handedly. But as soon as the great man opens his mouth, McEllroy realizes that he is a client just like any other. Maybe more so.

"It's bullshit that I even have to be here," Excelsior says, "What good are you if you can't even get me out of this bullshit court case?"

"Mr. Uh, Excelsior, uh, we've passed the point in the process where the case can be dismissed by the judge. Since you're not willing to settle — "

"It's not me, it's him. Them, the government." With a jerk of a gauntleted hand, he indicates Gus sitting the corner. Gus hooks a lung rocket in the corner of his ragged mouth.

"Uh, there's no smoking in my office," says McEllroy.

"Of course, we could settle," Gus says as he lights up anyway. He takes a long draw, then rolls the cigarette around between his thumb and forefinger. "But then we'll just have to keep paying. And paying. And paying. No, if we are going to fight this fight, we're going to fight it and win it so it stays won. So nobody else ever thinks to come looking for money."

"I'm not going to do it," says Excelsior.

"What do you mean you're not going to do it?" asks Gus. "You don't have to do anything. You just show up in a nice — I mean, your suit and sit there. It's got to be the easiest thing I've ever asked you to do."

"It's a sham. What are you going to do if I don't? Are you going to lock me up? With what? Where? I'm tired of this bullshit. That Cromoglodon thing destroys buildings and kills people and you leave him alone. Why? Because he's powerful. He gets to do whatever he wants because he's powerful. And I don't get to do anything I want? It's not fair. It's just not fair."

"It's not fair," Gus says, mocking Excelsior. "You sound just like a three-year old girl. Pull it together. Pretend like you're a man."

"Screw you and your tough-guy talk. It's all talk. That's all it is. What are you going to do, tough guy? Who's gonna stop me? You? Him?"

R. Lee McEllroy swallows uncomfortably. He wishes he were elsewhere.

"Don't let him scare you. He's an idiot," says Gus. McEllroy is not reassured. "Go on. Get out of here. I need a word in private with your client." McEllroy scurries from his own office.

Gus stubs out his cigarette on the sole of his boot. Then he looks at Excelsior for a long time. Excelsior breaks first.

"What? Why are you looking at me and not talking?"

"You know, soon I'll be dead. And since you don't seem to be getting any older, or wiser, I think you're going to outlive me. Outlive me and a whole bunch of others. And if you live long enough you're gonna be free of it. And then you can do what you want." Gus struggles to rise from the plush leather chair. His entire frame quivers with anger, "But I know what you did. I was there! We gave you your pass. We gave you the chance to earn it. To prove you were worth it."

Excelsior gets a faraway look in his eye and sinks into a couch. Gus advances on him.

"So you can play hero all you want. But I know. And unless you get your head on straight, unless you get back in this game, everybody else is gonna know too. You read me boy?"

After a moment Excelsior nods.

"You want that? You want all those people out there to know what kind of a person you really are?"

Excelsior shakes his head.

Gus walks to the office door and calls McEllroy back. "It's all right son, I gentled him down a might. He'll behave now."

CHAPTER FORTY-NINE
A Reasonable Disagreement

"All rise for the honorable Judge Perkins."

As the packed courtroom gets to its feet. Topper looks over at Excelsior. Jesus, he looks good in that silly costume. Red, white and blue. That full head of hair, strong jutting chin. He looks like all that is best about America stacked up in one place. And the sonofabitch is tall too. Where does this guy get off looking so young? He has to be 70 at least.

In that moment, Topper regrets taking the case. He feels like he is going to throw up. The jury is already swooning over Excelsior. This is hopeless.

"Would the counsel for the plaintiff please rise?" says the Bailiff.

A flash of anger brings Topper back to himself. "Larry, if you got a real job, maybe you could buy a new joke," he fires back.

The judge enters the courtroom. All business. Judge Perkins is not a man to tolerate nonsense. This kind of judge has cost Topper in the past. But this time Topper thinks it will work in his favor. If anyone is going to make nonsense speeches in this case it will be Captain Red White and Blue. Or better yet, his overblown legal counsel, McEllroy.

Topper looks over, and up, at Edwin. His tall friend looks positively Gothic in this setting. His grey suit is immaculate. He looks like the agent of all the ordinary, right and regular commerce of the world; the everyday events and assurances that keep it all on course.

Edwin's exceptional mind sees the law as complicated intellectual machinery. That's the right approach for contracts and corporate law, but not for litigation. Topper thinks that Edwin has never really been able to get his mind around litigation. Edwin is all finesse. He doesn't realize that sometimes facts make sense only when you beat them into shape. And that is what litigation is for.

Edwin certainly doesn't understand what role appearance and opinion play in the courtroom. How easily and subtly a jury can be swayed or seduced from one point of view to another. No, it was all an equation to Edwin. A very complicated and useful equation. Like a machine. Input here, output there. But this view left no room for magic. And legal magic is what Topper does best.

As he looks back and forth between Edwin and Excelsior, his stomach settles down. He remembers why he took this case. And how he can win it. Next to Edwin, this guy looks like a cross between a clown and a boyscout. Both are great figures for children. But for adults, for the modern world, for the continued progress of civilization, boy scouts are obsolete.

He also wants to do well by his friend. Edwin and Topper are very different. But the world never really fit either of them. And misfits have to stick together, don't they? Or else all the ordinary people will band together and stomp them flat.

Sometimes Topper feels very stupid around Edwin. But this, this trial, is something that he can do. And do better than the tall man. This is Topper's chance to come through. To do his part. To pay back all of the favors Edwin has done him over the years. The guy has thrown him an entire practice worth of business. Topper owes. And this is his chance to make good.

"Gentleman," begins Judge Perkins, "I'm going to give both of you the same advice — I don't care who you are, or the circumstances that brought you here. This is a court of law. You will respect it as such. As prejudicial to my character as it would be to hold such a great servant of this country as Excelsior to account at my bench, or in contempt of this court, I will do it. Here we hold men equal before the law."

Excelsior nods gravely.

"And the plaintiff, Mr. Windsor. This is an unusual, one might say outrageous, suit you bring. But you have grievances and they will be heard. I instruct you and your counsel to remember that we are not putting a hero on trial. We are settling a civil matter. It is a question of responsibility and, perhaps, compensation."

Edwin nods.

"All right then." Judge Perkins sits. "Commence." Perkins pounds the gavel a few times. "Court is in session."

"Ladies and Gentleman of the jury," Topper begins with a flourish of the hands. "My client is an ordinary, hard-working businessman. Perhaps his talents are unusual. He does have clients that are far from ordinary. But he is a businessman, a man of trade, if you will. He has never been convicted of any crime. In fact, the only time he has ever been charged is for an illegal right on red. And the case was thrown out, because while the turn was, in fact, illegal, the sign that indicated this to the general public had fallen into disrepair."

"Objection! The counsel for the defense can't see how this can possibly be relevant to the matter at the bar."

"Your Honor," Topper answers with infinite courtesy, "We all know what an upstanding member of the community Excelsior is. I am trying to emphasize that, in the eyes of the law, these two men are exactly the same. My client is tax-paying, law-abiding, as honest as the day is — "

"Enough," says Judge Perkins. "You've made your point. Objection overruled. Move along."

But Topper has no desire to move along. Because when he said, "As honest as the day," Excelsior had snickered. Topper's not about to let that go. "Excuse me, I didn't quite catch that," he says to Excelsior.

"My client didn't say anything," says McEllroy.

"Well of course you'd defend him. You're his defense attorney aren't you, Lee? Can you read that back from the record?" Topper asks the court reporter.

"I have it as a snigger," says the court reporter.

"A snicker?" asks Topper.

"No, no a snigger. Two g's"

"A snigger? Really?"

"Your Honor, please," protests the defense.

"I thought you would never ask." Judge Perkins drops his gavel. "Objection granted."

"He didn't object," objects Topper.

"Well then I'm objecting. Strike this nonsense from the record."

"Your Honor, he laughed at my client."

"Sniggered," says the court reporter.

Judge Perkins' head swims a little. Not five minutes into the trial and it was already falling apart. "Sniggered, snickered or guffawed, I want it struck from the record! As far as I'm concerned and the jury is concerned, it never happened. You got it?"

Topper says nothing.

"Now would you like to continue with your opening statement or can we strike the rest of that from the record?" says Judge Perkins.

"I'd like to continue, if it please the court," says Topper. The judge, beyond speech, waves his hand — get on with it already.

"My client is not a villain. He is not a criminal of any kind. Yet, for some reason, Excelsior has seen fit to treat him as one. We will show you how he has hounded my client. Destroyed his property. Assaulted his clients. Terrorized him and ruined his livelihood.

"That's right," Topper says with a close-to-the-ground-swagger, "He's made it impossible for my client to make a living."

"Objection! Your Honor!" says McEllroy. "Mr. Windsor works with known criminals, villains of the worst sort."

Topper smiles. "Your Honor, we will so stipulate. It is an agreed fact of this case that my client works with persons who are known to have a criminal record. But many people do. The law sees fit to deprive felons of the right to vote. Would the counsel for the defense also see fit to deny them professional services? Medical care? Employment? Legal counsel?

"The defense betrays a bitter prejudice of the worst kind. A prejudice that preys upon the disadvantaged and downtrodden of our society. Perhaps this prejudice is at the heart of Excelsior's criminal actions against my client."

Both the Judge and the defense team bristle. Topper moves on. "But that is not our case. That is not our concern."

Topper walks back across the courtroom. "No, we're going to show you that on May 15 at 2:45, Excelsior did willfully destroy the office of my client. And not just the office, the entire building, a valuable structure worth many millions of dollars.

"Excelsior claims to have been in pursuit of a dangerous felon. A man known as Lifto the Magnificent. Yes, the man had just committed a bank robbery. But he was on his way out of the building at the time Excelsior attempted to apprehend him. And thus, there was no reason to choose my client's place of employ as the site of this violently destructive takedown. He could simply have waited until Mr. Lifto was out on the sidewalk. There was simply no reason to destroy a perfectly good building. There was no reason for innocent people to die in the process. No reason other than the purest malice."

"Objection, Your Honor. Counsel is exaggerating."

"Your Honor, if you will examine exhibit 34 you will find a statement from Mr. Windsor's insurance company, complete with structural engineering assessment and a denial of claim on the basis that the damage was an "Act of Superpersons" and therefore not covered. Exhibits 35 'a' through 'm' are death certificates, including that of Mr. Windsor's beloved secretary Agnes Plantagenet. Her death has wrought grave physic harm to my client and has created a very real climate of terror in his mind."

"Objection overruled," said the Judge.

"We do not seek to damage this... great man's reputation. Far from it. First, we seek immediate injunctive relief. It is our hope that this court will see fit to place a restraining order on Mr. Excelsior that will prevent him from harassing my client any further. In addition, we seek compensation for property damage, emotional distress, and the defamation of character that comes from being the object of so mighty a hero's aggression."

Topper scans the jury. Some are with him, but a few aren't buying it. Time for a little extra heat.

"My client has great respect for Excelsior. So do I. I looked up to him as a child and, due to unfortunate genetics, I still do. But for one reason or another, this great man has lost his way. Ladies and Gentlemen of the jury, we must help him find it again. And the instrument of our assistance will be the law. An instrument directed by your good and fair judgement.

"And one more thing, ladies and gentleman of the jury. There is one more thing you should know. My client is willing — and has been willing — to settle out of court at any time. He is also willing to agree to total secrecy about the whole matter to protect the dignity of our great hero. The only thing preventing this timely resolution — the only reason this court has been convened and your private lives disrupted — is their stubborn refusal to be reasonable."

R. Lee McEllroy gets up from his chair. He admits to himself that the midget is better than he expected. Perhaps even inspired. Now he will proceed with caution. He pinches the bridge of his nose, takes a deep breath, and begins.

"Reasonable. An interesting word, Ladies and Gentleman of the jury. A seductive word. Reasonable. After all, who doesn't want to be reasonable? Likable. Nice. So as you decide this matter, I'll ask you to use the standards of a reasonable person. In fact, that is exactly what the law directs you to do in this matter. Use the standards of a reasonable person to determine, on the preponderance of evidence, how responsibility falls in these matters."

He glares at Topper and Edwin and makes sure the jury sees it happening. "We're going to show that there is nothing reasonable about the Plaintiff. In fact, the preponderance of evidence will show that he has a long history, as they have just admitted, of consorting with the worst sort of criminal. Villains, supervillains whatever you want to call them. If you believe, as one the earliest members of the supreme court did that, 'society is a fabric, woven together from the threads of our common action' then this man, Edwin Windsor, is that most irresponsible of souls who finds the loose threads and yanks on them for his personal profit."

Topper snorts. "Your Honor, I'm not even sure what all this means, but I'm pretty sure, we're going to have to object. If only on the grounds that Shakespeare over there is wasting our time."

McEllroy continues, "I mean to say that any reasonable person would recognize that what Mr. Windsor is doing is opening the gates for the barbarians. If we allow him to win this suit, then the worst elements in our society will be free to drag down our highest exemplar, Excelsior."

"Vague objection overruled. But counsel is instructed to use a mode of speech originating in this century," cautions Judge Perkins.

"Of course, Your Honor. So we're going to decide this matter on the preponderance of evidence. Preponderance. Which means, what does most of the evidence indicate to a reasonable person like you? Excelsior has devoted his entire life to protecting and defending people like you and me. To preserving our way of life. Years of service. And suddenly, he's going to throw that all away, for some irrational vendetta? Why would he do such a thing? Why, that sort of thing just doesn't seem reasonable. And that's exactly what we're going to show."

CHAPTER FIFTY
Get Him to Pop

"Call Eustace Eugene Rielly the 3rd."

Edwin turns his head and sees that Eustace has not given up on his dreams of supervilliany. For an instant, pity almost enters Edwin's hard heart. Despite his injuries, Dr. Loeb struggles to the witness box under his own power. One leg appears to be pinned in several places and a brace is screwed into his skull to keep his apparently broken spine from moving. He wears a cream suit with a Neru jacket, and tries to fix the courtroom in a gaze of terrible intensity. For all his dreams of true hatred, his eyes are nothing more than large, moist spotlights of pathos. He is as threatening as a wounded puppy.

"Did Excelsior really do all that damage, or did you stage that?" Edwin asks Topper.

"As your lawyer, I advise you not to answer that question. He looks great, doesn't he?"

As the bailiff struggles to help him into the witness' stand, Eustace gouges large chips from the polished woodwork with his metal neck brace. Dr. Loeb lets out a few high pitched moans. And it is when Dr. Loeb is at his most pathetic, that the hint of Edwin's sympathies snaps off sharply. Dr. Loeb failed to listen to Edwin. What else could he expect but misery?

"State your name for the record."

"Dr. — "

Topper slams his hand down on the table and coughs.

"Eustace Eugene Rielly," the words come out slowly, squeezing their way through a jaw that has been wired shut, "the Third." His headdress clatters as Eustace struggles to get his hand past his bolts and restraining arms and onto a bible. He sounds like a snake as the oath to "tell the truth, the whole truth and nothing but the truth" hisses out between clenched teeth.

"Mr. Rielly, I realize that you are in a great deal of pain, so I will try to keep this brief. I hope that the defense will be kind enough to do the same. Clearly, you've suffered enough already," says Topper. "Are you a client of Mr. Windsor's?"

"Yessssssssssss," he says.

"How were you injured?"

"I was assaulted," Eustace says. He has to try three times, to make it over the deep glottal gorge of the "au" that lurks in the middle of the word assaulted.

"Is the man who assaulted you in this courtroom?"

"Yesssssss."

"Can you point him out to the court?" Eustace raises his arm and points at Edwin. Then he bends his hand so that the tip of his finger points directly at Excelsior.

"I'm sorry Mr. Rielly, it's unclear who you're pointing at."

"Sssss- sssssORY. Can't turn."

"That's okay. For the record, whom are you indicating?"

"Him. Eck, Eck, ACK! ACKcelsior!"

Edwin has to admit, it is impressive to watch Topper work. In his personal life, Edwin finds Topper abrasive and ill-mannered, often thoughtless and sloppy and given over to an excess of all appetites — but that is only one side of the volatile equation that is Topper Haggleblat, world's most dangerous attorney at law.

Inside the courtroom Topper's manic energy is channeled and not a drop is wasted. For here, under the scrutiny of the judge and jury, every reaction, or overreaction or lack of reaction sways the case to one side or the other. Of course there are facts. Perhaps an objective reality exists, but here in the arena, where argument is pitted against argument, it is the way a fact is delivered that means everything.

When the defense makes a remark calculated to get into Topper's head, he ignores it. When he thinks he has something to gain, Topper rages as if the defense attorney is a monkey who has flung poo in the face of God himself. He pushes right up to the point of a contempt citation.

He works the judge back and forth across his patience until the old man sags in his robes like an exhausted prize-fighter. Topper pushes hardest and is the most annoying only when it will turn out that he is so solidly in the right, the Judge's own conscience will prohibit him from taking the other side. So it is that the short man radiates power and is a kind of giant in the chambers of the law.

As they leave the courtroom at the end of the day, Once again, Topper struggles to keep up with his long-legged friend. Edwin walks with his hands clasped behind his back and lowers his head slightly. He is in thought.

"Edwin, I'm concerned."

"Hmmm," says Edwin.

"Yes, as your lawyer I'm concerned."

"About what?" Edwin asks, not really wanting to know the answer.

"I think we're in trouble. In the case."

"Your argument has been excellent."

"Oh, why thank you. Thank you very much. But that's not the point. Before the trial, I had a talk with Judge Perkins. At the time I thought he was just a crotchety old bastard, but I think he was right."

"About what?" Edwin asks, paying Topper as little attention as he possibly can.

"He said we couldn't win."

Edwin stops so abruptly that Topper takes three steps past him. "So the problem is that you have said something to upset the judge?"

"No, no, no," Topper says, gesturing wildly. "Well, probably, but that's not my point. It's not Old Judge Bastard. He's not the problem. The problem here is the jury.

"Look, we've got a good argument. Hell, we've got a great argument. We've even got (and it's not often I get to say a thing like this) the Truth on our side. Yeah, Truth. The one with a capital-tits 'T'. But they've got Excelsior. A hero. In fact, THE friggin' hero — right? So all he has to do is just sit there. Just sit there and look like a hero. He keeps his mouth shut and the jury just basks in his glow. And the longer he sits there, the more they're gonna bask. And then, after they've basked long enough, they're going to decide in his favor."

"But he clearly did the wrong thing."

"Edwin," Topper says, shaking his head and chuckling a little, "I love you. I do. But you gotta understand, this isn't about the facts. It only seems like it's about the facts. Look, this is a trial. Which means we make the best case we can. If we do that well, we earn a chance of winning. It's kind of like buying a ticket to a Justice raffle. Except this time our odds of winning are so bad that it's more like a Justice Keno ticket."

"The problem is the jury."

"Yes, the jury. A jury of your peers. But Excelsior doesn't have any peers. And neither do you. So we get what everybody gets. A jury box filled with people who were too stupid to get out of jury duty. Hell, we'd be better off with a judge. Even Justice would be better off if the judge just decided the case. And we'd be better off. Hell, if it was anybody else but Perkins, we could just bribe the bastard and be done with it. But juries, juries are brutal. Hah! And they call justice a system."

298

"You are saying we should rig the jury?"

A wistful look crosses Topper's face. "Ah, if only. But we can't do that. You see these are ordinary people. Just regular jerks. They're not professionals. No code. They won't stay bribed. A crooked judge, he'll stay bribed. Because if word gets out that he won't stay bribed, then nobody can trust him and the bribe money dries up. And then he's no damned good to anybody. That's a sure-fire recipe for getting caught. And then you wind up with a 10-minute scandal that nobody pays attention to. But whatever, whatever, I'm preaching to the choir." Topper concludes with a lot of hand-waving.

Edwin is upset. Topper isn't making any sense. "So what do you suggest we do?"

"The only way is to get Excelsior to pop."

"Pop?"

"Pop, right there in the courtroom in front of everybody. He's got to lose his shit. So they can see that he's not perfect. Look, even if we prove everything, all he has to do is sit there with that bullshit midwestern-football-hero 'aw, shucks' charm. Well, the jury is going to think, 'Yeah, maybe he didn't do the right thing, but he's just folks. And he makes mistakes from time to time, but his heart's in the right place,' and they'll let him right off the hook.

"Sure, years later, when somebody else tears down the guy's facade, they'll think back and wonder if they did the right thing. But on the day, in the room, when it matters? They'll let him right off the hook. They'll sun themselves so much in his hero glow they'll get a friggin' sunburn — and they won't even notice when their skin peels off from his nuclear vision or whatever it is!"

"I'm afraid you're taking this a little too personally."

"Well of course I'm taking it PERSONALLY. That's how were going to stick it to this daffy, caped bastard. I hate to lose. You know how I hate to lose."

"Hmmm," says Edwin.

"Come on, Beanpole, you gotta help me think of something."

"Hmm," says Edwin, resuming his stride.

"Hmm? What hmm? What does hmm mean?"

"I have an idea."

CHAPTER FIFTY-ONE
Gus in the Hospital

Edwin has never killed a man. In his professional life he has almost always advised against it. The motives that lead one to murder are ill-informed. Justice and its darker cousin, revenge, are ill-served by murder. And crimes of passion are always, always more expensive than they first appear.

The way he sees it, if your object is to cause someone pain, killing that person is suboptimal because there is no pain after death. If you truly wish to revenge yourself upon another, force them to live in a set of unbearable circumstances. Oedipus is a good starting place. Arrange for a man to unwittingly kill his father and marry his mother, then reveal it to him. That is revenge. By comparison murder is simply pedestrian, ill-informed and wasteful.

And especially wasteful. When you kill a man you forfeit the benefit of his labor and expertise. Even slavery, as ruinously expensive as it is, is better than murder.

What Edwin rarely explains is that there are certain cases in which the benefits of killing a person greatly outweigh the costs of keeping them alive. Why else would political assassination exist?

And right now, Edwin is faced with one of those rare cases in which killing someone is the best thing to do. But that's only what he thinks, in the safety of his logical abstraction.

Gus is outside the courtroom. He puts a cigarette in his mouth, but before he can light it, he is overcome with a coughing fit. It's the kind of fit that might make a person think that killing Gus is a waste of time. He's clearly half-dead already. In fact, he might even drop dead before he stops coughing.

Edwin places his hand on Gus' back. "Are you all right?" asks Edwin. Still coughing, Gus looks over his shoulder. When he sees who it is, he jerks away from the contact.

"Get your hands off me, you shifty bastard."

Edwin is nonplussed by this insult. He offers Gus his handkerchief. "I thought you might need assistance."

"Even if I do, I'm not taking help from the likes of you."

Then Excelsior is there. He puts himself between Gus and Edwin. "You stay away from him," says Excelsior. Edwin raises his hands as if to suggest that he means no further harm. Excelsior ushers Gus away from the courthouse.

Edwin stands with his hands at his side and watches Excelsior and a dead man walk away. Very carefully, Edwin opens his right hand. A small needle drops to the ground. The needle is tipped with ricin, a deadly poison derived from the shell of castor beans. Even a few microns are poisonous. The needle itself is so delicate that it will soon be ground into oblivion by the shoes of the unsuspecting. The unsuspecting always make such wonderful accomplices.

Edwin nods to a photographer who has been snapping pictures of the whole exchange. The photographer has no idea why what he has photographed will be important, useful or even desired. Why would anyone want a photograph of a chance meeting with an old man?

Hours later, Excelsior is awakened by the angry squawk of the pager. He drags himself out of bed. What is it this time? Can't these emergencies wait until the morning? He squints at the vile plastic box. He blinks twice as he tries to make sense of the message. Then he is gone. He doesn't even bother to don his costume. He just grabs a pair of pants and shirt and flies out the window, without bothering to open it.

Within minutes he is standing in an Intensive Care Unit. The figure in the bed is obscured by tubes and wires. A variety of machines cluck and beep and slurp as they wrap Gus in a cold embrace of mechanical concern. Excelsior feels awkward, and powerless. Gus looks withered and weak. With his eyes closed lying helpless in the bed, he seems both a thousand years old and as innocent as a child.

But innocent he is not. Where the blanket has fallen off his chest, Excelsior can see the crisscross of scar tissue, medals awarded for a lifetime of living hard and fast. He wonders what it would be like to have scars, for the world to leave its mark upon your flesh in pain. He re-covers his oldest and only friend with the blanket.

A doctor enters the room. "Is it... cancer?" Excelsior asks.

The doctor snorts. "Yeah, it's cancer. He's had lung cancer. But that's not what put him here. He's had a massive stroke. The hits just keep on coming."

"Is he going to be okay?"

"Be okay? How should I know? I'm just a doctor. I would have told you he should have been dead 6 months ago. But he wasn't. As for the stroke, we'll have to see. There's some brain damage. How long it will last? How much of him will come back? We'll just have to wait and see."

"Wait and see? That's the best you can do?"

"I'm sorry, I'm just a doctor. I don't have superpowers."

The Doctor leaves. Excelsior doesn't know whether to sit or stand, to cry or remain stoic. He wishes that Gus' stroke was a giant monster he could punch. But of course it isn't.

His grief and confusion are interrupted by a small coughing noise. Excelsior does not turn. Then he hears it again, louder.

"Heh-HEM"

Excelsior turns to see a man he does not remember meeting. The man is small and vaguely piggish. This man knows so much about Excelsior he thinks he owns him. He opens his mouth and noise comes out.

He had intended to say, "I am Director Smiles. For the time being, I will be your liaison with the government." But what actually comes out is, "I am Directasquee — "

Smiles is scared shitless.

"I think you have the wrong room," Excelsior says, summoning what little patience he has.

"No," the Director says, sweating profusely, "I am Director Smiles, I will b-b-b-b-b-" As Smiles struggles with the future tense, Excelsior is sucked in by the suspense of his stutter. What is he trying to say? Will he make it past the second letter of the alphabet this time?

"b-b-b-b-b-b-b-b-b-b..."

In the midst of his terrified motorboat impersonation, Director Smiles decides that this "b" is unassailable. He gives up on the sentence and tries another one.

"I am in control of you now," says Director Smiles. He is pleased that he has gotten this sentence out in such good voice, with a real tone of authority. But when Excelsior's face collapses into a frown, Smiles realizes he may have made a mistake.

"You do NOT control me!" Excelsior picks the little man up by the front of his cheap suit. "I control you! You get it?" Excelsior twists his wrist and turns Director Smiles upside down. As small change falls out of the Director's pockets, Excelsior whispers, "I can end you any time I want. And if you don't leave me alone with my friend, I am going to end you."

"Government!" Smiles squeaks, by way of protest.

"Wait outside, we'll talk about it when Gus wakes up."

Excelsior stands a vigil over his friend. Smiles sits outside on the couch frantically messaging people from his phone. He is praying, to whatever committee of dark gods bureaucrats pray to in their secret, inefficient hearts, that Gus will pull through.

As the first fingers of dawn claw their way through the heavily louvered blinds, Excelsior raises his head. The lack of sleep hangs under his eyes. He looks to Gus. "It's a new day old man. It's a new day and I have to go. But you rest easy, I've got it from here."

Director Smiles awakes with a jerk. He realizes that Excelsior is watching him. Smiles is afraid before he can even fully wake up. "I have to go to court," says Excelsior. Smiles nods. "Is it your fault that I have to go to court?" Smiles nods again. Excelsior frowns. "Rule 1 — no more court cases." Smiles nods. "Rule 2 — you don't pick and choose the emergencies anymore. You send me everything, I choose what I'm going to help with."

"But you can't possibly — " Smiles protests.

"I can. And I will. Send me everything. If Gus wakes up, it takes priority." Smiles nods again. He opens his mouth to speak, but Excelsior is gone.

CHAPTER FIFTY-TWO
Excelsior Throws Down the Gauntlet

Excelsior takes the stand with surprising dignity for a man wearing a cape and tights.

"Hold up your right hand and solemnly swear, I promise to tell the truth, the whole truth and nothing but the truth."

Excelsior says nothing. The Bailiff starts to repeat the oath. Excelsior says, "This is bullshit."

Judge Perkins is so startled that he says, "Excuse me?"

"I said it's bullshit. That's the truth. That's what you wanted, right?"

"Son, I've never charged a man in tights with contempt before. But don't think that means I won't."

Excelsior holds up a small black box. "You know what this is? Of course you don't. This is a pager. A very special kind of pager. And when it goes off, it means that something bad is happening somewhere in the world. Very bad. The kind of bad only I can handle."

Judge Perkins pounds his gavel. "Mr. Excelsior, you will sit down! Or you WILL be held in contempt!" Excelsior reaches over and takes the gavel out of the judge's hand.

"I have a headACHE," Excelsior says as he crushes the gavel into dust. He turns back to the courtroom, "This pager has gone off three times since this bullshit trial started. I have never had to put up with this kind of nonsense before. He's a bad man. A very, very bad man," he says, pointing directly at Edwin Windsor.

"Objection!" Topper says. "The only bad man here is you. We have evidence, sworn affidavits!" Topper waves a pile of papers in the air. Excelsior squints and the papers are on fire. Topper drops the documents and stomps them out.

Edwin watches all of this as if it is happening on a television screen.

Excelsior continues, "Because I'm here at this farce of a trial, people are dying." He reads from the pager. "A bridge collapsed in Oregon. There's been a cave-in in Pennsylvania. And 134 brave souls are trapped on an experimental submarine at the bottom of the North Sea. These are all people I could be helping. But am I?"

"No, I'm sitting here listening to this criminal. And just because he hasn't been convicted doesn't mean he hasn't committed crimes."

"I have committed no crimes," says Edwin.

"He's an accessory to every major villain I've faced in the last five years. This man is the brains behind the bad guys. The guy, behind the guy, behind the guy. Now I have to listen to him insult me? Bullshit. This costing people's lives. I am out of here."

Topper shrieks, "As you can see, he's dangerous and unbalanced! Prone to fits of rage! He has an irrational hatred of my client. This man recognizes no law but his own." Excelsior's eyes flash again. Now the back of Topper's suit is on fire. He runs around in a circle trying to put it out.

Excelsior steps from the witness stand and walks to Edwin. "And you. If you've got a problem with me, be a man. Don't try and let the courts do your work. You want a piece of me? You chickenshit suit. You can have a piece of me. Any time. Any place. Anyway you want to go. We'll do it."

Edwin looks at him with infinite calm. Excelsior turns on his heel and walks towards the door. He thinks that the matter is concluded. But the sound of a chair scraping against the hardwood floor tells him he is mistaken. When he turns around, Edwin stands in the middle of the courtroom.

"Fine," says Edwin.

"Fine?" asks Excelsior, unable to believe what he is hearing.

"Your terms are acceptable."

"Oh, you don't know when to quit."

"If the time for quitting presents itself," says Edwin, "I will quit promptly and well. Let's settle this."

"So what's it going to be, Windsor?"

Topper looks at Edwin. The judge comes out from behind his bench. The reporters lean in. The sketch artist scribbles furiously, attempting to complete a drawing of Topper chasing his own flaming ass.

"Clubs," says Edwin.

"Clubs? You got to be kidding, you want to fight me with a club? You'll get killed. Besides, it's not your style."

"Golf clubs. Tomorrow, 8:15, Belvedere Country Club. If you win, the case is dropped and I no longer advise villains. If I win, you leave me, and my clients, in peace."

"Fine, I'll be there," says Excelsior.

CHAPTER FIFTY-THREE
The Front Nine

Edwin, Topper, Edwin's caddy and Judge Perkins have assembled on the first tee. The only way the Judge would agree to such an unusual form of arbitration was if he presided over it. And now the Judge is faced with this first ruling. Excelsior is late. As the Judge kicks one of the tee box markers he considers how long he should wait before declaring a forfeit.

The next time he looks up, his problem is solved. There, in the sky, is a wondrous sight. A man flying in cape and costume, but this time, his silhouette includes a bag of golf clubs. As Excelsior flies closer he calls out, "Is this Belvedere?"

"It is sir," answers the Judge, "and you are late."

"Sorry," Excelsior says, "all these damn golf courses look alike from the air." As Excelsior descends, a gust of wind buffets him. He twists and loses control of the golf bag. Clubs rain down on the first tee and everyone runs for cover.

"Oh, Jeeze," says Excelsior. His comment about finding the golf course is a lie. He had no idea that it would be so difficult to handle the golf clubs in flight. He has dropped them several times on the flight over.

"You know," says the Judge as he emerges from behind a golf cart, "if you kill me, you forfeit the match. I want that to be clear. Now, we will proceed with match play on a hole-over-hole basis. A hole that is tied is halved and does not push to the next hole. USGA rules will govern play. If you need a ruling, don't hesitate to ask. Good luck."

"Yeah," says Topper, "touch both clubs and come out swinging." The Judge gives Topper a stern look. Topper asks, "What, you gonna hold me in contempt of golf course?" Judge Perkins considers it.

Edwin ignores this exchange as he surveys the first hole. Par four, 421 yards. Not difficult, but at about 270 yards the fairway narrows dramatically. On any other day, he would be tempted to hit a long drive and push for a birdie. But not today.

Topper takes the driver from the caddy and hands it to Edwin. "Just belt the crap out if it."

"Three wood," says Edwin, not taking his eyes off the hole.

"Three wood?"

"Yes, please."

"I don't know if I can let you do that. He's gonna hit it a mile. You know he's gonna hit it a mile. You can't have this punk out-driving you."

"Topper, the only thing I care about is him outscoring me."

"All right, but don't come crying to me when you don't respect yourself in the morning."

Edwin steps up to his ball. He takes a quick practice swing. Then he very plainly, very simply hits the ball 230 yards down the middle of the fairway. It kicks high in the air and come to rest.

"Nice pitch," says Topper. "I like it. Reminds me of myself. Very short."

"Yes, I get it already," says Edwin.

As Excelsior takes the tee box, there's no way he could look more out of place. Even in an environment where men have taken pride in wearing plaid with plaid, the absurdity of a man in a cape playing golf cannot easily be explained. On top of which, Excelsior holds his driver as if it is a bird that he has crushed the life out of, and keeps on crushing, just to be sure. His practice swing is a cross between a slap shot and a seizure.

Topper laughs. He has finally found someone with an uglier swing than his own. One of the damned mocking the other. Edwin reserves judgement. The look of a swing matters little. What can he do with it? With this kind of thinking, Edwin tries to insulate himself from surprise. He believes that he is prepared for anything. Edwin is wrong.

With a grunt, Excelsior heaves the club backwards. As he begins his downswing, the corner of his cape wraps around his driver and locks off on itself. Excelsior lunges forward with all of his mighty strength. The club bends in half. Excelsior pulls himself off-balance and falls down just as the carbon fiber shaft explodes. Lying flat on his back, he tries to piece together what has just happened. The unmolested golf ball still sits on the tee.

Topper is overcome by a fit of hysterical laughter. The caddies snicker. Even Edwin permits himself a smile. Excelsior stands and brushes the club fragments from his hair. Only Judge Perkins manages to keep a straight face. "One," he proclaims solemnly.

"What do you mean? I didn't even touch the ball!"

"Rule 14," says the Judge, "forward motion made with the intent of fairly striking at and moving the ball. One stroke."

"What about my club?"

"I don't think it will do you much good now," says the Judge, with no humor.

Excelsior accepts another club from his caddy. This time he makes contact with the ball. There is an awful, hollow sound. The ball rises quickly, but leaks off to the right, disappearing into the rough nearly three hundred yards from the tee.

Edwin wins the first two holes without incident. After his drive, Excelsior removes his cape and plays as an ordinary man would. Badly, but without trying to take advantage of his considerable powers. On the fourth hole things get interesting again.

It's the first par five of the round. Straight open, straight ahead. The wide, welcoming fairway is marred only by a single pit bunker. Again Topper begs Edwin to use his driver. Edwin ignores him, as does his caddy. Edwin calmly knocks his ball 280 yards out into the middle of the fairway. Solid, but uninspired.

"That's noble work ya doing there, grinding it out," says Topper.

As Excelsior surveys the hole, he has a feeling that it is his time. This is the way it always happens. He starts off taking it on the chin. He gets knocked through buildings, maybe blasted by a few energy bolts. Then, just when everyone has started to lose hope, he rallies and wins the day in a spectacular fashion. Usually with an uppercut.

"Windsor, I'm going to put this one on the green for you."

"Best of luck," Edwin says.

"You don't think I can do it?"

"We'll find out soon enough."

Excelsior turns back to his ball. He's got it figured out. He has been tensing too many muscles. The muscles weren't doing anything useful. They were fighting each other rather than letting the physics of the swing work for him. But maybe, just maybe...

He takes the club back slow and accelerates mightily as it comes back through. His wrists unlock and BOOM! The head of the club is moving so fast when it hits the ball that the golf ball explodes.

"Son, I'm getting tired of your shenanigans," says the Judge. "Are you going to settle down and play golf, or are you going to keep this up the whole round?"

"But I'm not trying to…" Excelsior beats his club against the ground in brute rage.

"And that's another stroke," adds Topper cheerily.

"Aw come on!" protests Excelsior.

"Yeah, you big flying boy scout, you might as well just give up now," says Topper.

"No penalty," says the Judge, "Rule 5, paragraph 3 — if the ball breaks into pieces as the result of a stroke, the stroke shall be replayed without penalty."

"All right. Win one for the good guys. Throw me another ball there, caddy."

Topper sneers at the mention of the "good guys," but Edwin's face remains serene.

Excelsior smiles as he tees his second ball. Finally, something has gone his way. He has gotten a lucky break.

"Keep your head down," says his caddy. Keep your head down. Like you were in a war. And wasn't he? Excelsior has always believed that golf was a game for old, fat men, but now that he's in it, he is surprised by how much pressure the game is putting him under.

Excelsior strikes the ball well. It only flies 320 yards, but this does not bother Excelsior. He tells himself that he will have it figured out by the end of the round. His childlike joy at this shot slips away when he remembers that he has lost every hole up to now. But this is it. This is the turning point. No doubt about it.

Edwin plays a fairway wood for another 230 yards. This leaves him a straightforward pitch into the green. Topper watches it with a frown, "No imagination. No daring," Topper says.

"Would you be content with a hole in one?" asks Edwin.

"Only if it had style."

In spite of himself, Excelsior is beginning to like Topper. At least he's game. Unlike the bloodless ghoul he is matched against. What's the point of winning if you can't enjoy it? This time, Excelsior steps up to his ball with total confidence. His caddy hands him an iron as if it is some mighty weapon from a

315

Norse saga with a string of unpronounceable consonants for a name.

And then, in the long light of the early morning, with the strength of a god and perfect lie, Excelsior swings. The club head coils around his body even as his hips and shoulders begin to turn in the opposite direction. By the time the club head starts down, the momentum of the swing is transformed into a force of nature. His wrists unlock at the perfect moment. Just as the full power of the motion is about to be transferred into the ball, Excelsior lifts his head. The club hits the ground three inches behind the ball. Somehow, he manages to make enough contact that the ball squibs thirty yards down the fairway.

Excelsior realizes that he is going to lose this hole. And the next hole. And all the holes after that. And he will have to play all of them. Even though he knows how it will turn out. He sneaks a furtive look at the judge and wonders which rule and paragraph covered slaughter?

He tries to steady himself. He hates this game with every fiber of his being. It is a devilish creation. A way for the weak and decadent to mock the strong and virtuous. He could reduce this golf course to a wasteland with three quick passes.

His caddy taps him on the shoulder, "Yer still away." Make that four passes, thinks Excelsior. A fourth pass just to make sure all the caddies are dead.

Miraculously, mercifully, Excelsior's third shot makes the green. He misses his putt and leaves it six feet past the hole.

"Would you like to know what your problem is?" Edwin asks.

"People like you who make money off the misery and suffering of others?" Excelsior returns.

"No, no, no. With your game. You're not used to working at anything, it's all been given to you."

"How about you play your ball and I'll play my ball and you play a little side game of shut up," Excelsior counters.

Edwin sinks his putt. "Birdie," he says, as he wins another hole.

Now Excelsior thinks about losing. Losing the side, losing the match, losing the bet. He will have to grant Windsor free rein, allow him and his clients to operate with impunity. With each step it sinks in a little more. Because of him, the good guys are going to lose.

CHAPTER FIFTY-FOUR
The Turn

By the eighth hole, Edwin feels that he has the entire match within his grasp. Tie it on 9, win it on 10 does not seem out of the question. Then he will have the privilege of playing out the rest of the holes by himself. Just for the enjoyment of it.

You might think it would be a rare treat for Edwin to best someone with superpowers. But it is not. Excelsior has proved to be so little competition that Edwin isn't finding much joy in the game. It feels like uninspired work. Like hanging siding or bagging groceries. Something that requires a person to wear a one-piece jumpsuit. Edwin shudders at the thought.

He can not fathom why Excelsior has accepted this wager. It must be some vestigial sense of honor, highly irrational, yet still active in the herd. It doesn't really matter. Edwin knows how to exploit a lucky bounce when he gets it. And immunity from the world's most powerful superhero — and the ability to sell that protection — is certainly a lucky bounce. Some might see this as a license to steal, but Edwin doesn't think of it like that. He thinks of it as a license to print money. Steal, and you may get rich. Print money and you have power.

Edwin addresses his ball. He has never been more certain of his swing. But as the club makes contact with the ball, he feels a queer sensation in his hands. The ball leaves the tee with a frightening amount of topspin. The club head separates from the shaft and flies straight up. Something has gone horribly, horribly wrong.

There is Excelsior, grinning at Edwin's misfortune. Edwin ignores him. He's looking at his club. No defect is visible, but the shaft is twisted and mangled. It is unexplainable, undeniable. Somehow a perfect swing has resulted in an awful shot.

"What the hell did you do that for?" Topper asks. He grabs the club out of Edwin's hand. "What happened?" Edwin ignores Topper. His only concern is what to do now.

"I guess you'll just have to start hitting the driver," says Topper.

"Four wood," says Edwin.

"Four wood? FOUR WOOD! Are you out of your mind?!" Topper asks.

"I know I'll hit it straight."

"And you'll still have 220 yards left to go!"

"Then I will hit it again."

"Take the driver. Please, please take the driver."

"No matter what I hit, I'm not going to get it on the green. But I can put it in the fairway," says Edwin. With strain he adds, "It's not like I need better than a bogey to beat him on this hole."

"Exactly. And you're so far ahead — "

"Not as far ahead as I'm going to be." It is a controlling principle in Edwin's life to never leave a contest unsettled. He does not believe in leaving adversaries to dangle over shark-filled tanks. When he finishes business, he likes it to be concluded utterly and beyond redemption. The match will be over when Excelsior has lost. Not before. No matter how far ahead he gets, both hands will stay firmly on the club. Never mind Excelsior, golf itself is too cruel a game to take chances with.

Edwin banishes the freak accident from his mind. He is going to knock this one stiff, close with a bogey, and put the hole behind him. Or so he thinks. This time, the club head flies off at the top of his backswing. It bounces off the next tee box and rolls into the fairway. Edwin is aghast. How can this happen? Twice?

Excelsior tries to hold it in, but he cannot. A giggle slips out.

"Do you mind?" Edwin asks. Excelsior just keeps laughing.

"Hey! Body suit! Spandex! Yeah, Jazzercize. I'm talking to you," Topper says. "Man's trying to play a game here. Keep your yap shut." Excelsior holds his sides. He bites his lips. He tries thinking of a thousand other things. But it is no use. The giggles just keep coming. Tears stream down his face. He makes slobbery, slurping noises in the corners of his mouth as he fights for control. The judge is about to reprimand him, but it's so bad he asks, "Are you okay?"

Excelsior nods and lies with his head. He is very far from okay. He is GREAT. The best he's been in, well, forever really. He has CHEATED! It is the first time he has broken the rules and it feels GREAT!

At the top of Edwin's backswing, Excelsior had used his heat vision, for just an instant, to melt the shaft. And no one realizes. He is going to get away with it. He has gotten away with it! Twice. Now he just can't stop giggling about it.

As best they can, the golfing party ignores Excelsior's breakdown.

"Does that count as a stroke?" Edwin asks the judge.

"Did you start on the downswing?"

"No, but I intended to hit the ball."

"AHHHHHHH," shrieks Topper, "AHHHHHH! You never answer more than you absolutely have to! Any defense lawyer can tell you that!"

"He's right son," says the Judge

"So I'm lying three?"

"That is correct," says the Judge, "Still your shot."

Edwin considers his next move very carefully. The situation is fluid, uncertain. Causes are unknown. Outcomes are unclear. And, for the first time, he reappraises how much is at stake. "Three iron."

"Edwin, please, I'm begging you. Please, please, please hit the driver. Just blast it," says Topper. Edwin gets his own club and plays the hole. He finishes with a triple-bogey while Excelsior manages to hole a 30-foot putt for a double.

The hero has won a hole.

CHAPTER FIFTY-FIVE
The Back Nine

It's driving Topper crazy. He knows Excelsior is cheating. Topper doesn't know exactly how, but he knows that Excelsior has sabotaged Edwin's clubs. What bothers Topper about this situation is not the cheating. It's that it is unfair in an unfair way. Cheating is there so the little guy can level the playing field. It's not supposed to make the strong guys stronger or the fast guys faster. Excelsior is clearly breaking all the rules of breaking the rules. It's just wrong.

The judge doesn't care. The rules of golf weren't written with superpowers in mind. There is nothing about improving the path of a ball in flight; nothing about blowing your opponent's ball off course.

The worst is that Edwin refuses to notice. As his position in the match degenerates, Edwin speaks less and less. Surely that means that his powerful brain is working. But it doesn't take a genius to see that there is no thinking your way out of this situation. Something has to be done. And that something is cheating back.

As they walk to the next hole, Topper asks, "E, E, what's the matter?"

"Nothing."

"Look, we gotta do something. What's the play?"

"Everything is fine."

"I know how we can get him."

"By having a lower score on each hole," says Edwin, "I am aware of this already."

"Edwin," says Topper, clawing at the tall man's pant leg, "he's moving things with his mind!"

"That's ridiculous."

"E, you gotta know that he's cheating!"

Edwin says, "Please Topper, I'm in the middle of the match." Edwin lengthens his stride and leaves his little lawyer behind. That's when Topper decides it's his job to save the day.

On the eleventh hole, in the middle of Excelsior's backswing, Topper kicks Edwin's golf bag out of the caddy's hands. The bag crashes to the ground. This noise causes Excelsior to yank his drive high and way left.

"Do you MIND?!" Topper snaps at the caddy in mock horror, "Man's trying to play a match here. You do that again and you're fired."

Edwin raises an eyebrow. The judge says nothing, but surely he too must have his suspicions.

Excelsior's badly struck drive has sent his ball far out into a lake. It has come down behind a small island. Topper could not see the splash from where he was standing, but he knows there is no way the ball is dry. Excelsior confers with his caddy for a moment and then announces, "I'm just going to have a look." He flies over to the island.

"Sonofabitch!" Topper thinks "That ball is in the water. No way it's on that island, but he's going to go over there where no one can see. Pretend to look for a minute and — "

Excelsior cries out, "Found it!"

"That's my trick," thinks Topper. "He's going to beat us with my own trick!" The little man is fit to burst. Rage is always a destructive emotion. Topper's rage doubly so.

As everyone else makes their way down the fairway, Topper lags behind with Excelsior's weathered old caddy. "So," Topper asks, a little out of breath from his struggle to keep up with the taller man, "You like this guy?"

"He's all right," the caddy says noncommittally.

"C'mon, 'all right.' Get outta here, he's like everybody's hero. I mean the guy can fly."

"Noticed that. Not much of a golfer, though."

"Yeah, yeah, so don't you think it's kind of strange that he's winning?"

"Seen a lotta strange things on the golf course," he says. He lets his gaze linger on Topper.

"Well sure, I mean, you seen it all, right?"

"I'd appreciate it if you'd be coming to a point, young sir. It's my man's swing."

Excelsior hacks at his ball. It's an ugly swing for an ugly shot. But the ball leaps free of the swampy island and lands 20 yards short of the green. This island hop has shaved a great deal of length off the hole.

Edwin, bereft of fairway woods, plays two irons and a pitch to reach the green. A brilliant putt brings him within three feet of the cup. Par seems within reach. And par should be good enough to win the hole. Sure, Excelsior has a putt for birdie, but it's so far from the hole, there is no way he can make it. Is there?

The man in spandex hunches his mighty frame over his tiny putter. In the midst of intense concentration, Excelsior looks quite absurd. But he strikes the ball well, and it rolls to the very edge of the cup. "Birdie!" he cries out even before the ball goes in. But in one of those impossible, heartbreaking moments that golf always seems to deliver, the ball hangs on the edge of the cup.

"A shame," says Edwin, "a good putt." He starts to knock the ball in with his putter. But Excelsior says, "Wait." He squats down about ten yards behind the ball and looks at it. He blinks, and the ball jumps in.

"Didn't you see that!" screams Topper. "Tell me somebody saw that!" He runs over to the judge and asks, "Did you see that?"

"Yes. This hole to Excelsior. He's up by one."

"That was amazing. That was fantastic. That was TOTALLY UNREASONABLE!" says Topper.

On the next hole, Edwin hits a long, low, knock-down shot. It is away and over the hill before Excelsior can do anything about it. Topper's heart soars. Edwin isn't stupid. He can keep it up. He can win. Barring any high lobs over water, Edwin could be home free playing a bump-and-run kind of game. But on his second shot, right before Edwin makes contact with his ball, Topper sees a small whiff of smoke rise from the grass. Edwin's ball flies funny and lands in the sand trap just short of the green.

"Edwin," Topper says.

"If you won't let me concentrate on my game, I'm going to have to ask you to leave."

Damn that man, thinks Topper. Why won't he let himself be helped? Is Topper not good enough to help him?

On the seventeenth hole, Excelsior gives Topper his chance. The hole is a 210 yard par 3. The back of the green closely guarded by heavy woods. Edwin hits a 4 iron, playing it to the short side. It's safe, disciplined play, just like the rest of the round. But Topper doesn't watch the ball. Topper watches Excelsior. He sees him puff up his cheeks and blow out a puff of air.

This zephyr hits Edwin's ball and knocks it over the back of the green. The ball makes a horrible sound as it crashes into the trees. It is hopelessly lost. Edwin hits a provisional, and Excelsior pulls the same trick AGAIN. Topper is so angry, he can barely stand still.

"Well, I'll find one of them," Edwin says agreeably. He actually seems happy about being on the brink of absolute disaster.

What is wrong with him? Is it mind control? As they make their way to the green, Topper sneaks a ball from Edwin's bag. As Edwin and the caddies search deep in the woods, Topper stays close to the green. He finds a spot, flat, level and with a clear shot to the pin. And then, with the ease of a practiced master, he yells, "Found it!"

He conceals the ball in his hand, and bends over like he's just picked it up. Then he "replaces" the ball on the ground. As Edwin walks over Topper says, "Must have gotten a good kick off one of those trees."

Seemingly unaware of Topper's deception, Edwin chips it close and wins the hole with a par. The losing streak is broken, and the match is all tied going in to 18.

CHAPTER FIFTY-SIX
The Last Hole

As they approach the 18th tee, Topper has given his tall friend a chance. Now it is up to Edwin to see it through. But things do not look good. This final hole is the last par five on the course. Edwin has lost every par five today. But as Edwin takes the tee, Topper is heartened to hear his friend call for his driver.

"Oh. Get outta my way." Topper grabs the driver from Edwin's caddy and runs to his friend. "Knock the cover off the ball."

"I wouldn't be penalized for that, would I?" Edwin ask, looking to the judge, his face betraying just the hint of a smile.

"Your Honor," says the Judge.

Here it comes, thinks Topper. If he can just get through this swing, he's got it. As Edwin tees his ball, Topper sidles around behind Excelsior. As Edwin takes a practice swing, Topper reaches up and pinches Excelsior's right ass cheek as hard as he can.

Excelsior whirls around with a look of utter disbelief. "What do you think you're doing?"

"You're a fine piece of man-meat." Topper whispers. Excelsior looks at him as if he is considering stepping on him. Which he is. Topper doesn't care. Topper winks at him.

Wha-BOOM. While Excelsior is distracted, Edwin takes his shot. Edwin's ball leaves the tee like a missile. It has that unique trajectory only found in a perfectly struck drive. The ball is spinning backwards so quickly that the dimples on the ball impart lift. The ball defies gravity. For a moment the little white dot seems to obey the laws of a more elegant world. When it finally returns to earth it is in the middle of the fairway, 376 yards from the tee box.

Topper cheers unabashedly. Then he turns to Excelsior, "Nevermind big boy. It never would have worked out between us. You're too goody two-shoes for me."

Excelsior swings hard, but only managed to move the ball 320 yards. He tops his next shot, then puts his third on the green.

As Edwin approaches his ball, Topper is at a loss for another distraction. There just never seemed to be strippers around when you really needed them, he thinks. But then Edwin does something remarkable.

"Would you consider letting me borrow your three wood, in the interests of good sportsmanship?" Edwin asks Excelsior.

Excelsior is caught flat on his feet. A bad man, say, a villain, would have refused such a request in the interest of winning the match. But Excelsior stands for fair play. He can't do such a thing, at least not in front of other people. So Excelsior hands Edwin his club. But there is hatred in his heart as he does it. "Of course. Good luck."

Edwin takes a practice swing. Then another. The tension builds within Topper. He can't take it. Everything hangs on this swing.

When Edwin connects with the ball Topper thinks he's mis-hit it. But as the ball speeds away, he realizes the genius of the shot. It's another low runner. The ball stays six inches off the ground all the way to the front of the green. It bounces on the fringe and then rolls up to the pin. Topper goes nuts. He throws his hat in the air. He kisses the caddy's leg. He jumps up and down in front of Excelsior yelling, "Hunh? Hunh? How you like me now?"

In contrast, Edwin displays no emotion. He hands his club off and walks to the green as if no other outcome had been possible.

Excelsior's mouth hangs open in disbelief. The shot had been perfect. It simply hadn't gotten high enough in the air for him to interfere with. After all this. After that tremendous cheating rally over the last eight holes, Excelsior is going to lose. As Excelsior's caddy shoulders the clubs and heads to the green he says, "He's still got to sink that putt."

But the old caddy knows it to be a formality. The rules will have to be observed, but Edwin is within three feet of the hole and now has a putt for two-under par. An eagle. The old caddy knows his man has no chance. As he walks behind Edwin Windsor, he whispers, "Fine shot, sir."

Excelsior misses his 30 foot putt for a birdie, and taps in for a par. Edwin puts his ball in to win the match. "Yeah!" screams Topper, "the good guys win one! I mean the bad guys. I mean, us. I mean we won. We beat Excelsior."

Excelsior stares into the turf as if something irreplaceable is leaking out of him. Gus, fading away in the hospital, and now this? He was supposed to beat the man. How could he have lost? After all, Windsor is just a man.

The judge notices that Edwin is staring at his ball with a strange look on his face. He asks, "What is it?"

"It's the wrong ball."

"What?"

"I was playing a Penfold Heart. But it was a number three." Edwin holds up the ball so that the Judge can clearly read the number four imprinted on its dimpled surface.

"Mr. Windsor, that is a shame. But the rules are clear. Hole number 17 is forfeit. Hole and match to Excelsior."

Excelsior snaps out of it. He isn't sure what has just happened, but since it has gone his way, he isn't about to complain. Edwin walks over to him and extends his hand, "Good game."

"What? What are you doing? Have you lost your oversized mind?" screeches Topper.

"There are some things more important than winning. Excelsior understands that, even if you do not, Topper."

"You're completely insane. Your Honor, I'd like to declare this match void on grounds of insanity!"

Edwin looks down and smiles a sad smile at his little friend, "Topper, right has prevailed. As it always will in the end. I realize that now."

"Who are you? No, seriously, who in the hell are you? And what have you done with EDWIN WINDSOR?!"

Edwin turns on his heel and leaves the green.

"Don't you walk away from me, beanpole! Where do you think you are going? I worked hard for that fix and you just threw it away." Topper waddles after him as fast as his short legs will carry him. "And now you're going to get out of the business? How am I supposed to be your henchman?"

"Get in the car."

"You're clearly not in your right mind. I don't think someone as loony as you should be operating heavy machinery."

CHAPTER FIFTY-SEVEN
Out of Business?

Edwin eases the sedan out of the club's parking lot. The car is understated, powerful, and well-suited to the large man's size. Topper is barely able to see over the soft leather dash. They ride along in silence until Topper can stand it no longer.

"Well, I guess you're out of business," says Topper with an air of finality.

"Hmm," says Edwin.

"The bet. You said, if you lost, you'd stop advising villains."

"Hmm."

"So you're gonna welsh, right?"

"No, I will honor my agreement."

"But he was cheating his tight little pants off. You know that, right?"

"Yes, I know he was cheating."

"Then why'd you do it?"

"Golf? I enjoy golf."

"Okay," says Topper, realizing that Edwin is toying with him. "Then why'd you throw the match?"

"I didn't. You threw the match for me. Rather brilliantly, I thought."

"What! I got you back in the game. He was cheating! Cheating like crazy! Cheating like, like, like his head was on fire! I don't know. And you didn't do a thing about it. What? Was it some kind of mind control ray?" Edwin chuckles in that way Topper hates. The way that means that Topper has missed something big.

"So that is the only thing you noticed? That I was acting under the influence of a 'mind control' ray?"

"I noticed he was cheating."

"Anything else?"

"But he's a good guy. I mean he's THE good guy. He's not supposed to cheat. He can't cheat. What else is there to notice? That you lost? I noticed that you lost."

"Perhaps in the short term. But where does it net out? What's the final accounting, the bottom line?"

"Okay, I give up. I can't see how losing a bet — and I just lost $1000 to that battered old caddy because of you — I don't see how it nets out for anybody other than the guy who wins. Please explain to me, Mr. Mastermind, how that nets out."

"Someone has their hooks into him very deeply. I don't know what drives a man like him, but it's very, very bad. He's trying to atone for something. Something he believes to be awful. I would venture to say that he hasn't broken the "rules" since he was a child. But today! Today he broke loose. He felt the freedom of action. What it means to be a moral agent, rather than someone's puppet. Did you see the joy in his eyes?"

"And here I thought that just came from beating you?"

"After both clubs melted? There is no such thing as coincidence Topper. It is always, always your enemies conspiring against you."

"Okay, so what?"

"He's cheated. He just lost his moral center. Now he's adrift in a world of complex choices. He has rediscovered his soul, so to speak. But he threw away the owner's manual for it years ago. It is a fascinating predicament. He will need someone to turn to for guidance."

"Hoooo boy, that's rich. And it sounds like loser's limp to me. You're trying to tell me that if you zapped me with a ray that suddenly made me into Mother Friggin' Teresa — repenting my evil defense-lawyer ways — no longer defending drug dealers, embezzlers, wealthy pederasts — all the high-paying scum of the earth — giving up the whores and the cocaine, devoting myself to patient, non-profit work and girls who are as tall as they are wide — that I would have some kind of gratitude for you? And then I would come to you for a little fatherly advice?"

"The only way to overcome such a man is to break him down inch by inch. Excelsior is a man with no character. He has no real integrity, just a blind lust for victory. Now that he has cheated, now that he has realized the full range of his options, I expect him to fall apart under the weight of his own power."

"Seriously, I think you're cracked. Terribly strained from your ordeal and defeat. I advise you not to sign any contracts or make any big life decisions, because you are — "

"Topper — "

"Edwin, if you messed with my head like that, you'd be lucky if I didn't dress up in a fairy costume and pipe bomb your house. Seriously. If the most powerful man in the world comes unglued, GOD HELP US! God help us all."

Edwin smiles at his friend, "I would have thought you might have made that appeal a little farther south."

"What are you talking about? Sure, the devil is the patron saint of all defense lawyers, but God loves me. I'm meek." Topper leans out the window and yells at a nondescript white van driving slowly in the left lane. "Outta the way urinal puck! We're not getting any younger!" Then he pulls his head back in the car and continues as if nothing had happened, "That's why I'm going to inherit the earth."

CHAPTER FIFTY-EIGHT
The Trap is Baited

He doesn't trust me, thinks Director Smiles. He doesn't respect me. I have nothing he needs. I have no leverage. None of this is good for Smiles. He has bootlicked, backstabbed and connived his way to the top of the bureaucratic pile so that people would be forced to do what he said. And now Excelsior isn't playing along. When the others find out that Smiles can't control Excelsior, they will laugh. It will not be the knowing laugher of loving parents as they watch their children struggle to take their first steps. No, it will be the laughter of jackals who realize that one of their own will not survive his wounds and, for today at least, the feast will come without the effort of a hunt.

They will turn on him. And after he is gone, they will rename a section of the South Dakota state highway after him. If Smiles had to choose between bureaucratic death and real death, he'd take real death. Except he is pretty sure he doesn't have the guts it would take to kill himself.

So, mostly, he feels sorry for himself. Smiles is good at feeling sorry for himself. And it helps that the situation isn't fair. Why did Excelsior have to do what Gus said and not what Smiles said? After all, Smiles is Gus's boss. Maybe Excelsior doesn't understand that. Maybe Smiles should try telling him that. But every time he sees the hero, Smiles just locks up. He can't say what he wants to say. Everything just comes out wrong.

It isn't fair. And the way Smiles looks at it, it is his job, the government's job, to make sure everything is fair for everybody. If Smiles had stopped to think about it, he might have realized that this was the surest, shortest recipe for human misery ever invented. But he doesn't think about it. He's not in this game for the greater good. He's in it for power.

Yesterday, he received a request from a Senator from California. An oil rig was falling off its platform. It could have easily become an ecological disaster. And, of course, the oil company would have to shut down production. Which would have been a financial disaster as well. The only way to repair the platform was to use a gigantic crane ship. There are only two in the world, the Gargantua and the Pantagruel. And both of them are inconveniently in Dubai being used to construct islands shaped like Disney characters. It would have taken many months and many millions to bring one of them to repair the senator's oil rig.

But, as the Senator explained, Excelsior could save the day. He did not need a place to stand to lift that much weight. Wouldn't take him but a second. So if Director Smiles could find a free moment in the big guy's schedule, the favor would not be forgotten.

The thing is, this Senator is a member of the appropriations committee. He has direct influence on the disbursement of trillions of dollars. Smiles is no fool. If he can get this taken care of, he'll have a chip he can play in the big game. And you can never have too many of those chips. Besides, it would be easy for Excelsior. So Smiles messaged him with, "Ecological disaster, come quick!"

When Excelsior arrives, he explains the matter to him. Not in the chip-in-the-big-game way, but in the hero-providing-a-great-service-to-his-country way. Sure Smiles stutters a little bit, but all in all he doesn't do that bad of a job.

"I hate oil," Excelsior says, "It takes forever to get it out of my suit. There's got to be another way."

"Not for nearly a year,"

"No." says Excelsior. Then he flies away.

Thinking Excelsior was well out of earshot, Smiles shrieks, "You come back here!" In an instant, Excelsior returns. He floats an inch in front of Smiles' face. "I said NO." Smiles quivers with terror. Excelsior disappears in an instant, but Smiles shakes for many minutes afterwords.

When the terror wears off, the self-pity sets in. But it doesn't last long. Smiles is spineless and contemptible, but he isn't weak. He isn't completely powerless. He walks to his office with a scowl on his face. He needs to get something on Excelsior. Or give him something he wants. But what could it be? What do you get the man who can do anything? What do you get on the man that nothing can hurt? For all his big talk and pain-in-the-ass, tough-guy attitude, Gus has something on Excelsior. He thinks he's so much better than Smiles. But Smiles now realizes that Gus has been playing the game just like everybody else. Everything is politics.

Smiles knows he can play politics better than Gus. Because he's smarter than Gus. Isn't he? He'll get something on Excelsior, and then he'll have the biggest chip in the biggest game around. Oh yeah, nobody will tell him what to do. Even the president will be nice to him. Nobody will ever play Smiles again. He'll be above the game.

He sits at his desk. On it is an envelope with the words "The solution to your problem" printed in black magic marker. Smiles can't believe what he finds inside.

It is a brief detailing how Edwin Windsor poisoned Gus. There are pictures of the device, a chemical description of the poison, and several 8x10s of Edwin patting Gus on the back. Edwin's hand is circled in red. Oh, this is good. This is exactly what he needs to get into Excelsior's good graces. Not enough to control him, but certainly enough to open up detanté.

Smiles almost considers that this might be a set up. He almost wonders who would benefit from Edwin Windsor being the target of the most powerful man in the world. He almost checks to make sure that having Edwin out of the way will be to his advantage. Almost.

If he was smarter, or more cunning, he might consider blackmailing Edwin with this evidence, getting as much money out of him as he can, and then still unleashing Excelsior upon him. Director Smiles thinks of none of this. He allows himself to be played. What does he care? He's getting what he wants out of the deal. What would he think if he knew that Edwin Windsor had prepared that envelope especially for him?

CHAPTER FIFTY-NINE
The Reckoning

Edwin stands in the ruins of his building. After the extensive damage done by the conflict between Lifto and Excelsior, the entire building was deemed more expensive to repair than to simply rebuild. So, the structure is totaled — dead as it stands. As Edwin shuffles through the dust and the debris, he is philosophical about waste, destruction and loss.

Everything has its natural and unavoidable consequence. He can see that now. He can see something of the whole pattern, inevitable and inexorable. All of this destruction is a consequence of what came before.

Edwin is surprised to find that he is not afraid. Ever since Agnes's death, long-forgotten feelings and emotions have coursed through him. Most of these spasms have been unpleasant. He has struggled, not only to keep control of his thoughts, but to remember the words that are used to describe emotions. It has been so long since he felt anger, greed, hope, fear, sadness, joy — any of them. But now, Edwin is calm, resolved, resigned to his fate.

"Jesus, you can't go home again can ya?" says Topper, as he emerges from the darkness. "Just look what they have done with the place."

"What are you doing here?"

"I'm looking for you, you morose bastard. I was worried I would find you here. This is no good for you. Lingering in the past."

Now Edwin feels a little fear. But not for himself. "You should go. It's not safe."

"Well if it's not safe for me, then it's certainly not safe for you. You're not as resourceful as I am."

"Excelsior is coming for me."

"Then what are you doing here? You gotta run. You gotta hide."

Edwin smiles at his little friend. "No, Topper, the time for running and hiding — the time for playing it small — has passed. This is the reckoning."

There is a beeping. It is the sound of a large truck backing up. Men in white jumpsuits throw open the doors. Inside is The Cromoglodon. He senses a chance at freedom and roars, rattling the panels of the truck that contains him.

Edwin reaches into his pocket and triggers the fear. The Cromoglodon moves to the back of the truck and cowers. Edwin reaches out to the beast. "It's all right," he says, even as his hand stays firm on the trigger. The Cromoglodon moves towards him. Edwin lowers the intensity of the fear. When The Cromoglodon touches him, Edwin deactivates the electrodes. Relief floods through The Cromoglodon, and he holds Edwin's hand, weeping with joy.

"You see," Edwin says, "he is not completely lost. He is trainable. All that is needed is the proper reinforcement mechanism. We may yet civilize him." Edwin gives The Cromoglodon a pat on the head, as one might pat a dog, and walks away. The Cromoglodon shuffles after him on his knees, unwilling to leave his master's side.

"Oh," says Topper, "okay, you're gonna get revenge for what Excelsior did to Agnes. I like to see that passion in you Edwin. Revenge is what keeps me young."

"Revenge isn't the point Topper. There is work to be done here. My work. And even if I find pleasure in it, it must be done all the same."

"But what if The Cromoglodon can't kill Excelsior. What if Excelsior can't be killed?"

Edwin sets his jaw. A slight tension ripples across his brow. "Then we are doomed."

There is a sonic boom and Excelsior appears before them.

"Windsor, I'm going to enjoy this," says Excelsior.

Edwin gives The Cromoglodon a little pat on the shoulder, "Go on. Get him." The Cromoglodon looks unsure.

"Look at me, Windsor," says Excelsior.

But Edwin is still coaxing The Cromoglodon. "It's okay. You go ahead."

Excelsior lunges for Edwin. His fingers stop mere millimeters from Edwin's throat. No one is more surprised at this than Edwin. He and Excelsior look down. The Cromoglodon has grabbed Excelsior. For a moment, all is still. Then The Cromoglodon lifts Excelsior into the air and slams him into the ground. The concussion knocks Edwin and Topper from their feet.

Excelsior is hurt, but he's not stunned. He's been thinking about the last time this happened. And he's got a few more things to try. The last time, he had tried to match brute strength with brute strength. He won't make that mistake again. Even as he feels his ribs compress as they contact the ground, beams of energy leap out from his eyes. The smell of burning flesh fills his nostrils. He laughs. The Cromoglodon's face is burning.

The Cromoglodon bellows in pain. He takes his other hand and smashes the palm of it into Excelsior's face. His fingers find Excelsior's eyeballs and press. Excelsior blinks. It's an involuntary reflex. The back of Excelsior's eyeballs get hot and he lets the beams drop. Using his legs, he kicks The Cromoglodon high into the air. As the beast recedes into the

343

sky, Excelsior realizes that The Cromoglodon's shirt is displaying an advertisement for painkillers.

As they watch the struggle, Topper turns to Edwin and says, "Let's make it interesting. I'll put twenty dollars on Excelsior."

Edwin does not look away from the fight. "If Excelsior wins, he's going to kill me."

"Yeah, right, so you're clearly betting on the other guy," says Topper, still cheery.

"And he'll probably kill you as well."

"Ah, whatever. At least I'll die twenty dollars richer. And that way I'll be less upset about getting killed," Topper says with a smile.

The Cromoglodon literally hits the ground running. As he lumbers towards Excelsior, the caped hero fills his lungs with air. The Cromoglodon bellows with rage and braces for impact, but he never gets there. Hurricane force winds hold him back as Excelsior breathes out. The Cromoglodon fights against the current of air. His fingers clench and unclench in frustration. He's dying to get a hold on Excelsior.

Edwin says to Topper, "You see, one-dimensional thinking. If The Cromoglodon would only step to the side."

"Yeah. I think you should just pay up now," says Topper.

Excelsior grows red in the face and starts to sputter. He has run out of air, but The Cromoglodon has not run out of anger. He crashes into Excelsior. Using his forearms like an ape, he bludgeons Excelsior to the ground. Excelsior rolls out from underneath the blows and soars into the sky. The Cromoglodon stands there, trying to figure out what's going on. Now he's all worked up. He wants something to smash. But the something he was smashing just flew away.

"I can't believe it!" says Topper. "The BUM! He ran away. What a cowar — " Before Topper can finish his sentence, Excelsior comes streaking out of the sky and hits The

Cromoglodon at a terrific speed. The Cromoglodon is pushed backwards. His feet leave large furrows in the earth, but he does not fall. He whirls to face his attacker, but Excelsior is already gone.

Excelsior swoops down and hits him again. This time The Cromoglodon slumps to a knee. He coughs up some blood.

"I got some bad news," says Topper. "I think I'm winnin' twenty bucks."

This time, Excelsior is really cooking. He means to break The Cromoglodon's spine. No more holding back. He gets in the slot and pours it on. It feels good. But just as he is about to hit The Cromoglodon, something happens. His target disappears. Then earth leaps up and hits him in the face. Then it does it again. And again. Things go black.

The Cromoglodon has grabbed Excelsior by the cape. He's beating Excelsior against the ground like a rug. A very dirty rug that The Cromoglodon is very, very angry with.

Topper tries to hand Edwin a $20 bill. Edwin ignores him.

Now Excelsior is unconscious on the ground. The Cromoglodon stands over him and gives a triumphant roar. As he bends to deliver the coup de grace, Edwin triggers the fear.

The Cromoglodon scurries to Edwin's side. In The Cromoglodon's mind, Edwin does not cause the pain. Edwin is the one who stops the pain. Edwin has worked hard to cultivate this illusion. "That's enough," he says.

Edwin reaches into his pocket for a walkie-talkie. He keys the mike and says, "We're a go." Men in jumpsuits emerge from the truck. They rush to Excelsior, put him on a stretcher and bring him to Edwin. "Is he dead?" Edwin asks.

As if in response, Excelsior stirs slightly. From a long way away he asks, "What are you going to do to me?"

"I'm going to reason with you," answers Edwin.

CHAPTER SIXTY
Hero of Villain?

When Excelsior wakes up, the first thing he sees is Edwin Windsor. Edwin sits in a plush leather chair on a wooden platform raised off the crude floor. Next to the chair there is a small side table with a pot of tea and a video projector. Edwin sips the tea and asks. "How are you feeling?" His concern almost sounds genuine.

"A little woozy," says Excelsior. The room smells musty to him. He sees worklights strung on the ceiling. When he tries to move he realizes that he cannot. This has never happened before. Excelsior is not happy. He struggles vigorously, but gets nowhere.

"I don't know what you're trying to do, Windsor, but when I break free, I'll take care of you."

"Of that I have no doubt," says Edwin, placing the cup in its saucer. He crosses his legs and says, "but I thought we might have a little talk first."

"There's nothing to talk about. You're a monster. Plain and simple."

Edwin considers monstrosity. "Perhaps," he says, "perhaps I am a monster. But one thing is certain. I am not a barbarian." Edwin removes a pristine white handkerchief from his jacket pocket. Then he leans down and wipes some of the grime from

Excelsior's face. Excelsior tosses his head from side to side but there is nothing he can do.

"Hold still," Edwin commands. He pours a bit of tea into his handkerchief and rubs at a stubborn spot on Excelsior's forehead. Excelsior gnashes at him with his teeth. It's the only resistance he can offer.

Edwin avoids the bite. "With those manners, I will certainly not be offering you tea."

"What have you done to me?"

"I have placed you in a cardboard tube, and then filled the tube with quick setting epoxy. It has tensile strength almost equal to titanium. Remarkable substance. Especially because, to unbind it, all I need do is apply this reactant," Edwin says, holding up a small vial of liquid."

"It doesn't matter. You're just a villain like all the rest. And someday I will defeat you."

"Really? Why not today? Why not now?"

Again, Excelsior struggles against his prison. Again he fails to break free. Edwin wasn't kidding, this stuff is strong. Excelsior thought he might break it if he were at full strength, but the beating took a lot out of him. More than he likes to admit. Excelsior scans the strange room again. All he needs is a window, a little —

"Sunlight?" Edwin asks. "I am afraid not. We are six stories underground. This is all that is left of my building. Sub-basement 3B, I think it is. I am certain this room has never seen the light of day."

"How did you know?"

"You mentioned it in a magazine interview in 1974. It's never wise to reveal the source of your powers. Actually, it's never wise to reveal anything. It's a mistake I'm sure you won't be making again. Don't take it so hard. Even without research it would have been easy enough to deduce. A simple order-of-magnitude calculation. Where else could so much energy come from? From what you eat? How many calories of energy would you have to exert to lift a battleship? No, it simply has to be the sun. Unless you yourself are a fusion reactor."

Excelsior turns his head to hide his expression. The last thing he wants is Edwin gloating over his shame.

"There is no shame in defeat," says Edwin, "There is only shame in avoidable defeat — in, to be perfectly honest, stupidity."

Excelsior whips his head back and forth. "Your ass is mine Windsor. I'll come for you. Nothing on earth is going to stop me from getting you."

"You're really not much of a hero, are you?"

Excelsior struggles some more. Sweat breaks out on his face. He yells at the top of his lungs. Finally, realizing that he is truly helpless, he sighs and speaks the truth: "I used to be."

Edwin has another sip of tea. He tries to imagine what Excelsior would be like if he were really a hero. It is not easy. "You never were a hero. You just thought you were."

"Great," says Excelsior, "now you're going to lecture me?"

"No." says Edwin. "I am going to offer you a choice." He triggers a walkie-talkie and says "Go." There is a slithering noise as a hose leading into the middle of the room swells and belches wet concrete onto the floor.

"What are you doing?"

"I am building a monument to your last battle."

"You what?"

"Right up there," Edwin says, pointing to the surface, "will be your memorial. A large bronze statue, with the legend, 'Upward, ever upward.'"

"Why are you doing this?" asks Excelsior, eyeing the concrete as it oozes closer and closer.

"So no one will ever forget your sacrifice. I don't see why you are so upset. This is your chance to die as a hero."

"Is this because I destroyed your office?"

"No."

"This isn't fair. This ISN'T FAIR!" Excelsior pounds his head against the floor.

"Fair?" Edwin laughs. The concrete oozes across the floor. It has almost reached Excelsior's face. "Fair has nothing to do with it. There is only what I can do, and what I will do."

"Okay Windsor, what do you want?"

"You don't have anything I want. You don't seem to have anything at all."

"Then why are you doing this?"

"I told you, I am here to offer you a choice." Edwin holds up the vial of reactant. "I can free you — "

"Free me. Go ahead, that's my choice!"

"Calm down. You haven't heard the other option."

"Are you insane?"

"I don't think so. I think I am perfectly rational. I can free you, or I will generously agree to bury you in concrete."

"What's generous about that?"

"Well, I am doing all of this at my own expense."

"That's no choice, let me out of this thing," Excelsior says as the concrete reaches the tip of his chin.

"I think burial is the way you want to go with this one. That is, if you're serious about being a hero." Edwin activates the video projector. Motes of dust dance in the beam and an image forms on the far wall.

On the wall Excelsior sees a picture of a candlelight vigil held in front of a memorial wall decorated with hundred of flowers.

"They're holding a vigil for me? Because I'm gone?" Excelsior asks hopefully.

"No. It is not for you. Look closer." Edwin advances to a picture of a young girl. "This is Stephanie Mills, 25. She worked in an office below mine. She and seventeen of her co-workers fell to their death when you knocked part of the top off Windsor Tower."

Next, Edwin shows him a picture of a man with a plain, honest face. Now the projector shows that this picture is tacked to the memorial wall. Next to it the words, 'Daddy, we miss you' are written in crayon. "Thomas Sarah, bank clerk, father of three daughters. He is one of the people who was killed when Stephanie and her co-workers landed."

"I didn't kill them, I was fighting Lifto." Even as Excelsior says it, it rings false in his ears. He has the feeling again. The feeling that everything is going wrong. The feeling of a plane falling apart in his fingers.

"You chose to fight Lifto in the city," says Edwin. "You could have apprehended him at another place. Another time. You could have let the police do it."

"None of the police are strong enough."

"Not by themselves, but they could have maintained a cordon. Perhaps I could have talked him into surrendering."

"But I had to save them. Save the people from villains like Lifto and The Cromoglodon."

"But you didn't," says Edwin, clicking relentlessly through pictures of the departed and the ones they left behind. A young girl, no more than three, but seeming ancient as she stands next to an open grave.

And next, an arm protruding from rubble. Cars, still on fire in the first light of dawn. The eerily peaceful face of a dead woman on a mortuary table. "Don't you see, you killed all of them."

"Hey, everybody makes mistakes," Excelsior scrambles to think of the phrase that Gus always uses, "Sometimes you gotta break a few eggs. Right? That's no reason to do this."

"I am trying to help you. I'm giving you a chance to be a hero. For the first time in your life."

"What do you mean. I am THE hero!"

"Ah, the hero. Heroic in every way. Always doing what is best and right and true. Is that what you are?"

"Turn the concrete off and we can talk about it," Excelsior says. The grey slush surrounds his body. It is heavy and cold. Excelsior starts to shiver.

"But I can't turn the concrete off. No one can. There has to be a continuous pour or else it won't set up correctly. There are concrete trucks lined up for a mile for you. So let us speak quickly. Do you always do what's right?"

"Yeah, sure. I mean I make mistakes but pretty much, yeah."

"But you don't choose, Excelsior. You don't make mistakes. Other people tell you what to do and you make their mistakes. You only do what you are told. Don't you?"

"Yeah that's right, I was just doing what I was told," Excelsior says, eager to shift the blame. Eager to say anything that will get him out of this horrible situation.

"You are not describing a hero, Excelsior. You are describing a puppet."

"I'm nobody's puppet. And I'm sick of hearing that. This is sick. This is wrong. That's why you're the villain. And I'm the hero. Can't you see that?"

"No, I can't." Edwin activates the next slide. It is a picture of a beautiful village in Africa. Children play. Bright fabrics dry in the sun. The people of the village stand tall and proud. "Uganda," Edwin says. He advances to the next slide. It is the same village, now utterly destroyed. The huts are burnt. The body of a child lies bloating in the sun.

"Hey, I didn't have anything to do with that. I've never been to Uganda. I've never even heard of it."

"That is my point. You've never been there. Hundreds of thousands of people die in a terrible genocide. And the mighty Excelsior does nothing."

"But I didn't know! They didn't tell me!"

"But they could have. And you know that a man who is serious about doing good — a hero — would have found out. He would have asked. Might have wondered what more good

352

he could have done. But you did not. What of the typhoon that just ravaged Hong Kong? You saved Miami, why not Hong Kong?"

"Hey I can't be everywhere. I can't save everybody."

"Ah, you were busy. Bigger crisis on the other line. And what was that crisis? What was so important that it kept you from saving several hundred lives and averting billions of dollars of property damage?" Edwin reveals the next image. It is Excelsior crushing Telstar 9. "Ah, yes, here you are destroying a perfectly good communications satellite, while accosting the one client I have who I am certain has never committed a crime."

"What? Why didn't they tell me?" In his confusion, Excelsior stops thinking about himself for the first time in a long time.

"They didn't tell you because they didn't care. You have given your power over to men with no conscience."

"This is wrong. It's all wrong. I never wanted..."

"I know. That's why I'm giving you a chance to make it right."

The wreckage of Singapore Airlines Flight 209 fills the wall. On the side of the fuselage he can clearly see the indentation of his hand on the scarred and twisted metal.

"To make it right," Edwin says again.

Excelsior huffs through his nostrils like a wounded animal. Slow ripples move through the concrete. His tears feel hot on his face. He's tired, so tired. Tired of losing. Tired of doing the wrong thing. Tired of feeling like this. His neck muscles are sore from holding his head above the rising concrete.

"You want to be a hero. But you have become the villain."

"No," says Excelsior.

"Sooner or later, the world will figure it out. And then you will go from being loved to being reviled."

"No, it's not true," Excelsior says, trying to convince himself. "You killed Gus."

"Yes, and now you are all alone. Who do you have to live for?"

"But you're a bad man, a murderer," Excelsior says, clinging to the last rung of the ladder.

"So are you. You've killed thousands. I killed one man. One man had to die to give you a chance to save the world from yourself."

"This is wrong." Excelsior protests. He knows it's wrong. But the feeling is still with him. Windsor is a bad man, but is it possible that Excelsior is somehow worse?

"If I let you go, more innocent people are going to die. Do you want more innocent people to die?"

"No. It's not my fault." Excelsior tries to say this with conviction, but fails. It rings false even in his ears.

"You are right. It is not your fault. You are who you are. No one man should have so much power."

"But I can do good. I've done good!" Has he really? Excelsior can only think of one or two times when it was good. Really good. The pure win he craved so much. The other times...

"You've tried. But every time you have saved someone, you've made the rest of us weaker. You've made the heroism of ordinary people seem insignificant."

"I didn't mean to..." says Excelsior, but he has seen it over the years. Once, people were surprised and grateful when he showed up. Then they came to expect it. To feel that they were owed. That's why there was a team of people to cover it up when he failed.

"But you did. And if you leave this room, you will continue to do harm. Someone else will mislead you, or misuse you. More innocents will die. Don't you see? You are the only person who is strong enough to defeat you. You are the only person who can save the world from yourself."

Is it true? Could it be true?

"Are you hero enough to fall on your own sword? Do you have the courage it will take to die with honor?" Edwin doesn't like the word "honor." Honor is the revered lie that allows a shrewd man to trick a simple man into dying for a cause. Edwin watches Excelsior closely to discover how well the modern myth of honor is holding up.

For a time, both men are silent. Excelsior blinks several times in a slow rhythm of realization. Edwin feels sweat on his palms. Is this it? Has he done it?

Excelsior blows the concrete away from the corner of his mouth and says, "You're right Windsor. Leave me here. Better I should die a hero."

Excelsior lays his head down and lets the concrete wash over him.

Edwin rises and buttons his suit jacket. He sees that only the side of Excelsior's head and his ear are visible above the thick grey slurry. Edwin bends down to the ear and whispers. "This is not revenge. This is not a perfect remedy. This is not a perfect world." Edwin watches as the concrete rises above the level of Excelsior's ear. He watches Excelsior shiver as the cold, grey ooze floods into his ear canal.

Fitting and proper, thinks Edwin, extinction for the whole breed. He turns and leaves Excelsior to his tomb.

When Edwin emerges from the tunnel, he has to shield his eyes against the harsh work lights. He walks down the long line of concrete trucks. He passes truck after truck, unable to describe what he feels. His stride lengthens. There is much work to be done. Tonight, Edwin will rest. Tomorrow, he will begin in earnest. After all, there's a whole world out there. And Edwin means to have it all.

CHAPTER SIXTY-ONE
The Man in Room Three

The duty nurse's station. Terminal ward. This is where the people with money come to die. And nothing attracts friends and family to a hospital like a sick relative with money. Most of the time this disgusts Nurse Kim. All that fighting and scrabbling. But that's the odd thing about the man in room number three. He's got the finest treatment that money can buy, but no family has ever come to visit him. He's listed as John Doe. How does John Doe get such good insurance coverage?

Nurse Kim doesn't know why visitors would come here. It's not like it matters. There's a saying that floats around hospital wards: don't screw up so bad that you kill a dead person. And that describes everybody in this ward, dead, but kept alive through the miracle of medical science.

It's not like the gentleman in room three was breathing for himself or pumping his blood on his own. Even his assisted vitals were crappy. So when Kim finishes her round she doesn't give him another thought.

Then the alarm goes off. The gentleman in room number three is crashing. She calls a code and goes to save him. She hurries, but she doesn't run. There's no point. The monitor has told her that the man's heart has stopped, so they'll have to defib him anyway. Most of the patients here are vegetables, so there's no harm in a little extra brain death. It's not like he had really been alive anyway. Unplug the machines and he's gone. In fact, the most likely explanation for all of this is that one of the machines has failed.

But when Kim reaches the doorway, she stops dead in her tracks. The dead man in room number three is sitting up in his bed. He's pulling the last of his ventilation tube free. He looks at Kim and spits a wad of blood and phlegm on the floor.

"Where is he?" the man asks.

"Who?" says Kim, because she can't think of anything else to say to a man risen from the dead.

"Excelsior."

"You mean the hero? He's dead. They had a funeral and everything. The president was there."

"Bullshit. Was there a body?"

"W-w-what?"

"Did they find a body?"

"N-n-no."

The man swings his legs out of the bed and tries to stand. His legs have atrophied and won't hold him. He slides onto the floor. "Well, yippie ki-yay," he says, disgusted at his weakness.

"Take it easy," says Nurse Kim, "You've been in bed for a long time." She checks his chart rather than going to help him. This man has a crazy light in his eye that she's not comfortable with. "Three months."

The man curses and struggles to get to his feet. After a minute he claws his way back onto the bed. As Nurse Kim watches this, she asks, "Where do you have to be in such a hurry, Mister Doe?"

"Heh, John Doe, huh? My name's Augustus, but all my lady friends call me 'Gus.'"

"Well, why are you in such a hurry, Gus?"

"I'm going to go find him. I'm going to find Excelsior."

"But he's dead."

"If they didn't find a body, he's still alive. Being a hero is not the kind of thing you get to quit." Gus says this with an air of disgust. He scans the around the room. "Where are my boots?"

"You don't have any personal effects Mr. Doe. Besides, you couldn't possibly leave in your condition."

"Can't do anything else," says. He falls back onto his pillow in exhaustion. "There's rules you know."

Nurse Kim has no idea what he's talking about, but his voice is so raspy it causes her pain. "Can I get you a glass of water?"

"The bad guys don't get to win. No matter what. It's not over. It's never over." Gus is wracked by another coughing fit.

"Please, Mr. Doe, calm down. A man in your condition, you'll kill yourself."

"No," croaks Gus, growing weaker by the second. "Not yet. I've got a funeral to go to. A tall man. A man so tall, they'll have to build a custom casket."

"You're delirious. Let me get you some water."

"Water? Yeah. And find me some cigarettes. I could just about kill for a cigarette," says Gus as he passes out.

If you liked this book, the kindest thing you can do for the author is to tell a friend, or (better yet a stranger) about it. Why not write a review on amazon or goodreads?

The World's Most Dangerous
About the Author Blurb.

You know those "About the Author" blurbs that list a series of credentials and accomplishments so impressive that they make you feel that if you don't buy a book, everyone will recognize you for the uncultured Phillistine* that you are? This is not that kind of author blurb. This is the other kind.

This is an About the Author blurb that actually tells you about the author. This blurb it will tell you that Patrick has been shot, has fallen off a mountain, was once framed for a crime he did not commit, that he has gambled with his rent money and knows how to replace the water pump in a 1966 Chrysler. It will also explain that, like a lost boy raised by wolves, he was brought up by economists and knows how to interpret the strange dances and guttural utterances of their dismal tribe.

But most of all this blurb wants you to know that Patrick can write. That he puts words and concepts and characters together in a way that will make your synapses light up like an accident in an unlicensed fireworks factory. Yes, a substance that powerful will eventually be made illegal. But before that happens, you've got a chance to go to www.patrickemclean.com to get more of his writing.

If you don't use this chance, Patrick won't hold it against you. After all, he's a nice, easy-going kind of guy. But this Blurb will know. And believe me, this is one "About the Author" blurb you don't want to cross.

Editor's Note: Patrick put an extra l in Phillistine here just to make sure it STAYED down. Don't let him fool you. He's also a little dangerous. Especially with a consonant close to hand.

Made in the USA
Middletown, DE
25 June 2016